ARTEMIS

ANDY WEIR

DEL REY

3 5 7 9 10 8 6 4 2

Del Rey, an imprint of Ebury Publishing
20 Vauxhall Bridge Road,
London SW1V 2SA

Penguin
Random House
UK

Del Rey is part of the Penguin Random House group of companies whose
addresses can be found at global.penguinrandomhouse.com

First published in the US in 2017 by Crown Publishers, an imprint of the
Crown Publishing Group, a division of Random House LLC, a Penguin
Random House Company, New York

Published in the UK in 2017 by Del Rey, an imprint of Ebury Publishing

www.penguin.co.uk

A CIP catalogue record for this book is available from the British Library

Hardback ISBN 9780091956943
Trade Paperback ISBN 9780091956950

Printed in the UK by Clays Ltd, St Ives PLC

Penguin Random House is committed to a sustainable future for
our business, our readers and our planet. This book is made
from Forest Stewardship Council® certified paper.

ARTEMIS

Also by Andy Weir:

The Martian

For Michael Collins, Dick Gordon, Jack Swigert,

Stu Roosa, Al Worden, Ken Mattingly, and Ron Evans.

Because those guys don't get nearly enough credit

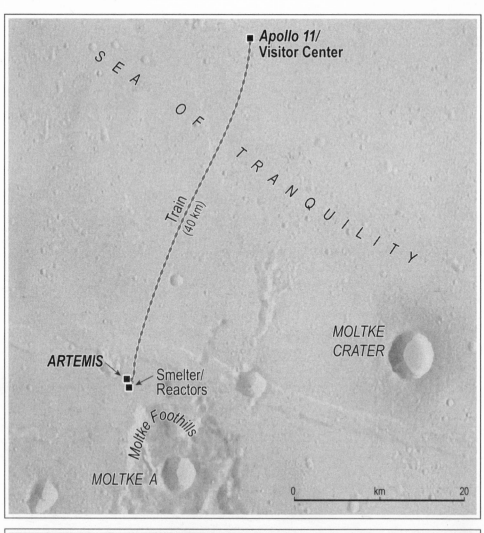

SEA OF TRANQUILITY

Apollo 11/
Visitor Center

Train
(40 km)

ARTEMIS

Smelter/
Reactors

Moltke Foothills

MOLTKE
CRATER

MOLTKE A

0   km   20

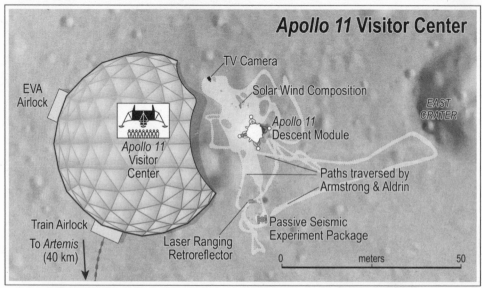

Apollo 11 Visitor Center

EVA
Airlock

Apollo 11
Visitor
Center

Train Airlock

To *Artemis*
(40 km)

TV Camera

Solar Wind Composition

Apollo 11
Descent Module

EAST
CRATER

Paths traversed by
Armstrong & Aldrin

Laser Ranging
Retroreflector

Passive Seismic
Experiment Package

0   meters   50

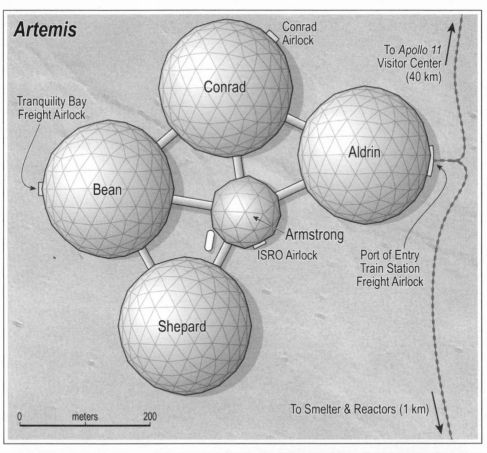

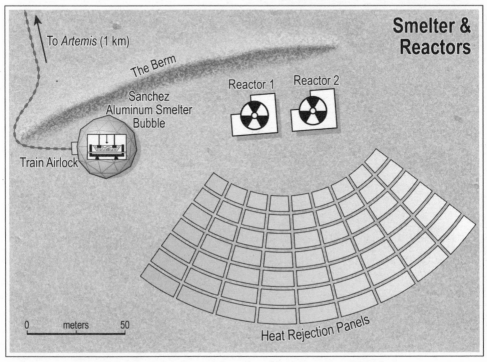

ARTEMIS

I bounded over the gray, dusty terrain toward the huge dome of Conrad Bubble. Its airlock, ringed with red lights, stood distressingly far away.

It's hard to run with a hundred kilograms of gear on—even in lunar gravity. But you'd be amazed how fast you can hustle when your life is on the line.

Bob ran beside me. His voice came over the radio: "Let me connect my tanks to your suit!"

"That'll just get you killed too."

"The leak's huge," he huffed. "I can *see* the gas escaping your tanks."

"Thanks for the pep talk."

"I'm the EVA master here," Bob said. "Stop right now and let me cross-connect!"

"Negative." I kept running. "There was a pop right before the leak alarm. Metal fatigue. Got to be the valve assembly. If you cross-connect you'll puncture your line on a jagged edge."

"I'm willing to take that risk!"

"I'm not willing to let you," I said. "Trust me on this, Bob. I know metal."

I switched to long, even hops. It felt like slow motion, but it was the best way to move with all that weight. My helmet's heads-up display said the airlock was fifty-two meters away.

I glanced at my arm readouts. My oxygen reserve plummeted while I watched. So I stopped watching.

The long strides paid off. I was really hauling ass now. I even left Bob behind, and he's the most skilled EVA master on the moon. That's the trick: Add more forward momentum every time you touch the ground. But that also means each hop is a tricky affair. If you screw up, you'll face-plant and slide along the ground. EVA suits are tough, but it's best not to grind them against regolith.

"You're going too fast! If you trip you could crack your face-plate!"

"Better than sucking vacuum," I said. "I've got maybe ten seconds."

"I'm way behind you," he said. "Don't wait for me."

I only realized how fast I was going when the triangular plates of Conrad filled my view. They were growing *very* quickly.

"Shit!" No time to slow down. I made one final leap and added a forward roll. I timed it just right—more out of luck than skill—and hit the wall with my feet. Okay, Bob was right. I'd been going way too fast.

I hit the ground, scrambled to my feet, and clawed at the hatch crank.

My ears popped. Alarms blared in my helmet. The tank was on its last legs—it couldn't counteract the leak anymore.

I pushed the hatch open and fell inside. I gasped for breath and my vision blurred. I kicked the hatch closed, reached up to the emergency tank, and yanked out the pin.

The top of the tank flew off and air flooded into the compartment. It came out so fast, half of it liquefied into fog particles from the cooling that comes with rapid expansion. I fell to the ground, barely conscious.

I panted in my suit and suppressed the urge to puke. That was way the hell more exertion than I'm built for. An oxygen-deprivation headache took root. It'd be with me for a few hours, at least. I'd managed to get altitude sickness on the moon.

The hiss died to a trickle, then finished.

Bob finally made it to the hatch. I saw him peek in through the small round window.

"Status?" he radioed.

"Conscious," I wheezed.

"Can you stand? Or should I call for an assist?"

Bob couldn't come in without killing me—I was lying in the airlock with a bad suit. But any of the two thousand people inside the city could open the airlock from the other side and drag me in.

"No need." I got to my hands and knees, then to my feet. I steadied myself against the control panel and initiated the cleanse. High-pressure air jets blasted me from all angles. Gray lunar dust swirled in the airlock and got pulled into filtered vents along the wall.

After the cleanse, the inner hatch door opened automatically.

I stepped into the antechamber, resealed the inner hatch, and plopped down on a bench.

Bob cycled through the airlock the normal way—no dramatic emergency tank (which now had to be replaced, by the way). Just the normal pumps-and-valves method. After his cleanse cycle, he joined me in the antechamber.

I wordlessly helped Bob out of his helmet and gloves. You should never make someone de-suit themselves. Sure, it's doable, but it's a pain in the ass. There's a tradition to these things. He returned the favor.

"Well, that sucked," I said as he lifted my helmet off.

"You almost died." He stepped out of his suit. "You should have listened to my instructions."

I wriggled out of my suit and looked at the back. I pointed to a jagged piece of metal that was once a valve. "Blown valve. Just like I said. Metal fatigue."

He peered at the valve and nodded. "Okay. You were right to refuse cross-connection. Well done. But this still shouldn't have happened. Where the hell did you get that suit?"

"I bought it used."

"Why would you buy a used suit?"

"Because I couldn't afford a new one. I barely had enough money for a used one and you assholes won't let me join the guild until I own a suit."

"You should have saved up for a new one." Bob Lewis is a former US Marine with a no-bullshit attitude. More important, he's the EVA Guild's head trainer. He answers to the guild master, but Bob and Bob alone determines your suitability to become a member. And if you aren't a member, you aren't allowed to do solo EVAs or lead groups of tourists on the surface. That's how guilds work. Dicks.

"So? How'd I do?"

He snorted. "Are you kidding me? You failed the exam, Jazz. You super-duper failed."

"Why?!" I demanded. "I did all the required maneuvers, accomplished all the tasks, and finished the obstacle course in under seven minutes. *And*, when a near-fatal problem occurred, I kept from endangering my partner and got safely back to town."

He opened a locker and stacked his gloves and helmet inside. "Your suit is your responsibility. It failed. That means *you* failed."

"How can you blame me for that leak?! Everything was fine when we headed out!"

"This is a results-oriented profession. The moon's a mean old bitch. She doesn't care *why* your suit fails. She just kills you when it does. You should have inspected your gear better." He hung the rest of his suit on its custom rack in the locker.

"Come on, Bob!"

"Jazz, you almost died out there. How can I possibly give you

a pass?" He closed the locker and started to leave. "You can re-
take the test in six months."

I blocked his path. "That's so ridiculous! Why do I have to put
my life on hold because of some arbitrary guild rule?"

"Pay more attention to equipment inspection." He stepped
around me and out of the antechamber. "And pay full price when
you get that leak fixed."

I watched him go, then slumped onto the bench.

"Fuck."

I plodded through the maze of aluminum corridors to my home.
At least it wasn't a long walk. The whole city is only half a kilometer across.

I live in Artemis, the first (and so far, only) city on the moon.
It's made of five huge spheres called "bubbles." They're half un-
derground, so Artemis looks exactly like old sci-fi books said a
moon city should look: a bunch of domes. You just can't see the
parts that are belowground.

Armstrong Bubble sits in the middle, surrounded by Aldrin,
Conrad, Bean, and Shepard. The bubbles each connect to their
neighbors via tunnels. I remember making a model of Artemis
as an assignment in elementary school. Pretty simple: just some
balls and sticks. It took ten minutes.

It's pricey to get here and expensive as hell to live here. But a
city can't just be rich tourists and eccentric billionaires. It needs
working-class people too. You don't expect J. Worthalot Richbas-
tard III to clean his own toilet, do you?

I'm one of the little people.

I live in Conrad Down 15, a grungy area fifteen floors under-
ground in Conrad Bubble. If my neighborhood were wine, con-
noisseurs would describe it as "shitty, with overtones of failure
and poor life decisions."

I walked down the row of closely spaced square doors until I got to my own. Mine was a "lower" bunk, at least. Easier to get into and out of. I waved my Gizmo across the lock and the door clicked open. I crawled in and closed it behind me.

I lay in the bunk and stared at the ceiling—which was less than a meter from my face.

Technically, it's a "capsule domicile" but everyone calls them coffins. It's just an enclosed bunk with a door I can lock. There's only one use for a coffin: sleep. Well, okay, there's another use (which also involves being horizontal), but you get my point.

I have a bed and a shelf. That's it. There's a communal bathroom down the hall and public showers a few blocks away. My coffin isn't going to be featured in *Better Homes and Moonscapes* anytime soon, but it's all I can afford.

I checked my Gizmo for the time. "Craaaap."

No time to brood. The KSC freighter was landing that afternoon and I'd have work to do.

To be clear: The sun doesn't define "afternoon" for us. We only get a "noon" every twenty-eight Earth days and we can't see it, anyway. Each bubble has two six-centimeter-thick hulls with a meter of crushed rock between them. You could shoot a *howitzer* at the city and it still wouldn't leak. Sunlight definitely can't get in.

So what do we use for time of day? Kenya Time. It was afternoon in Nairobi, so it was afternoon in Artemis.

I was sweaty and gross from my near-death EVA. There was no time to shower, but I could change, at least. I lay flat, stripped off my EVA coolant-wear, and pulled on my blue jumpsuit. I fastened the belt then sat up, cross-legged, and put my hair in a ponytail. Then I grabbed my Gizmo and headed out.

We don't have streets in Artemis. We have hallways. It costs a lot of money to make real estate on the moon and they sure as hell aren't going to waste it on roads. You can have an electric cart or scooter if you want, but the hallways are designed for foot traffic. It's only one-sixth Earth's gravity. Walking doesn't take much energy.

The shittier the neighborhood, the narrower the halls. Conrad Down's halls are positively claustrophobic. They're just wide enough for two people to pass each other by turning sideways.

I wound through the corridors toward the center of Down 15. None of the elevators were nearby, so I bounded up the stairs three at a time. Stairwells in the core are just like stairwells on Earth—short little twenty-one-centimeter-high steps. It makes the tourists more comfortable. In areas that don't get tourists, stairs are each a half meter high. That's lunar gravity for you. Anyway, I hopped up the tourist stairs until I reached ground level. Walking up fifteen floors of stairwell probably sounds horrible, but it's not that big a deal here. I wasn't even winded.

Ground level is where all the tunnels connecting to other bubbles come in. Naturally, all the shops, boutiques, and other tourist traps want to be there to take advantage of the foot traffic. In Conrad, that mostly meant restaurants selling Gunk to tourists who can't afford real food.

A small crowd funneled into the Aldrin Connector. It's the only way to get from Conrad to Aldrin (other than going the long way around through Armstrong), so it's a major thoroughfare. I passed by the huge circular plug door on my way in. If the tunnel breached, the escaping air from Conrad would force that door closed. Everyone in Conrad would be saved. If you were in the tunnel at the time . . . well, it sucks to be you.

"Well, if it isn't Jazz Bashara!" said a nearby asshole. He acted like we were friends. We weren't friends.

"Dale," I said. I kept walking.

He hurried to catch up. "Must be a cargo ship coming in. Nothing else gets your lazy ass in uniform."

"Hey, remember that time I gave a shit about what you have to say? Oh wait, my mistake. That never happened."

"I hear you failed the EVA exam today." He tsked in mock

disappointment. "Tough break. I passed on my first try, but we can't all be me, can we?"

"Fuck off."

"Yeah, I got to tell you, tourists pay *good* money to go outside. Hell, I'm headed to the Visitor Center right now to give some tours. I'll be raking it in."

"Make sure to hop on the really sharp rocks while you're out there."

"Nah," he said. "People who *passed* the exam know better than to do that."

"It was just a lark," I said nonchalantly. "It's not like EVA work is a real job."

"Yeah, you're right. Someday I hope to be a delivery girl like you."

"Porter," I grumbled. "The term is 'porter.'"

He smirked in a very punchable way. Thankfully we'd made it to Aldrin Bubble. I shouldered past him and out of the connector. Aldrin's plug door stood vigil, just as Conrad's did. I hurried ahead and took a sharp right just to get out of Dale's line of sight.

Aldrin is the opposite of Conrad in every respect. Conrad's full of plumbers, glass blowers, metalworkers, welding shops, repair shops . . . the list goes on. But Aldrin is truly a resort. It has hotels, casinos, whorehouses, theaters, and even an honest-to-God park with real grass. Wealthy tourists from all over Earth come for two-week stays.

I passed through the Arcade. It wasn't the fastest route to where I was going, but I liked the view.

New York has Fifth Avenue, London has Bond Street, and Artemis has the Arcade. The stores don't bother to list prices. If you have to ask, you can't afford it. The Ritz-Carlton Artemis occupies an entire block and extends five floors up and another five down. A single night there costs 12,000 slugs—more than

I make in a month as a porter (though I have other sources of income).

Despite the costs of a lunar vacation, demand always exceeds supply. Middle-class Earthers can afford it as a once-in-a-lifetime experience with suitable financing. They stay at crappier hotels in crappier bubbles like Conrad. But wealthy folks make annual trips and stay in nice hotels. And my, oh my, do they shop.

More than anywhere else, Aldrin is where money enters Artemis.

There was nothing in the shopping district I could afford. But someday, I'd have enough to belong there. That was my plan, anyway. I took one more long look, then turned away and headed to the Port of Entry.

Aldrin is the closest bubble to the landing zone. Wouldn't want rich people dirtying themselves by traveling through impoverished areas, right? Bring them straight into the pretty part.

I strolled through the large archway into the port. The massive airlock complex is the second-largest chamber in the city. (Only Aldrin Park is larger.) The room buzzed with activity. I slid my way between workers who efficiently glided to and fro. In town, you have to walk slowly or you'll knock over tourists. But the port is for professionals only. We all know the Artemis Longstep and can get a good head of steam going.

At the north side of the port, a few commuters waited near the train airlock. Most were headed to the city reactors and Sanchez Aluminum's smelter, a kilometer south of town. The smelter uses insane amounts of heat and extremely nasty chemicals, so everyone agrees it should be far away. As for the reactors . . . well . . . they're nuclear reactors. We like those far away too.

Dale slithered over to the train platform. He'd be going to the Apollo 11 Visitor Center. Tourists love it. The half-hour train ride provides stunning views of the moon's terrain, and the Visitor Center is a great place to look at the landing site without ever leaving pressure. And for those who do want to venture outside to get a better view, Dale and other EVA masters are ready to give them a tour.

Just in front of the train airlock there was a huge Kenyan flag. Beneath it were the words "You are now boarding Kenya Offshore Platform Artemis. This platform is the property of the Kenya Space Corporation. International maritime laws apply."

I stared daggers at Dale. He didn't notice. Damn, I wasted a perfectly good bitchy glare.

I checked the landing zone schedule on my Gizmo. No meat-ship today (that's what we call passenger ships). They only come about once a week. The next one wouldn't be for three days. Thank God. There's nothing more annoying than trust-fund boys looking for "moon poon."

I headed to the south side, where the freight airlock stood ready. It could fit ten thousand cubic meters of cargo through in a single cycle, but bringing it in was a slow process. The pod had arrived hours earlier. EVA masters had brought the entire pod into the airlock and gave it the high-pressure air cleanse.

We do everything we can to keep lunar dust from entering the city. Hell, I hadn't even skipped the cleanse after my faulty valve adventure earlier that day. Why go through all that hassle? Because lunar dust is *extremely* bad to breathe. It's made of teeny, tiny rocks, and there's been no weather to smooth them out. Each mote is a spiky, barbed nightmare just waiting to tear up your lungs. You're better off smoking a pack of asbestos cigarettes than breathing that shit.

By the time I got to the freight airlock, the giant inner door stood open and the pod was being unloaded. I slid up to Nakoshi, the head longshoreman. He sat at his inspection table and examined the contents of a shipping box. Satisfied that it contained no contraband, he closed the box and stamped it with the Artemis symbol—a capital *A* with the right side styled to look like a bow and arrow.

"Good morning, Mr. Nakoshi," I said cheerfully. He and Dad had been buddies since I was a little girl. He was family to me, like a beloved uncle.

"Get in line with the other porters, you little shit."

Okay, maybe more like a distant cousin.

"Come on, Mr. N," I wheedled. "I've been waiting on this shipment for weeks. We talked about this."

"Did you transfer payment?"

"Did you stamp the package?"

He maintained eye contact and reached under the table. He pulled out a still-sealed box and slid it toward me.

"I don't see a stamp," I said. "Do we have to do things this way every damn time? We used to be so close. What happened?"

"You grew up and became an underhanded pain in the ass." He set his Gizmo on top of the box. "And you had so much potential. You pissed it away. Three thousand slugs."

"You mean twenty-five hundred, right? Like we agreed?"

He shook his head. "Three thousand. Rudy's been sniffing around. More risk means more pay."

"That seems more like a Nakoshi problem than a Jazz problem," I said. "We agreed to twenty-five hundred."

"Hmm," he said. "Maybe I should give it a detailed inspection then. See if there's anything in here that shouldn't be. . . ."

I pursed my lips. This wasn't the time to make a stand. I brought up my Gizmo's banking software and initiated the transfer. The Gizmos did whatever magic shit computers do to identify each other and verify.

Nakoshi picked up his Gizmo, checked the confirmation page, and nodded with approval. He stamped the box. "What's in there, anyway?"

"Porn, mostly. Starring your mom."

He snorted and continued with his inspections.

And that's how to smuggle contraband into Artemis. Pretty simple, really. All it takes is a corrupt official you've known since you were six years old. *Getting* the contraband to Artemis . . . well, that's another story. More on that later.

I could have picked up a bunch more packages to deliver around, but this one was special. I walked over to my cart and hopped in the driver's side. I didn't strictly need a cart—Artemis wasn't set up for vehicles—but it got me around faster, and I could deliver more stuff that way. Since I'm paid per delivery it was worth the investment. My cart is a pain in the ass to control, but it's good at carrying heavy things. So I decided it was male. I named him Trigger.

I paid a monthly fee to store Trigger at the port. Where else would I keep him? I have less space at home than a typical Earth prisoner.

I powered Trigger up—there's no key or anything. Just a button. Why would anyone steal a cart? What would you do with it? Sell it? You'd never get away with it. Artemis is a small town. No one steals shit. Well, okay, there's some shoplifting. But no one takes carts.

I motored out of the port.

I wound Trigger through the opulent passageways of Shepard Bubble. It was a far cry from my sleazy neighborhood. The hallways of Shepard feature wood paneling and tasteful, noise-absorption carpeting. Chandeliers hang every twenty meters to provide light. Those, at least, aren't stupidly expensive. We've got plenty of silicon on the moon, so glass is locally made. But still, talk about ostentatious.

If you think *vacationing* on the moon is expensive, you don't want to know what it costs to live in Shepard Bubble. Aldrin is all overpriced resorts and hotels, but Shepard is where wealthy Artemisians live.

I was headed to the estate of one of the richest richfucks in town: Trond Landvik. He'd made a fortune in the Norwegian telecom industry. His home occupied a big chunk of Shepard's ground floor—stupidly huge, considering it was just him, his daughter, and a live-in maid. But hey, it was his money. If he wanted to have a big house on the moon, who was I to judge? I just brought him illegal shit as requested.

I parked Trigger next to the estate entrance (one of the entrances, anyway) and rang the buzzer. The door slid open to reveal a bulky Russian woman. Irina had been with the Landviks since the dawn of time.

She stared at me wordlessly. I stared back.

"Delivery," I finally said. Irina and I had interacted a zillion times in the past, but she made me state my business every time I came to the door.

She snorted, turned, and walked inside. That was my invitation to enter.

I made snide faces at her back while she led me through the mansion's foyer. She pointed down the hall and walked in the opposite direction without saying a word.

"Always a pleasure, Irina!" I called after her.

Through the archway, I found Trond reclining on a sofa, wearing sweats and a bathrobe. He chatted with an Asian man I'd never seen before.

"Anyway, the moneymaking potential is"—he saw me enter and flashed a wide smile—"Jazz! Always good to see you!"

Trond's guest had an open box next to him. He smiled politely and fumbled it closed. Of course, that just made me curious when I normally wouldn't have given a shit.

"Good to see you too," I said. I dropped the contraband on the couch.

Trond gestured to the guest. "This is Jin Chu from Hong Kong. Jin, this is Jazz Bashara. She's a local gal. Grew up right here on the moon."

Jin bowed his head quickly, then spoke with an American

accent. "Nice to meet you, Jazz." It caught me off guard and I guess it showed.

Trond laughed. "Yeah, Jin here is a product of high-class American private schools. Hong Kong, man. It's a magical place."

"But not as magical as Artemis!" Jin beamed. "This is my first visit to the moon. I'm like a kid in a candy store! I've always been a fan of science fiction. I grew up watching *Star Trek*. Now I get to live it!"

"*Star Trek?*" Trond said. "Seriously? That's like a hundred years old."

"Quality is quality," Jin said. "Age is irrelevant. No one bitches about Shakespeare fans."

"Fair point. But there aren't any hot alien babes to seduce here. You can't *quite* be Captain Kirk."

"Actually"—Jin Chu held up a finger—"Kirk only had sex with three alien women in the entire classic series. And that number assumes he slept with Elaan of Troyius, which was implied but never made clear. So it might just be two."

Trond bowed in supplication. "I will no longer challenge you on anything *Star Trek*–related. Are you going to the Apollo 11 site while you're here?"

"*Absolutely*," Jin said. "I hear there are EVA tours. Should I do one, you think?"

I piped in. "Nah. There's an exclusion perimeter around the whole site. The Viewing Hall in the Visitor Center gets you just as close."

"Oh, I see. Guess there's no point, then."

Suck it, Dale.

"Anyone want tea or coffee?" Trond offered.

"Yeah, please," Jin said. "Dark coffee if you have it."

I slumped into a nearby chair. "Black tea for me."

Trond vaulted over the back of the couch (not as exciting as it sounds—remember the gravity here). He slid to the credenza and picked up a wicker basket. "I just got some high-end Turkish coffee. You'll love it." He craned his neck toward me. "Jazz, you might like it too."

"Coffee's just a bad kind of tea," I said. "Black tea is the only hot drink worth having."

"You Saudis do love your black tea," Trond said.

Yes, *technically* I'm a citizen of Saudi Arabia. But I haven't been there since I was six. I picked up a few attitudes and beliefs from Dad, but I wouldn't fit in anywhere on Earth nowadays. I'm an Artemisian.

Trond got to work on our drinks. "Talk amongst yourselves, it'll be a minute." Why not have Irina do it? I don't know. I don't know what the hell she was for, honestly.

Jin rested his arm on the Mystery Box. "I hear Artemis is a popular romantic destination. Are there a lot of newlyweds here?"

"Not really," I said. "They can't afford it. But we do get older couples trying to spice things up in the bedroom."

He looked confused.

"Gravity," I said. "Sex is totally different in one-sixth G. It's great for couples who've been married a long time. They get to rediscover sex together—it's like new."

"I never thought of that," Jin said.

"Lots of prostitutes in Aldrin if you want to find out more."

"Oh! Uh, no. Not my thing at all." He hadn't expected a woman to recommend hookers. Earthers tend to be uptight on that topic, and I've never understood why. It's a service performed for a payment. What's the big deal?

I shrugged. "If you change your mind, they run about two thousand slugs."

"I won't." He laughed nervously and changed the subject. "So . . . why is Artemisian money called slugs?"

I put my feet up on the coffee table. "It's short for soft-landed grams. S-L-G. Slug. One slug gets one gram of cargo delivered from Earth to Artemis, courtesy of KSC."

"It's technically not a currency," Trond said from the credenza. "We're not a country; we can't have a currency. Slugs are pre-purchased service credit from KSC. You pay dollars, euros, yen, whatever, and in exchange you get a mass allowance for shipment to Artemis. You don't have to use it all at once, so they keep track of your balance."

He carried the tray over to the coffee table. "It ended up being a handy unit for trade. So KSC is functioning as a bank. You'd never get away with that on Earth, but this isn't Earth."

Jin reached forward to get his coffee. As he did, I got a look at the box. It was white with stark black text that read ZAFO SAMPLE—AUTHORIZED USE ONLY.

"So this couch I'm on is an Earth import, right?" Jin said. "How much did it cost to bring here?"

"That one weighs forty-three kilograms," Trond said. "So it cost forty-three thousand slugs to have it shipped."

"What does a typical person make?" asked Jin. "If you don't mind me asking, that is."

I grabbed my tea and let the cup's warmth seep into my hands. "I make twelve thousand a month as a porter. It's a low-paying job."

Jin sipped his coffee and made a face. I've seen it before. Earthers hate our coffee. Physics dictates that it tastes like shit.

Earth's air is 20 percent oxygen. The rest is stuff human bodies don't need like nitrogen and argon. So Artemis's air is *pure* oxygen at 20 percent Earth's air pressure. That gives us the right amount of oxygen while minimizing pressure on the hulls. It's not a new concept—it goes back to the Apollo days. Thing is, the lower the pressure, the lower the boiling point of water. Water boils at 61 degrees Celsius here, so that's as hot as tea or coffee can be. Apparently it's disgustingly cold to people who aren't used to it.

Jin discreetly put the cup back on the table. He wouldn't be picking it up again.

"What brings you to Artemis?" I asked.

He drummed his fingers on the ZAFO box. "We've been working on a business deal for months. We're finally closing the deal, so I wanted to meet Mr. Landvik in person."

Trond settled into his couch and picked up the box of contraband. "I told you, call me Trond."

"Trond it is," Jin said.

Trond tore the wrapping off the package and pulled out a dark wooden box. He held it up to the light and looked at it from several angles. I'm not much for aesthetics, but even I could tell it was a thing of beauty. Intricate etchings covered every surface and it had a tasteful label written in Spanish.

"What have we here?" Jin asked.

Trond flashed a shit-eating grin and opened the box. Twenty-four cigars, each in its own paper holder, rested inside. "Dominican cigars. People think Cubans are the best, but they're wrong. It's all about the Dominicans."

I smuggled a box of those things in for him every month. Got to love regular customers.

He pointed to the door. "Jazz, would you mind closing that?"

I headed to the doorway. A starkly functional hatch hid behind the finely appointed wall panels. I slid it closed and spun the handle shut. Hatches are pretty common in upscale homes. If the bubble loses pressure, you can seal your house and not die. Some people are paranoid enough to seal their bedrooms at night just in case. Waste of money if you ask me. There's never been a pressure loss in Artemis's history.

"I have a special air-filtration system in here," Trond said. "The smoke never gets out of this room."

He unwrapped a cigar, bit the end off, and spit it into an ash-tray. Then he put the cigar in his mouth and lit it with a gold lighter. He puffed several times and sighed. "Good stuff . . . good stuff."

He held the box out toward Jin, who politely waved it away. Then he offered it to me.

"Sure." I grabbed one and slipped it into my breast pocket. "I'll smoke it after lunch."

That was a lie. But why would I turn down something like that? I could probably get a hundred slugs for it.

Jin furrowed his brow. "I'm sorry, but . . . cigars are contraband?"

"Ridiculous, really," said Trond. "I have a sealed room! My smoke doesn't bother anyone! It's injustice, I tell you!"

"Oh, you're so full of shit." I turned to Jin. "It's fire. A fire in Artemis would be a nightmare. It's not like we can go outside. Flammable materials are illegal unless there's a really good reason for them. The last thing we want is a bunch of idiots wandering around with lighters."

"Well . . . I guess there's that." Trond fiddled with his lighter. I'd smuggled it in for him years ago. Every few months it needed new butane. More money for me.

I took another swig of warm tea and pulled out my Gizmo. "Trond?"

"Right, of course." He pulled out his own Gizmo and held it next to mine. "Still four thousand slugs?"

"Mm-hmm. But fair warning: I have to bump it to forty-five hundred next time. Things got more expensive for me recently."

"Not a problem," he said. He typed while I waited. After a moment, my screen popped up the transfer verification. I accepted and the transaction was complete.

"All good," I said. I turned to Jin. "Nice to meet you, Mr. Jin. Have fun while you're here."

"Thanks, I will!"

"Have a good one, Jazz." Trond smiled.

I left the two men behind to do whatever they were up to. I didn't know what it was, but it sure as hell wasn't aboveboard. Trond did all sorts of shady shit—that was why I liked him. If he'd brought a guy all the way to the moon, there was something way more interesting going on than "a business deal."

I rounded the corner and left through the foyer. Irina gave me a nasty look as I departed. I wrinkled my nose at her. She closed the door behind me without saying goodbye.

I was just about to hop into Trigger when my Gizmo beeped. A porter job had just popped up. I had seniority and proximity, so the system offered it to me first.

"PICKUP LOCATION: AG-5250. MASS: ~100KG. DROP-OFF LOCATION: UNSPECIFIED. PAYMENT: 452ğ."

Wow. Four hundred fifty-two whole slugs. Roughly a tenth of what I'd just made from a box of cigars.

I accepted. I had to make money somehow.

Dear Kelvin Otieno,

Hi. My name's Jasmine Bashara. People call me Jazz. I'm nine years old. I live in Artemis.

Ms. Teller's my teacher. She's a good teacher even though she took away my Gizmo when I played with it during class. She gave us homework to send email to kids at the KSC complex in Kenya. She assigned me your address. Do you speak English? I can speak Arabic too. What do you speak in Kenya?

I like American TV shows and my favorite food is ginger ice cream. But usually I eat Gunk. I want to get a dog but we can't afford one. I hear poor people can have dogs on Earth. Is it true? Do you have a dog? If you have a dog please tell me about your dog.

Does Kenya have a king?

My dad's a welder. What does your dad do?

Dear Jazz Bashara,

Hello. I am Kelvin and I am also nine. I live with my mom and dad. I have three sisters. They're jerks and the two older ones beat me up. But I'm getting bigger and someday I'll beat them up. I'm just kidding, boys should never hit girls.

Kenyans speak English and Swahili. We do not have a king. We have a president and a National Assembly and a Senate. Grown-ups vote for them and they make the laws.

My family doesn't have a dog but we have two cats. One of them just comes around to eat, but the other one is very nice and sleeps on the couch all the time.

My dad is a security officer for KSC. He works at Gate 14 and he makes sure only people who are allowed to go in can go in. We live in assigned housing in the complex and my school is in the complex too. Everyone who works

for KSC gets free school for their kids. KSC is very generous and we are all grateful.

My mom stays at home. She takes care of all of us kids. She is a good mother.

My favorite food is hot dogs. What's Gunk? I've never heard of that.

I love American TV shows. Especially soap operas. They are very exciting even though my mom doesn't want me watching them. But we have good internet here so I watch when she's not looking. Please do not tell her. Haha. What does your mom do?

What do you want to be when you grow up? I want to make rockets. Right now I make models of rockets. I just finished a model of a KSC 209-B. It looks very nice in my room. I want to make real rockets someday. The other kids want to be pilots for the rockets but I don't want to do that.

Are you white? I hear everyone in Artemis is white. There are many white people here at the complex. They come from all over the world to work here.

Dear Kelvin,

It's too bad you don't have a dog. I hope you get to make rockets someday. Real ones, not models.

Gunk is food for poor people. It's dried algae and flavor extracts. They grow it here in Artemis in vats because food from Earth is expensive. Gunk is gross. Flavor extracts are supposed to make it taste good but they just make it taste gross in other ways. I have to eat it every day. I hate it.

I'm not white. I'm Arabic. Sort of light brown. Only about half the people here are white. My mom lives on Earth somewhere. She left when I was a baby. I don't remember her.

Soap operas are lame. But it's okay for you to like lame stuff. We can still be friends.

Do you have a yard at your house? Can you go outside anytime you want? I can't go outside until I'm sixteen because those are the rules for EVAs. Someday I'll get my EVA license and go outside as much as I want and no one can tell me no.

Building rockets sounds like a neat job. I hope you get that job.

I don't want a job. When I grow up I want to be rich.

Armstrong sucks. It's a damn shame such an awesome guy got such a shitty part of town named after him.

The grinding thrum of industrial equipment oozed from the walls as I guided Trigger along the old corridors. Even though the heavy manufacturing plants were fifteen floors away, the sound still carried. I pulled up to the Life Support Center and parked just outside the heavy door.

Life Support is one of the few places in town that has genuine security protocols. You don't want just anyone wandering in. The door had a panel you could wave your Gizmo over, but of course I wasn't on the approved list. From there I had to wait.

The pickup request was for a package approximately one hundred kilograms. No problem for me. I can lift twice that without breaking a sweat. Not many Earth gals can say that! Sure, they have six times the gravity to deal with, but that's their problem.

Other than mass, the request was vague. No info on what it was or where it was going. I'd have to find that out from the customer.

Artemis's Life Support is unique in the history of space travel. They don't process carbon dioxide back into oxygen. Yes, they have the equipment to do that and batteries to last months if needed. But they have a much cheaper and virtually infinite supply of oxygen from another source: the aluminum industry.

Sanchez Aluminum's smelter outside town produces oxygen

from processing ore. That's what smelting is, really. Removing oxygen to get pure metal. Most people don't know it, but there's a ridiculous amount of oxygen on the moon. You just need a shit-load of energy to get it. Sanchez produces so much oxygen by-product that they not only make rocket fuel on the side, they supply the city with all our breathable air and still end up vent-ing the excess outside.

So we actually have more oxygen than we know what to do with. Life Support regulates the flow, makes sure the incoming supply from the Sanchez pipeline is safe, and separates out the CO_2 from used air. They also manage temperature, pressure, and all that other fun stuff. They sell the CO_2 to Gunk farms, who use it to grow the algae poor people eat. It's always about economics, am I right?

"Hello, Bashara," came a familiar voice from behind.

Shit.

I put on my fakest smile and turned around. "Rudy! They didn't tell me the pickup was from you. If I'd known, I wouldn't have come!"

Okay, I won't lie. Rudy DuBois is a seriously good-looking man. He's two meters tall and blond as a Hitler wet dream. He quit the Royal Canadian Mounted Police ten years ago to become Artemis's head of security, but he still wears the uniform every day. And it looks good on him. Really good. I don't like the guy, but . . . you know . . . if I could do it with no consequences . . .

He's what passes for law in town. Okay, sure, every society needs laws and someone to enforce them. But Rudy tends to go the extra mile.

"Don't worry," he said, pulling out his Gizmo. "I don't have enough evidence to prove you're smuggling. Yet."

"Smuggling? Me? Golly gee, Mr. Do-Right, you sure get some strange notions."

What a pain in my ass. He'd been gunning for me ever since an incident when I was seventeen. Fortunately, he can't just deport people. Only the administrator of Artemis has that authority. And she won't do it unless Rudy provides something compelling. So we do have *some* checks and balances. Just not many.

I looked around. "So where's the package?"

He waved his Gizmo over the reader and the fireproof door slid open. Rudy's Gizmo was like a magic wand. It could open literally any door in Artemis. "Follow me."

Rudy and I entered the industrial facility. Technicians operated equipment while engineers monitored the huge status board along one wall.

With the exception of me and Rudy, everyone in the room was Vietnamese. That's kind of how things shake out in Artemis. A few people who know one another emigrate, they set up a service of some kind, then they hire their friends. And of course, they hire people they know. Tale as old as time, really.

The workers ignored us as we wound between machinery and a maze of high-pressure pipes. Mr. Đoàn watched from his chair in the center of the status wall. He made eye contact with Rudy and nodded slowly.

Rudy stopped just behind a man cleaning an air tank. He tapped the man on his shoulder. "Pham Binh?"

Binh turned around and grunted. His weathered face wore a permanent scowl.

"Mr. Binh. Your wife, Tâm, was at Doc Roussel's this morning."

"Yeah," he said. "She's clumsy."

Rudy turned his Gizmo around. The screen showed a woman with bruises on her face. "According to the doc, she has a black eye, a hematoma on her check, two bruised ribs, and a concussion."

"She's clumsy."

Rudy handed me the Gizmo and punched Binh squarely in the face.

In my delinquent youth I'd had a few run-ins with Rudy. I

can tell you he's a strong son of a bitch. He never punched me or anything. But one time he restrained me with one hand while typing on his Gizmo with the other. I was trying really hard to get away too. His grip was like an iron vise. I still think about that sometimes late at night.

Binh crumpled to the ground. He tried to get to his hands and knees but couldn't. When you can't get off the ground in the moon's gravity, you are seriously out of it.

Rudy knelt down and pulled Binh's head off the ground by the hair. "Let's see . . . yes that cheek is swelling up nicely. Now for the black eye . . ." He rabbit-punched the barely conscious man in the eye then let his head fall to the ground.

Binh, now in a fetal position, moaned, "Stop . . ."

Rudy stood and took his Gizmo back from me. He held it so we could both see. "Two bruised ribs, right? The fourth and fifth on the left side?"

"Looks like it," I agreed.

He kicked the prone man in the side. Binh tried to cry out but had no breath to scream with.

"I'll just assume he has a concussion from one of those head punches," Rudy said. "Wouldn't want to take things too far."

The other techs had stopped to watch the spectacle. Several of them were smiling. Đoàn, still in his chair, had the slightest hint of approval on his face.

"This is how it's going to go, Binh," Rudy said. "Whatever happens to her happens to you from now on. Got that?"

Binh wheezed on the floor.

"Got that?!" Rudy asked, louder this time.

Binh nodded fervently.

"Good." He smiled. He turned to me. "There's your package, Jazz. Approximately one hundred kilograms to be delivered to Doc Roussel. Charge it to the Security Services account."

"Got it," I said.

That's how justice works around here. We don't have jails or fines. If you commit a serious crime, we exile you to Earth. For everything else, there's Rudy.

After that "special delivery" I did a few more mundane pickups and drop-offs. Mostly items from the port to home addresses. But I did nab a contract to move a bunch of boxes from a residence back to the port. I love helping people move. They usually tip well. That day's move was pretty modest—a young couple relocating back to Earth.

The woman was pregnant. You can't gestate a baby in lunar gravity—it leads to birth defects. And you can't raise a baby here, anyway. It's terrible for bone and muscle development. When I moved here I was six years old—that was the minimum age for residency back then. Since then they've bumped it up to twelve. Should I be worried?

I was just moving on to the next pickup when my Gizmo screeched at me. Not the ring of a phone call, not the bleep of a message, but the *scream* of an alarm. I fumbled it out of my pocket.

> FIRE: CU12-3270—LOCKDOWN ENACTED. ALL NEARBY VOLUNTEER PERSONNEL TO RESPOND.

"Shit," I said.

I threw Trigger into reverse and backed up until I found a patch of hallway wide enough for a U-turn. Now facing the right way, I sped to the ramps.

"Jazz Bashara responding," I said to my Gizmo. "Current location Conrad Up Four."

The central safety computer noted my report and popped up a map of Conrad. I was one of many dots on that map, all converging on CU12-3270.

Artemis doesn't have a fire department. We have volunteers. But smoke and fire are so deadly here the volunteers have to know how to breathe with air tanks. So all EVA masters and EVA trainees are automatically volunteers. Yes, there's an irony there.

The fire was on Conrad Up 12—eight floors above me.

I screeched along the ramps up and up to CU12, then sped along the corridors toward the third ring. From there, I had to find the lot that was approximately 270 degrees from true north. It didn't take long—a crowd of EVA masters had already converged.

A red light flashed over the thick door to the address. The sign above read QUEENSLAND GLASS FACTORY.

Bob was on-scene. As the ranking guild member present, the fire was his responsibility. He gave me a quick nod to acknowledge my presence.

"Okay, listen up!" he said. "We've had a full-fledged fire inside the glass factory, which has burned off all the available oxygen in the room. There are fourteen people inside—all of them made it to the air shelter in time. There are no injuries, and the shelter is working properly."

He stood in front of the door. "We can't just wait for the room to cool like we normally would. This factory creates glass by reacting silicon with oxygen, so they have large tanks of compressed oxygen in there. If those tanks burst, the room will contain the explosion, but the people inside will have no chance. And if we let fresh oxygen in the whole thing will blow."

He shooed us away from the doorway to make an empty area. "We need a tent right here, sealed to the wall around the doorway. We need an inflatable accordion tunnel *inside* the tent. And we need four rescue workers."

The fire brigade, well trained, got on it immediately. They built a cube skeleton out of hollow pipes. Then they taped plastic to the wall around the fireproof door, draped it over the skeleton, and taped the edges together. They left the rear flap open.

They hoisted an accordion tunnel into the tent. This was no small task—unlike the makeshift tent, inflatable tunnels were made to hold pressure. They're thick and heavy, designed to rescue people from air shelters when there's a complete vacuum outside. A bit of an overkill in this scenario, but it's the equipment we had.

The tent wasn't very large, and the tunnel occupied most of the space inside. So Bob pointed to the four smallest responders. "Sarah, Jazz, Arun, and Marcy. Get in."

The four of us stepped forward. The others put air tanks on our backs, breather masks on our faces, and goggles over our eyes. One by one we tested our gear and gave a thumbs-up.

We crowded into the tent. It was a tight fit. Bob stood a metal cylinder just inside. "The air shelter is along the west wall. A total of fourteen people inside."

"Copy. Fourteen," said Sarah. A fully licensed EVA master with the most tenure out of the four of us, she was the insertion team's leader. The other fire brigade volunteers taped the tent flap closed, except for one corner, which they left slightly open.

Sarah cranked the valve on the cylinder and it sprayed a fog of carbon dioxide into the tent. It's a sloppy process, displacing oxygen, but we didn't need to expel every last atom. We just needed to get the percentage as low as possible. After a minute, she cranked the valve shut again and the people outside sealed that last corner of the tent.

She felt the door. "Hot," she said. We were about to open a door into a room just waiting to blow up. We weren't going to add oxygen, but it was still unnerving.

She keyed the fire unlock code into the door panel. Yes, a code. Once a fireproof room's alarms go off, the doors and vents seal immediately. The people inside can't get out—they have to get into an air shelter or die. Seem harsh? Well, it's not. A fire spreading in town would be far worse than a few people dying in a sealed room. Artemis does *not* fuck around with fire safety.

At Sarah's command, the door clicked open and heat from inside filled our tent. I immediately broke into a sweat.

"Jesus," said Arun.

The factory was thick with smoke. Some corners glowed red with heat. If there'd been any oxygen to spare, they would've certainly been aflame. Along the far wall, I could just make out the shape of the industrial air shelter.

Sarah wasted no time. "Jazz, you're with me up front. Arun and Marcy, stay here and hold the back of the inflatable."

I joined Sarah. She grabbed one side of the tunnel's front opening and I grabbed the other. Arun and Marcy did the same with the back half.

Sarah walked forward and I kept pace. The accordion-style tunnel expanded along behind us, with Arun and Marcy holding the rear steady.

Reacting silicon with oxygen creates a lot of heat. Hence the fireproof room. Why not just melt sand like they do on Earth? Because we don't have sand on the moon. At least, not enough to be useful. But we do have plenty of silicon and oxygen, which are by-products of the aluminum industry. So we can make as much glass as we want. We just have to make it the hard way.

The primary reaction chamber stood just ahead of us. We'd have to get the tunnel around it to reach the trapped workers. "Probably a hot spot," I said.

Sarah nodded and led us around in a wide arc. We didn't want to melt a hole in our rescue tunnel.

We reached the shelter hatch and I knocked on the small, round window. A face appeared—a man with watering eyes and ash-covered face. Most likely the foreman, who would have entered the shelter last. He gave me a thumbs-up and I returned the gesture.

Sarah and I stepped into the tunnel, then clamped the hoop around the shelter's hatch. That was easy, at least. It's exactly what the tunnel was designed for. Still at the tent, Arun and Marcy pressed their end of the tunnel against the plastic and taped it in place. We'd created an escape route for the workers, but it was full of unbreathable air from the room.

"Ready to blow it out?" Sarah yelled.

"Sealed and ready!" Arun called back.

The folks outside cut a slit in the plastic. Smoke from the tunnel leaked into the hallway, but the brigade already had fans and filters ready to minimize its spread.

"Tent's open! Blow it out!" Arun yelled.

Sarah and I exchanged a glance to confirm we were both ready. Together, we took a deep breath and popped the vent releases on our air tanks. The escaping gas pushed the smoke along with it, down the tunnel and out into the hallway. Soon, the tunnel had "breathable" air inside. Conrad Up 12 would have a sooty smell for days.

We both coughed when we tried the air, but it wasn't too bad. It didn't have to be pleasant. It just had to be non-toxic. Satisfied that it wouldn't kill the workers, Sarah cranked the handle to the air-shelter hatch.

To their credit, the workers filed out in a fast, controlled line. My respect for Queensland Glass went up a notch. They kept their employees well trained for emergencies.

"One! Two! Three! . . ." Sarah counted off each person as they passed. I kept my own count to confirm.

Once she reached fourteen, I called out, "Fourteen! Confirmed!"

She looked into the shelter. "Empty shelter!"

I did the same. "Empty shelter! Confirmed!"

We followed the coughing, choking workers down the tunnel to safety.

"Good work," said Bob. Other volunteers were already fitting oxygen masks on the singed employees. "Jazz, we have three moderately wounded—second-degree burns. Give them a ride to Doc Roussel. The rest of you, shove that tent and tunnel into the room and reseal the fire door."

For the second time that day, Trigger and I served as an ambulance.

In the end, the oxygen tanks didn't blow up. Still, Queensland Glass was destroyed. A shame—they'd always been solid on fire safety. Never even had a single infraction. Bad luck, I guess. Now they'd have to rebuild from scratch.

Still, their well-maintained air shelter and regular fire drills had saved a lot of lives. Factories can be rebuilt. People can't. It was a win.

That evening, I hit my favorite watering hole: Hartnell's Pub.

I sat in my usual seat—second from the end of the bar. The first seat used to be Dale's, but those days were over.

Hartnell's was a hole in the wall. No music. No dance floor. Just a bar and a few uneven tables. The only concession to ambience was noise-absorption foam on the walls. Billy knew what his customers valued: alcohol and silence. The vibe was completely asexual. No one hit on people at Hartnell's. If you were looking to score, you went to a nightclub in Aldrin. Hartnell's was for drinking. And you could get any drink you wanted, as long as it was beer.

I loved the place. Partially because Billy was a pleasant bartender, but mainly because it was the closest bar to my coffin.

"Evenin', luv," said Billy. "Heard there was a fire today. Heard you went in."

"Queensland Glass," I said. "I'm short so I got volunteered. The factory's totaled but we got everyone out all right."

"Right, well the first one's on me, then." He poured a glass of my favorite reconstituted German beer. Tourists say it tastes like shit but it's the only beer I've ever known and it works for me. Someday I'll buy an intact German beer to see what I'm missing. He set it in front of me. "Thanks for your service, luv."

"Hey, I won't say no." I grabbed the free beer and took a swig. Nice and cold. "Thanks!"

Billy nodded in acknowledgment and went to the other end of the bar to serve another customer.

I brought up a web browser on my Gizmo and searched for "ZAFO." It was a conjugation of the Spanish verb *zafar*, meaning "to release." Somehow I doubted Mr. Jin from Hong Kong brought something with a Spanish name. Besides, "ZAFO" was in all-caps. Probably an acronym. But for what?

Whatever it was, I couldn't find any mention of it online. That meant it was a secret. Now I *really* wanted to know what it was. Turns out I'm a nosy little shit. But right at that moment, I didn't have anything else to go on, so I mentally set it aside.

I had this bad habit of checking my bank account every day, as if compulsively looking at it would make it grow. But the banking software wasn't interested in my dreams. It gave me the dismal news:

ACCOUNT BALANCE: 11,916ğ

My entire net worth was about 2.5 percent of my goal of 416,922 slugs. That's what I wanted. That's what I *needed*. Nothing was more important.

If I could just get into the damned EVA Guild, I'd pull down serious income from then on. Tours are big money. Eight customers per tour at 1,500ğ each. That's 12,000ğ per tour. Well, 10,800ğ after I pay the guild their 10 percent.

I could only give two tours a week—a limitation enforced by

the guild. They're cautious about their members' radiation exposure.

I'd be making over 85,000ğ a month. And that's just from
tours. I'd also try to get a job as a probe wrangler. They're the
EVA masters who bring the probes to the freight airlock and
unload them. Then I'd have access to shipments *before* Nakoshi
inspected them. I could sneak contraband in right then or set it
aside for later recovery with a sneaky midnight EVA. Whatever
worked best. Point is, I could cut Nakoshi out entirely.

I'd keep living like a pauper until I'd saved up the money I
needed. Accounting for living expenses, I could probably get it
done in six months. Maybe five.

As it was, on my porter's salary with smuggling on the side, it
would take approximately forever.

Goddamn, I wish I'd passed that fucking test.

Once I'd taken care of the 416,922ğ, I'd still be making a
bunch of money. I could afford a *nice* place. My shithole coffin
only cost eight thousand a month, but I couldn't even stand up in
it. And I wanted my own bathroom. That doesn't seem like a big
deal, but it is. I realized that around the hundredth time I had
to walk down a public hallway in my nightie to take a midnight
piss.

For fifty thousand a month—well within what I'd be earn-
ing—I could get a condo in Bean Bubble. A nice one with a living
room, bedroom, bathroom, and its own shower. No more communal anything. I could even get a place with a cook nook. Not
a kitchen—that'd be stupidly expensive. They have to be in their
own fire containment rooms. But a cook-nook burner was allowed to get up to 80 degrees Celsius and could have a 500-watt
microwave.

I shook my head. Someday, maybe.

I guess my pained expression was visible even from the far
end of the bar. Billy walked over. "Oi, Jazz. Why so glum?"

"Money," I said. "Never enough money."

"I hear ya, luv." He leaned in. "So . . . remember when I con-tracted your services for some pure ethanol?"

"Sure," I said. In a concession to basic human nature, Arte-mis allows liquor even though it's flammable. But they draw the line at pure ethanol, which is *incredibly* flammable. I smuggled it in the usual way and only charged Billy a 20 percent markup. That's my friends-and-family rate.

He looked left and right. A couple of regulars minded their own business. Other than that we were alone. "I want to show you somefin' . . ."

He reached under the bar and pulled up a bottle of brown liq-uid. He poured some into a shot glass. "Here. 'Ave a sip."

I could smell the alcohol from a meter away. "What is it?"

"Bowmore single-malt scotch. Aged fifteen years. Give it a try, on the 'ouse."

I'm never one to turn down a free drink. I took a sip.

I spat it out in disgust. It tasted like Satan's flaming asshole!

"Huh," he said. "No good?"

I coughed and wiped my mouth. "That is *not* scotch."

He looked at the bottle with a frown. "Huh. I had a bloke on Earth boil the liquids off then send me the extract. I reconsti-tuted it with water and effanol. Should be exactly the same."

"Well, it's not," I rasped.

"Scotch is an acquired taste. . . ."

"Billy, I've swallowed better-tasting stuff that came out of people."

"Bugger." He put the bottle away. "I'll keep working on it."

I gulped beer to wash the taste away.

My Gizmo beeped at me. A message from Trond:

"Free tonight? Can you drop by my place?"

Meh. I was just starting my evening beers.

"It's late. Can it wait?"

"Best if handled tonight."

"I'm just sitting down to dinner . . ."

"You can drink dinner later. This is worth your time, I promise."

Smartass.

"Looks like I have to cash out," I told Billy.

"Pull the other one!" he said. "You've only had one pint!"

"Duty calls." I handed him my Gizmo.

He took it to the register. "One pint. Lowest tab I ever rung you for."

"I won't make a habit of it."

He waved my Gizmo over the register then handed it back to me. The transaction was done (I'd long ago set up my account to accept Hartnell's as a "no-verify" point of purchase). I slid the Gizmo into my pocket and headed out. The other patrons didn't say goodbye or even acknowledge me. God, I love Hartnell's.

Irina opened the door and frowned at me like I'd just pissed in her borscht. As usual, she wouldn't let me pass without stating my business.

"Hi, I'm Jazz Bashara," I said. "We've met over a hundred times. I'm here to see Trond at his invitation."

She led me through to the dining-hall entrance. The smell of delicious food hung in the air. Something meaty, I thought. Roast beef? A rare delicacy when the nearest cow is 400,000 kilometers away.

I peeked in to see Trond sip liquor from a tumbler. He wore his usual bathrobe and chatted with someone across the table. I couldn't see who.

His daughter Lene sat next to him. She watched her father talk with rapt fascination. Most sixteen-year-olds hate their parents. I was a *huge* pain in the ass to my dad at that age (nowadays I'm just a general disappointment). But Lene looked up to Trond like he put the Earth in the sky.

She spotted me then waved excitedly. "Jazz! Hi!"

Trond gestured me in. "Jazz! Come in, come in. Have you met the administrator?"

I walked in and—holy shit! Administrator Ngugi was there. She was just . . . there! Hanging out at the table.

Fidelis Ngugi is, simply put, the reason Artemis exists. When she was Kenya's minister of finance, she created the country's entire space industry from scratch. Kenya had one—and only one—natural resource to offer space companies: the equator. Spacecraft launched from the equator could take full advantage of Earth's rotation to save fuel. But Ngugi realized they could offer something more: policy. Western nations drowned commercial space companies in red tape. Ngugi said, "Fuck that. How about we don't?"

I'm paraphrasing here.

God only knows how she convinced fifty corporations from thirty-four countries to dump billions of dollars into creating KSC, but she did it. And she made sure Kenya enacted special tax breaks and laws just for the new megacorporation.

What's that, you say? Favoring a single company with special laws isn't fair? Tell that to the East India Tea Company. This is global economics, not kindergarten.

And wouldn't you know it, when KSC had to pick someone to run Artemis for them, they picked . . . Fidelis Ngugi! That's how shit gets done. She pulled money out of *nowhere*, created a huge industry in her formerly third-world country, and landed herself a job as ruler of the moon. She had run Artemis for over twenty years.

"Bwuh—" I said eloquently. "Shaa . . ."

"I know, right?!" said Lene.

Ngugi's traditional *dhuku* headscarf counterpointed her modern, Western-style dress. She stood politely, walked toward me, and said, "Hello, dear." Her Swahili-accented English rolled so smoothly off her tongue I wanted to adopt her as my grandma right then and there.

"J-Jasmine," I stammered. "I'm Jasmine Bashara."

"I know," she said.

What?

She smiled. "We have met before. I hired your father to install an emergency air shelter in my home. He brought you along. That was back when the administrator's quarters were in Armstrong Bubble."

"Wow . . . I don't remember that at all."

"You were very young. Such an adorable little child, hanging on her father's every word. How is Ammar these days?"

I blinked a couple of times. "Uh . . . Dad's fine. Thanks. I don't see him much. He's got his shop and I've got my work."

"He is a good man, your father," she said. "An honest businessman and a hard worker. One of the best welders in town, as well. It's too bad you had a falling-out."

"Wait, how did you know we—"

"Lene, it's been lovely to see you again. You're so grown-up now!"

"Thanks, Administrator!" Lene beamed.

"And Trond, thank you for a delicious meal," she said.

"Any time, Administrator." Trond stood up. I couldn't believe he was in his bathrobe! He had dinner with the most important person on the moon and he wore his bathrobe! Then he shook Ngugi's hand like they were equals or something. "Thanks for coming by!"

Irina showed up and led Ngugi away. Was there a hint of admiration on the grumpy old Russian's face? I guess even Irina had her limits. You can't hate *everyone*.

"Holy shit, dude," I said to Trond.

"Pretty cool, huh?" Trond turned to his daughter. "All right, pumpkin, time for you to skedaddle. Jazz and I have business to discuss."

She groaned the way only teenage girls can. "You always send me away when things get interesting."

"Don't be in such a hurry. You'll be a cutthroat business asshole soon enough."

"Just like my dad." She smiled. She reached to the floor and picked up her crutches. They were the kind that gripped the upper arm. She got them both into position with ease and brought herself vertical. Her legs hung free. She kissed Trond on the cheek, then walked out on the crutches without her feet touching the ground.

The car accident that killed her mother had paralyzed Lene for life. Trond had money coming out his ass, but nothing could buy back his daughter's ability to walk. Or could it? On Earth, Lene was confined to a wheelchair, but on the moon, she could easily move around on crutches.

So he hired VPs to manage most of his companies and relocated to Artemis. And just like that, Lene Landvik could walk again.

"Bye, Jazz!" she said on her way out.

"Bye, kiddo."

Trond swirled his drink. "Have a seat."

The dining table was huge, so I picked a chair a couple of spaces away from Trond. "What's in the glass?"

"Scotch. Want some?"

"Maybe a taste," I said.

He slid the glass across to me. I took a sip.

"Ohhh yeahhh . . ." I said. "That's better."

"Didn't know you were a scotch gal," he said.

"Not normally. But I had an awful approximation of it earlier today, so I needed a reminder of what it's supposed to be like." I offered the tumbler back.

"Keep it." He went to the liquor credenza, poured a second glass, and returned to his seat.

"So why was the administrator here?" I asked.

He put his feet up on the table and leaned back in his chair. "I'm hoping to buy Sanchez Aluminum and I wanted her blessing. She's fine with it."

"Why would you want an aluminum company?"

"Because I like building businesses." He preened theatrically. "It's my thing."

"But aluminum? I mean . . . isn't that sort of blah? I get the impression it's struggling as an industry."

"It is," said Trond. "Not like the old days, when aluminum was king—each bubble required *forty thousand tons* of aluminum to build. But now the population has plateaued and we're not making new bubbles anymore. Frankly, they would have gone out of business long ago if it weren't for their aluminum monopropellant fuel production. And even that barely turns a profit."

"Seems like you missed the gravy train. Why get in now?"

"I think I can make it hugely profitable again."

"How?"

"None of your business."

I held up my hands. "Sheesh. Touchy. Fine, you want to make aluminum. Why not start your own company?"

He snorted. "If only it were that easy. It's impossible to compete with Sanchez. Literally impossible. What do you know about aluminum production?"

"Pretty much nothing," I said. I settled back in my chair. Trond seemed chatty tonight. Best to let him get it out of his system. And hey, as long as he talked I got good booze.

"First, they collect anorthite ore. That's easy. All they have to do is pick up the right rocks. They have automated harvesters running day and night. Then they smelt the ore with a chemical and electrolysis process that takes a shitload of electricity. And I do mean a shitload. Sanchez Aluminum uses *eighty percent* of the city reactors' output."

"Eighty percent?" I'd never thought about it before, but two

27-megawatt nuclear reactors was a bit much for a city of two thousand people.

"Yeah, but the interesting part is how they pay for it."

He pulled a rock from his pocket. Wasn't much to look at—just a gray, jagged lump like all the other lunar rocks I'd ever seen. He tossed it toward me. "Here. Have some anorthite."

"Yay, a rock." I plucked it out of the air as it approached. "Thanks."

"It's made of aluminum, oxygen, silicon, and calcium. Smelting separates it into those base elements. They sell the aluminum—that's the whole point. And they sell the silicon to glassmakers and the calcium to electricians for next to nothing—mainly to get rid of it. But there is one by-product that's incredibly useful: oxygen."

"Yeah, and that's what we breathe. I know."

"Yeah, but did you know Sanchez gets free power in exchange for that oxygen?"

He had me there. "Really?"

"Yup. It's a contract that goes back to the early days of Artemis. Sanchez makes our air, so Artemis gives Sanchez as much power as they want—completely free of charge."

"They don't have to pay an electric bill? Ever?"

"As long as they keep making oxygen for the city, that's right. And power is the most expensive part of smelting. There's just no way I can compete. It's not fair."

"Oh, poor billionaire," I said. "Maybe you should have some moors installed so you can pine on them."

"Yeah, yeah, rich people are evil blah, blah, blah."

I emptied my glass. "Thanks for the scotch. Why am I here?"

He cocked his head and looked at me. Was he carefully choosing his words? Trond never did that.

"I hear you failed your EVA exam."

I groaned. "Does *everyone* in town know about that? Do you

all meet up and talk about me when I'm not around or something?"

"It's a small town, Jazz. I keep my ear to the ground."

I slid my glass over to him. "If we're going to talk about my
failures, I'll want another scotch."

He passed me his full glass. "I want to hire you. And I want
to pay you a lot."

I perked up. "Well, okay then. Why didn't you open with that?
What do you need smuggled in? Something big?"

He leaned forward. "It's not smuggling. It's an entirely different enterprise. I don't know if it's even in your comfort zone.
You've always been honest—at least with me. Do I have your
word that this will stay between us? Even if you turn down the
job?"

"Of course." One thing I picked up from Dad: Always keep
your bargains. He worked within the law and I didn't, but the
principle was the same. People will trust a reliable criminal
more readily than a shady businessman.

"That power-for-oxygen deal is the only thing standing between me and the aluminum industry. If Sanchez stops supply-
ing oxygen, they'll be in breach of contract. Then I'll step in and
offer to take it over. Same deal: free oxygen for free power."

"Where would you get the oxygen?" I asked. "You don't have
a smelter."

"No rule says it has to be smelted. The city doesn't give a shit
where the oxygen comes from, so long as it comes." He steepled
his fingers. "For the last four months, I've been collecting oxygen
and storing it away. I have enough to supply the entire city's
needs for over a year."

I raised an eyebrow. "You can't just take city air and keep it.
That's monumentally illegal."

He waved his hand dismissively. "Please. I'm not an idiot. I
bought the oxygen fair and square. I have standing contracts
with Sanchez for regular deliveries."

"You're buying oxygen from Sanchez so you can take over the oxygen contract from Sanchez?"

He smirked. "They make so much oxygen the entire city doesn't breathe it fast enough. They sell it cheap to anyone who wants it. I bought it slowly, over time, through various shell businesses so no one would know I'm hoarding."

I pinched my chin. "Oxygen is pretty much the definition of flammable. How'd you get the city to let you store so much?"

"I didn't. I built huge holding tanks outside Armstrong Bubble. They're in the triangle formed by the connector tunnels of Armstrong, Bean, and Shepard. Totally safe from idiot tourists, and if anything goes wrong, they'll just leak into the vacuum. They're connected to Life Support's systems, but they're separated by a physical valve outside. No harm can come to the city."

"Huh." I spun my glass on the table. "You want me to stop Sanchez's oxygen production."

"Yes, I do." He stood from his chair and walked over to the liquor credenza. This time he selected a bottle of rum. "The city will want a fast resolution and I'll get the contract. Once that happens, I won't even have to build my own smelter. Sanchez will see the futility of trying to make aluminum without free power and they'll let me buy them outright."

He poured himself a fresh drink and returned to the table. There, he opened a panel to reveal a bunch of controls.

The room lights faded and a projection screen came to life on the far wall.

"Are you a supervillain or something?" I gestured to the screen. "I mean, come on."

"Like it? I just had it installed."

The screen showed a satellite picture of our local area in Mare Tranquillitatis. Artemis was a tiny blob of circles brilliantly illuminated by sunlight.

"We're in the lowlands," Trond said. "There's plenty of olivine and ilmenite around. Those are great for making iron, but if you want aluminum you need anorthite. It's rare around here, but the highlands are *littered* with it. So Sanchez's harvesters operate in the Moltke Foothills three kilometers south of here."

He turned on his Gizmo's laser pointer and pointed to a region south of the city.

"The harvesters are almost completely autonomous. They only call home for instructions if they get stuck or can't figure out what to do next. They're an essential part of the company's operations, they're all in one place, and they're completely unguarded."

"Okay," I said. "I see where this is going. . . ."

"Yeah," he said. "I want you to sabotage those harvesters. Take them all out at once. And make sure they can't be repaired. It'll take Sanchez at least a month to get replacements shipped here from Earth. During that time they'll get no new anorthite. No anorthite means no oxygen production. No oxygen production means I win."

I folded my arms. "I don't know if this works for me, Trond. Sanchez has like a hundred employees, right? I don't want to put people out of their jobs."

"Don't worry about that," Trond said. "I want to *buy* the company, not ruin it. Everyone will keep their jobs."

"Okay, but I don't know anything about harvesters."

His fingers flew over the controls and the display changed to a picture of a harvester. It looked like something from a catalogue. "The harvesters are Toyota Tsukurumas. I have four of them in my warehouse, ready for use."

Whoa. Okay. Something the size of a harvester would have to be shipped in chunks and assembled here. Plus, it would have to be done in secret so no one asked awkward questions like "Say, Trond, why is your company assembling harvesters?" He'd had his people on this for a long time.

He must have seen the gears turning in my head. "Yeah. I've been working on this for a while. Anyway, you're welcome to examine my harvesters for as long as you want. All in secrecy of course."

I got out of my chair and walked up to the screen. Man, that harvester was a beast. "So it's my problem to find a weakness in these things? I'm not an engineer."

"They're automated vehicles without any security features at all. You're clever, I'm sure you'll come up with something."

"Okay, but what happens if I get caught?"

"Jazz who?" he said theatrically. "The delivery girl? I barely know her. Why would she do such a thing? I'm baffled."

"I see how it is."

"I'm just being honest. Part of the deal is your word that you won't drag me down if you get caught."

"Why me? What makes you think I can even pull this off?"

"Jazz, I'm a businessman," he said. "My whole job is exploiting underutilized resources. And you are a *massively* underutilized resource."

He stood and walked to the credenza for another pour. "You could have been anything. Didn't want to be a welder? No problem. You could have been a scientist. An engineer. A politician. A business leader. Anything. But you're a porter."

I scowled.

"I'm not judging," he said. "Just analyzing. You're really smart and you want money. I need someone who's really smart and I have money. Are you interested?"

"Hmm . . ." I took a moment to think. Was it even possible?

I'd need access to an airlock. There are only four airlocks in the whole city and you have be a licensed EVA Guild member to use them—their control panels check your Gizmo.

Then there was the three-kilometer trip to the Moltke Foothills. How would I do that? Walk? And once I was there, what would I do? The harvesters would have cameras and film everything in a 360-degree arc for navigational purposes. How would I sabotage them without getting spotted?

Also, I smelled bullshit in the air. Trond had been squirrely and evasive about his reasons for getting into aluminum. But it was *my* ass on the line if something went wrong, not his. And if I got caught I'd get exiled to Earth. I probably couldn't *stand up* on Earth, let alone live there. I'd been in lunar gravity since I was six.

No. I was a smuggler, not a saboteur. And something smelled off about the whole thing.

"I'm sorry, but this isn't my thing," I said. "You'll have to find someone else."

"I'll give you a million slugs."

"Deal."

Yo, Kelvin,

What's new? Haven't heard from you in a few days. Did you get into the chess club?

What kind of junior high chess club has entrance requirements, anyway? Are they so impacted with applicants they have to turn some away? What, like they don't have enough chess boards? Only so many tables? Limited number of pocket-protectors?

My school is trying to put me in the gifted classes. Again. Dad totally wants me to go, but why should I? I'm probably just going to be a welder. I don't need differential calculus to stick pieces of metal together. Sigh . . .

Hey, so what happened with Charisse? Did you ask her out? Or talk to her? Or indicate in any way that you exist? Or are you sticking with your brilliant plan to avoid her at all costs?

Jazz,

Sorry, I've been busy with extracurricular stuff lately. Yes, I got into the chess club. I played several games to establish my skill level and they rated me at 1124. That's not very good, but I'm studying and practicing to become better. I play against my computer every day and now I'll get to play against people too.

Why don't you join the gifted classes? Academic achievement is a great way to honor your parents. You should consider it. I'm sure your father would be very proud. My parents would love it if I could get into the advanced classes. But math is hard. I keep my grades up, but it's hard.

I have resolve, though. I want to make rockets, and you can't do that without math.

No, I haven't talked to Charisse. I'm sure she wouldn't be interested in a boy like me. Girls like boys who are big and strong and who beat up other boys. I'm none of those things. If I talked to her, I would just get humiliated.

Kelvin,

Dude.

I don't know where you're getting info about girls but you're WRONG. Girls like boys who are nice and make us laugh. We DON'T like boys who get in fights and we don't like boys who are stupid. Trust me on this. I'm a girl.

Dad has me helping out around the shop. I can solo the simpler jobs. He pays me, which is nice. But he stopped my allowance now that I have an income. So now I'm working for a little bit more than I was getting for free. Not sure I'm on board with that plan but whatever.

Dad's having problems with the Welders' Guild. Around here, you can either be freelance or part of the guild. And the guild doesn't like freelancers. Dad doesn't have a problem with guilds as a rule, but he says the Welders' Guild is "mobbed up." I guess they're pretty much owned by Saudi organized crime. Why Saudi? I don't know. Almost all the welders here are Saudis. We're just the people who ended up controlling the welding industry.

Anyway, the guild forces people to join with bullshit tactics. Not like in movies where they threaten you or anything. Just rumormongering. Floating stories that you're dishonest and you do shitty work. Stuff like that. But Dad spent his whole life building a reputation. The fake rumors just bounce off. None of his customers believe them.

Go Dad!

Jazz,

That's too bad about the Welders' Guild. There are no unions or guilds at KSC. It's a special administrative zone and the normal laws that help unions don't apply. KSC has a lot of power in the Kenyan government. There are many special laws for them. But KSC is a boon to all of us and they deserve special treatment. Without them we would be poor like other African countries.

Have you ever considered moving to Earth? I'm sure you could become a scientist or an engineer and make a lot of money. You're a citizen of Saudi Arabia, right? They have lots of big corporations there. Lots of jobs for smart people.

Kelvin,

Nah. I don't want to live on Earth. I'm a moon gal. Besides, it would be a huge medical hassle. I've been here more than half my life, so my body is used to $1/6$th of your gravity. Before I could go to Earth I'd have to do a bunch of exercise and take special pills to stimulate muscle and bone growth. Then I'd have to spend hours every day in a centrifuge . . . bleh. No thanks.

Talk to Charisse you chickenshit.

I slinked along a huge corridor on Aldrin Down 7. I didn't really have to sneak around—at this ungodly hour, no one was in sight.

Five a.m. was a largely theoretical concept to me. I knew it existed, but I rarely observed it. Nor did I want to. But this morning was different. Trond insisted on secrecy, so we had to meet before normal working hours.

Barn doors towered every twenty meters. The lots here were few and large, a testament to how much money these businesses had handy. Trond's company workshop was labeled only with a sign reading LD7-4030—LANDVIK INDUSTRIES.

I knocked on the door. A second later, it slid partially open. Trond poked his head out and looked both ways down the hall.

"Were you followed?"

"Of course," I said. "And I led them straight to you. Turns out I'm not very bright."

"Smartass."

"Dumbass."

"Come in." He gestured me forward.

I slipped in and he immediately closed the door. I didn't know if he thought this was stealthy or what. But hey, he was paying me a million slugs. We could play 007 if he wanted.

The workshop was effectively a garage. A *huge* garage. Seriously, I'd kill to have that space. I'd make a little house in one corner and then, I don't know, install fake grass in the rest of it? Four identical harvesters, each in its own bay, filled the room.

I walked over to the nearest harvester and looked up at it. "Wow."

"Yeah," Trond said. "You don't realize how big they are until you see one up close."

"How did you get them into town without anyone knowing?"

"It wasn't easy," Trond said. "I had them shipped here in pieces. Only my most trusted people even know about it. I pieced together a staff of seven mechanics who know how to keep their mouths shut."

I scanned the cavernous workshop. "Anyone else here?"

"Of course not. I don't want anyone knowing I hired you."

"I'm hurt."

The harvester stood four meters tall, five meters wide, and ten meters long. Reflective material coated the hull to minimize solar heating. Each of the beast's six wheels was a meter and a half across. The bulk of the machine was a huge, empty basin. Powerful hydraulics on the front and a hinge on the rear provided the basin's dumping mechanism.

The front of the harvester had a scoop with associated articulation. There was no passenger compartment, of course. Harvesters were automated—though they could be remote-controlled when necessary. A sealed metal box rested where you might expect a cockpit. It bore the Toyota logo, along with the word "Tsukuruma" in a stylish font.

Roll-around toolboxes and maintenance equipment surrounded the harvester wherever the workers had left off at the end of their shift.

"Okay," I said, taking in the scene. "This is going to be a challenge."

"What's the problem?" Trond walked over to one of the wheels and leaned against it. "It's just a robot—it doesn't have any defenses. Its only AI is for pathing. I'm sure you and a big tank of acetylene could figure something out."

"This thing is a *tank*, Trond. It's not going to be easy to kill." I walked partially around the harvester and got a closer look at the undercarriage. "And it's got cameras everywhere."

"Of course it does," said Trond. "It needs them to navigate."

"It sends video back to its controllers," I said. "Once it goes offline, the controllers will roll back to footage to see what happened. They'll see me."

"So cover up any identifying marks on your EVA suit," Trond said. "No problem."

"Oh there's a problem. They'll call the EVA masters to ask what the hell's going on, and then the EVA masters will come out to get me. They won't know who I am, but they can drag my ass back inside and have a *Scooby-Doo* moment when they pull my helmet off."

He walked around to my side of the harvester. "I see your point."

I ran my hands through my hair. I hadn't showered that morning. I felt like I was a wad of grease that had been dipped in a vat of dirtier grease. "I need to come up with something that has a delayed effect. So it'll happen *after* I get back inside."

"And don't forget, you've got to total the things. If there's anything left to fix, Sanchez's repair crews will have them up and running in days."

"Yeah, I know." I pinched my chin. "Where's the battery?"

"In the forward compartment. The box with the Toyota logo on it."

I found a primary breaker box near the forward compartment. Inside were the main breakers to protect the electronics from power surges or shorts. Worth noting.

I leaned up against a nearby tool cabinet. "When they're full, they take their stuff to the smelter?"

"Yeah." He picked up a wrench and threw it into the air. It lofted toward the ceiling.

"Then they . . . what? Dump their load and go back to Moltke?"

"After they recharge."

I ran my hand along the sleek, reflective metal of the basin. "How big's the battery?"

"Two point four megawatt hours."

"Wow!" I turned to him. "I could arc-weld with that kind of juice."

He shrugged. "Hauling a hundred tons of rock takes energy."

I climbed under the harvester. "How does it deal with heat rejection? Wax state-change material?"

"No idea."

When you're in a vacuum, getting rid of heat is a problem. There's no air to carry it away. And when you have electric power, every Joule of energy ultimately becomes heat. It might be from electrical resistance, friction in moving parts, or chemical reactions in the battery that release the energy in the first place. But ultimately it all ends up as heat.

Artemis has a complex coolant system that conveys the heat to thermal panels near the reactor complex. They sit in the shade and slowly radiate the energy away as infrared light. But the harvesters had to be self-contained.

After some searching, I found what I was looking for. The heat-rejection system valve. I recognized the type immediately— Dad and I had attached many of these in the past while repairing rovers.

"Yeah. It's wax," I said.

I saw Trond's feet approach. "What's that mean?" he asked.

"The battery and motor housings are encased in a solid wax reservoir. Melting the wax takes a lot of energy, so that's where the heat goes. The wax lines are surrounded by coolant pipes. When the harvester comes home to recharge, they pump cold water into those pipes to re-chill the wax, then pull the newly heated water back out. Then they cool the water off at their leisure while the harvester gets back to work."

"So can you make the harvesters overheat?" he asked. "Is that your plan?"

"It's not that simple. There are safeties to prevent overheating. The harvesters would just shut down until they cooled off. Sanchez's engineers would fix the problem right away. I have a different idea."

I wriggled out from under the harvester, stood, and stretched my back. Then I climbed the side and dropped into the basin. My voice echoed as I spoke. "Can any of its cameras see in here?"

"Why?" he asked. "Oh! You're going to ride a harvester to the Moltke Foothills!"

"Trond, can the cameras see in here?"

"No. Their purpose is navigation. They point outward. Hey, how will you get out of the city? You don't have airlock privileges."

"Don't worry about it." I climbed out of the basin and dropped four meters to the ground. I pulled a chair toward me, spun it around, and straddled it. I rested my chin on my palm and got lost in thought.

Trond sidled over. "So?"

"Thinking," I said.

"Do women know how sexy they look when they sit like that?"

"Of course."

"I *knew* it!"

"Trying to concentrate."

"Sorry."

I peered at the harvester for several minutes. Trond wandered aimlessly around the bay and fiddled with tools. He was an entrepreneurial genius, but he had the patience of a ten-year-old.

"Okay," I finally said. "I have a plan."

"Yeah?" Trond dropped a socket driver and scurried over. "Do tell."

I shook my head. "Don't worry about the details."

"I like details."

"A lady's got to have her secrets." I stood up. "But I'll completely destroy their harvesters."

"That sounds great!"

"All right," I said. "I'm going home. I need a shower."

"Yeah," said Trond. "You really do."

Once I got back to my coffin, I threw off my clothes faster than a drunk prom date. On with a bathrobe and off to the showers. I even paid the extra 200ğ for a soak in a tub. Felt good.

I spent the day doing deliveries as usual. I didn't want some perceptive asshole to notice a break in my routine immediately before a huge crime got committed. Just a normal day. No need to look at me whistling innocently. I worked until about four p.m.

I went home, lay down (it's not like I could stand up), and did some research. I envy one thing about Earthers—they get much faster internet. We have a local network in Artemis that's handy for slug transactions and email, but when it comes to web searches, all those servers are back on Earth. And that means an absolute minimum of four seconds' wait for every request. The speed of light just isn't as fast as I'd like.

I drank so much tea I had to jog to the communal bathroom every twenty minutes. After hours of work, I came to a conclusion: I really wanted my own bathroom.

But by the end of it I had a plan. And like all good plans, it required a crazy Ukrainian guy.

.   .   .

I pulled Trigger up to the ESA Research Center and parked in the narrow hallway.

Space agencies around the world were the first to rent property in Artemis. In the old days, Armstrong Ground was the best real estate in town. Since then, four more bubbles sprang up, and the space agencies remained. Their once cutting-edge design was now two decades out of date.

I hopped off Trigger and went into the labs. The first room, a tiny reception area, was a throwback to the days when real estate was much more limited. Four hallways led off at odd angles. Some of the doors couldn't be opened if others were open. The ergonomic abortion was the result of seventeen governments designing a laboratory by committee. I went through the center door, down the hallway almost to the end, and into the microelectronics lab.

Martin Svoboda hunched over a microscope and reached absently for his coffee. His hand passed three beakers of deadly acid before he grabbed the mug and took a sip. I swear that idiot's going to kill himself someday.

He'd been assigned to Artemis by ESA four years ago to study microelectronic manufacturing methods. Apparently, the moon has some unique advantages in that area. The ESA lab is a highly coveted posting, so he must've been good at his job.

"Svoboda," I said.

Nothing. He hadn't noticed me come in and didn't hear me speak. He's like that.

I smacked him on the back of the head and he jerked away from the microscope. He smiled like a child seeing a beloved aunt. "Oh! Hi, Jazz! What's up?"

I sat on a lab stool opposite him. "I need some mad science from you."

"Cool!" He spun his stool to face me. "What can I do?"

"I need electronics." I pulled schematics out of my pocket and handed them over. "This. Or something like it."

"Paper?" He held the schematics like they were a urine sample. "You wrote them on paper?"

"I don't know how to use drafting apps," I said. "Just—what do you think?"

He unfolded the paper and frowned at my scribblings. Svoboda was the best electrical engineer in town. Something like this shouldn't be a challenge for him.

He turned the sketch sideways. "Did you draw this with your left hand or something?"

"I'm not an artist, okay?"

He pinched his chin. "Art quality aside, this is an elegant design. Did you copy it from somewhere?"

"No, why? Is something wrong?"

He raised his brow. "It's just . . . it's really well done."

"Thanks?"

"I never knew you were so talented."

I shrugged. "I found electronics tutorials online and worked from there."

"You taught yourself?" He looked back to the schematic. "How long did it take?"

"Most of the afternoon."

"You learned all this *today*?! You'd make a great scientist—"

"Stop." I held up my hand. "I don't want to hear it. Can you make it or not?"

"Sure, sure," he said. "When do you need it?"

"The sooner the better."

He tossed the schematics on the lab table. "I can have it for you tomorrow."

"Great." I hopped off the stool and whipped out my Gizmo. "How much?"

He hesitated—never a good sign during negotiations.

He'd done odd jobs for me for years, mostly removing antipiracy chips from smuggled electronics. He usually charged 2,000ğ for freelance work. Why was this time different?

"Two thousand slugs?" I suggested.

"Hmm," he said. "Would you consider a trade?"

"Sure." I put my Gizmo away. "Need something smuggled in?"

"No."

"I see." Goddammit, I'm a smuggler! Why did people keep asking for other shit?!

He stood and gestured for me to follow. I went with him to the back corner of his lab where he did his off-book work. Why buy your own equipment when the taxpayers of Europe will buy it for you?

"Behold!" He gestured to the table.

The item in the middle wasn't much to look at. Just a small, clear plastic box with something inside. I took a closer look. "Is that a condom?"

"Yes!" he said proudly. "My latest invention."

"The Chinese beat you by seven centuries."

"This is not your everyday condom!" He slid a thermos-size cylinder over to me. It had a power cable and a hinged top. "It comes with this."

I opened the top. Tiny holes inside adorned the walls and a rounded metal cylinder stood mounted to the bottom. "Um. Okay . . ."

"I can make a profit by selling these kits for three thousand slugs each."

"Condoms only cost fifty slugs. Why would anyone buy this?"

He grinned. "It's reusable!"

I blinked. "Are you shitting me?"

"Not at all! It's made of a thin but durable material. Good for hundreds of uses." He pointed to the rounded metal part of the device. "After each use, you turn the condom inside-out and put it on this cylinder—"

"Ew."

"Then you turn on the cleaner. There's a liquid cleanse cycle and then a high temperature bake for ten minutes. After that it's sterile and ready to use again—"

"Oh God, no."

"You should probably rinse it off first—"

"Stop!" I said. "Why would *anyone* want something like this?"

"Because it saves money in the long run, and it's less prone to failure than a normal condom."

I gave him my most dubious glare.

"Do the math," he said. "Normal condoms cost way too much. No one manufactures them locally—there's no raw materials to make latex. But *my* product will last through two hundred uses, minimum. That's *ten thousand slugs* of savings."

"Huh . . ." Now he was speaking my language. "Okay, maybe it's not so crazy after all. But I don't have money to invest right now. . . ."

"Oh, I'm not looking for investors. I need someone to test it."

"And you think *I've* got the dick for the job?"

He rolled his eyes. "I need to know how it feels for the woman."

"I'm not having sex with you."

"No, no!" He winced. "I just want you to use it the next time you have sex. Then tell me how it affected your experience."

"Why don't you bang a girl and ask her yourself?"

He looked at his shoes. "I don't have a girlfriend and I'm terrible with women."

"There are brothels all over Aldrin! High-end, low-end, whatever you want."

"That's no good." He crossed his arms. "I need data from a woman who is having sex *for fun*. The woman has to be sexually experienced, which you definitely are—"

"Careful . . ."

"And likely to have sex in the near future. Which, again—"

"Choose your next words wisely."

He paused. "Anyway. You see what I'm after."

I groaned. "Can't I just pay you two thousand slugs?"

"I don't need money. I need testing."

I glared at the condom. It *looked* normal enough. "So it's effective? You're sure it won't break or anything?"

"Oh, definitely. I've run it through a battery of tests. Stretching, pressure, friction, you name it."

A disturbing thought popped into my head. "Wait. Have you used this one?"

"No, but it wouldn't matter if I had. The cleaning process renders it sterile."

"Are you kidd—" I stopped myself and took a breath. Then, as calmly as I could, I said, "It would matter, Svoboda. Maybe not biologically, but psychologically."

He shrugged.

I deliberated for a moment, then finally said, "Okay, it's a deal. But I'm not promising to run out and get laid."

"Sure, sure," he said. "Just . . . whenever the next time it comes up naturally, you know?"

"Yeah, all right."

"Excellent!" He picked up the condom box and cleaning device and handed them to me. "Call me if you have any questions."

I took the items gingerly. Not my proudest moment, but logically speaking there was nothing wrong with it. I was just doing some product testing, right? That's not weird, right?

Right?

I started to leave. Then I stopped and turned back toward him. "Hey . . . have you ever heard of something called ZAFO?"

"No, should I have?"

"Nah, don't worry about it. I'll drop by tomorrow afternoon to pick up the device."

"It's my day off. Want to meet at the park instead? Say, three p.m.?"

"That works," I said.

"Can I ask what this thing is for?"

"Nope."

"Okay. See you tomorrow."

Conrad Down 6.

I drove Trigger down the familiar hallways and tried to ignore the sinking feeling in my gut. I knew every crooked hallway, every shop, and every scratch on every wall. I could close my eyes and tell where I was just from echoes and background noise.

I rounded the corner to Crafters Row. The best tradesmen in town worked here, but there were no flashing signs or advertisements. They didn't need to draw in customers. They got their business through reputation.

I parked in front of CD6-3028, got out, and hesitated at the door. I turned away in a moment of cowardice, steeled myself, then turned back and rang the buzzer.

A man with a weathered face answered the door. He had a well-trimmed beard and wore a white *taqiyah* (head covering). He stared at me quietly for a moment, then said, "Huh."

"Good evening, Father," I said in Arabic.

"Are you in trouble?"

"No."

"Do you need money?"

"No, Father. I am independent now."

He furrowed his brow. *"Then why are you here?"*

"Can a daughter not visit her father simply to honor him?"

"Cut the crap," he said in English. "What do you want?"

"I need to borrow some welding equipment."

"Interesting." He left the door open and walked into the shop. That was as much invitation as I was going to get.

Not much had changed over the years. The fireproofed workshop was hot and cramped, as they all were. Dad's meticulously organized equipment hung on the walls. A worktable dominated one corner of the room next to a collection of welding masks.

"Come on," he said. I followed him through the back door into the residence. The tiny living room was palatial compared to my humble shithole.

Dad's place had two coffin bunks along one wall. Very common among lower-class Artemisians. Not as nice as bedrooms, but they allowed privacy, which was good. I grew up in that house. I did . . . stuff in that bunk.

He had a cook nook with an actual flame-based stove. One of the few advantages to living in a fireproofed room. Way better than a microwave. You might think a real stove meant tasty meals, but you'd be wrong. Dad did his best, but Gunk is Gunk. There's only so much you can do with algae.

There was one big change, though. Along the back wall a meter-wide sheet of metal ran from the floor to the ceiling—it wasn't even close to vertical. I'd estimate 20 to 30 degrees off true.

I pointed to the new feature. "What the hell is that?"

Dad looked over to it. "It's an idea I came up with a while ago."

"What's it for?"

"Work it out."

Ugh! If I had a slug for every time he'd said that in my life . . . Never a straight answer—everything had to be a goddamn learning experience.

He crossed his arms and watched me like he always did during these little quizzes.

I walked over and touched the sheet. Very sturdy, of course. He never did anything half-assed. "Two-millimeter sheet aluminum?"

"Correct."

"So it doesn't need to handle lateral force . . ." I ran my finger along the intersection of the sheet and the wall. I felt small bumps every twenty centimeters. "Spot welds? That's not like you."

He shrugged. "It might be a stupid idea. I'm not ready to commit."

Two hooks jutted out from the top of the sheet, just centimeters from the ceiling. "You're going to hang something on it."

"Correct. But what?"

I looked it up and down. "This weird angle is the key . . . got a protractor I could borrow?"

"I'll save you the trouble," he said. "It's twenty-two point nine degrees from vertical."

"Huh . . ." I said. "Artemis's longitude is twenty-two point nine . . . ah. Okay, I got it." I turned to face him. "It's for prayers."

"Correct," he said. "I call it a prayer wall."

The moon always points the same face toward Earth. So, even though we're in orbit, from our point of view, Earth doesn't move. Well, *technically*, it wobbles a bit because of lunar libration, but don't worry your pretty little head about that. Point is: Earth is fixed in the sky. It rotates in place and goes through phases, but it doesn't move.

The ramp pointed at Earth so Dad could face Mecca while praying. Most Muslims here just faced west—that's what Dad had done all my life.

"How will you use it?" I asked. "Special straps or something? I mean—it's almost vertical."

"Don't be ridiculous." He put both hands on the prayer wall and leaned forward onto it. "Like this. Simple and easy. And it's more in keeping with Qiblah than facing west on the moon."

"Seems silly, Dad. It's not like Muslims in Australia dig a hole and face down. You think Muhammad's going to be impressed?"

"Hey," he said sharply, "if you're not going to practice Islam, you don't get to talk about the Prophet."

"All right, all right," I said. I pointed to the hooks. "What are those for?"

"Work it out."

"Ugh!" I said. Then I grudgingly added, "For attaching a prayer rug?"

"Correct." He walked to a table near the cook nook and sat in one of the chairs. "I don't want to poke holes in my usual prayer rug, so I ordered another one from Earth. It'll be here in a few weeks."

I sat in the other chair, where I'd had countless meals throughout my life. "Do you have a shipping manifest number? I can arrange to get it here faster—"

"No, thanks."

"Dad, there's nothing illegal about pulling strings to—"

"No, thanks," he said, a little louder this time. "Let's not argue about it."

I gritted my teeth but kept quiet. Time for a change of subject. "Weird question: Have you ever heard of something called 'ZAFO'?"

He raised an eyebrow. "Isn't that an ancient Greek lesbian?"

"No, that's Sappho."

"Oh. Then no. What is it?"

"No idea," I said. "Just something I saw in passing and wondered about."

"You've always been curious. You're great at finding answers too. Maybe you should put your genius to work on something useful for a change."

"Dad," I said with a hint of warning in my voice.

"Fine." He folded his arms. "So you need welding equipment?"

"Yeah."

"Last time you had access to my equipment it didn't go well."

I stiffened. I tried not to break eye contact, but I couldn't help myself. I looked at the floor.

He took a softer tone. "I'm sorry. That was uncalled-for."

"No, it wasn't," I said.

We had an uncomfortable silence—we'd mastered that art over the years.

"Well . . ." he said awkwardly. "So . . . what do you need?"

I cleared my head. I didn't have time for gnawing guilt. "I need a torch, a couple tanks of acetylene, a tank of O_2, and a mask."

"What about neon?" he asked.

I winced. "Right, yeah. Neon, of course."

"You're getting rusty," he said.

I didn't need neon. But I couldn't tell him that.

When you weld aluminum, you need to flood it with a non-reactive gas to keep the surface from oxidizing. On Earth they use argon because it's massively abundant. But we don't have noble gases on the moon, so we have to ship them in from Earth. And neon weighs half as much as argon, so that's what we use. It didn't matter to me, because I'd be working in a vacuum. No oxygen to oxidize the metal. But I didn't want him to know that. Also, I'd be cutting steel, not aluminum. But again—no reason to share that with Dad.

"So, what's this for?" he asked.

"I'm installing an air shelter for a friend."

I'd lied to Dad more times than I could count, especially when I was a teen. But every time—every damn time—it tied my stomach in knots.

"Why doesn't your friend hire a welder?" he asked.

"She did. She hired me."

"Oh, so you're a welder now?" He widened his eyes theatrically. "After years of telling me you didn't want to do it?"

I sighed. "Dad. It's just a friend who wants an air shelter in her bedroom. I'm barely charging her for it." Residential air shelters were common, especially among recent immigrants. Newcomers tend to be paranoid about the whole "deadly vacuum outside" thing. It's irrational—Artemis's hull is extremely safe—but fear isn't logical. In practice, personal air shelters quickly become closets.

"What's the illegal part?" he asked.

I gave him a hurt look. "Why would you assume there's—"

"What's the illegal part?" he repeated.

"Her apartment's in Armstrong up against the inner hull. I have to weld the shelter directly to it. The city requires all sorts of extra inspections if you weld to the inner hull and she can't afford them."

"Hmf," he said. "Pointless bureaucracy. Even the most rank amateur couldn't damage a six-centimeter plate of aluminum."

"I know, right?!" I said.

He folded his arms and frowned. "Darned city getting in the way of business . . ."

"Preach."

"All right. Take what you want. But you have to reimburse me for the acetylene and neon."

"Right, of course," I said.

"You all right? You look kind of pale."

I was about ready to puke. Lying to Dad transported me back to my teen years. And let me tell you: there's no one I hate more than teenage Jazz Bashara. That stupid bitch made every bad decision a stupid bitch could make. She's responsible for where I am today.

"I'm fine. Just a little tired."

Dear Jazz,

I got a big poster of the *Roosa* for my birthday. What a magnificent ship! It's the largest spaceliner ever built! It can hold up to two hundred passengers! I'm learning all about it. I'm a little obsessed, but who cares? It's fun.

The ship is a marvel! It has full centripetal gravity, with a radius large enough that no one will get dizzy. It even helps people adjust to lunar gravity! They gradually slow the rotation over the seven-day trip to the moon. So when people first board, the passenger decks are at 1 g, and by the time they reach the moon, they're at $1/6$th g. They do the reverse on the way back to get folks accustomed to 1 g again. How cool is that?

I still don't understand the "Uphoff-Crouch Cycler Orbit," though. I get that it's a ballistic orbit that goes back and forth between the Earth and the moon, but it's really weird. It's like . . . start at Earth, then it's at the moon seven days later, then it flings up way out of the Earth–moon plane and comes back to the moon fourteen days later . . . somewhere in there it just sits in an elliptical orbit around Earth for a couple of weeks . . . I don't get it. And I won't try. Point is, it's an awesome ship.

Someday, when I'm a rich rocket designer, I'm going to visit Artemis. We can have tea.

Hey, when you and your dad moved to Artemis, did you go there on the *Roosa*?

Dear Kelvin,

Nah, the *Roosa* hadn't been built yet when we moved here. We came over on the *Collins*, the only spaceliner that existed at the time. It was ten years ago (I was only six), so I don't remember all the details. But I remember we didn't have artificial gravity. It was zero-G everywhere. I had a shitload of fun bouncing around!

You got me curious about the orbit stuff, so I looked it up. It seems pretty straightforward. The ship goes through a cycle with each step taking seven days: Earth -> Moon -> (deep space out of Earth–moon plane) -> Moon -> Earth -> (deep space in the Earth–moon plane) -> Earth. And it repeats that over and over. If the moon stood still they could just go back and forth, but it's moving around Earth once per month, which complicates the hell out of the cycler.

I looked up the math behind how orbits work and then checked their numbers against those equations. It was pretty simple, you can do it in your head.

Dear Jazz,

Maybe *you* can do it in your head. I would give anything to be as smart as you. But I'm not. That's okay. I work hard instead, and you're lazy as hell.

Dear Kelvin,

How dare you call me lazy! I'd come up with a scathing retort but, meh, I'm just not motivated.

Hey, I need advice. Edgar and I are going on our fourth date. We've been making out a lot (just kissing, nothing else). I want to escalate, but I don't want to move too fast—I'm not ready to get naked yet. Any recommendations?

Dear Jazz,

Boobs.

Dear Kelvin,

Seriously? That simple?

Dear Jazz,

Yes.

4

The next morning, I woke up naked in a plush, comfortable bed.

No, there wasn't anyone with me. Get your mind out of the gutter. I just wanted to get a taste of what life would be like once I got that million slugs.

I stretched out my arms and arched my back. What a fantastic night's sleep!

Unlike my shitty coffin, this room had excellent noise insulation. No neighbors waking me up with screaming arguments or loud sex. No booming hallway conversations bleeding in. No drunk idiots stumbling into walls.

And the bed! I could lie across it width-wise and still fit! Plus the sheets and blankets were softer than velvet. The bedding felt better against my skin than my own pajamas.

The room cost 2,000ğ a night. When I got my payday from Trond, I'd get a bed like this in my beautiful noise-proof apartment.

I checked my Gizmo. Eleven in the morning?! Wow, I really slept!

I slid out of the warm sheets and walked over to the bathroom—the *private* bathroom. No robe, no dudes checking me out in the hall, just me and my bladder headed to take care of business in peace.

I went through my morning ritual, including an extra-long shower. Private shower—another thing for my list of future amenities. Water's expensive in Artemis, but it's not like we throw it away. It's a closed system, so what you really pay for is water purification. The hotel room had a graywater-reuse shower. The first twenty liters were fresh water (that lasted about three minutes). After that, it reheated your used water and gave it back to you. You could be in there as long as you wanted and you'd only use twenty liters. Important note: Do not pee in a graywater-reuse shower.

I threw on an insanely comfortable terrycloth robe and wrapped my hair in a towel-turban.

Time to work on the next step of my evil plan. This time I didn't need to do any research. I just needed to brainstorm. I lay back on the Bed Jazz Never Wanted to Leave and let my mind wander.

The problem: How would I get out of the city?

Airlocks won't obey commands from non–EVA Guild members. There's a good reason for that. The last thing you want is some untrained dipshit playing around with airlock controls. A misused airlock is a fast and efficient way to kill everyone in a bubble.

So, to use an airlock control panel, you have to wave your Gizmo over it. It verifies that you're part of the guild. It's a simple idiot-proofing scheme that's very effective. But no idiot-proofing can overcome a *determined* idiot. There's a flaw in the system.

For safety reasons, airlocks don't have security on their *outer* doors. If you're in a leaky EVA suit and scrambling to safety, the last thing you want to see is "VERIFYING AUTHORIZATION. . . ." I just needed someone to operate the controls from the outside. Someone . . . or something.

I left the hotel room because the front desk called to say I had to check out or they'd charge me for another night. Then I drove

Trigger to Armstrong Down 4. Or, as the locals called it, Little Hungary. The Hungarians owned all the metalworking shops. Just like the Vietnamese owned Life Support and Saudis owned welding.

I pulled up next to the workshop of Dad's colleague Zsóka Stróbl, who was apparently named during a severe vowel famine. She was a pressure-vessel specialist. When Dad got a contract to install an air shelter, he usually bought one from Zsóka. She made high-quality product and Dad's all about quality.

I parked Trigger and rapped on the door. Zsóka slid it open a crack, peeked out with one eye, and spoke with a thick accent. "You want what?"

I pointed to myself. "It's me, Mrs. Stróbl. Jazz Bashara."

"You are daughter of Ammar Bashara," she said. "He good man. You were nice little girl. Now you are bad."

"Okay . . . look, I want to talk to you about something—"

"You are unmarried and have sex with many men."

"Yes, I'm quite the harlot."

Her son, Isvan, had banged more dudes than I ever had. I resisted the urge to tell her. "I just need to borrow something for a couple of days. I'm willing to pay you a thousand slugs for it."

She opened the door a little wider. "Borrow what?"

"Your HIB."

Zsóka had been around for the construction of both Bean and Shepard Bubbles. Bubble construction is a hell of a job (pays well too).

She and dozens of other metalworkers had made the slightly curved triangles that stacked on a frame to form the hull. The EVA masters assembled the pieces and added enough rivets to make a shitty, leaky pressure seal. Then Life Support kept the bubble fed with enough air to counteract the leaks while welders made the real seals from inside. Dad made good money off those jobs, I remember.

Ethical metalworkers like Zsóka regularly inspect their work.

But how do you look at the outside of the hull without being a trained, licensed EVA master? With a hull-inspection bot. "HIB" for short.

They're really just R/C cars with claws instead of wheels. The outer hulls of Artemis are covered in handles to ensure access for maintenance. HIBs use those handles to get wherever they want. Seems inefficient, eh? Well, it's the only way to climb up the side of a bubble. The aluminum isn't magnetic, suction cups and propellers don't work in a vacuum, and a rocket engine would be stupidly expensive.

"Why you want HIB?" she asked.

I'd worked out a lie in advance. "The Shepard relief valve is leaking. Dad was the one who installed it. He wants me to check the weld site."

Keeping Artemis at constant pressure is tricky. If people use more power than usual, the city becomes slightly over-pressurized. Why? The power becomes heat, which increases the air temperature, and that makes the pressure go up. Normally, Life Support pulls air out of the system to compensate. But what if that doesn't work?

So as a fail-safe, the city has relief valves in every bubble. If the pressure gets too high, they'll open and let air out until it's back to normal.

"Your father never makes bad weld. Must be other problem."

"I know that and you know that, but we have to rule it out."

She thought it over. "How long you need?"

"Just a couple of days."

"One thousand slugs?"

I pulled out my Gizmo. "Yeah. And I'll pay in advance."

"You wait." She slid the door closed.

After a minute, Zsóka opened the door again and handed me a case. I checked inside to make sure everything was there.

The mechanical bug was thirty centimeters long. Its four

movement claws were folded into their stow position and the tool arm formed a "7" shape along the top of the robot. That arm had a high-definition camera on the end and basic clamping and grabbing actuators. Perfect for poking at things and recording the results—exactly what you need when remotely inspecting a hull. And also what I needed for my nefarious plan.

She handed me the remote—a sleek little device with knobs and joysticks surrounding a video screen.

"You know how to use?"

"I read the manual online."

She frowned. "You break, you pay for fix."

"This is just between you and me, right?" I hovered my finger over my Gizmo screen. "The Welding Guild's always looking for excuses to shit-talk Dad—I don't want to give them ammo."

"Ammar is good man. Good welder. I will not tell."

"So we have a deal?"

She pulled out her Gizmo. "Yes."

I fired off the funds transfer and she accepted.

"You bring back. Two days." She returned to her shop and closed the door.

Yeah, she was grumpy and thought I was a bimbo. But you know what? I wish everyone was like her. No chitchat, no bullshit, no pretense of friendship. Just goods and services exchanged for money. The perfect business partner.

I did a little shopping in Bean Bubble. It was more expensive than I like, but I needed specialty clothing. Artemis has a small Muslim population (including my dad), so there are a few stores that cater to them. I found a long tan dress with simple colors and a stylish embroidered pattern. It was suitable for even the most conservative Muslim gal. I also bought a dark-green niqab.

I considered brown or black, but the dark green counterpointed the tan dress for an earthy ensemble. Just 'cause I was planning a heist, that didn't mean I couldn't look good doing it.

Okay, you can stop pretending you know what a niqab is. It's a traditional Islamic headwear that covers the lower face. Combined with a hijab (head cloth) to cover my hair, only my eyes were visible. Great way to wear a mask without arousing suspicion.

Next, I had to get a new Gizmo. I couldn't use my own—that would leave a digital trail of all the illegal shit I was about to do. I could just see Rudy reviewing my Gizmo's logs and building a case. No thanks. Life's a pain in the ass when you have a cop constantly on your ass. I needed a false identity.

Lucky for me it's easy to set up a false identity here. Mainly because nobody cares who you are. Things here are set up to prevent identity theft, not aliases. If you tried to steal a *real* person's identity you'd fail miserably. As soon as your victim found out they'd report it and Rudy would use your Gizmo to track you down. Where would you run? Outside? Hope you can hold your breath.

I went online and converted a few hundred slugs into euros. Then I used those euros to buy slugs from KSC under the name Nuha Nejem. It only took ten minutes of internet activity. It would have been even faster if I were on Earth, but we have that four-second ping time from here.

I stopped at home and dropped off my Gizmo. Time to become Nuha Nejem.

I went to the Artemis Hyatt, a small hotel on Bean Up 6 with little flair but reasonable prices. They saw a lot of business from ordinary people taking a once-in-a-lifetime vacation. I'd only been there once before, on a date with a tourist. The room was pleasant enough, but I'm not the best judge. I only got a good look at the ceiling.

The whole hotel was one long hallway. The "front desk" was a closet-size kiosk with a single employee. I didn't recognize him, which was good. It meant he wouldn't recognize me.

"I greet," I said with a thick Arabic accent. Between that and my traditional clothes, everything about me screamed tourist.

"Welcome to the Artemis Hyatt!" he said.

"Needing Gizmo."

He was used to broken-English conversations. "Gizmo? You need a Gizmo?"

"Gizmo." I nodded. "Needing."

I could see his thought process. He could try to figure out which reservation I was under, but as a Saudi woman, it would be under my husband's name. That would take a lot of panto-mime and miscommunication to work out. Easier just to set up the Gizmo for me. It's not like it cost the hotel anything.

"Name?" he said.

I didn't want to be too eager. I looked at him with confusion.

He patted himself on the chest. "Norton. Norton Spinelli." Then he pointed to me. "Name?"

"Ah," I said. I patted my own chest. "Nuha Nejem."

He typed away on his computer. Yes, there was an account for Nuha Nejem, and no one had linked a Gizmo to it. It all made sense. He pulled a weathered Gizmo from under the counter. It was an older model with the words PROPERTY OF ARTEMIS HYATT stenciled on the back. With a few keystrokes, he got everything set up. Then he handed me the Gizmo and said, "Welcome to Artemis!"

"I thank," I said with a smile. "I thank many. Moon is much excitement!"

I had a fake identity. Time for Phase Two.

I brought up the map app on my new Gizmo and pretended to navigate with it. Obviously, I didn't need a map to get around Artemis, but it was 'all part of my tourist act. I wandered inef-ficiently across town to the Port of Entry. I carried a big purse, of course. What tourist woman would be without one?

Now for the tricky part.

Everyone knew me at the port. I was there every day and my sparkling personality was hard to forget. That's not ideal when you're trying to sneak around. But today I wasn't Jazz Bashara. I was Nuha Nejem, Saudi tourist.

I headed to the waiting area next to the train airlock and joined a crowd of tourists. All the seats were taken and dozens more people stood around. Several families had obnoxious kids bouncing off the walls. In this case, "bouncing off the walls" is not just a figure of speech. The overstimulated kids were *literally* bouncing off the walls. Lunar gravity is the worst thing to ever happen to parents.

"This is so cool!" said a dumb blonde to her trust-fund boyfriend. "We're about to take the moonorail!"

Ugh. Only tourists called it that. It's not even a monorail! It runs on parallel tracks, just like trains on Earth.

By the way, we also hate it when people call us "Loonies" or when they call Artemis the "City in Space." We're not in space—we're on the moon. I mean, technically we're "in space" but so is London.

I digress.

The train finally arrived. I pretended to be enthralled by its approach like everyone else. It was just a single car, not the long-ass trains Earthers are used to. It slowed to a crawl next to the docking port and inched forward until it connected. After a click and a kachunk, the round entry hatch opened up to reveal the conductor.

Shit! It was Raj! He wasn't supposed to be there! He must have switched shifts with someone.

Raj and I grew up together. We went to the same schools. We were teenagers together. We weren't close friends or anything, but we saw each other every day for most of our lives. My dress and hijab might not be enough of a disguise.

He stepped through the aperture and adjusted his uniform—

a silly, nineteenth-century-style, navy-blue outfit with brass buttons and a conductor's cap. Giddy folks returning from the Apollo 11 site exited the train. Many of them carried souvenirs from the Visitor Center: lunar modules carved from local rocks, Apollo 11 mission patches, and so on.

Once everyone de-trained, Raj called out in a clear, loud voice, "*This* is the 2:34 p.m. traaaain to Apollo Eleeeeeven! All abooooooard!" He held out a vintage-looking brass ticket shredder. Of course, there were no paper tickets to shred. It was just decoration surrounding a payment pad.

I closed the niqab a little tighter and walked with a hunch. Maybe if I changed my body language I wouldn't be as recognizable. Passengers filed past Raj, waved their Gizmos over the shredder, and walked through an antechamber into the train.

He made sure there was only one person in the antechamber at a time. He was sneaky about it, mostly by standing in people's way. It was easier than explaining, "If there's a pressure failure, the antechamber door will close. The city will be safe but you'll die."

When my turn came, I looked down to avoid eye contact. My Gizmo beeped and popped up a text blurb:

CITY OF ARTEMIS: 75ğ TRAIN FARE.

Raj didn't notice me. I breathed a sigh of relief and stepped into the train.

The seats had all been taken and I was ready to stand for the whole trip, but a tall black guy saw me and stood up. He said something in French and pointed to his seat. A true gentleman! I bowed to him and sat down. I rested my purse in my lap.

Once the last passenger boarded, Raj followed and sealed both antechamber doors along the way. He walked to the front of the train and spoke over the intercom. "Welcome to the Lunar Express! This is the 2:34 p.m. service to the Apollo 11 Visitor

Center. Our scheduled arrival time is 3:17 p.m. Please keep your hands and feet inside the vehicle at all times!"

A snicker rippled through the passengers. It was a stupid-ass joke, but comedic gold to the tourists.

The train set off. It was utterly smooth. No rocking, no shaking, nothing like that. It ran on an electric motor (obviously) and the tracks never had to deal with the warping effects of weather. Plus, there wasn't much weight on them, compared to Earth tracks.

Each row of seats had a porthole window. Passengers eagerly took turns looking at the drab, rocky landscape. Why did it excite them so much? It's a bunch of gray rocks. Who gives a shit?

A frumpy Midwestern woman giggled at her window and turned to me. "Isn't it amazing?! We're on the *moon!*"

"*Ma'alesh, ana ma'aref Englizy,*" I said with a shrug.

She turned to another passenger. "Isn't it amazing?! We're on *the moon!*"

Nothing like a language barrier to make people leave you alone.

I brought up an Arabic gossip webzine on my Gizmo. I just wanted an excuse to keep my head down. Fortunately, Raj was manning the controls and facing away.

By the time we arrived, I had learned all about the latest scandal in the Saudi royal family. The crown prince had cheated on his wives. Two of them had filed for divorce under the Islamic law of Khula, but the other two were standing by him. I was halfway through reading the queen's quote on the situation when the train came to a stop.

The familiar sounds of the docking procedure clanged through the car and Raj shouted "End of the liiine!"

He walked to the door and opened it. "Apollo 11 Visitor Center! Have an excellent stay!"

We all crowded out of the train and found ourselves in a gift shop. Some folks stopped there, but most of us continued forward to the Viewing Hall. That entire side of the center was floor-to-ceiling windows looking out over the landing site.

A well-manicured docent greeted the crowd as we approached the glass. I averted my eyes. Yet another person I knew. Goddamn, it's annoying to commit crimes in a small town.

Gunter Eichel had emigrated to Artemis ten years earlier with his stepsister, Ilsa. They came because they were ostracized in Germany for being a couple. Yes, really. That's why they emigrated. We don't care what people do, sex-wise, as long as everyone's a consenting adult. (Though some folks stretch the definition of "adult.")

Anyway, he and I weren't friends or anything. My disguise would be fine.

He waited for people to conglomerate, then launched into his presentation. "Welcome to Tranquility Base. Come on up to the glass, there's plenty of room for everyone."

We moved forward and lined up against the giant windows. The lander sat where it had been for the last century, alongside experimental packages that the old-time astronauts had laid out.

"You may notice the Viewing Hall windows follow a weird path," Gunter said. "Why not just a half-circle or a straight line? Well, we have a rule that nothing is allowed within ten meters of *any part* of an Apollo landing site. The definition of 'any part' includes the lander, equipment, tools, the commemorative plaque, and even the footprints left behind by the astronauts. The Viewing Hall is built so that each window is just over ten meters from the nearest part of the site. Feel free to wander along the hall to get a look from different angles."

Some of the tourists had already walked along the serpentine wall. But with Gunter's suggestion, several more began the trek.

"If you're nervous about a pane of glass separating you from the vacuum of space, don't be. These windows are *twenty-three centimeters* thick to protect you from the radiation. That has a side effect of making them the *strongest* part of the Visitor

Center's hull. And, I'm proud to point out, the glass was man-ufactured right here on the moon. A small amount of regolith dust was added to darken it. Otherwise the sunlight from outside would be blinding."

He gestured to the landing site. "The *Eagle*, named after the national bird of the United States, landed July twentieth, 1969. What you see here is the *Eagle*'s Descent Stage. Astronauts Neil Armstrong and Buzz Aldrin took the Ascent Stage back into lunar orbit at the end of their mission."

The tourists pressed against the windows, entranced at what they saw. I took a long look myself. Hey, I'm not made of stone. I love my city and its history. The *Eagle* is a big part of that.

"Every Apollo mission planted an American flag," Gunter said. "So where is it? Well, when the Ascent Stage lifted off, the exhaust knocked the poor flag over. Then, the dust that had been kicked up covered it. If you look closely on the ground, just to the left of the *Eagle*, you can see a small patch of white. That's the only bit of the flag still visible."

The crowd murmured as people pointed out the white bit to one another.

"For later missions, they figured out to put the flags farther away."

A small chuckle came from the crowd.

"Interesting side note: All the other flags have been exposed to unfiltered sunlight during lunar days for over a hundred years. They've been bleached completely white now. But Tran-quility Base's flag is under a thin layer of regolith. So it probably still looks like it did back in 1969. Of course, no one is allowed to enter or modify the landing site to take a look."

He clasped his hands behind his back. "We hope you enjoy the history and beauty of Tranquility Base. If you have any ques-tions, don't hesitate to ask me."

Behind the crowd, Bob Lewis and two other EVA masters stood next to a doorway labeled EVA PREPARATION AREA.

Gunter gestured to the trio. "We offer curated EVAs to those who are interested. It's an amazing experience and allows you to look at the site from angles the Viewing Hall can't provide."

Usually, Dale would be there among his peers, but today was a Saturday. He was devoutly Jewish and off at Artemis's only synagogue, Congregation Beth Chalutzim.

A small crowd gathered around the EVA masters while the remaining (poorer) people stayed at the windows. I shuffled along with the EVA gang, trying to stay toward the middle. I didn't want to get too close to Bob.

The masters divided us into three groups of eight. I ended up with Bob. Goddammit.

Each master took their group aside and explained the basics of how things were going to work. I stood in the back of my group and averted my eyes.

"Okay, listen up," Bob said. "I will be in a full EVA suit while you will be in what we call 'hamster balls.' You are not allowed to bring anything sharp with you, because you would puncture your ball and die. There will be no horseplay. You will walk, not run. You will not bounce around or ram each other." He shot a withering glare to a couple of teens in the group.

"There is a one-meter-high fence around the landing site to protect it from you. The fence delineates the ten-meter boundary beyond which no one may pass. *Do not attempt to get past the fence.* If you do, I will terminate the EVA and you *will* be deported to Earth."

He paused a moment to let that sink in. "While outside, you will follow my instructions immediately and without question. You will stay within sight of me at all times. You may explore in any direction you choose, but if I radio that you are too far away for my comfort, you will return to me. Are there any questions?"

One small Asian man raised his hand. "Um, yes, the docent mentioned there's radiation out there? How dangerous is it?"

Bob answered the question with practiced ease. "The EVA

will last approximately two hours. In that time, you will receive less than one hundred microsieverts of radiation—about the same dosage you get from a set of dental X-rays."

"Then why is the Visitor Center shielded?" asked Nervous Guy.

"All structures on the moon, including the Visitor Center, are shielded for the benefit of the people who live and work here. It's fine to be exposed once in a while but not all the time."

"And what about you? You go outside all the time, right?"

Bob nodded. "I do. But each EVA master only does two tours per week, to keep their exposure to a minimum. Anything else?"

Nervous Guy looked down. If he had any further questions, he was too intimidated to ask.

Bob held out his payment panel. "The price for this EVA is one thousand, five hundred slugs each."

The tourists ran their Gizmos over it one at a time. I wedged myself in the middle of the pack and paid along with them. I frowned at my Gizmo as it reported my dwindling account balance. This get-rich-quick scheme was costing me a lot of money!

Bob led us to the antechamber. As the most senior EVA master present, he got to take his group out first.

Deflated hamster balls hung on racks throughout the room. Next to each one was a hard-shelled backpack. The far wall had a large hatch and associated control panel. Beyond it was an airlock large enough to fit an entire tour group.

Bob pulled one of the backpacks off the wall. "This is a scurry pack. You'll have it on your back during the EVA. This is your life support system. It adds oxygen and removes carbon dioxide as needed. It keeps the air at the correct pressure and temperature."

He turned the scurry pack sideways to reveal a headset Velcroed to the side. "You'll have this headset on during the EVA. It's an open channel. All nine of us will be on it. Also, your scurry pack will report any problems to me if they arise."

Nervous Guy raised his hand. "How do we operate it?"

"You don't," said Bob. "It's completely automated. Don't screw with it."

I listened with fake fascination. Of course I knew all about scurry packs. Hell, as part of my training, I'd been given several deliberately broken packs and told to identify the problems. I got every one of them right too.

Bob pointed to a line of lockers. "Put your personal items and anything else you don't want to carry in those lockers there. Keep your Gizmos with you."

The excitement level jumped a notch. The tourists were all smiles and giddy conversation. I went to the locker nearest me and waved my Gizmo. It clicked open. Now it was initialized to my Gizmo, so only I'd be able to open it again later. Elegant design—even Nervous Guy was able to work it out without extra questions.

I put my purse in the locker, then cast my eyes askance to see if anyone was watching me. No one was.

I pulled the HIB out of my purse and set it on the floor next to the locker bank. I couldn't get it completely out of sight, but at least it was partially occluded. I slipped the remote control into a holster I had strapped to my inner thigh.

From there, we all donned scurry packs under Bob's watchful eye. Then, one by one, he sealed us each into our hamster balls. There were some stumbles and falls along the way, but most people adapted to the balls well. It's not that hard.

Bob pulled his own EVA suit out of a locker and put it on in three minutes. Damn, he was fast. The fastest I ever got into mine was nine.

We all lined up behind him, some more gracefully than others. He waved his Gizmo over the airlock controls and the inner hatch popped open. He ushered us into the airlock.

I got in first and rolled to the corner. I faced the wall, pulled the remote out from under my dress, and activated the HIB. It came to life in the prep room and fired up its camera. I could now see everything from the HIB's vantage point as well as my own.

Bob was paying attention to the tourists, which meant he was facing away from the HIB. The tourists had their eyes locked on the outer door—the last barrier between them and an exciting experience on the moon. Also, hamster balls are pretty dark when you're inside. They're made to shield the occupant from harsh sunlight.

So this was my chance. I had the HIB scamper forward on its adorable little claws. It darted into the airlock beside the second-to-last tourist's hamster ball. Then it hid in the corner.

Bob sealed the inner door and got to work on the outer door cranks. Nothing fancy for outer airlock doors—just manual valves. Why not a sleek computer system? Because valves don't crash or reboot. This is not something we take chances with.

The air hissed out of the room and our hamster balls became more rigid. Bob continually checked his readouts to make sure all eight of us had solid seals. Once the airlock was in vacuum, he addressed us over the radio.

"All right. Opening the outer door now. The tour area's been cleared of any sharp rocks. But if you see something that could possibly puncture your ball, don't mess with it. Just tell me."

He opened the outer door, and the gray, lifeless landscape lay beyond.

The tourists oohed and aahed. Then they all tried to talk at the same time on the open channel.

"Keep chatter to a minimum," Bob said. "If you want to talk to a specific person, call them with your Gizmo. The shared channel is for tour-related instructions and questions."

He stepped outside and gestured for us to follow.

I rolled out onto the moon with everyone else. The scratchy lunar regolith crunched under my ball. The flexible polymer skin blocked most of the incoming sunlight. But that meant it all became heat. The inner layers of polymer were good insulators, but not perfect. Within seconds of stepping into the sunlight, I could feel the warmth in my air.

The scurry pack fired up one of its fans, sucked in the warm air, and blew it out cold.

Just like harvesters, hamster balls have to deal with the pain in the ass that is heat rejection. But you can't encase a person in wax. So what did the scurry pack do with all that heat? Dump it into a big block of ice.

Yup. Good old frozen water. A couple of liters of it. Water is one of the best heat absorbers in all of chemistry. And melting the ice takes even more energy. That was really the limiter to how long a hamster ball excursion could be: how long that block of ice would last. It worked out to be two hours.

Bob closed the outer door once we were all through and led us toward the landing site. I'd left my little HIB buddy (I decided his name was Hibby) in the airlock on purpose.

It was a short walk around the arc of the Visitor Center.

I joined everyone else right up against the fence. Remember when I told Jin Chu the view was just as good from the Visitor Center? I lied. It's way cooler from outside. You really feel like you're there. Well, I mean, you *are* there. But you know what I mean.

I took a moment to admire Neil and Buzz's old stomping grounds. It really was a sight. That was my history right there.

Then it was back to work.

The tourists fanned out to examine the site from different angles. Some of them waved to the Visitor Center windows, though we couldn't see in. From our side the windows were mirrors. It's a hell of a lot lighter outside than in.

I faced away from Bob as if I were admiring the lunar desolation. I pulled out the remote and fired up the HIB again. You might be wondering how a simple remote-control unit could send radio waves capable of penetrating an Artemis hull. It's hard to broadcast through two six-centimeter aluminum sheets and a meter of ground-up rock.

Pretty simple, actually. Like everything else in town, it sent data through the wireless communications network. The city had receivers and repeaters atop every bubble, even the Visitor Center. Wouldn't want to leave the EVA masters mute, right? There's no more powerful tool for safety than communication. So Hibby's controller could talk to him without any problems.

The airlock was in vacuum—the default state of all airlocks. Right now, the next tour group was getting prepped by their EVA master. I had a short window of opportunity.

I had Hibby crawl to the outer door. The screen highlighted areas that he could grab to climb. Fantastic AI assist. All I had to do was tell him where to go and he worked out the rest.

He grabbed pipes, valve handles, and other protuberances to climb up the door. I had him anchor himself against a reenforcement rib and grab the hatch handle.

He needed two claws to get enough force to turn the handle, but it worked. After three full handle revolutions, the door was ajar. I had him drop to the ground. He automatically spun as he fell and landed on his claws. Man, he was fun to play with! I made a mental note to buy one after I was rich.

Like a cat sneaking into a room, Hibby nudged the airlock door open and slipped through. Then he closed the door behind him.

I looked over my shoulder to make sure no one was watching. Most tourists were up against the fence and Bob just scanned the scene. No one was breaking rules or in danger, so he was content.

I had Hibby push the door closed, climb up it, and reseal the hatch. From there, I told him to get to the apex of the Visitor Center dome. A perfect place to stay out of sight. He climbed merrily up the side, finding a convoluted but effective path of handles and grips he could reach. It took him two minutes to reach the top.

I put him in power-save mode and re-holstered the remote. I looked back to the dome of the Visitor Center and couldn't even see the apex from the ground. Perfect.

Phase Two complete. I spent the rest of the tour checking out the *Eagle*. It's amazing to think people actually landed here in that thing. You couldn't get me to do that for a million slugs.

Well, okay. I'd do it for a *million* slugs. But I'd be nervous about it.

Dear Kelvin,

Sean fucked up.

I love the man and he makes me howl in bed. But my God he can be stupid sometimes.

He got ahold of some pot—bought it off a tourist. We needed a place to party. Problem is, around here, if you smoke you'll set off fire alarms. So where would we go?

I had the perfect solution: Dad's new shop!

Dad's expanding the business right now. He leased a second location. He's bringing in new equipment, interviewing welders to staff it, the whole nine yards.

It's not up and running yet—half the equipment hasn't even arrived. So it's just this big, mostly empty room that I know the lock code to. And hey, smoking in a fire-rated workshop is the responsible thing to do! Protecting the city from fire and all that. So I offered it up.

We had a party. Nothing big. Just a few of Sean's friends and me. We got good and stoned. Then Sean and the guys started playing with the equipment. I should have stopped them, but everyone was laughing and having a good time. I didn't want to break the mood, you know?

Anyway, turns out Dad had filled the acetylene tanks that day. So while Sean and his idiot friends sword-fought with the torch handles, the gas-feed lines were actually live. Someone must have rolled a knob or something, because when they clashed the metal on metal it made a spark.

The whole room caught fire, the alarms went off, and it automatically sealed itself off. We were trapped in there and we barely got to the air shelter in time. We all crammed in and waited for the fire brigade.

Long story short: No one got hurt, but the room was trashed. Rudy (the nosy Mountie asshole) wanted to have me deported, but the fire destroyed all the pot, so he had no evidence of illegal flammables.

Dad was PISSED OFF. He yelled at me like never before—went on and on about how much money he'd sunk into that location and how it went up in flames because of me. And that just got me mad, because, you know, I could have died. The least he could do is ask if I'm okay, right?

We really got into it. He said I had to stop seeing Sean. As if he got a say in my love life! And then he went off on that same tired shit he always slings about me wasting my potential.

I am so fucking sick of the word "potential." I'm sick of hearing it from Dad, from teachers, and every goddamn "adult" I meet.

I told him he had no say in who I date! He kept banging on about how I could "make a difference" with a mind like mine, Sean's a waste of my time, blah, blah, blah. It's my life, I'll do what I want with it!

I grabbed some of my things and got the hell out of there. I'm staying with Sean for now. So much nicer than Dad's place. Sean's only twenty-three and his place has its own bedroom and bathroom. He doesn't work his ass off just to barely survive like everyone wants me to do. He's a bookie and he covers all his own bets. He's saving up to buy a table at the Starlite Casino. It's in Aldrin Bubble!

I'll find a job and stock up enough money until I can afford my own place. Or maybe not. Sean and I might just keep living together.

Dear Jazz,

I'm so sorry to hear you've had a falling-out with your father. I know you're mad, but please consider reconciling with him, even if you don't want to live in his home. There's nothing more important than family.

In other news, I got a job at KSC! I'm just an assistant loadmaster and I weigh cargo pods all day, but it's a start! After a provisional period, they say they'll train me in payload balancing. It's very important that a payload be properly secured and balanced or the launch could fail.

If I work my way up to loadmaster, I'll be able to afford trade school for my sisters. Then, once they are all trained in skills, the four of us will be able to support our parents. Mom and Dad will finally be able to retire. It's a long way off, but my sisters and I are working hard to make it happen.

Dear Kelvin,

Sorry for the slow reply. These past two weeks have been pretty hectic. Sean and I got in a fight but then made up (I'll spare you the details, it's all cool now).

Congrats on the job!

Some Saudi guys dropped by the other day and told me they'd set me up as a welding apprentice if I wanted. There are at least five master welders in town who want me in their shop. The Hungarian machinists also dropped by. They figured welding and machining are similar in that they both involve metal. I don't follow their logic. Anyway, they think I'd be good at that.

After that, the word got out that I'm available or something. A bunch of tradesmen have contacted me. Plumbers, electricians, glassworkers, you name it. I'm suddenly the belle of the ball. Yes, I have a reputation for being good at whatever I set my mind to, but this is ridiculous.

I smell Dad. This has his fingerprints all over it. He's got influence with the craftsmen in town. Either he directly asked them to talk to me, or they're just doing it because employing Ammar Bashara's daughter would mean a strong business relationship with him.

I turned them all down. I don't hate Dad or anything. I'm just trying to make my own way, you know? Also, to be blunt: Those professions are a lot of hard work.

I got a job as a porter. It's just a temporary gig to have some spending money. Sean pays the rent, but I don't want to rely on him for everything, you know? Anyway, I like it because I can work as much or as little as I want. There's no structure or boss or anything. I get paid per pickup or delivery.

In other news, Sean is banging other women. We never declared exclusivity. I moved in because I had nowhere else to go. So I guess that's a weird situation, but it's okay. We worked out some rules. The main one is: Neither of us

can bring anyone back to Sean's place. Go bang somewhere else. For me it's largely academic. I'm not interested in juggling men. One's plenty.

No, I don't like it. But Sean was very up front about all this from day one, so I can't complain. We'll just see how it goes.

5

The next morning, I lay in my coffin and screwed around with the HIB remote.

Hibby came to life right when I told him to. His charge was at 92 percent. No solar panels for my little Hibby, unfortunately. Why would the designers put those in? HIBs are supposed to be used a couple of hours at a time, then come back inside.

I had him climb down the arc of the Visitor Center dome to just above the train airlock. Then, I had to wait. I dicked around on my Gizmo for a bit, mostly reading the Arabic gossip site. The queen actually sided with the wives against her own son! Can you believe that?! You know you're a fuckup when your own mother tells you so.

Finally, the first train of tourists arrived at the Visitor Center. Hibby climbed down off the dome and onto the train car itself. The train ran perfectly on time. After ten minutes it departed for Artemis with my little stowaway aboard.

HIBs have a nice battery life, but they sure as hell can't walk forty kilometers across lunar terrain. So Hibby was riding back to town in style. Nothing but the best for my little buddy!

I killed more time on my favorite gossip site while I waited for the train to get back to Artemis.

Oh my God! I could not *believe* the shit the prince's second wife was saying about him in the press. That's just *mean*! Still, I can empathize with any woman who's been cheated on. I've been that woman. And honey, it sucks.

The train made it back to town and I had Hibby scamper onto Aldrin Bubble. Things got easy from there. Now I was using Hibby to do exactly what he was designed to do.

He crawled along the outer hull of Aldrin, then across the top of the Aldrin–Conrad Connector tunnel, and then onto Conrad. I had him take up position at the apex of Conrad.

Then it was back to low-power mode for Hibby and back to trashy royal family gossip for me.

ATTENTION: YOU ARE ENTERING ALDRIN PARK. THE PARK IS NOT PROTECTED BY A DOUBLE HULL. IF YOU HEAR THE BREACH ALERT IMMEDIATELY GET TO THE NEAREST AIR SHELTER. AIR SHELTERS ARE DENOTED WITH BLUE FLAGS AND CAN BE FOUND THROUGHOUT THE PARK.
ADMISSION:
NON-RESIDENTS - 750ǧ
RESIDENTS—FREE

I waved my Gizmo across the reader and the booth door opened. Free entry for me, of course. Who says there's no such thing as an Artemisian citizen?

I stepped into the booth and waited for the outer door to seal. Once it did, the inner door opened, letting me into the park. I stepped into the sunlight. Yes, sunlight.

Aldrin Park occupies the top four floors of the bubble. Instead of the everything-proof walls found around the rest of the city, this area was protected by enormous panes of glass—the same kind the Apollo 11 Visitor Center used. Proudly manufactured right here on the moon.

It was three p.m. Nairobi time (and therefore three p.m.

Artemis time), but physically it was lunar "morning." The sun hovered at the horizon and cast its light onto the park. The glass protected park-goers from the harsh radiation and UV that would otherwise have roasted us alive.

I still had time before my meeting with Svoboda. I took a walk.

The park's design was simple and elegant. The circular grounds met with glass walls. The terrain was mostly flat with a few artificial hills here and there, all covered in grass. Real, honest-to-God grass. That was no small achievement.

I moseyed along the perimeter, looking out at the moon. I've never seen the appeal of lunar landscape. It's just . . . nothing. I guess people like that? Some sort of Zen shit? Not me, though. To me, the most beautiful thing out there was the rest of Artemis.

The city shined in the sunlight like a bunch of metallic boobs. What? I'm not a poet. They look like boobs.

To the west, Conrad Bubble dominated the view. It might be grungy and impoverished on the inside, but the outside was just as pretty as its sisters.

Southwest, the smaller Armstrong Bubble sat like a spider in the middle of a web. Farther along that line, Shepard Bubble sat there full of richfucks. I didn't think it was possible for a half-sphere to look arrogant, but it did. Bean Bubble sat between Conrad and Shepard, both symbolically and geographically. It'd be my future home if all this scheming worked out. It was farthest from me.

I looked to the north. The Sea of Tranquility stretched out as far as I could see. Gray hills and jagged boulders dotted the terrain all the way to the horizon. I wish I could say it was all magnificent desolation and crap like that, but it's not. The land around Artemis is crisscrossed with tire tracks and utterly denuded of rocks. We have a lot of masonry here. Guess where people get the rocks.

I walked to the center of the park, toward the Ladies.

Real trees would have been too much to arrange. But the park featured a very realistic sculpture of a cinnamon tree. Two statues stood beneath it. One was Chang'e, the Chinese goddess of the moon. The other was Artemis, the Greek goddess our fair city was named after. The two women stood frozen in laughter, Chang'e's hand on Artemis's forearm. They seemed to be in the middle of some friendly girl talk. Locals knew them as the Ladies. I walked up and leaned against the "tree."

I looked up to the half Earth in the sky.

"No smoking in the park," said a raspy old voice.

The groundskeeper was at least eighty years old. He'd been a fixture since the park opened.

"Do you see a cigarette in my hand?" I said.

"I caught you once before."

"That was ten years ago."

He pointed to his eyes and then to me. "Watching you."

"Let me ask you something," I said. "Who moves all the way to the moon just to mow lawns?"

"I like plants. And my joints hurt. The gravity here's easy on my arthritis." He looked up at Earth. "Once the wife died, I didn't have much reason to stay there."

"Hell of a trip for an old man," I said.

"I used to travel a lot for work," he said. "I don't mind."

Svoboda showed up exactly on time, as usual. He carried a bag over his shoulder and smiled. He pointed to me and the goddess statues. "Hey, look at that! Three hot moon babes hanging out!"

I rolled my eyes. "Svoboda, someday I'll teach you how to talk to women."

He waved to the groundskeeper. "Hey, I know you. You're Mike, right?"

"Nope," said the groundskeeper. He shot me a look. "I'll leave you and your john alone. No sex on the grass."

"Try not to age to death on the way home, gramps," I said.

He waved over his shoulder as he walked away.

"Did you finish it?" I asked Svoboda.

"Yup, got it right here!" He handed the bag over to me.

I peeked inside. "Thanks."

"Did you get a chance to test that condom yet?"

"It's been twenty-four hours. What kind of sex life do you think I have?"

"Whatever, I don't know. Just asking." He scanned the park. "I don't come here often enough. It's a nice place to relax."

"If you like flying debris, yeah." The park was infamous for this. If you're from Earth, no matter how much you mentally prepare yourself, you always throw too hard. Your friend ten meters away—the intended receiver—will watch a ball sail over their head to the other side of the park. And don't get me started on Frisbees. Between the low gravity and low air pressure they're a complete mystery to tourists.

"I like it," Svoboda said. "It's the only 'natural' place in town. I miss open spaces."

"Plenty of open space outside to look at," I said. "And you can hang out with friends in a bar more easily than a park."

His face lit up. "We're friends?"

"Sure."

"Cool! I don't have many of those. You're my only friend with boobs."

"You *really* need to work on how you talk to women."

"Yeah, okay. Sorry."

I wasn't mad. It barely registered. I was too busy obsessing about my plans.

This was it. All the pieces were in place. I had the welding equipment, the custom electronics, and the HIB was ready. My breathing got short and my heart nearly beat right out of my chest. My little caper wasn't theoretical anymore. I was actually going to do this.

· · ·

That night, I repaired the leaky valve in my EVA suit. And I gave the whole suit a thorough inspection. Then I gave it another one. I'd never admit it to Bob, but he was dead right about my shoddy inspection work before the test. It was my problem to make sure my suit wouldn't kill me. And this time I made *damn* sure everything was in perfect working order.

I got some sleep, but not much. I'm not a brave person and I never claimed to be. This was it. The rest of my life hinged on how well I did.

I awoke at four a.m. Then I was too antsy to wait any longer.

I walked to the Port of Entry, collected Trigger and my EVA suit, and drove through the corridors of the sleeping city to Conrad Airlock. No one was there this time of morning. I dropped off my EVA gear and the big sack of equipment for my heist, stowing it all in the antechamber so it wouldn't be visible to anyone walking by.

I drove the now-empty Trigger *back* to his parking space at the port. Tip: If you're going to commit a major crime, don't leave your car at the crime scene while you do it.

I walked back to Conrad Airlock and closed myself into the antechamber. I just had to hope no one walked in on me or I'd have some 'splainin' to do.

I used duct tape to cover all identifying marks on my EVA gear. Serial numbers, license number, the big patch reading J. BASHARA on the front . . . that sort of thing. Then I brought Hibby back online. He perked right up.

Under my instruction, Hibby crawled down the arc of Conrad's hull to the airlock. He turned the crank to open the outer door. Then he dropped to the ground, nosed his way in, and shut the door behind him. He turned the crank again, sealing the door, then came over to the inner door.

I watched my little buddy through the round porthole window as he grabbed the manual valves to let air from Artemis into the airlock. A quick hiss, then the airlock had equalized with the city. Hibby turned the inner door's crank and opened it up.

I stepped into the airlock and patted him on the head. "Good boy." I powered him down and stowed him in a locker in the antechamber, along with his remote.

Well. There it was. An airlock all ready for use and the control panel was none the wiser. I flipped off the control panel just to assert dominance. It didn't seem impressed.

I suited up. I timed myself, of course. It's an EVA master thing. I took eleven minutes. Damn. How did Bob do it in three? The guy was a freakin' prodigy.

I fired up the suit's systems. Everything came online just as it should. I ran a pressure test. As instructed, the suit over-pressurized a little and monitored its status. This was the best way to check for leaks. No problems.

I stepped into the airlock, sealed the inner door, and started the cycle. Once it was done, I opened the outer door.

Good morning, Moon!

It's not dangerous to do a solo EVA, in and of itself. EVA masters do it all the time. But I was doing an EVA *in secret*. No one even knew I'd be out there. If I had a problem, no one would think to look for me. There'd just be a very attractive dead body out on the surface for however long it took someone to notice.

I made sure my microphone was off, but left the receiver on to the public EVA channel. If someone else ventured outside I'd damn well want to know about it.

My two oxygen tanks had sixteen hours of oxygen total. And I'd brought six more tanks with eight hours each. Way more than I'd need (I hoped), but I was playing it safe.

Well . . . I can't quite say "playing it safe" when I'm on an EVA and planning to fire up a welding torch on a moving rock harvester. But you know what I mean.

My CO_2-removal system reported green status, which was good, because I don't like dying. In the old days, astronauts needed expendable filters to collect CO_2. Modern suits sort the CO_2 molecules out through some complicated use of membranes and the vacuum outside. I don't know the details, but it works as long as the suit has power.

I checked my suit readouts again and made sure all the values were in the safe range. *Never* count on your suit's alarms to warn you. They're well designed, but they're the last resort. Safety begins with the operator.

I took a deep breath, hoisted the duffel over one shoulder, and got to walking.

First I had to walk all the way around the city. Conrad's airlock faced north, and Sanchez Aluminum's smelter was south. That took me a good twenty minutes.

Then it took me two hours to get to the smelter-reactor complex a kilometer away. It was disconcerting to see Artemis recede into the distance. Hey, look, it's the only place for humans to survive on this whole rock. Wave goodbye!

I finally made it to the base of what we call the Berm.

When they designed Artemis, someone said, "What if there's an explosion at the reactor? It's, like, a thousand meters from town? That'd be bad, right?" A bunch of nerds furrowed their brows and pondered this. Then one of them said, "Well . . . we could put a bunch of dirt in the way?" They gave him a promotion and a parade.

I embellished the details there, but you get my point. The Berm protects the city from the reactors in the event of an explosion. Though the hulls would probably do that just fine. It's all about redundant safety. Interestingly, we don't need protection from radiation. If the reactors ever melt down it won't matter. The city is shielded all to hell.

I sat down and rested at the base of the Berm. I'd had a long walk and needed a rest.

I turned my head inside the helmet, bit a nipple (try not to get excited), and sucked some water out. The suit's temperature systems also chilled the water. Hey, I spent a lot of money on that suit. It was quality gear when it wasn't malfunctioning and ruining my guild exam.

I gave a mighty grunt and started climbing. Five meters at a 45-degree angle. It might not seem like much, especially in lunar gravity. But when you're wearing a hundred kilograms of EVA suit and hauling another fifty of equipment, believe me, it's work.

I wheezed, gasped, and swore my way up the Berm. I think I invented some new profanities, I'm not sure. Is "fusumitch" a word? I finally made it to the top and surveyed the lands beyond.

The reactors lived in irregular-shaped buildings. Dozens of pipes led away to hundreds of shiny thermal panels lying on the ground.

Reactors on Earth dump heat into lakes or rivers. We're a bit dry here on the moon, so we dump our heat via infrared light emitted into space. It's century-old technology, but we haven't come up with anything better.

The smelting facility sat two hundred meters from the reactors. It was a mini bubble thirty meters across, with a hopper on one side. The hopper ground rocks into a coarse grit and put it in sealed cylindrical containers. The containers were sealed into pipes, which forced them into the facility with air pressure. Like an old-school pneumatic tube system from the 1950s. If you're going to have a bunch of air pumps and vacuum-management systems in your facility anyway, you may as well take advantage of them.

The train airlock stood on the other side of the bubble. The train tracks leading to it diverged into two lines. One ran to the airlock, the other to the unmanned silo car that transported rocket fuel to the port.

I dropped a couple of meters down the Berm and found a position where I could lie back and watch the scene. I had no idea what kind of schedule the harvesters had, so I would just have to wait.

And wait.

And fucking wait.

If you're curious, there were exactly fifty-seven rocks within reach. I sorted them from smallest to largest, then changed my mind and sorted them from most spherical to least spherical. Then I tried making a regolith castle, but it ended up being more of a lump. Regolith particles are barbed and they stick together well, but there's only so much you can do with EVA gloves. I could just about manage little half-spheres of dirt. I made a scale model of Artemis.

All told, I waited four hours.

Four. Goddamn. Hours.

Finally, I caught a glint of sunlight on the horizon. A harvester returning to port! Thank God. I stood and prepared the duffel for travel again. (I'd alphabetized my equipment out of boredom, first in English, then in Arabic.)

I hopped down the Berm. The harvester and I converged on the smelter from different directions. I got there first.

I crept around the bubble to stay out of sight of the harvester's cameras. No real reason to do that—it's not like anyone would be watching the feeds. I continued along the bubble wall until I got sight of the harvester. There it was, in all its giant shiny glory.

The harvester backed up to the hopper, latched into place, and slowly raised the front of its basin.

Thousands of kilograms of ore tumbled into the hopper. A brief cloud of dust accompanied the avalanche but almost immediately disappeared. No air to keep it afloat.

Having taken a good dump, the basin returned to level and the harvester sat idle. Mechanical arms reached out to attach the charging cable and coolant lines. I wasn't sure how long it would take to recharge, but I wasted no time.

"One million slugs," I said.

I climbed up the side of the harvester and threw my gear into the basin. Then I dropped into the basin myself. Easy enough.

I expected a long wait during the recharge, but it only took five minutes. I have to hand it to Toyota, they know how to make rapid-recharge batteries. The harvester lurched forward and just like that, we were on our way.

My plan was working! I giggled like a little girl. Hey, I'm a girl, so I'm allowed. And besides, no one was watching. I pulled an aluminum stock rod from the duffel, climbed to the top of the harvester, and held it out like a sword. "Onward, mighty steed!"

Onward we went. The harvester headed southwest toward the Moltke Foothills at the breakneck speed of five kilometers per hour.

I watched the smelter bubble and reactors disappear in the distance and grew uneasy again. Don't get me wrong, this wasn't the farthest I'd been from the Shire or anything. The train to the Visitor Center is over forty kilometers. But this was the farthest I'd ever been from *safety*.

The landscape grew rocky and jagged as we entered the foothills. The harvester didn't even slow down. It might not have been fast but damn, it had torque.

We hit the first of many boulders and I almost flew out of the basin. I barely kept all my gear inside. Harvesters are not luxury cars. How did the rocks even stay put on the trip back? The harvesters must've been a little more cautious on their way home. Still, the bumpy ride was better than walking. That incline would have killed me.

Finally, we leveled off and things got smooth again. I pushed the duffel off of me and climbed back to the top. We'd made it to the collection zone.

The wide, flat plain had been denuded of rocks over years of harvesting. Good. Finally some smooth sailing. The cleared area was roughly a circle. I spotted three other harvesters at the clearing's edge, scooping rocks into their basins. My harvester rumbled to the edge and dropped its scoop.

I tossed my gear out of the basin and hopped after it. At this point there was no way to avoid nav cameras. I just had to hope some Sanchez employee hadn't randomly decided to bring up the feeds to impress his girlfriend.

I collected the gear and dragged it under the harvester with me.

The first step was to attach myself and my gear to the under-carriage. Harvesters don't stay still for long and I didn't want to scurry after it. I upended the duffel to prep my equipment.

First was the tarp. It was heavy, fiber-reinforced plastic with grommets in the corners so you could tie it down. I laced nylon rope through the grommets and affixed it to some jack-points on the hull. Now I had a hammock. I crawled into my new secret lair and pulled my welding equipment up with me.

The harvester lurched forward. I guess it had loaded some rocks into its basin and decided to move forward for another bite. I had no warning because, hey, no sound. A minor incon-venience—I hadn't loaded the spare oxygen tanks into my ham-mock yet.

I looked over to the spare tanks. Okay. Not the end of the world. I could come back later to—

A huge boulder, destabilized by the fresh hole at its base, tipped forward onto the tanks. A pathetic fart of air escaped from underneath, briefly kicking up dust. Then there was noth-ing. And that was the end of my reserve air tanks.

"Oh, *come on!*" I yelled.

I took a moment to calculate how fucked I was.

I checked my arm readout. Six hours of oxygen left in the main supply. Two more hours in the emergency reserve. I had another tank for welding. I could attach it to my suit's universal valve, but that would defeat the purpose of the whole trip. I needed that oxygen for my nefarious plans.

So, eight hours of breathable air. Was this still doable?

Artemis was three kilometers away. The trip had a lot of rough terrain but it was also downhill. Call it two hours.

My original plan had been to wait until night (clock-night I mean, not actual lunar night) and then sneak in when everyone was asleep. But I didn't have enough air to wait that long. I'd have to enter in the middle of the day.

New plan: the ISRO airlock. It led into Space Agency Row in Armstrong Bubble. There'd be a few confused nerds and someone might say "um . . ." but I'd just keep walking. With the sun visor down, no one would see my face. And, unlike the Conrad airlock, it wouldn't be littered with EVA masters.

Okay, problem sorta solved. That meant I had six hours before I had to leave the collection area. Ninety minutes per harvester. Time to hustle.

I got as comfortable as I could in my hammock and assembled the welding gear. I laid the acetylene and oxygen tanks between my legs to keep them stable. On the harvester's undercarriage, I eyeballed ten centimeters from the coolant valve and scratched a three-centimeter circle there with a screwdriver. That's where I had to cut.

I flipped down my helmet's sun visor. I'd duct taped a welding lens shade to the middle. I cranked the acetylene valve, set the torch mixture to ignition mode, sparked it, and—

. . . it didn't start.

Um.

I tried again. Nothing. Not even sparks.

I checked the acetylene tank. No flow problems. What the hell?

I flipped up the visor and inspected the sparker. Dad taught me to use a flint sparker because an electric one is "another thing to break." It was just a piece of flint and steel grooves attached to a springy handle. Nothing complicated about it. This was thousand-year-old technology we're talking about here. Why wasn't it working?

Oh.

Right.

When flint strikes steel, it knocks microscopic flecks of metal into the air. The metal burns because of some complicated crap related to surface area and oxidization rates. Basically, it rusts so fast that the reaction heat makes fire.

Fun fact: Oxidizing requires oxygen. Flint and steel won't work in a vacuum. All right. No need to panic. A welding flame is just acetylene and oxygen on fire. I adjusted the valves and set the mixture to be a trickle of acetylene amongst a torrent of oxygen. Then I scraped the sparker right in front of the nozzle.

Sparks! Boy did they ever fly! That oxygen made the metal flecks go apeshit. But I'd got too far. There wasn't enough acetylene to ignite the flame itself. I added a bit more to the mix and tried again.

This time, the shower of sparks managed to light a sputtering, inconsistent flame. I spun the valves back to a normal mix and the flame settled into a familiar, stable shape.

I breathed a sigh of relief and flipped my visor down. I held the torch steady despite the clunky EVA suit. Pain in the ass. But at least I didn't have to deal with molten metal. This was a cut, not a join. When you cut, you aren't melting metal. You actually turn it into an oxidized gas. Yeah, it's that hot.

The actual cutting was a lot easier than I expected. It took less than a minute. The little three-centimeter circle of steel plopped down on my chest, followed by a blob of molten wax. The wax bubbled and re-hardened almost instantly.

My positioning was perfect. I'd cut into the wax reservoir without nicking the coolant lines nearby. I didn't care about the health of the coolant system, but I didn't want the harvester to call home about a coolant leak. The small daub of wax that fell on me wouldn't be enough loss to worry the harvester. At least, I hoped not.

I pulled a pressure valve from my duffel. I'd bought six of them from Tranquility Bay Hardware the day before (one per harvester and two spares). Standard pressure connector on one side, three centimeters raw pipe on the other. I jammed the connector into the hole. I'd done well on my cut—it was a snug fit. I fired up the torch again (with the same oxygen-crazy ignition mix as last time) and grabbed a rod of stock aluminum. I needed a strong, airtight seal around the valve.

I'd done a million valve installations with Dad as a kid. But never in an EVA suit. And unlike the cut, this time I was melting stock metal to make a seal.

If I screwed up, a blob of molten metal would fall on me and bore a hole straight through my suit. Holes in EVA suits are bad.

I got as far to the side as I could—if I screwed up, maybe the Aluminum Droplet of Doom would miss me. I got to work and watched the aluminum puddle grow. The droplet trembled along the weld site, then finally seeped upward into the crack above it. My heartbeat returned to somewhere near normal. Thank God for surface tension and capillary action.

I was careful, and took my time. I worked around the valve slowly, trying to keep my body from being directly underneath. Finally, I finished the deed.

I'd installed a pressure valve into the wax reservoir. Now it was time for the dastardly part of my plan.

I attached the line from my welding oxygen tank to the valve and cranked the flow to full.

Sure, the reservoir was full of wax, but there were gaps. And believe me, when you blow fifty atmospheres of air into a pressure vessel, it finds the gaps. Once the tank equalized with the compartment, I *very carefully* closed the valve and disconnected the tank line.

I slid out from under the harvester. I watched it for a second to make sure the damn thing wasn't about to move. I don't like making the same mistake twice.

The scoop crunched forward, grabbed a few hundred rocks, and dropped them in the basin. It reached down for another bite. Okay, I had time to climb aboard.

I hopped on the nearby wheel and hoisted myself onto the frame. I reached the breaker box and opened the little door. Inside, it was just like Trond's harvester's breaker box, with the same four lines connecting to it. Not a surprise—they were the same model. Still, I unclenched a little upon seeing it.

Harvesters have breakers all over to stave off electrical problems, but the last line of defense is the main breaker. All power runs through it. It's the "fuse" that protects the battery.

I pulled a homemade contraption from my duffel. It consisted of two jumper-cable clamps on thick-gauge wire, which led to a high-voltage relay switch. The relay was wired into the buzzer on a battery-powered alarm clock. Simple as that. The relay would trip when the clock's alarm went off. Not exactly rocket science, and it sure as hell wasn't pretty, but it would work.

I connected the positive and negative poles of the main power line with my contraption. Nothing happened, of course. The relay was open. But once the alarm went off (set for midnight that evening), the relay would close and the battery would short out. And the short would bypass the breaker box entirely, so the normal fail-safes wouldn't work.

When you short out a 2.4 megawatt-hour battery, it gets very, very hot. Like, *extremely* hot. And it'd be sitting in a sealed reservoir full of wax and compressed oxygen. And the reservoir was an airtight compartment. Let me give you the math on that:

Wax + oxygen + heat = fire.

Fire + confined volume = bomb.

(Bomb + harvester) × 4 = 1,000,000ğ for Jazz.

And it would happen long after I had safely returned to town. They could look as closely as they wanted at the video footage, they wouldn't know who I was. And I had another trick up my sleeve. . . .

I checked my arm readouts. I had to hope Svoboda's device worked as advertised. He'd never failed me before, at least.

Back in my coffin, the device Svoboda had made for me would be powering up. I affectionately named it the "alibi-o-mat." I'd slotted my Gizmo into it before I'd gone on this little adventure.

The alibi-o-mat poked at my Gizmo screen with little probes that had the same capacitance as a human finger.

It typed in my passcode and started surfing the internet. It brought up my favorite Saudi gossip websites, some funny videos, and a few internet forums. It even fired off some emails I'd composed in advance.

Not the perfect alibi, but it was pretty good. If anyone asked where I was, I'd say I was at home surfing the internet. Hardly an uncommon thing to do. And the data logs from my Gizmo and the city's network would back that up.

I checked the time. The whole procedure—from attaching the hammock to installing my harvester-killing-device—had taken forty-one minutes. This was doable! I'd make it back in plenty of time! One harvester down, three to go.

I crawled back under the now-doomed harvester, collected my gear, and crawled back out. All the while I was careful not to get crushed by the giant wheels. Even in lunar gravity the harvester was heavy enough to squish me like a grape.

I assumed the next harvester would be a hundred meters away or so on some other edge of the collection zone. But instead, it was *three meters from my face*. What the hell was it doing there?!

It didn't dig. It didn't load. It just "looked" at me, its high-resolution cameras re-focused slightly as I stood up. It could only mean one thing: Someone at Sanchez Aluminum had taken manual control of this harvester.

They'd spotted me.

Dear Jazz,

I'm very worried about you. I haven't heard from you in over a month. You haven't answered any of my emails. I found your father's email address through his welding business website and contacted him. He doesn't know where you are and he's very worried too.

Artemis's public contact directory has 7 people named Sean. I contacted all of them and none are the Sean who knows you. I guess your Sean didn't want his information public? Anyway, that was a dead end too.

Dear Kelvin,

Sorry you got worried. I wish you hadn't contacted Dad.

Things have not gone well lately. Last month Sean got a visit from an angry mob. About fifteen guys. They beat the shit out of him. He wouldn't talk about it afterward, but I knew what it was about. It's a thing people do here. It's called a "morals brigade."

Some things really piss people off. Enough that they'll form up and punish you, even though you didn't break any laws. Sean is a horny guy—I knew that. And I knew he had other girls.

But I didn't know he was screwing a fourteen-year-old.

We've got people from all over Earth here. Different cultures have very different sexual morals, so Artemis doesn't have age-of-consent rules at all. As long as it's not forced, it's not rape. And the girl was consenting.

But we're not savages here. You might not get deported to Earth, but you'll definitely get your ass kicked. I assume some of those guys were the girl's relatives. I don't know.

I'm an idiot, Kelvin. A complete idiot. How could I not see what Sean was? I'm only seventeen and he was hot for me from day one. Turns out I'm on the older end of his preference range.

I've got nowhere to stay. I can't go back to Dad. I just can't. The fire destroyed all that equipment he'd bought. And he had to pay for the damage to the room itself. Now he can't expand the business at all. Hell, he can barely keep afloat. How can I go crawling back after doing something like that?

I ruined my father with my stupidity.

And I ruined myself too, by the way. When I walked out on Sean, I had a couple hundred slugs to my name. I couldn't rent a room with that. I couldn't even eat proper food.

I'm living on Gunk. Every day. Unflavored, because I can't afford extracts. And . . . oh God, Kelvin . . . I don't have anywhere to live. I sleep where I can. Areas without a lot of people in them. High floors where it's godawful hot or low floors where it's freezing. I stole a blanket from a hotel laundry room just to have something to sleep under. I have to keep moving every night to stay a step ahead of Rudy. It's against the rules to be homeless. And he's been *gunning* for me since the fire. He'll use any excuse he can to get rid of me.

If he catches me I'll get deported to Saudi Arabia. Then I'll be broke, homeless, *and* have gravity sickness. I have to stay here.

I'm sorry to dump all this on you. I just don't have anyone else to talk to.

Do NOT offer me money. I know that'll be your first instinct, but don't. You have four sisters and two parents to take care of.

Dear Jazz,

I don't know what to say. I'm devastated. I wish I could do something for you.

Things haven't been great here either. My sister Halima announced that she's pregnant. The father is apparently a military man of some kind and she doesn't even know his last name. There's going to be a baby to take care of soon, and it throws a wrench into all our plans. Originally, I was going to pay for Halima's education, then she'd pay for Kuki's education while I saved up money for Mom and Dad's retirement. Then Kuki would pay for Faith's education and so on. But now Halima won't be doing anything but taking care of her baby and we'll have to fund her. Mom got a job as a clerk at a grocery store on the KSC campus. It's the first job she's had in her life. She seems to like it, but I wish she didn't have to work at all.

Dad will have to work many more years. Kuki is now saying she'll get an unskilled labor job somewhere to bring in money. But she's selling her future!

We should count our blessings. Halima will be a good mother. And my family will soon have a new child to cherish. We are all healthy and we have each other.

You may be homeless, but at least it's in the relatively clean, safe streets of Artemis instead of some Earth city. You have a job and are making some money. Hopefully more than you are spending.

Difficult times, my friend, but there is a path. There must be. We will find it. Let me know if there's anything I can do to help you.

6

"Okay, this is some bullshit," I said to the harvester.

The other two harvesters also rolled toward me. Probably to make sure I couldn't hide behind a rock to get away. Their controllers now had me on camera from multiple angles. Whee.

I later learned what had happened: The boulder that murdered my air tanks made quite a thump—the harvester felt the tremor. They have very sensitive equipment in their wheels to detect ground vibration. Why? Because they dig on mountainsides. If there's an avalanche brewing, the controllers want to know right away.

So the harvester called home to report the tremor. Back at Sanchez's control center, workers checked the previous couple minutes' video. They wanted to know if a wall of stony death was about to eat their multimillion-slug harvester. Guess what they saw! Me disappearing into the undercarriage! So they sent another harvester to see what the hell I was up to.

Then they called the EVA masters. I don't know exactly how the conversation went, but I assume it was something like this:

Sanchez controllers: "Hey! Why are you fucking with our harvester?!"

EVA masters: "We're not."

Sanchez: "Well, someone is."

EVA masters: "We'll go kick their ass. Not because we care

about you, but because we want to continue our stranglehold monopoly on EVAs. Also, we're a bunch of assholes."

So right now, the EVA masters were forming a posse to drag me back to Artemis. After that would come beatings, deportation, gravity sickness in Riyadh, and things generally going downhill from there.

I stopped to think about this new situation. There was no way I'd get back into town before an angry mob of EVA masters came out looking for me. So there was no point in aborting. May as well finish the job before the epic game of lunar hide-and-seek began.

The posse would use a freight rover for fast travel. They can go ten kilometers per hour. The uphill climb would slow them a bit. Call it six kilometers per hour. I had a half hour before they arrived.

Subtlety time was over. My plan to make shit happen after I got home was gone. Sanchez would recall all the harvesters for inspection. Mechanics would then go over each one with a fine-toothed comb and undo my hard work.

I had to permanently destroy all four harvesters within the next thirty minutes. On the plus side, Sanchez's controllers had been kind enough to put them all next to me.

Okay, first things first. I grabbed a pair of wire cutters from my duffel, leapt onto the harvester that spotted me, and clambered to the top. The primary and secondary comm systems were both mounted to the highest point of the cab for maximum range. The harvester (now under human control no doubt) shimmied forward and back—probably trying to shake me off. But harvesters just aren't very fast. I kept my balance easily and made short work of all four antennas. They were a little thicker than the wire cutters were designed for, but I got it done. It stopped dead as soon as the fourth antenna dropped. Harvesters are programmed to sit idle if they lose connection. You wouldn't want your harvester wandering around on its own, right?

I leapt directly to the roof of the next harvester over—the one I'd just meticulously turned into a time bomb. All that work for nothing. Sigh.

Snip, snip, snip, snip!

The other two harvesters backed away.

"Oh, no you don't!" I said. I leapt from the roof and hit the ground running. I caught up with ease.

I climbed to the top of my third victim and got to snipping. Like its brethren, it stopped dead as soon as the last antenna was gone.

I had a bit of a run to catch up to the last one, but I got there soon enough. I snipped three of the antennas and was just about to get the fourth when my left side exploded with pain and I flew through the air. Well, not "air." Vacuum. You know what I mean.

I smacked into the ground and rolled.

"Whu?" I said. It took me a second, but I realized what happened. Those *asswipes* at Sanchez had made the harvester smack me with its front-loader scoop!

Sons of bitches! That could have ruptured my suit! Sure, I was trashing their property but you don't *kill* someone for that, do you?!

Oh, it was *on*.

The harvester dropped its scoop halfway down and rolled toward me.

I got to my feet, ran in front of the main camera, and flipped it my middle finger. Then I bashed it with the cutters in my other hand. No more visual data for you, assholes.

"Whoever you are, we know you're out there," I heard over the main EVA channel. It was Bob Lewis. Dammit! Of course the guild would send their most skilled member to lead the posse. "Don't make this hard. If we have to physically restrain you, risking our safety, we'll make you pay for it."

He had a point. Contrary to space movies, fighting in an EVA suit is monumentally dangerous. I had no intention of doing that.

If they caught up to me I'd just surrender. This had become a game of tag.

One problem at a time. I still had Killdozer to deal with. Without the front camera, it flailed around trying to find me. The wheels might not move fast, but the raw power behind that scoop could really whip it back and forth.

The scoop slammed to the ground a meter to my left. Pretty good guess, but not good enough. I hopped into the scoop and crouched down. I was taking a gamble here. The scoop had very accurate weight sensors and my mass would surely be detectable. I hoped the controller wasn't paying enough attention.

The scoop reared up again, and when it did I leapt. Between my leap and the scoop's upward motion, I went way the hell higher than I'd intended.

"Well, shit," I said as I reached the top of the arc. I think I was about ten meters off the ground, but I'll never know for sure. I do know that when I landed on the harvester's roof I damn near broke my legs.

After a moment of reflection on the wisdom of my plan, I reached over and snipped the remaining antenna. The harvester stopped thrashing instantly.

"Whew." I'd temporarily disabled all four harvesters. Now to permanently disable them.

I started with the harvester that I'd already sabotaged. I climbed up the side as I had done before and opened the breaker box. I reached into my relay box and pawed at the alarm settings on the clock. I couldn't press the buttons, of course. The clock was designed for use by human fingers, not ham-fisted EVA gloves.

Okay, if I couldn't set the alarm time, I'd use a less subtle approach. I disconnected both alligator clips, yanked the relay out from between them, and cut the insulation off their cables. I tied the cables into a crude knot and reconnected the alligator clips to the battery poles.

Then I *hauled ass*.

By removing the relay, I'd created a new device known as a "wire." The battery was shorted and was absolutely *shitting* heat.

I ran full-speed to the nearest boulder and slid behind it. Nothing happened right away. I peeked around the edge. Still nothing.

"Hmm," I said. "Maybe I should—"

Then the harvester exploded. Like . . . *exploded*. Way the hell larger than I expected. Shrapnel flew in all directions. The blast forced the chassis into the ground so hard it bounced up, did a half flip, and landed on its roof.

I thought I was far enough from the explosion but no, not even close. Chunks of twisted metal bashed my boulder while smaller bits of wreckage rained from above.

"Oh, right," I said. I'd forgotten to account for the other explosive in there: the hydrogen fuel-cell battery. All that hydrogen had met the oxygen at high temperature and they'd had a brief chat.

The rock shielded me from the initial blast, but it was useless against the debris that came down from above. I belly-crawled to one of the other harvesters while tufts of dust erupted around me. Reminder: There's no air here. If something gets flung into the sky, it comes back down *as fast as it was going when it left*. It was raining bullets.

Through pure luck, I made it to the harvester and cowered under it for a while. I waited until the storm abated and crawled out to check my handiwork.

The victim harvester was totaled. Hell, you could barely tell it used to be a vehicle. The chassis was a wreck of twisted metal and a good 50 percent of the harvester was now evenly distributed across the collection zone. I checked the time. The whole process had taken ten minutes. Not bad, but I'd have to speed things up for the other three.

First, though, I picked through the wreckage, found a sheet of metal about two meters square, and dragged it to the far side of my Boulder of Protection. I leaned it against the edge to make a rudimentary shelter.

There. Technically I'd made a moon base. I sat in Fort Jasmine for a few minutes, converting my other relay cables to simple jumpers.

Then I got to work on the second harvester. At least this time there was no need for a hammock. The harvester wouldn't be going anywhere.

Now that I had the hang of firing up a torch in a vacuum, things went much faster. Also, I didn't bother marking the site first. I just did it from memory. Nothing quite like experience to speed your hand. I cut the hole, installed the valve, and filled the reservoir with air.

Then I shorted the battery, ran to my metal plate, crawled under it, and waited. And this time, I didn't look back like a moron.

I felt the explosion through the ground and readied myself for the "rain of terror." Would the metal plate be thick enough?

Dents appeared in the plate. Scary as hell, but it protected me from the hail. I waited until the dents stopped and checked the ground nearby to see if the puffs of dust had stopped. It would have been better if I could just hear things. Vacuum's refusal to convey sound is a real pain in the ass.

I crept out and nothing killed me, so everything seemed to be in order. I came around the rock to see another demolished harvester.

I checked the time on my arm readouts. Another ten minutes had passed. "Dammit!"

If the posse was efficient, they'd be on-site in another ten minutes. I still had two more harvesters to trash. If I left either of them operational, Sanchez Aluminum would still be able to get ore, still be able to make oxygen, and Trond would be keeping that million slugs.

The biggest time sink was when I had to run and hide from

the debris. I knew what I had to do—I just didn't like it. I'd have to blow the remaining two at the same time.

Please don't quote that last sentence out of context.

I prepared each of the remaining harvesters for kaboominess. Both were now full of oxygen, their breaker boxes open, and my jumper cables dangling from their positive poles.

I laid all the welding equipment under one of the harvesters. Now that I was in a hurry, I wouldn't be able to drag all that shit home with me. But I couldn't leave stuff with BASHARA WELDING COMPANY written all over it for people to find.

Eh. A million slugs. I'd buy him new stuff. *Better* stuff.

I stood at one harvester and looked to the other twenty meters away. This would be tricky. A long-forgotten rational part of my brain piped up. Was this really a good idea? (One million slugs.) Yup! I'm fine!

I shorted out one battery, ran to the other harvester, and shorted it too. I almost made it back to the shelter before the first one blew.

Almost.

The landscape ahead flashed bright with the blast. Tufts of dust burst around me as harvester bits diligently obeyed the laws of physics. No time to go around the boulder. I half climbed, half leapt over it. I tried for a graceful tuck-and-roll, but ended up with more of a flail-and-flop.

"Did you see that?!" came a voice over the radio.

"You're broadcasting on Main," said Bob.

"Shit."

The posse had been talking on some other channel to keep me from hearing them. That one guy screwed up. So now I knew they'd seen the explosion. They were close.

I waited for the second explosion, but it never came. When I got brave enough, I peeked around my rock to see one harvester still unharmed.

"What the fu—" I began. But then I saw it: The survivor was

pocked with superficial damage from the other harvester's explosion. My jumper had been severed cleanly in half by a piece of shrapnel. The two ends hung from their poles. The battery wasn't shorted anymore, and it hadn't had time to get hot enough to touch off the explosion.

I spotted a glint of light across the harvesting zone. The EVA masters had come. I looked back at the remaining harvester. Fifteen meters of ground to cross to get back to it, plus however long it would take me to fix the jumper. Then I looked at the glint again—now identifiable as a rover, just a hundred meters away, and coming at me fast.

I wouldn't make it. They'd be on me in a shot. I had to leave the one harvester behind.

"Shit!" I said. I knew it was the right decision, but that didn't mean I had to like it. I fled the crime scene.

Minor problem with running away from people on the moon: Your footprints are very obvious. I beelined out of the collection zone and left a blatant trail any idiot could follow. No way around that. The whole area had long since been cleared of everything but dust.

Once I got into natural terrain I had options—the highlands are riddled with everything from pebbles to boulders.

I stepped onto a rock and jumped to the next rock over. Then I jumped to the next one and so on. I continued my high-stakes game of The Floor Is Lava for the next twenty minutes. I never had to touch the dusty ground at all. Try following *that* trail, Bob.

The next bit was equal parts boring and stressful. I had several kilometers to cover, all the while looking over my shoulder. It wouldn't take the posse long to figure out I was headed home. Then they'd hop in their rover and catch up to me.

They'd drive along the shortest route home (I hoped), so I took a roundabout path. Nothing resembling a straight line. Artemis was only three kilometers away from the collection zone, but I walked five kilometers on my crazy circuitous route. The rocky landscape of the foothills provided lots of boulders and berms to block any direct line of sight to me.

It worked. I don't know what route the posse took, but they never got eyes on me.

I finally reached the base of the Moltke Foothills. The Sea of Tranquility stretched all the way to the horizon. Artemis shined in the extreme distance, probably a good two kilometers away. I suppressed the queasy feelings that came with realizing how isolated I was. No time for that shit right now.

I needed a new strategy. I couldn't hopscotch my way any farther. A vast field of gray powder separated me from home. Not only would I leave a trail, I'd be visible for kilometers around.

Time for a rest. For the moment, at least, I wasn't out in the open. I found a suitable boulder and sat in the shade. I turned off all my LEDs, even the ones in the helmet, and covered my arm readouts with tape.

Shadows on the moon are stark and black. No air means no light diffusion. But I wasn't in total darkness. Sunlight reflected off nearby rocks, dirt, hills, and so on, and some of that snuck around to hit me. Still, I was functionally invisible compared to the shine of the landscape.

I turned my head to the water nipple and slurped down a good half liter. EVAs are a sweaty business.

Good thing I'd taken a break. Five minutes into my rest I spotted the posse driving back to town. They were a fair distance away from me—on the straight-line course to the city.

The rover, designed for four passengers, had seven EVA masters piled on it. It looked like a clown car speeding across the flatlands. Judging by the rooster tail of dust it kicked up, they were moving as fast as they could. At that speed on the bumpy terrain they'd have no chance of spotting me. What the hell were they thinking?

"Aww, fuck," I said.

They didn't need to find me. They just needed to beat me back to town. Then they could guard every airlock. Eventually I'd run out of air and have to surrender.

"Shit! Damn! Crap! Ass! Son of a bitch!" It's important to vary your profanities. If you use the same one too often it loses strength. I fumed in my suit for a minute more, then calmed down and got to scheming.

Okay, this sucked but it came with advantages. They would beat me to town. Fine. But that meant they wouldn't be patrolling for me in Tranquility. I'd been stressing out about how to sneak across the flatlands but now that wasn't a problem.

I stood up, turned my LEDs back on, and pulled the tape off my arm readouts.

There'd be an EVA master on the lookout at every airlock. And they wouldn't just be hanging around inside. They'd be outside, where they could see me coming and sound the alarm.

I had a plan, but first I had to get next to the city itself. That was step one.

Conrad's airlock faced north, the Tranquility Bay Company's freight airlock in Bean faced northwest, the Port of Entry in Aldrin faced east, and the ISRO's airlock in Armstrong faced southeast. So the biggest "blind spot" in their coverage would be the southwest.

I bounced along the gray nothingness for an hour, taking a wide, circular course so as to approach from the right direction. I kept my eyes out for trouble as the domes of home grew on the horizon. The last hundred meters were pure stress. Once I entered the shadow of Shepard Bubble I felt a lot safer. I'd be hard to spot in the darkness.

Finally, I leaned against Shepard's hull and breathed a sigh of relief.

Okay. I'd made it to town. Now the trick was getting in.

I couldn't walk the perimeter of town to get where I needed

to be. I'd be spotted for sure. Time to make like Hibby and use those maintenance handholds.

The handles had been designed with EVA suits in mind—the perfect width for grabbing with giant gloves. It only took me ten minutes to climb the arc of the sphere. I hunkered down once I got to the peak. Not because I was worried about EVA masters—they'd all be too close to other bubbles to get eyes on me. No, my problem was basic geography. Shepard and Aldrin are separated only by Armstrong, and Armstrong is only half their height. So right that moment, anyone in Aldrin Park would be able to see me.

It was still pretty early in the morning, so hopefully there wouldn't be too many park visitors. Plus, anyone who did see me would probably assume I was a maintenance worker doing her job. Still . . . I was perpetrating a caper and preferred not to be noticed.

I climbed down the other side of Shepard and onto the connector tunnel between it and Armstrong. It wasn't exactly gymnastics. The tunnel is three meters wide.

Once I made it to Armstrong Bubble, I climbed over it too. Thanks to Armstrong's smaller size, it went considerably faster than my Shepard climb. Then I catwalked across the Armstrong–Aldrin Connector.

Aldrin was more of a challenge. I climbed up part of the way, but couldn't go to the peak. Well, I *could*, but I shouldn't. It's one thing to wander around on a bubble hull, but if I climbed on the glass of Aldrin Park right in front of people's faces, it would raise a few eyebrows. "Mommy, why is Spider-Man on the moon?"—no thanks.

Instead, I stopped climbing halfway up—just below the glass panels—and moved sideways, shimmying from handle to handle and working my way around the bubble. Soon, the Port of Entry came into view. Closest to me was the rail antechamber where train cars docked with the port. No train there at the moment, though. Next to that was the huge circular door to the freight airlock.

Bob Lewis stepped out of the train alcove.

"Oh shit!" I said. I'd been so careful coming around the arc of Aldrin! I'd moved slowly to make sure I'd see any EVA master before he could see me. But I didn't know Bob was *inside* the damn alcove. That's *cheating*, Bob!

He was doing rounds. Once a marine always a marine. He hadn't looked up yet but he would soon. I had a second, maybe two, to react.

I let go of the handles and slid down the dome. I tried to aim my feet at the ground—maybe if I landed just right I could control the impact. But no. No. I'm not graceful. I got the worst of both worlds: I hit the ground hard and completely off-balance.

I landed like a sack of shit. But I landed on the other side of the alcove and didn't break anything. Good thing sound doesn't travel in a vacuum, because Bob surely would have heard that landing. Whatever. A clumsy, awkward success is still a success.

I hugged the wall of Aldrin and crept away from the port until I couldn't see Bob anymore. I wasn't sure where his "patrol route" would take him, but I knew he wouldn't stray far from the port's airlock. I continued until I was well clear of the port and sat down with my back against the bubble.

Then I waited. I couldn't see the train alcove from my new position, but I could see the tracks leading away from town.

The train appeared on the horizon half an hour later. Owing to the small size of the moon, our horizon is only two and a half kilometers away, so I didn't have long before it arrived at the station.

I waited for the train to pull into the alcove and dock with the port. Then I crept along my side of the alcove.

This was the first train of the day. Most of the passengers would be employees of the Visitor Center itself. They loaded up quickly and the train was ready for its return trip.

It emerged from the alcove. It takes a while to get something that size up to speed, so it wasn't going very fast yet.

I leapt forward and grabbed the front wheel housing. It wasn't the best grip, but I held on with all my might. The train dragged me along, my legs bouncing off the terrain. Okay, maybe this wasn't the best plan I'd ever concocted, but it kept a train between me and Bob, which was all I wanted.

The train accelerated, faster and faster. I hung on for dear life. At this speed, any sharp rock could puncture my suit. I couldn't let myself dangle for the whole trip. I had to put my legs somewhere.

I reached up and grabbed the edge of a window—I had to hope no one was sitting there. I pulled myself up and put my feet on the wheel housing. I wanted to peek through the window to see if I'd been spotted, but I resisted the urge. People might not notice a few fingers outside a window, but they'd probably notice a big EVA suit helmet.

I tried not to move. It'd be pretty spooky for people in the train if they heard noise coming from the wall from outside. Attack of the Moon Woman Who Made Bad Life Decisions.

We puttered along the lazy path toward the Visitor Center. By now you've probably figured out my plan. The posse was guarding all the *Artemis* airlocks, but had they thought to guard the one at the Visitor Center?

Even if they had, they couldn't beat me there. This was the first train.

The trip took forty minutes, as usual. I managed to sit sort of comfortably on the wheel housing. It wasn't too bad.

I spent the trip brooding about my predicament. Even if I could make it back inside without getting caught, I was screwed. Trond had hired me to destroy four harvesters. I only trashed three. Sanchez's engineers would undo my sabotage to the survivor and get it back to work. Their production would be reduced, but they'd still make their oxygen quota.

Trond wouldn't pay me for this debacle, and I wouldn't blame him. Not only had I failed, I'd made things harder on him. Now Sanchez Aluminum knew someone was gunning for them.

"Damn . . ." I said as my stomach knotted up.

The train slowed as it approached the Visitor Center. I hopped off and stumbled to a stop while the train continued on to its alcove.

I bounded over to the Visitor Center and worked my way along the arc of its dome. The *Eagle* came into view as I rounded the hull. It almost seemed to disapprove. *Tsk, tsk.* My *crew would never pull shit like this.*

Then I saw a glorious sight: The EVA airlock was completely unguarded!

Hell yeah!

I rushed to the airlock and opened the outer door, hopped in, and closed the hatch behind me. I cranked the repress valve and heard the hiss of glorious air come at me from all directions.

Even though I was in a hurry, I waited through the air cleanse. Hey, I may be a smuggler, saboteur, and all-around asshole, but I'd never leave my EVA suit dirty.

The cleanse finished and I was clean as a whistle.

Back in town! I'd have to find somewhere in the Visitor Center to hide my EVA gear, but that wouldn't be a problem. I'd stow it in as many tourist lockers as it took, then come back later with a big container. I'm a porter—I'd just say I was there for a pickup. It wouldn't even look weird.

I opened the inner airlock door and stepped into salvation.

Except it wasn't salvation. It was shit. I stepped into shit. The smile on my face quickly changed to a "freshly caught carp" expression.

Dale stood in the antechamber, his arms folded and a half smirk on his face.

Dear Jazz,

Are you all right? I've been worried. I haven't heard from you in a couple of weeks.

Dear Kelvin,

Sorry, I had to shut off my Gizmo service for a while to save money. I've got it back on now. It's been tough. But I'm starting to get above water.

I made a new friend. Every now and then I scrape together enough money to get a beer at this hole-in-the-wall in Conrad. I know it's stupid to spend money on booze when you're homeless, but booze makes homelessness bearable.

Anyway, there's a regular there named Dale. He's an EVA master, mostly working out of the Apollo 11 Visitor Center. He does tourist EVAs, stuff like that.

We got to talking and, I don't know why, but I ended up telling him my problems. He was shocked at my fucked-up situation and offered to lend me some money. I assumed it was a play to get in my pants so I turned him down. I don't have a problem with prostitutes, but I don't want to be one.

But he swore up and down that he just wanted to help me out as a friend. Accepting that money was the hardest thing I've ever done, Kelvin. But I was out of options.

Anyway, I had just enough to pay deposit and first month on a capsule domicile. It's so small I have to step outside to change my mind (rim shot!) but at least it's a home. And true to his word, Dale never expected anything in return. Perfect gentleman.

And believe it or not I'm even dating a guy. His name is Tyler. It's early days, but he's really sweet. He's kind of shy, polite to everyone, and sort of a Boy

Scout when it comes to rules. So the opposite of me in every way. But we really click. We'll see how it goes.

You know what? I've been selfish lately. I've been so focused on me I didn't even ask about you. How are you handling things?

Dear Jazz,

Good for you! I was worried your experience with Sean would put you off men forever. See? We're not all bad.

I have my job at KSC, for which I'm very grateful. I even got a promotion. I'm a loadmaster-in-training now. In a couple months, I'll be a full loadmaster and I'll get a raise.

Halima is six months pregnant now, and we're all preparing for the baby. We've worked out a rotation so that my other sisters can take care of the baby while Halima stays in school. Mom, Dad, and I will keep working. Dad was almost ready to retire, but now he'll have to work another five years at least. What choice do we have? There's just not enough money otherwise.

Dear Kelvin,

You're a loadmaster-in-training? Does that mean you sometimes set up cargo pods unsupervised? Because there are a lot of people in Artemis who smoke.

Dear Jazz,

I'm listening . . .

7

I stared at Dale like he'd grown a dick out of his forehead. "How . . . ?"

"What else would you do?" He took the helmet from my unresisting hands. "You had to know the posse would cover all the Artemis entrances. That just leaves the Visitor Center."

"Why aren't you with the posse!"

"I am with the posse. I'm the guy who volunteered to guard the Visitor Center. I would've been here sooner, but this was the first train out. Given the timing, I'm guessing we caught the same ride."

Shit. Some criminal mastermind I was.

Dale set my helmet on a bench, then took my hand and unclamped the seals on the glove. He rotated the glove at the wrist and pulled it off. "You went too far this time, Jazz. Way too far."

"You're going to lecture me on morality?"

He shook his head. "Are you ever going to let that go?"

"Why should I?"

He rolled his eyes. "Tyler's gay, Jazz. Gay as Oscar Wilde wearing sequins walking a pink poodle with a tiara on his head."

"The poodle has a tiara?"

"No, I meant Oscar Wilde—"

"Right, right, that makes more sense. Anyway: Fuck you."

Dale groaned. "It was never going to work for you two. Never."

"And that makes it okay for you to fuck my boyfriend?"

"No," he said softly. He took my other glove off and sat it on the bench. "We shouldn't have been screwing while you two were still together. I was in love and he was confused, but that doesn't make it okay. It was wrong."

I looked away. "But you still did it."

"Yeah, I did. I betrayed my best friend. If you think that doesn't kill me inside you really don't know me."

"Poor you."

He scowled. "I didn't 'recruit' him, you know. If I weren't there he would have left you on his own. He'd never be happy with a woman. It has nothing to do with you. You know that, right?"

I didn't respond. He was right, but I was in no mood to hear it. He gestured for me to turn around. I did as instructed and he detached my life-support pack.

"Don't you want to tell your EVA buddies you caught me?"

He carefully set the pack on the bench. "This is a big deal, Jazz. It's not just an ass-beating. You could get deported. You blew up Sanchez Aluminum's harvesters. Why the hell did you do that?"

"What do you care?"

"I still care about you, Jazz. You were my best friend for years. I don't regret falling in love with Tyler, but I know I did wrong."

"Thanks," I said. "When I can't sleep at night because I know you're nailing the only man I ever loved, I'll just remember that you feel guilty. All better."

"It's been a year. When does your victimhood expire?"

"Fuck you."

He leaned against the wall and stared at the ceiling. "Jazz, give me a reason not to call the EVA posse. Anything."

I forced some logic through the swirling vortex of anger in my brain. I had to be a big girl—just for a minute. I didn't have to like it, but I had to do it.

"I'll give you a hundred thousand slugs." I didn't have 100,000ğ. But I'd get it if I could trash that last harvester.

He raised his brow. "Okay, that's a pretty good reason. What the hell is going on?"

I shook my head. "No questions."

"Are you in trouble?"

"That's a question."

"Fine, fine." He folded his arms. "What about the posse?"

"Do they know it's me?"

"No."

"Then you don't have to do anything. Just forget you saw me here."

"Jazz, there are only forty people in the whole city who have EVA suits. It's a small pool to investigate. And the EVA masters will *definitely* investigate. Not to mention Rudy."

"I have contingencies for that. All you have to do is keep your mouth shut."

He mulled it over. Then he flashed a smile. "Keep your hundred thousand. I want something else: I want to be friends again."

"A hundred and fifty thousand," I countered.

"One evening a week. You and me at Hartnell's. Just like the old days."

"No," I said. "Either take my money or feed me to the EVA mob."

"Jazz, I'm trying to play ball, here, but you don't get to jerk me around. I don't want money. I want to reconnect. Take it or leave it."

"Fff—" I began, but I suppressed the "uck you" in my throat. I found a limit to my pride somewhere in there. He could destroy my life with a Gizmo call. I had no choice.

"—fffine," I finished. "Once a week. Doesn't mean we're friends, though."

He heaved a sigh of relief. "Thank God. I didn't want to ruin you."

"You already ruined me."

He winced at the barb. Good.

He pulled out his Gizmo and dialed. "Bob? You still out there? . . . Okay, I'm just checking in. I'm at the Visitor Center and just suiting up now. . . . Yeah, I got the first train in. I searched the whole center. No one's here but me and a couple of workers starting their day."

He listened on the Gizmo for some time, then said, "All right. I'll be outside in fifteen minutes . . . okay, I'll radio when I'm outside."

He hung up. "Well, I'm off to search for the mysterious saboteur."

"Have fun with that," I said.

"Tuesday, eight p.m. at Hartnell's."

"All right," I mumbled.

I finished getting out of my suit with Dale's assistance. Then I helped Dale into his.

When I got home, I flopped onto my back. Good God I was exhausted. Even my shitty coffin seemed comfortable. I pulled my Gizmo out of the alibi-o-mat. I checked the web and email history. The device had done its job.

I sighed in relief. I'd gotten away with it. Sort of. I could expect some questions from Rudy and the guild, but I had my story straight.

There was a message on the Gizmo from Trond: **"That last delivery you made was missing an item."**

I messaged back: **"Apologies for the delay. I'm working on how to get that last package to you now."**

"Understood."

I needed a plan for that last harvester before I talked to Trond again. But what the hell could I do? Time for another scheme. No idea what form it would take, but I had to think of something.

Next thing I knew I woke up from an unscheduled nap. I still had my shoes on and the Gizmo in my hand. The day's exhaustion and previous night's shitty sleep had caught up with me, I guess. I checked the time and discovered I'd been asleep four hours.

Well, at least I was rested.

I walked laps around Conrad Ground for almost an hour. It wasn't for my health. I needed to get into the Conrad airlock's antechamber without being spotted.

The HIB was still in a locker in that antechamber. I'd promised Zsóka I'd return it to her within two days, and that deadline was fast approaching. But every time I passed the damn airlock, someone was nearby. So I just kept walking.

I also wanted to steer clear of the EVA Guild for a bit. They'd given up the search after five hours. Right about now they'd be investigating anyone who had access to an EVA suit. I had my Gizmo activity as an alibi, but I preferred not to answer questions at all. Best not to interact with the folks near the airlock.

After four entire laps, I finally caught a window where no one was around. I darted in, waved my Gizmo to open the locker, grabbed the HIB and its remote, then got the hell out of there.

I had a smug little smile on my face as I headed out of the antechamber. The perfect crime. Then I walked right into Rudy.

It was like walking into a brick wall. Well, not quite. If you get going fast enough, you might actually damage a brick wall. I dropped the HIB case because I'm a clumsy oaf.

Rudy watched it fall for a moment then casually plucked it out of the air.

"Good afternoon, Jazz," he said. "I've been looking for you."

"You'll never take me alive, copper," I said.

He looked at the case. "Is this a hull-inspection bot? Why would you need one of these?"

"Feminine hygiene. You wouldn't understand."

He handed it back to me. "We need to talk."

I put Hibby under my arm. "Ever heard of Gizmos? You can talk to people from *anywhere*."

"I suspect you wouldn't answer if I called."

"Oh, you know how it is," I said. "I get all flustered when a handsome boy calls. Anyway, nice talking to you."

I walked on. I expected him to grab my arm or something, but he just kept pace beside me.

"You know why I'm here, right?"

"No idea," I said. "Is it something Canadian? Do you need to apologize for shit that isn't your fault? Or hold a door open for someone twenty meters away?"

"I assume you heard about the Sanchez harvesters?"

"You mean that top news story on every local website? Yeah, I heard about it."

He clasped his hands behind his back. "Did you do it?"

I put on my best shocked expression. "Why would I do something like that?"

"That was going to be my follow-up question," he said.

"Has someone accused me?"

He shook his head. "No, but I pay attention to what's going on in my city. You have an EVA suit and you're a criminal. Seemed like a good place to start my investigation."

"I was in my coffin all night," I said. "Check my Gizmo activity if you don't believe me. I hereby give you permission to check that out—just to save you the trouble of getting Administrator Ngugi to authorize it."

"I'll take you up on that," he said. "I've also had a request from Bob Lewis of the EVA Guild. He wants last night's location info for everyone who owns an EVA suit. Do you give permission for me to give him your data?"

"Yes. Go ahead. That should put things to rest."

"Maybe for Bob," he said. "But I'm something of a suspicious soul. Just because your *Gizmo* was in your coffin all night, that doesn't mean *you* were. Have you got any witnesses?"

"No. Contrary to popular belief, I usually sleep alone."

He raised an eyebrow. "Sanchez Aluminum is angry. The EVA Guild is upset too."

"Not my problem." I rounded a corner without warning to throw him off, but he kept up. He must have known I was going to do that.

Dick.

"Tell you what"—he pulled out his Gizmo—"I'll pay you one hundred slugs to tell me the truth."

"Whu . . . huh?" I stopped walking.

He typed on his Gizmo. "One hundred slugs. Direct transfer from my personal account to yours."

My Gizmo beeped. I pulled it out of my pocket:

ACCOUNT TRANSFER FROM RUDY DUBOIS: 100ǧ. ACCEPT?

"What the hell are you doing?" I demanded.

"Paying for the truth. Let's have it."

I declined the transaction. "This is weird, Rudy. I already told you the truth."

"Don't you want a hundred slugs? If you're already telling me the truth, just take the money and tell me again."

"Go away, Rudy."

He gave me a knowing look. "Yeah. I thought so."

"Thought what?"

"I've known you since you were a little delinquent. You don't want to admit it, but you're just like your father. You have his business ethics."

"So?" I pouted and looked away.

"You'll lie all day if we're just talking. But if I *pay* for the truth, that makes it a business deal. And a Bashara *never* reneges on a deal."

I ran out of smartassed things to say. It's rare, but it happens once in a while.

He pointed to Hibby. "That HIB would be a great way to open an airlock without authorization."

"I suppose."

"You'd have to get it outside first."

"I suppose."

"You could probably sneak it out with a tourist EVA."

"You getting at something, Rudy?"

He tapped on his Gizmo. "There are no surveillance cameras on airlocks. We're not a police state. But there is a security camera in the Visitors Center gift shop."

He turned the screen to face me. There I was, walking through the gift shop in my disguise. He paused the playback. "According to the transaction she made to get on the train, her name is Nuha Nejem. Strange thing is, her Gizmo is offline now. She's about your height, build, and skin color, wouldn't you say?"

I leaned in to look at the screen. "You know there's more than one short Arab woman on the moon, right? Besides, she's wearing a niqab. Have you *ever* seen me in traditional clothes? I'm not what you'd call a devout Muslim."

"Neither is she." He swiped the screen a few times. "The train has a security camera too."

Now his Gizmo showed video from the train. The nice French guy stood up and offered me his seat. I bowed to him and sat down.

"Chivalry isn't dead," I said. "Good to know."

"Muslims don't bow to people," Rudy said. "Even Muhammad didn't let anyone bow to him. They bow to Allah and no one else. Ever."

Shit. I really should have known that. Maybe I should have paid attention when I was young—before Dad gave up on bringing me into the faith.

"Huh," I said. "Don't know what to tell ya."

Rudy leaned against the wall. "I've got you this time, Jazz. This isn't some minor smuggling. It's a hundred million slugs' worth of property damage. You're going down."

I shook a little. Not from fear. From rage. Didn't that asshole have better things to do than micromanage my life?! *Leave me the fuck alone!*

I don't think I hid it very well.

"What's the matter? No comeback?" he said. "You didn't do this for fun. This has 'work-for-hire' written all over it. Tell me who hired you, and I'll put in a good word with the administrator. It'll keep you from getting deported."

I kept my mouth a thin line.

"Come on, Jazz. Just tell me it was Trond Landvik and we can all move on with life."

I tried not to react, but I failed. How the hell did he know that?

He read my expression. "He's been selling Earthside holdings to amass a huge slug balance. He must be planning to buy something big in Artemis. Sanchez Aluminum, I'm guessing."

He must have wanted Trond pretty bad. He was willing to pass up an opportunity to take me down once and for all. But still . . . rolling on Trond? Not my style. "I don't know what you're talking about."

He put the Gizmo back in his pocket. "Why do you have a HIB?"

"I'm delivering it. I'm a porter. Delivering shit's my whole job."

"Who sent it? And who is it going to?"

"Can't tell you," I said. "Discretion about deliveries is guaranteed. I have a reputation to uphold."

He stared me down for a moment, but I didn't break my expression.

He frowned, then stepped back. "Fine. But this isn't going away. Powerful people are very angry."

"Then they're angry at someone else. I didn't do anything."

Then, to my utter surprise, he turned and walked away. "You'll be in over your head soon. When that happens, give me a call."

"Wha—" I began. But then I clammed up. If he wasn't taking me in, I sure as hell didn't want to break the spell.

This didn't make sense. Rudy had been after me for years. This was pretty damned solid evidence. Enough to convince the administrator, I was sure. She'd chuck my reprobate ass down to Earth without a second thought.

If he really wanted Trond, why not arrest me? If I was facing deportation, I'd be way more likely to rat out Trond, right?

What the hell?

I needed a drink. I stopped off at Hartnell's, sat in my usual seat, and signaled Billy. Time to drown my misery in alcohol and testosterone. I'd have a few cheap beers, throw on something sexy, head to an Aldrin nightclub, and go home with a good-looking guy. Hey, I could even give Svoboda's condom a trial run. Why not?

"All right, luv?" said Billy. "Try this batch. New formulation."

He pushed a shot glass forward and grinned from ear to ear.

I eyed it suspiciously. "Billy, really, I just want a beer."

"Give 'er a try. Just a sip and your first beer's on the 'ouse."

I spent a moment in deliberation, but decided a free beer was a free beer. I sipped the shot.

I have to admit: I was surprised. I thought it would taste terrible, like last time. But instead, it tasted terrible in an entirely new way. The flaming hot misery of before was gone, only to be replaced with something savory and foul. I spat it out.

Unable to speak, I pointed to the beer taps.

"Hrm," Billy said. He pulled me a pint and handed it over. I gulped at it like a lost desert traveler who found an oasis.

"Okay," I said, wiping my mouth. "Okay. Was that horserad-ish? I swear there was horseradish in there."

"No, it's rum. Well, rum extract and effanol."

"How the fuck did you start with rum and end up with this?"

"I'll give it another go later," he said. "Must be somefin' in the effanol removal process. I do have a vodka to try out if you're game."

"Maybe later," I said. "Right now I want another beer."

My Gizmo buzzed. A message from Trond: **"Concerned about that last package."**

"Shit," I mumbled. I had no idea how to kill that last har-vester.

"Putting final details on delivery plan now."

"I am presently a dissatisfied customer. Urgency on delivery is required."

"Understood."

"Maybe I should find another porter to deliver? If you're too busy."

I frowned at my Gizmo.

"Don't be an asshole."

"Let's talk this over in person. I'm available all day."

"I'll be over in a bit." I put the Gizmo back in my pocket.

"You look pissed," said Billy. "And I don't mean drunk."

"Customer-service issue," I said. "Gonna have to smooth it over in person."

"Cancel that second beer, then?"

I sighed. "Yeah. I guess I better."

I walked up to the Landvik estate's main entrance and rang the chime.

No answer. Huh. That was odd. Where was Irina and her trademark scowl? I'd already worked out some choice smartass things to say to her.

I rang again. Still nothing.

That's when I noticed the damage on the door. Just a little scuffing at the edge. Right about where you'd put a crowbar if you wanted to break in. I winced. "Aww, come on . . ."

I pushed open the door and peeked into the foyer. No sign of Irina or Trond. A decorative vase lay on the ground next to its usual display pedestal. A splash of bright-red blood on the wall—

"Nope!" I said.

I spun on my heel and stormed back into the hallway. "Nope, nope, nope!"

Dear Kelvin,

For the next shipment I'll need three kilograms of loose tobacco, fifty packets of rolling papers, twenty lighters, and ten cans of lighter fluid.

I found us a new revenue stream: spray-foam insulation. Turns out it's great for noise insulation, and believe me, noise is a real problem here. Especially in the shittier areas of town like where I live. The foam's flammable once it dries, so it's contraband. But if we can sell silence to folks in low-rent neighborhoods, they'll pay anything to get it.

As for special orders, I landed us a whale. He wants La Aurora brand Dominican cigars. You'll have to special order them. Pay whatever you need for rush shipment to Kenya. We're going to make a mint off this guy. He'll probably want a new batch every month, so stock up.

Last month's profits were 21,628ğ. Your half is 10,814ğ. How do you want it?

How are your sisters? Did you get everything squared away with Halima's asshole ex-husband?

Dear Jazz,

Okay, I'll get all those items in the next supply probe. It launches in nine days. Great idea on the foam insulation. I'll poke around and find the best noise-reduction-to-mass ratio and send you a case. We'll see how it sells.

Please convert my share to euros and wire it to my German account.

Yes, Halima's husband has been dealt with. He's no longer trying to get custody of Edward. He never wanted it, anyway. He just wanted me to buy him off. So I did. Thank God for our operation, Jazz. I have no idea what my family would do without it.

Kuki just headed off to college in Australia. She's training to become a civil engineer. We're all very proud of her. Faith is getting good grades in high

school, though she's a little more interested in boys than we'd like. And Margot is turning out to be quite an athlete. She's now a first-string forward for her football team.

How are things in your life? How's Tyler?

Dear Kelvin,

Tyler is great. He's the sweetest, kindest man I've ever been with. I'm not the mushy sort, and I never thought I'd say something like this: Seriously, he might be worth marrying. We've been together a year and I still love him. That's **unheard-of** for me.

He's the opposite of what Sean was in every way. Tyler is considerate, loyal, devoted to me, and a total sweetheart. Plus, he's not a pedophile, which is a major bonus over Sean. God, I can't believe I ever dated that asshole.

In other news, Dale's been teaching me how to do EVAs. He's a great teacher. It's a lot of work and it's a dangerous skill set to learn. And the EVA Guild is more clannish than a religious cult. But now that they know I'm training to become one of them, they're starting to warm up to me.

Man, once I get my EVA cert, I'll be *rolling* in cash. The money I can make from tours is massive!

And it won't just be me raking it in. You'll benefit too. I'll ditch the porter gig and get a job as a probe wrangler. Then I won't have to bribe Nakoshi anymore. Kelvin, my friend, the future's bright.

Dear Jazz,

That's great to hear.

There's been a wrinkle over here at KSC. They just announced that they'll be upping their launch schedule. As part of that push, they're expanding the payload loader department. There'll be another loader team working at the same time as mine. I can't be in both places at once, so we'll miss out on half the launches.

But I have an idea: How would you feel about adding another person to our group? I'd make sure it's someone we can trust. I know a lot of loaders who could use the extra cash. We wouldn't need to make them an equal partner but maybe cut them in for 10 percent?

Dear Kelvin,

To be honest, I'm not thrilled with the idea. I trust you with my life. But I don't know these other loaders for shit. We'd have to talk about any candidates very thoroughly. The more people involved, the higher the chance that it all comes tumbling down.

Still, you make a good point about missing half the launches. That hits me right in my greed bone.

Dear Jazz,

How about after you join the EVA Guild? We won't have Nakoshi's share to deal with anymore. It'll be a net-neutral effect and we'll be able to expand. The increased launch schedule means more product for us. We'll come out ahead.

Dear Kelvin,

I like your thinking. Okay, start looking around for someone. But for fuck's sake be subtle.

Dear Jazz,

Subtle? I never thought of that. I guess I should take that flyer off the company billboard.

Dear Kelvin,

Smartass.

8

I jogged away from the Landvik estate. Without breaking stride, I whipped out my Gizmo and texted Rudy: **"Trouble at Landvik estate. Blood on scene. Get there now."**

He texted back: **"On my way. Stay put until I get there."**

"Nope," I replied. The Gizmo rang as Rudy tried to call me. I ignored it and broke into a full run.

"Dammit," I hissed. "It's never easy."

I only touched the ground every seven or eight meters. I kicked off the walls when rounding corners so I wouldn't have to slow down.

Alan's Pantry was an upscale place, considering it sold junk food and kitschy souvenirs. It was less of a convenience store and more of a hotel gift shop—with appropriately jacked-up prices. I didn't have time to be picky.

"Can I help you, madam?" asked the clerk. He wore a three-piece suit. Who the hell wears formal clothes at a convenience store? I shook it off. No time to be judgmental.

I grabbed the largest bag I could find—a cloth sack with a picture of the moon on it. Really fucking original. I shoveled junk-food packets into it from every shelf, paying no attention to what I took. I had a vague impression of a bunch of chocolate bars and twenty flavors of dried Gunk. I'd take inventory later.

"Madam?" said the clerk.

I pulled a jug of water from the cooler, shot over to the counter, and upended the bag. "All this," I said. "Fast."

The clerk nodded. I had to hand it to him—he went as fast as he could. Didn't ask questions, didn't give me shit. Customer's in a hurry? Okay, then he's in a hurry too. I give Alan's Pantry five stars.

Once the items were spread out on the counter so none of them were touching each other, he pressed a button on the register. The computer identified everything and came up with a total.

"One thousand four hundred fifty-one slugs, please."

"Jesus," I said. But no time to argue. Money would be useless to me soon. I waved my Gizmo across the payment pad and okayed the transaction.

I shoveled everything into the bag and ran out. I hustled down the corridor and dialed my Gizmo. A confirmation dialog popped up before it connected:

YOU ARE CALLING EARTH. THE COST IS 31ğ PER MINUTE. CONTINUE?

I confirmed it and listened for the ringing.

"Hello?" said the accented voice on the other end.

"Kelvin, it's Jazz," I said. I rounded a corner and bounced toward the Bean Connector tunnel.

After a four-second delay, Kelvin's response came. "Jazz? You're calling directly? What's wrong?"

"I'm in deep shit, Kelvin. I'll explain later, but I have to make an alias right fucking now. I need your help." I stormed through the connector, cursing the god-awful communication latency.

"Okay. What can I do?"

"I don't know who might be after me, so I can't assume my banking info is private. I need you to set up a KSC account under an alias for me. I'll pay you back later, of course."

Four infuriating seconds later: "Okay, understood. How about a thousand US dollars? That'll be around six thousand slugs. And what name do you want it under?"

"Six thousand slugs is great, thanks. Put it under . . . I don't know . . . something Indian this time? How about Harpreet Singh?"

I shot through Bean Bubble. Bean was mostly a sleepy bedroom community. The corridors were long and straight. Perfect for a gal who's running like hell. I picked up a huge head of steam.

"Okay, I'll make it happen," said Kelvin. "It'll take about fifteen minutes. When you have a chance, drop me a line and explain what's going on. At least let me know you're safe."

"Thanks a million, Kelvin. Will do. Jazz out."

I hung up and turned off the Gizmo. I had no idea what was going on, but I sure as hell wasn't going to walk around with a tracking beacon on my ass.

I ran to the main concourse of Bean Ground. The nearest hotel was called the Moonrise Inn. Pretty stupid name, if you think about it. Artemis is the only city in existence that *can't* see a moonrise. But whatever. Any inn would do.

Just as I had done with Nuha Nejem, I picked up a hotel Gizmo for Harpreet Singh. An Arab looks the same as an Indian to clueless hotel clerks.

Okay. Alias taken care of. I'd be Harpreet Singh for the foreseeable future. Tempting though it was to check into the hotel right then, I wasn't willing to hide in plain sight. I had to go where literally no one would see me.

I knew just where to go.

DOUBLE HOMICIDE IN ARTEMIS

Business magnate Trond Landvik and his bodyguard
Irina Vetrov were found dead today at Landvik's estate
in Shepard Bubble. Artemis has only had five other mur-

ders in its history and this is the lunar city's first double homicide.

Constable Rudy DuBois, acting on a tip, found the bodies at 10:14 a.m. The door had been forced open and both victims had been stabbed to death. Evidence indicates that Vetrov died attempting to protect her employer and may have inflicted significant damage on the attacker.

Landvik's daughter, Lene, was at school during the time of the murders.

The bodies have been transported to the clinic of Dr. Melanie Roussel for pathological examination.

Lene Landvik is set to inherit her father's sizeable fortune when she turns eighteen. Until then, the estate will be managed by the Oslo-based law firm of Jørgensen, Isaksen & Berg. The heiress was unavailable for comment.

The article went on, but I didn't want to read any more. I put the Gizmo on the cold metal floor. I huddled in a corner, hugged my knees, and buried my face.

I tried to hold back the tears. I really did. My panicked flight had kept me amped with a sense of purpose. But once I was safe, the adrenaline wore off.

Trond was a good guy. Maybe a little underhanded and he wore that stupid bathrobe everywhere, but he was a good guy. And a good dad. God, who was going to take care of Lene? Mutilated in a car crash as a kid and then orphaned at age sixteen. Jesus, what a shitty draw. Sure, she had money but . . . fuck . . .

It didn't take a degree in criminology to figure out it was revenge for the sabotage. Whoever did it would want me dead too. Maybe they didn't know I was the one who did the sabotage, but I wasn't going to bet my life on it.

So now I was hiding from a murderer. And, side note, I'd

never get that million slugs, even if I trashed the last harvester. It's not like Trond and I had a written contract. I'd done it all for nothing.

I shivered in the freezing confines of the access nook. I'd been there before, long ago when I was homeless. Ten years of struggling to stay afloat and now I was right back where I started.

I sobbed into my knees. Quietly. That's another skill I learned back in the day: how to cry without making too much noise. Wouldn't want anyone in the hall to hear me.

The nook was a tiny triangular space with a removable panel so maintenance workers could get at the inner hull. There wasn't even room to lie down. My coffin was a *palace* compared to this. Tears stung my face as they turned ice cold. Bean Down 27 was a great place to hide, but it was frigid. Heat rises, even in lunar gravity. So the lower you go, the colder it gets. And no one puts heaters in maintenance nooks.

I wiped my face and picked up my Gizmo again. Well, Harpreet's Gizmo, but you know what I mean. My own Gizmo sat in the corner of my nook with the battery removed. Administrator Ngugi would only release a Gizmo's location info if there was a good reason, but "wanted for questioning in a double homicide" was a pretty good reason.

I had to make a decision right then. A decision that would affect the rest of my life: Would I go to Rudy?

Surely he cared more about murder than my smuggling operation. And I'd be a lot safer if I just came clean. He might be an asshole, but he was a good cop. He'd do everything he could to protect me.

But he'd been looking for a reason to deport me since I was seventeen. He already knew Trond was screwing with Sanchez Aluminum, so it's not like I'd provide useful information. And I assumed the "amnesty for ratting out Trond" offer was off the table—Trond was dead. So if I went to Rudy, I would:

a) Give him all the evidence he needed to get me deported, and

b) Not help him solve the murders at all.

No, fuck that. Keeping my head down and my mouth shut was the only way to come out of this alive and still living on the moon.

I was on my own.

I looked over my supplies. Probably a few days' worth of food and water. I could use the public restrooms down the hall when no one was looking. I wasn't going to just stay in the nook, but for the moment I didn't want to be seen. At all. By anyone.

I sniffled back the last of my tears and cleared my throat. Then I called Dad's number through a local proxy service. No one would know that Harpreet Singh called Ammar Bashara.

"Hello?" he answered.

"Dad, it's Jazz."

"Oh, hi. Weird, my Gizmo didn't recognize your number. How'd the project go? Are you done with the equipment?"

"Dad, I need you to listen to me. Really listen."

"Okay . . ." he said. "This doesn't sound good."

"It's not." I wiped my face again. "You have to get out of the house and away from the shop. Stay with a friend. Just for a few days."

"What? Why?"

"Dad, I messed up. I messed up bad."

"Come over. We'll work it out."

"No, you have to get out of there. Did you read about the murders? Trond and Irina?"

"Yes, I saw that. Very unfort—"

"The killers are after me now. They might go after you for leverage because you're the only person I care about. So get the hell out of there."

He was silent for a while. "All right. Meet me at the shop and we'll go stay with Imam Faheem. He and his family will take care of us."

"I can't just hide—I need to find out what's going on. You go to the imam's. I'll contact you when it's safe."

"Jazz"—his voice quavered—"leave this to Rudy. It's his job."

"I can't trust him. Not now. Maybe later."

"You come home right now, Jasmine!" His voice had risen a full octave. "For the love of Allah, don't tangle with murderers!"

"I'm sorry, Dad. I'm so sorry. Just get out of there. I'll call you when this is over."

"Jasmi—" he started, but I hung up.

Another benefit to the proxy service: Dad couldn't call me back.

I cowered in the nook the rest of the evening. I darted out to go to the bathroom twice, but that was it. I spent the rest of the time just fearing for my life and compulsively reading the news.

I woke up the next morning with cramped legs and a sore back. That's the thing about crying yourself to sleep. When you wake up, the problems are still there.

I pushed the access panel aside and rolled out onto the corridor floor. I stretched out my complaining muscles. Bean Down 27 didn't get many people coming through, especially this early in the morning. I sat on the floor and ate a hearty breakfast of unflavored Gunk and water. I should have stayed hidden in the nook but I just couldn't take the cramped quarters any longer.

Sure, I could just hide out and hope Rudy caught the killer, but it wouldn't help. Even if he succeeded, the people behind it would send another one.

I took another bite of Gunk.

It was all about Sanchez Aluminum.

Duh.

But why? Why were people killing each other over a bygone industry that didn't even make much money?

Money. It's always about money. So where was the money? Trond Landvik hadn't become a billionaire by randomly guessing at shit. If he wanted to make aluminum, he had a tangible, solid reason. And whatever it was, it got him killed.

That was the key. Before I worked on *who* I had to figure out *why*. And I knew where to start: Jin Chu.

He was the guy at Trond's house the day I delivered the cigars. He was from Hong Kong, he had a box labeled "ZAFO," and he tried to hide it from me. That's all I had.

I poked around online, but I couldn't find anything about him. Whoever he was, he kept a low profile. Or he'd come to Artemis under an alias.

That cigar delivery felt like forever ago but it had only been four days. Meatships come once a week and there had been no departures in that time. Jin Chu was still in town. He might be dead, but he was still in town.

I finished my "breakfast" and put the packaging back in my nook. Then I sealed the nook, straightened my rumpled jumpsuit, and headed out.

I hit a secondhand shop in Conrad and bought a hell of an outfit: a bright-red miniskirt so short you could almost call it a belt, a sequined top that exposed my midriff, and the tallest heels I could find. I topped it off with a large red patent-leather handbag.

Then off to a hair salon for a quick updo and voilà! I was now a floozy. The girls at the salon rolled their eyes at me as I checked myself out in the mirror.

The transformation was disturbingly easy. Sure, I have a nice body, but I wish it had been a *little* more effort to become so trashy.

. . .

Travel's a bitch. Even when it's a once-in-a-lifetime vacation.

You leak money like a sieve. You're jet-lagged. You're exhausted all the time. You're homesick even though you're on vacation. But all of those hassles pale in comparison to the food.

I see it all the time here. Tourists love to sample our local cuisine. Problem is: Our cuisine sucks. It's made of algae and artificial flavors. Within a few days the Americans want pizza, the French want wine, and the Japanese want rice. Food makes you comfortable. It's how you recenter.

Jin Chu was from Hong Kong. He'd eventually want proper Cantonese food.

The types of people who have one-on-one meetings with Trond are business magnates or, at the very least, highly important people. Those people travel a lot. They learn to stay where the food's good.

So we had an important, travel-savvy guy from Hong Kong who'd want home cooking. One establishment fit the bill perfectly: the Canton Artemis.

The Canton, a five-star hotel in Aldrin bubble, catered to the Chinese elite. Owned and operated by Hong Kong business interests, they provided a homelike experience to high-end travelers. And most important, they had a proper Cantonese breakfast buffet. If you're from Hong Kong and you have unlimited money, the Canton is where you stay.

I walked into the plush, well-adorned lobby. It was one of the few hotels in town that had an honest-to-God lobby. I guess when you charge 50,000ğ a night for a room, you can waste a little space on presentation.

I stood out like a sore thumb in my prostitute regalia. A few heads turned in my direction then turned away in disdain (though the male heads took a little longer). An old Asian lady manned the concierge desk. I walked straight up without a hint of shame. Internally, I was embarrassed as all hell—I did my best to hide it.

The concierge gave me a look that told me I'd offended her and her great ancestors. "Can I help you?" she asked with a slight Chinese accent.

"Yeah," I said. "I've got a meeting here. With a client."

"I see. And do you have this client's room number?"

"Nah."

"Do you have his Gizmo ID?"

"Nah." I pulled a compact out of my handbag and checked my ruby-red lipstick.

"I'm sorry, madam"—she looked me up and down—"I'm unable to help you if you don't have his room number or some other proof that you've been invited."

I shot her a bitchy glare (I'm good at that). "Oh, he wants me here all right. For an hour." I set the compact on her desk and fished around in my handbag. She leaned away from the compact like she might catch a disease from it.

I pulled out a piece of paper and read: "Jin Chu. Canton Artemis. Arcade District. Aldrin Bubble." I put the paper away. "Just call the fuckin' guy, okay? I got other customers after this."

She pursed her lips. Hotels like the Canton wouldn't contact a guest just because someone claimed to be meeting them. But rules get bent where sex is involved. She typed a few keystrokes on her computer, then picked up the phone.

She listened for a while, then hung up. "I'm sorry, but there's no answer."

I rolled my eyes. "You tell him he still has to pay!"

"I'll do no such thing."

"Whatever!" I snatched up the compact and tossed it back in my purse. "If he shows up, tell him I'm in the bar."

I stomped off.

So he wasn't in. I could stake out the lobby—the bar had a great view of the entrance—but that could take all day. I had a different plan.

That lipstick adjustment earlier hadn't just been for show. I'd placed the compact so I could see the concierge's computer screen in the mirror. When she looked up Jin Chu, it popped up his room number: 124.

I reached the bar and hopped up on the stool second from the corner. Habit, I guess. I glanced through the lobby to the elevators. A beefy security guard stood nearby. He wore a suit and nice shoes, but I know muscle when I see it.

A guest walked up, waved his Gizmo, and the elevator opened. The guard watched but didn't seem too interested.

A few seconds later, a couple approached. The woman waved her Gizmo and the doors opened. The guard stepped forward and spoke to them briefly. She said something and he returned to his post.

No sneaking aboard the elevator. You had to be a guest or with a guest.

"What can I get for ya?" said a voice from behind.

I turned to face the bartender. "Have you got Bowmore fifteen-year single-malt?"

"Indeed we do, ma'am. But I should warn you it's seven hundred fifty slugs for a two-ounce pour."

"Not a problem," I said. "Round it up to a thousand and keep the change. Charge it to my date: Jin Chu, Room 124."

He typed on his register, confirmed the name matched the room number, and smiled. "Right away, ma'am. Thank you."

I stared at the elevators and waited for the guard to take a break or something. The bartender returned with my drink. I took a sip. Oh, man . . . good stuff.

I poured a little out on the floor for Trond. He was a sneaky moneygrubber who would break any laws that got in his way.

But he was good to the people in his life and he didn't deserve to die.

All right. How would I get past the goon at the elevator? Distract him? Probably wouldn't work. He was a trained security guard and his whole job was controlling access. He wasn't likely to fall for bullshit. Maybe I could find someone tall or fat and literally hide behind them? Hmm, that seemed a little too "Buster Keaton" to actually work.

I felt a tap on my shoulder. An Asian man in his mid-fifties sat next to me. He wore a three-piece suit and an ugly comb-over.

"*Purai?*" he asked.

"Huh?" I said.

"Eh . . ." He pulled out his Gizmo and gestured to it. "*Purai?*"

"English?" I asked.

He typed on his Gizmo then turned it to face me. The text read: **Price?**

"Oh," I said. Well, that's what I got for dressing like a prostitute and hanging out in a bar. It was nice to know I had an alternate career path if smuggling didn't work out. I glanced at the elevators and their guardian, then back to my john.

"Two thousand slugs," I said. Seemed reasonable. I was rocking that miniskirt.

He nodded and typed up the transaction on his Gizmo. I put my hand over his to stop him.

"After," I said. "Pay after."

He seemed puzzled but agreed.

I stood from the bar and downed my Bowmore. I assume everyone in Scotland gasped in psychic pain.

My little friend took my arm like a gentleman and we walked through the lobby. We got to the elevators, he waved his Gizmo, and we stepped aboard arm in arm. The guard glanced but said nothing. He saw this sort of thing a hundred times a day.

You're probably imagining a high-rise hotel with twenty-five floors or something, but remember this is Aldrin Bubble. The Canton only had three floors. My customer pressed *1*. Excellent, that was the floor I needed.

The elevator took us to the first floor and we stepped into the plush hallway. Shit, everything was decorated here. Soft carpet, crown molding, paintings on the walls, the works. Each door boasted its room number in gold relief digits.

My date took me down the hall past Room 124. We stopped at 141. He waved his Gizmo by the lock and the door clicked open.

I made a show of pulling out my Gizmo and looking at it. I frowned at the blank screen as if it had an important message. He watched with interest.

"Sorry, I have to make a call," I said. I pointed to the Gizmo for emphasis. Then gestured for him to go into the room. He nodded and walked in.

I held the Gizmo up to my ear. "Rocko? Yeah, it's Candy. I'm with a customer. What? Oh no she didn't!" I closed Grandpa's room door so I could talk to my pimp in private. He'd probably wait a good fifteen minutes before he figured out I left.

Sure, I was ditching a horny businessman, but I hadn't taken his money. I was ethically in the clear.

I slinked down to Room 124. I looked left and right. No one else in the hall. I pulled a screwdriver from my gaudy purse and jimmied the lock. All right, Jin Chu. Let's see what you're up to.

I pushed open the door. A grizzled Latino man sat on the bed, his right arm in a sling. He gripped a Bowie knife in his left hand.

He shot to his feet. "*Tu!*" he yelled.

"Uh—" I began.

He lunged.

Dear Jazz,

Glad to hear about the sales of the foam insulant. We're making a killing! I'll send another two cases in the next probe.

I have a candidate picked out for our "employee." His name is Jata Masai. He's a recently hired assistant loader. He's a friendly man but private. Reclusive. He mentioned he has a wife and two daughters, but that's about all I know. He never eats lunch with the other loaders in the cafeteria—he brings a lunchbox instead. To me this means he's short on money.

Wife. Two kids. Needs money. Assistant loader. I like that combo. I haven't approached him about it yet, obviously. I hired a private investigator to learn everything about him. I'll send you her report as soon as she delivers it. If you like what you see, I'll recruit him.

How are things with Tyler?

Dear Kelvin,

Make it two cases of foam insulant. Yes, please send the report on Jata when it's available.

Tyler and I are done. I don't want to talk about it.

9

My mind went into overdrive.

Okay, so a guy was coming at me with a knife. He had a wounded arm, probably from Irina while she was being murdered. That meant he wanted to kill me too.

Irina was strong, trained, and armed, but she still lost a knife fight to this guy. What chance did I have? I can't fight for shit. And running wasn't an option either. I was in heels and a tight skirt.

I had one chance, and it relied on me guessing where he was going to stab. I was a helpless, exposed girl with no weapon. Why waste time? Just slit my throat.

I jerked my purse to my neck just in time to block his attack. His lightning-fast strike slashed the purse open and the contents spilled out. That would have been my throat. He assumed I'd be halfway through dying after that assault, so he left himself a little open.

I grabbed his bad arm with one hand and punched it with the other. He cried out in pain. He lashed at me with the knife, but I twisted out of the way. I hung on and kicked off the doorframe to torque his injured arm as much as I could. Maybe if his pain was bad enough, he'd be distracted and I could run away.

He screamed in rage and used the arm to hoist me into the air. Okay, that wasn't part of my plan. He lifted me bodily over his head and swung me down toward the hotel room's floor. This was my chance. It would hurt, but it was a chance.

I let go of his arm right before hitting the floor. It didn't lessen the blow. I smashed into the ground on my side. My ribs exploded with pain. I wanted to curl up and moan but I didn't have the time. I was free—if only for a second.

He stumbled. He'd just had 55 kilograms of Jazz on his arm and it suddenly fell off. I pushed through the pain in my side and got to my knees. With every ounce of strength I had, I slammed my shoulder into his back. "Lefty" was off balance and wasn't expecting an attack. He tumbled into the hallway.

I fell backward into the hotel room and kicked the door shut. It locked automatically. Less than a second later, I heard the first resounding *thump* as Lefty tried to force his way back in.

I scrambled to the nightstand next to the bed and dialed the phone.

"Front Desk," came the immediate reply.

I tried to sound panicked. It wasn't hard. "Hey! I'm in Room 124 and there's some guy pounding on the door! I think, he's drunk or something. I'm scared!"

"We'll send security right up."

"Thanks."

Lefty flung himself against the door a second time.

I hung up and limped to the door. I peeked through the peephole. Lefty reared back and took another running leap at the door. Another rattling thump, but the door was unaffected.

"Metal door, metal deadbolt!" I yelled. "Fuck you!"

He'd backed up to take another run when the elevator doors at the end of the hall opened. The beefy security guy stepped forward. "Something I can help you with, sir?"

A few other room doors opened up. Confused guests peeked at the action. Lefty hadn't exactly been quiet. He took stock of the situation and of the very large security guard. This wasn't something he could stab his way out of. He looked at the door longingly, then scampered off.

The guard straightened his tie, walked up, and knocked on my door.

I opened it a crack. "Uh, hi?"

"Are you all right, ma'am?" he asked.

"Yeah. It was just weird is all. Aren't you going after him?"

"He had a knife. Best to let him go."

"I see."

"I'll stick around in the hall for a while to make sure he doesn't come back. Rest easy."

"Okay, thank you." I closed the door.

I took a moment to recenter.

Lefty was in Jin Chu's room because . . . why? He had no way of knowing I'd come. He wasn't there for me. He must have been there for Jin Chu.

A Latino assassin. And wouldn't you know it, Sanchez Aluminum was owned by Brazilians. Shit, I know companies get pissed when you trash their stuff, but murder? *Murder?!*

I looked through the peephole again. The guard stood nearby. I was safer than I'd been all day. All right. Time to search the room.

Man. Must be nice to be rich. The room had a king-size bed, a tidy workstation in one corner, and a bathroom with a graywater reuse shower. I heaved a sigh. My dreams of a nice place had died with Trond.

I tossed the room. No point in subtlety. I found the usual stuff you'd expect for a business traveler: clothes, toiletries, et cetera. What I *didn't* find was a Gizmo. And judging by the condition of the room (at least the condition it was in before I trashed it), there hadn't been a struggle. That was all good news for Jin Chu. It meant he probably wasn't dead. Most likely scenario: Lefty came to kill him but he wasn't home. So Lefty waited. Then I showed up and ruined everything.

You're welcome, Jin Chu.

I was about to leave when I noticed the safe in the closet. It's one of those things you don't even pay attention to. The wall-mounted safe had an electronic lock with instructions on how to set it. Pretty simple, really. It starts disarmed. You put your shit in it, then set the code. It'll keep that code until you check out.

I tried the handle and it didn't open. Interesting. When one of those wall safes isn't in use it's ajar.

Time to become a safecracker. Those things aren't exactly made to protect the crown jewels.

The contents of my now-destroyed purse lay strewn across the floor. I found the makeup compact and slapped it against my palm several times. I opened it to a mess of crumbled powder. I held it up to the safe and blew across the surface.

Brown, dusty makeup clouded the air around the safe. I stepped back and waited for it to clear up. Dust takes a long time to settle in Artemis. Atmosphere plus low gravity equals particles taking forever to fall.

Eventually the area cleared up. I took a good look at the keypad. A layer of makeup covered everything, but three of the buttons had more dust on them than the others. The *0*, the *1*, and the *7*. Those were the ones with finger grease on them. With a hotel like the Canton, you could bet they cleaned everything in the room between guests. So those numbers had to be the digits Jin Chu chose for his combination.

According to the instructions on the safe, you set a four-digit code.

Hmm. A four-digit code with three unique numbers. I closed my eyes and did some math. There'd be . . . fifty-four possible combinations. According to the instructions, the safe would lock down if it got three incorrect combinations in a row. Then the hotel staff would have to open it with their master code.

I replayed my brief interaction with him in my head. He was

on Trond's couch . . . he drank Turkish coffee while I had black tea. We talked about—

Aha! He was a *Star Trek* fan.

I typed 1-7-0-1 and the safe clicked open. NCC-1701 was the registration number of the starship *Enterprise*. How did I know that? I must have heard it somewhere. I don't forget stuff.

I opened the safe door and found the mysterious white case— the one Jin Chu had tried to hide from me. The outside still read ZAFO SAMPLE—AUTHORIZED USE ONLY. All right, now we were getting somewhere!

I popped open the case to discover . . . a cable?

It was just a coiled cable, maybe two meters long. Had someone taken the secret device and left the power cable behind? Why do that? Why not take the whole case?

I looked at the cable more closely. Actually, it wasn't a power cord. It was a fiber-optic cable. Okay, so it was for data. But what data?

"Okay. Now what?" I asked myself.

The door beeped and slid open. Svoboda stepped into his studio apartment and dropped his Gizmo on the shelf near the door.

"Hi, Svobo," I said.

"*Svyate der'mo!*" He put his hand on his chest and panted.

I'd smuggled in so many illegal chemicals for him over the years he'd given me the keypad-code for his apartment. It was just easier for me to deliver that way.

I leaned back in his desk chair. "I need some work from you."

"Jesus Christ, Jazz!" he said, still breathing heavily. "Why are you in my apartment?"

"I'm in hiding."

"What's with your hair?"

I'd changed back into normal clothes, but I still had my whore-do. "Long story."

"Are those sparkles? You have sparkles in your hair?"

"*Long story!*" I pulled a square of wrapped chocolate from my pocket and tossed it to him. "Here. I read somewhere you should always bring a gift when visiting a Ukrainian."

"Ooh! Chocolate!" He caught the morsel and unwrapped it. "Rudy came by the lab today asking about you. He didn't say why, but scuttlebutt is you're involved in those murders?"

"The guy who killed them wants to kill me."

"Wow," he said. "This is serious. You should go to Rudy."

I shook my head. "And get deported? No thanks. I can't trust him. I can't trust anyone right now."

"But you're here." He smiled. "So you trust me?"

Huh. It never occurred to me *not* to trust Svoboda. He was way too "Svoboda" to be sinister. "I guess so."

"Awesome!" He snapped the chocolate in two and handed me half. He popped the other half in his mouth and savored it.

"Oh, hey," he said with his mouth full. "Did you get a chance to test the condom?"

"No, I haven't had sex in the *two days* since you gave me the condom."

"Okay, okay," he said.

I picked up the ZAFO box and tossed it to him. "I need you to tell me what this is."

He plucked it out of the air and read the label. "Huh. ZAFO. You asked me about that earlier."

"Yeah. Now I have a sample. What can you tell me about it?"

He opened the box and pulled the cable out. "It's a fiber-optic data cable."

"What's it for?"

He peered at one end. "Nothing."

"What?"

He held both ends of the cable up. "These aren't connectors. They're caps. This cable can't be used for anything. Not without connectors, anyway."

"So what's the point? It's just a useless cable?"

"No idea," he said. He coiled it up and put it back in the box. "Is it related to the murders?"

"Maybe," I said. "I don't know."

"Okay, I'll take it to the lab right now. I'll get you some answers tonight."

I pulled out my Harpreet Gizmo. "Two thousand slugs?"

"What?" He gave me a look like I'd pissed on his mother's grave. "No. Nothing. The price is nothing. Jesus."

"What's wrong?" I said.

"You're in trouble. I'm helping you because you're my friend."

I opened my mouth to speak, but couldn't think of what to say.

He whipped his Gizmo from the shelf. "I assume you're using an alias. Give me its ID."

I shared my new contact info with him. He nodded curtly when his Gizmo received it. "Okay, 'Harpreet,' I'll call you when I have something."

I'd never seen him so annoyed. "Svoboda, I—"

"Forget it. It's cool." He forced a smile. "I just thought that would be assumed, is all. You need somewhere to stay?"

"Uh, no. I've got a hideout set up."

"Of course you do. Lock up when you leave." He left a little faster than necessary.

Well, shit. I didn't have time for male ego or whatever the hell that was about. I had to hurry off to my next scheme.

"All right, Lefty," I mumbled to myself. "Let's see how well connected you are. . . ."

Evening is the Arcade District's busiest time of day. It's when the richfucks come out to play. Freshly fed and liquored up, they hit the shops, casinos, brothels, and theaters. (If you haven't seen lunar acrobats in action, you don't know what you're missing. Hell of a show.)

It was perfect. People *everywhere*. Just what I needed.

Arcade Square (which is a circle) sat in the center of Aldrin Ground, right in the middle of everything. It was only a collection of benches and a few potted trees—the sort of thing you see in every town square on Earth, but an incredible luxury here.

I glanced around and didn't see Lefty anywhere. Very helpful of him to have a sling on. It made him easy to spot. Someday when I died and went to hell I'd thank Irina for slashing him.

Drunks and revelers crisscrossed the square. Tourists packed the benches and chatted or took pictures of one another. I pulled out my Gizmo and turned it on.

And when I say "my Gizmo" I mean my *real* Gizmo. It powered up and showed the familiar wallpaper—a picture of a Cavalier King Charles spaniel puppy. What? I like puppies.

I discreetly placed the Gizmo on the ground and kicked it under a nearby bench.

The bait was set. Now to see if anyone came nibbling.

I walked into the Lassiter Casino. It had wide windows looking out over Arcade Square so I could observe from a safe distance. Plus, it had a reasonably priced buffet on the third floor right up against those windows.

I paid for the all-you-can-eat Gunk bar with Harpreet's Gizmo.

The trick with Gunk is to steer clear of stuff trying to taste like other stuff. Don't get the "Tandoori Chicken" flavorant. You'll just be disappointed. Get "Myrtle Goldstein's Formulation #3." That's good shit. No idea what the ingredients are. It could be termite carcasses and Italian armpit hair for all I know. I don't care. It makes the Gunk palatable, and that's what matters.

I took my bowl to a window table and sat down. I nibbled Gunk and sipped water, never taking my eyes off the bench where I'd stowed the Gizmo. It got boring after a while, but I stuck with it. This was a stakeout.

Could Lefty track my Gizmo? If he could, it'd give me an idea of how powerful he was. It would mean he had connections all the way to the top.

"Mind if I join you?" said a familiar voice behind me.

I jerked my head around to look.

Rudy. Shit. "Uh . . ." I said eloquently.

"I'll take that as a yes." He seated himself and rested a Gunk bowl on the table. "As you can imagine, I have a few questions."

"How did you find me?!"

"I tracked your Gizmo."

"Yeah, but it's way down there!" I pointed to the windows.

He looked out over the Arcade. "Yes, imagine my surprise when your Gizmo turned on in the middle of Arcade Square. That's pretty careless. Doesn't seem like you at all."

He took a bite of Gunk. "So I figured you'd be watching from a safe distance. This is a nice, cheap buffet and a perfect vantage point. Wasn't hard to work out."

"Well, aren't you Mr. Clever." I stood. "I'll just be on my way—"

"Sit down."

"No, I don't think I will."

"Sit *down*, Jazz." He shot me a look. "If you think I won't tackle you here and now, think again. Eat your Gunk and let's talk."

I settled back into my seat. There was no way I could take Rudy in a fight. I tried once, back when I was seventeen and stupid as shit. It didn't go well. The guy had muscles of iron. Magnificent, stallion-like muscles of iron. Did he work out? He had to, right? I wondered what he looked like working out. Would he be sweaty? Of course he'd be sweaty. It'd be all dripping down those muscles in rivulets of—

"I know you didn't commit the murders," he said.

I snapped back to reality. "Aww, I bet you say that to all the girls."

He pointed to me with his spoon. "I know you blew up the Sanchez harvesters, though."

"I didn't have anything to do with that."

"Do you expect me to believe the sabotage, the murders, and you hiding out are all unrelated?" He scooped a bite of Gunk from his bowl and ate it with perfect table manners. "You're in the middle of all this, and I want to know what you know."

"You know everything I know. You should work on the murders instead of the petty vendetta you've got against me."

"I'm trying to save your life, Jazz." He put his napkin on the table. "Do you have any idea who you antagonized with that sabotage?"

"*Alleged* sabotage," I said.

"Do you know who *owns* Sanchez Aluminum?"

I shrugged. "Some Brazilian company."

"They're owned by O Palácio, Brazil's largest and most powerful organized crime syndicate."

I froze.

Shit, shit, shittity shit!

"I see," I said. "Spiteful bunch, are they?"

"Yes. They're the old-fashioned, 'kill you to make a point' kind of mafia."

"Wait . . . no . . . that can't be right. I've never even heard of these guys."

"It's possible—just possible—that I know more about organized crime in my city than you do."

I put my forehead in my hands. "You've got to be shitting me. Why the *hell* does the Brazilian mob own a lunar aluminum company?! The aluminum industry's in the toilet!"

"They're not in it for the profits," Rudy said. "They use Sanchez Aluminum to launder money. Artemisian slugs are an unregulated, largely untracked quasi-currency and the city has iffy identity verification at best. We're a perfect haven for money laundering."

"Oh God . . ."

"You have one thing going for you: They don't have a strong presence here. This isn't an 'operation' to O Palácio. It's just an avenue for creative accounting. But it would seem they do have at least one enforcer on-site."

"But . . ." I started. "Wait . . . let me think this through . . ."

He rested his hands on the table and waited politely.

"Okay," I said. "Something doesn't add up here. Did Trond know about O Palácio?"

Rudy sipped his water. "I'm sure he did. He was the kind of man who researched everything before making a move."

"Then why did he knowingly fuck with a major crime syndicate to take over a failing industry?"

For the first time in my life, I saw confusion on Rudy's face.

"Stumped, eh?" I said.

I glanced out at the Arcade and froze.

There was Lefty. Right next to the bench where I'd hidden my Gizmo.

I guess Rudy saw the color disappear from my face. "What?" he asked. He followed my gaze out the windows.

I shot him a glare. "That guy with his arm in a sling is the killer! How'd he know where my Gizmo is?"

"I don't know—" Rudy began.

"You know what else organized crime does?" I said. "They bribe cops! How the *fuck* did that guy track my Gizmo, Rudy?!"

He held both hands out. "Don't do anything rash—"

I did something rash. I flipped the table and hauled ass. Rudy would have to fight off a slowly tipping table before he could give chase.

I'd worked out my escape route in advance, of course. I ran straight across the casino floor and through an "Employees Only" door in the back. They were supposed to keep it locked but they never did. It led to the main delivery corridors that connected all the Aldrin casinos. I knew those tunnels well—I'd made hundreds of deliveries there. Rudy would never catch me.

One thing, though . . . he wasn't chasing me.

I slid to a stop in the corridor and watched the door. I don't know why—I guess I wasn't thinking well. If Rudy had barged through I would have lost valuable running-like-hell time. But he didn't.

"Huh," I said.

I channeled my inner "dumbass in a horror movie" and walked back to the door. I opened it a crack and peeked through. No sign of Rudy, but a crowd had gathered near the buffet.

I slinked back through the casino and joined the crowd. They had good reason to gawk.

The window near our table was shattered. A few jagged spikes of glass stuck out from the frame. We don't have safety glass here. Importing polyvinyl butyral is too expensive. So our windows are good old-fashioned neck-slicing deathtraps. Hey, if you want to play life safe, don't live on the moon.

An American tourist in front of me nibbled on a Gunk bar and craned his neck to see over the crowd. (Only Americans wear Hawaiian shirts on the moon.)

"What happened?" I asked.

"Not sure," he said. "Some guy kicked the window out and jumped through. It's three stories to the ground. Think he's dead?"

"Lunar gravity," I reminded him.

"But it's like thirty feet!"

"Lunar grav—never mind. Was the guy dressed in a Mountie uniform?"

"You mean bright-red clothes and a weird hat?"

"That's the *ceremonial* uniform," I said. "I mean a duty uniform. Light shirt, dark pants with a yellow stripe?"

"Oh, Han Solo pants. Yeah, he had those on."

"Okay, thanks." Pfft. Han Solo's pants have a *red* stripe. And it's not even a stripe—it's a bunch of dashes. Some people have no education.

Rudy hadn't chased me. He'd gone after Lefty. The Arcade-level entrance was three floors down and across a huge lobby. It would have taken at least two minutes for Rudy to get there by conventional means. I guess he'd picked a faster route.

I peered into the Arcade along with the other onlookers. Both Rudy and Lefty seemed to be long gone. Too bad—I would have loved to see Rudy beating the shit out of that bastard and cuffing him.

But I guessed this meant Rudy wasn't part of a plot to kill me. And hey, now Lefty had Rudy to deal with. All in all, not a bad outcome.

Not that I was happy. I still didn't know how Lefty found my Gizmo.

My hidey-hole on Bean Down 27 was barely okay for sleeping and too damned small for anything else.

So I sat on the floor in the corridor. On the rare occasions when I heard someone coming, I skittered into my hutch like the cockroach I am. But mostly, I had the hall to myself.

First thing I wanted to know: Did Rudy catch Lefty? I scanned local news sites and the answer was no. Murders are extremely rare in Artemis. If Rudy'd caught the killer, it would be on every front page. Lefty was still out there.

Time for some research. My subject: Sanchez Aluminum. I tapped away on Harpreet's Gizmo to look up public info about the company.

They employed about eighty people. That may not sound like much but in a town of two thousand it's pretty significant. Their

CEO and founder was Loretta Sanchez, from Manaus, Brazil. She had a doctorate in chemistry with a specialty in inorganic processes. She invented a system to cheaply implement the FFC Cambridge Process to deoxidize anorthite by minimizing loss in the calcium chloride salt bath via . . . I stopped caring around there. Point was, she was in charge, and (though the article didn't mention it) she was mobbed up all to hell.

Of course, the harvester sabotage was all over the news. In response, Sanchez had implemented tight security. Their offices in Armstrong Bubble no longer allowed visitors. They'd restricted smelting-facility access to core personnel only. They even had humans (not just computers) directly checking company IDs on the train to the smelter.

Most important, they weren't taking any chances with that last harvester. They'd contracted the EVA Guild to guard it, with EVA masters working in shifts to have two people physically with the harvester at all times.

There was a certain pride in knowing I caused an entire company to shit themselves. They'd tried to kill me. Repeatedly. And it wasn't just an O Palácio thing either. Someone in the Sanchez control room had ordered a harvester to smush me when I was out on the surface, remember? There was some *flawed* company culture going on over there.

Bastards.

The Gizmo buzzed in my hand—a notification from my email client.

I might have been on the run for my life, but I wasn't willing to go without email. I just had it running through a proxy so no one could tell which Gizmo I used to check in. The proxy server was on Earth somewhere (I think in the Netherlands?), so everything was slow as shit. It only updated once per hour. Better than nothing.

I had fifteen messages, fourteen of which were Dad desperately trying to get in touch with me. "Sorry, Dad," I said to myself. "You don't want none of this, and I don't want none of it on you."

The fifteenth email was from Jin Chu.

> Ms. Bashara. Thank you for saving my life—your actions at the hotel kept me safe. At least, I assume the woman in my room was you—you're the only other (surviving) person involved in this plot-gone-wrong. Now that I'm aware of the threat, I have made arrangements for my safety and I am staying hidden. Can we meet? I would like to arrange for your safety as well. I owe you that. —Jin Chu

Interesting. I ran a few scenarios in my head and settled on a plan.

> Ok. Meet me at my father's welding shop tomorrow at 8am. The address is CD6-3028. If you're not there by 8:05 I'm gone.

I set an alarm on my Gizmo for four a.m. and crawled into my rathole.

10

The thing that sucks about life-or-death situations is how boring they can be.

I waited in Dad's shop for three hours. I didn't have to show up at five a.m., but I'd be damned if I was going to let Jin Chu show up before I did.

I leaned a chair against the back wall of the shop, right next to the air shelter where I'd snuck my first cigarette. I remember I damn near puked from all the smoke that built up but hey, when you're a rebellious teen and you think you're making a statement, it's worth it. "Take that, Daddy!"

God, I was such a dipshit.

I checked the clock on the wall every ten seconds as eight a.m. approached. I fiddled with a handheld blowtorch to pass the time. Dad used it to shrink seals onto pipe fittings. It wasn't "welding," but you had to do it in a fireproof room, so he offered it as one of his services.

I kept my finger by the ignition trigger. It wasn't a gun (there were no guns in Artemis) but it could hurt someone if they came too close. I wanted to be ready for anything.

The far door opened at 8:00 on the dot. Jin Chu stepped through gingerly. He hunched his shoulders and darted his gaze around like a frightened gazelle. He spotted me in the corner and waved awkwardly. "Uh . . . hi."

"You're punctual," I said. "Thanks."

He stepped forward. "Sure, I—"

"Stay over there," I said. "I'm not feeling super-trusting today."

"Yeah okay, okay." He took a breath and let it out unevenly. "Look, I'm really sorry. It wasn't supposed to go like this. I just thought I could make a few bucks, you know? Like a finder's fee?"

I tossed the blowtorch from one hand to the other. Just to make sure he saw it. "For what? What the hell is going on around here?"

"For telling Trond and O Palácio about ZAFO. In separate, confidential transactions, of course."

"I see." I scowled at the weaselly little shit. "And then you made *more* money by selling out Trond to O Palácio when their harvesters blew up?"

"Well, yeah. But it's not like that was going to stay secret. Once he took over the oxygen contract they woulda worked it out."

"How did they find out I did the sabotage?"

He looked at his feet.

I groaned. "You are *such* an asshole!"

"It's not my fault! They offered me so much money!"

"How did you even know I did it?"

"Trond told me. He gets chatty when he's drunk." He frowned. "He was a cool guy. I didn't think anyone would get hurt, I just—"

"You just thought you'd stir up a billionaire and a mob syndicate and nothing would happen? Fuck you."

He fidgeted for a few seconds. "So . . . do you have the ZAFO sample? The case from my hotel room?"

"Yes. Not here, but it's safe."

"Thank God." He loosened up a bit. "Where is it?"

"First tell me what ZAFO is."

He winced. "It's kind of secret."

"We're past secrets now."

He looked truly pained. "It's just . . . it cost a *lot* of money to make that sample. We had to launch a dedicated satellite with a centrifuge to grow it in low-Earth orbit. I'll be *super-duper* fired if I go home without it."

"Fuck your job. People got *murdered*! Tell me why!"

He let out a heavy sigh. "I'm sorry. I'm just so sorry. I didn't want any of this to happen."

"Apologize to Lene Landvik," I said. "She's the crippled teenager who's now an orphan."

Tears formed in his eyes. "No . . . I have to apologize to you too."

The door opened again. Lefty stepped in. His right arm still hung in a sling. His left arm, however, held a knife that could gut me like a trout.

I shook all over. I wasn't sure if it was terror or rage. "You son of a bitch!"

"I'm so sorry," Jin Chu sobbed. "They were gonna kill me. This was the only way I got to live."

I clicked the trigger and the blowtorch flamed to life. I held it out at arm's length toward the approaching Lefty. "Which part of your face you want crème brûléed, asshole?"

"You make it hard, I make it hurt," said Lefty. He had a thick accent. "This can be quick. Doesn't have to hurt."

Jin Chu covered his face and cried. "And I'm going to get fired too!"

"Goddammit!" I yelled to him. "Will you stop whining about your problems during my murder?!"

I grabbed a pipe from the workbench. There was something weird about being on the moon fighting for your life with a stick and some fire.

Lefty knew if he lunged I could block with the pipe and give him a face full of blowtorch. What he didn't know was that I had a more complicated plan.

I swung the pipe with all my strength at a wall-mounted

valve. The resounding metal-on-metal clank was followed by the scream of high-pressure air. The valve shot across the room and smacked into the far wall.

While Lefty paused to consider why the hell I'd done that, I leapt to the ceiling (not hard here—the average person can jump three meters straight up). At the top of my arc, I blasted a fire sensor with the blowtorch.

Red lights blinked and the fire alarm blared throughout the room. The door slammed shut behind Jin Chu. He jerked around in shock.

As soon as I hit the ground, I bounded into the air shelter and slammed the door behind me. Lefty was hot on my heels, but he didn't catch up in time. I spun the crank to seal myself in. Then I jammed the pipe into the crank spokes and held on to the other end.

Lefty tried to turn the crank from the other side, but he couldn't overcome my leverage advantage.

He glared at me through the air shelter's small round window. I flipped him off.

I could see Jin Chu clawing at the door, trying to get out. Of course it was no use. It was a fireproof room's door—solid metal and clamped shut with a mechanical interlock that could only be opened from the outside.

The foggy airflow from the broken valve slowed and petered out. Dad's wall valves connected to gas cylinders that he refilled every month.

Lefty stormed to the workbench and grabbed a long, steel rod. He came back to my shelter, breathing heavily. I got ready for a life-or-death game of circular tug-o-war.

He panted and wheezed as he stuck the rod into the handle. He pushed hard, but I was able to hold firm. By all rights, he should have won—he was bigger, stronger, and had better leverage. But I had one thing he didn't: oxygen.

The gas that had just filled the room? Neon. Dad had wall-mounted neon valves because he used it so much when welding aluminum.

The fire system had sealed the air vents, so the workshop was full of inert gas. You don't notice neon when you breathe it. It just feels like normal air. And the human body has no way to detect a *lack* of oxygen. You just plug along until you pass out.

Lefty fell to his hands and knees. He shook a bit, then collapsed to the floor.

Jin Chu lasted a little longer. He hadn't exerted himself as much. But he succumbed a few seconds later.

Let's meet so I can protect you. Did he really think I'd fall for that?

I pulled out Harpreet's Gizmo and dialed Rudy's number. I didn't want to, but I had no choice. Either I could call him or the fire brigade volunteers would when they arrived. May as well get a jump on it.

Artemis didn't have a police station. Just Rudy's office in Armstrong Bubble. Its holding cell was nothing more than a repurposed air shelter. In fact, it was Dad who'd installed it. Air shelters don't have locks, of course. That would massively defeat the purpose. So Rudy's "cell" had a metal chain with a padlock around the crank. Crude, but effective.

The usual occupants of the cell were drunks or people who needed to cool off after a fistfight. But today it held Lefty.

The rest of the room wasn't much larger than the apartment I'd grown up in. If Rudy had been born a few thousand years earlier, he would have made a good Spartan.

Jin Chu and I sat handcuffed to metal chairs.

"This is some bullshit," I said.

"You poor, innocent thing," said Rudy without looking up from his computer.

Jin rattled his handcuffs. "Hey, I actually *am* innocent! I shouldn't be here."

"Are you fucking kidding?!" I said. "You tried to kill me!"

"That's not true!" Jin pointed to Lefty's cell. "*He* tried to kill you. I just set up the meet. If I hadn't he would have killed me on the spot!"

"Chickenshit!"

"I value my life more than yours. Sue me. We wouldn't be in this mess if you hadn't been so *blatantly obvious* with your sabotage!"

"Fuck you!"

Rudy pulled a squirt bottle from his desk and sprayed us both. "Hush," he said.

Jin winced "Now, that's just unprofessional!"

"Quit bitching," I said, shaking the water off my face.

"You may be used to taking shots in the face, but I'm not," he said.

Okay, that was a good one. "Go fuck yourself," I said.

The door opened and Administrator Ngugi stepped in. Because why the hell not?

Rudy glanced over. "Hmm. You."

"Constable," Ngugi said. She looked over to me. "Jasmine. How are you, dear?"

I showed her my handcuffs.

"Is that necessary, Constable?"

"Is it necessary for you to be here?" Rudy asked.

I could have sworn the temperature dropped ten degrees.

"You'll have to excuse the constable," Ngugi said to me. "We don't see eye-to-eye on everything."

"If you'd stop coddling criminals like Jazz, we'd get along better."

She waved her hand as if shooing a bug. "Every city needs an underbelly. It's best to let the petty criminals do their thing and focus on bigger issues."

I grinned. "You heard the lady. And I'm the pettiest of them all. So lemme go."

Rudy shook his head. "The administrator's authority over me is questionable at best. I work directly for KSC. And you're going nowhere."

Ngugi walked over to the air shelter and peeked through the window. "So this is our murderer?"

"Yes," said Rudy. "And if you hadn't spent the last decade hampering my attempts to drive out organized crime, those murders wouldn't have happened."

"We've been through this, Constable. Artemis wouldn't exist without syndicate money. Idealism doesn't put Gunk on people's plates." She turned to face Rudy. "Did the suspect have anything to say?"

"He refuses to answer questions. He wouldn't even tell me his name—but according to his Gizmo, his name is Marcelo Alvarez and he's a 'freelance accounting consultant.'"

"I see. How sure are you that this is the man?"

Rudy turned his computer to face Ngugi. The screen showed medical lab results. "Doc Roussel dropped by earlier and got a blood sample from him. She says it matches the blood found at the crime scene. Also, the wound on his arm is consistent with the knife Irina Vetrov had in her hand."

"The blood DNA matched?" Ngugi said.

"Roussel doesn't have a crime lab. She compared blood type and enzyme concentrations—they matched. If we want a DNA comparison we'll have to send samples to Earth. It'll take at least two weeks."

"That won't be necessary," Ngugi said. "We only need enough evidence to warrant a trial, not to convict him."

"Hey!" Jin Chu interjected. "Excuse me! I demand to be released!"

Rudy squirted him with the bottle.

"Who is this man?" Ngugi asked.

"Jin Chu from Hong Kong," Rudy said. "Couldn't find any record of where he works and he isn't forthcoming about it. He set a trap so Alvarez could kill Bashara, but claims he did it under duress. Alvarez was going to kill him if he didn't."

"We can hardly blame him for that," she said.

"Finally! Someone with common sense!" Jin said.

"Deport him to China," said Ngugi.

"Wait, what?" Jin said. "You can't do that!"

"Of course I can," she said. "You were complicit in a plot to murder someone. Coerced or not, you're not welcome here."

He opened his mouth to protest again and Rudy pointed the squirt bottle at him. He thought better of it.

Ngugi sighed and shook her head. "This is troubling. Very troubling. You and I . . . we're not friends. But neither of us wants murder in our city."

"On that, at least, we agree."

"And this is new." She clasped her hands behind her back. "We've had murders before, but it's always been a jealous lover, an angry spouse, or a drunken brawl. This was professional. I don't like it."

"Was your gentle hand with petty crime worth it?" Rudy asked.

"That's not fair." She shook off the gloom. "One thing at a time. There's a meatship launching today for the *Gordon* cycler. I want Mr. Jin on it. Deport to Hong Kong with no legal complaints. Hang on to Mr. Alvarez for now. We need to collate the evidence for the courts in . . . where's he going?"

"Landvik was Norwegian and Vetrov was Russian."

"I see," said Ngugi.

If you commit a serious crime, Artemis deports you to the *victim's* country. Let their nation exact revenge on you for it. It's only fair. But Lefty—I guess I should call him Alvarez—had killed people from two different countries. Now what?

"I'd like you to let me pick this one," Rudy said.

"Why?"

Rudy looked to the cell. "If he cooperates I'll send him to Norway. If not, he'll go to Russia. Where would you rather be tried for murder?"

"Excellent strategy. I see you're a little Machiavellian yourself."

"That's not—" Rudy began.

"You should release Jasmine, though, don't you think?" she said.

Rudy was taken aback. "Certainly not. She's a smuggler and a saboteur."

"*Allegedly*," I said.

"Why do you care so much about Jazz?" he asked.

"Sanchez Aluminum is a Brazilian company. Do you want to deport her to Brazil? She'd be lucky to last a day there before O Palácio killed her. Does she deserve to die?"

"Of course not," Rudy said. "I recommend Deportation Without Complaint to Saudi Arabia."

"Declined," Ngugi said.

"This is ridiculous," he said. "She's clearly guilty. What is your fixation with this girl?"

"Girl?" I said. "I'm twenty-six!"

"She's one of us," Ngugi said. "She grew up here. That means she gets more leeway."

"Bullshit," Rudy snapped. I'd never heard him swear before. "There's something you're not telling me. What is it?"

Ngugi smiled. "I'm not deporting her, Constable. How long would you like to keep her handcuffed here?"

Rudy thought it over, then pulled a key from his pocket and unlatched my handcuffs.

I rubbed my wrists. "Thanks, Administrator."

"Stay safe, dear." She walked out of the office.

Rudy glared as she left, then he shot me a look. "You're *not* safe. You're better off confessing to your part in this and getting deported to Saudi Arabia. It's easier to hide out there than here."

"You're better off eating shit," I said.

"O Palácio won't give up just because I caught their fixer. You can be sure they'll send another one on the next meatship."

"First of all: duh," I said. "Second off: *I* caught him, not you. And finally . . . how'd he track my Gizmo?"

Rudy frowned. "That does bother me."

"I'll be on my way. If you need to reach me, you know the identity I'm using." He'd confiscated my Harpreet Gizmo when he arrested me. I picked it up off his desk. "You've had plenty of opportunities to kill me and haven't done it."

"Thanks for the vote of trust. You should stay around me for your own safety."

It was tempting. But I couldn't. I didn't know what my next move would be, but it would definitely be something I couldn't do with Rudy watching.

"I'm better on my own, thanks." I turned to Jin Chu. "What's ZAFO?"

"Suck a dick!"

"Get out," Rudy said to me. "Come back if you want protection."

"Fine, fine," I said.

Hartnell's had its usual crowd of quiet, borderline alcoholics. I knew each of them by face, if not name. There were no strangers that day, and none of the regulars even glanced my way. Business as usual at my watering hole.

Billy poured me a pint of my usual grog. "Aren't you on the run or somefin'?"

I wiggled my hand. "Kind of."

Was Alvarez the only thug O Palácio had in town? Maybe. Maybe not. I mean, how many people would you assign to your lunar mafia money-laundering operation? At least I knew one thing: They couldn't have sent anyone new. Not yet. It takes weeks to get here from Earth.

"Is it wise to come 'round your favorite pub then?"

"Nope. It's one of the stupidest things I've ever done. And that's a field of *intense* competition."

He threw a towel over his shoulder. "Then why?"

I swigged my beer. "Because I made a deal."

Billy looked past me to the entrance and widened his eyes. "Cor! There's a face I haven't seen in an age!"

Dale walked up to his old stool next to mine and sat down. He grinned from ear to ear. "A pint of your worst, Billy."

"On the house for ya!" Billy said. He filled a pint for Dale. "How's me favorite arse bandit?"

"Can't complain. Still do, though."

"Har!" He slid the pint to Dale. "I'll leave you two hatebirds alone."

Dale sipped his beer and smirked at me. "I wasn't sure if you'd show."

"Deal's a deal," I said. "But if someone shows up to kill me I might need to leave early."

"Yeah, about that. What's going on? Rumor has it you're tangled up in the murders."

"Rumor's right." I drained my glass and tapped it twice on the bar. Billy slid me another—he'd poured it in advance. "I was the next intended victim."

"Rudy caught the murderer, right? The news sites say it's some Portuguese guy?"

"Brazilian," I said. "Doesn't matter. They'll just send another one after me. I've got a short break at best."

"Shit, Jazz. Is there anything I can do?"

I stared him in the eyes. "We're not friends, Dale. Don't worry about me."

He sighed. "We could be. In time, maybe?"

"I don't see it happening."

"Well, I've got one evening a week to change your mind." He smiled at me. Smug little fucker. "So why'd you do the harvester job?"

"Trond was going to pay me a big pile of money."

"Yeah, but . . ." He looked pensive. "I mean, it's not your style. It was risky—and you're really smart. You don't take risks unless you have to. You're not desperate for cash or anything, so far as I know. I mean, yeah, you're poor. But you're stable. Do you owe loan sharks or something?"

"No."

"Gambling debt?" he asked.

"No. Stop it."

"Come on, Jazz." He leaned in. "What's the deal? This doesn't make sense to me."

"Doesn't have to make sense to you." I checked my Gizmo. "We have three hours and fifty-two minutes left until midnight, by the way. Then it won't be 'evening' anymore."

"Then I'm just going to spend three hours and fifty-two minutes asking the same question."

Pain in my ass . . . I sighed. "I need 416,922 slugs."

"That's . . . a very specific number. Why do you need it?"

"Because fuck you, that's why."

"Jazz—"

"No!" I snapped. "That's all you're getting."

Awkward silence.

"How's Tyler?" I asked. "Is he . . . I don't know. Is he happy?"

"Yeah, he's happy," said Dale. "We have our ups and downs like any couple, but we work at it. Lately he's frustrated with the Electricians' Guild."

I snickered. "He's always hated those fuckers. Is he still non-guild?"

"Oh, of course. He'll never join. He's a very good electrician. Why would he go out of his way to get paid less?"

"Are they squeezing him?" I asked. One of the downsides of having almost no laws: monopolies and pressure tactics.

Dale seesawed his hand. "A little. Some rumormongering and deliberate price undercutting. Nothing he can't handle."

"If they go too far let me know," I said.

"What would you do?"

"Dunno. But I don't want anyone fucking with him."

Dale held up his glass. "Then I pity anyone who fucks with him."

I clinked my glass against his and we both took a sip.

"Keep him happy," I said.

"I'll sure as hell try."

My Harpreet Gizmo buzzed. I pulled it out to take a look. It was a message from Svoboda: **"This ZAFO shit is amazing. Meet me at my lab."**

"Just a sec," I said to Dale. I typed out a response.

"What did you find out?"

"It'd take too long to type. Besides, I want to show you what it can do."

"Hmm," I said.

"Problem?" Dale asked.

"A friend wants to meet. But last time I met someone it was an ambush."

"Need backup?"

I shook my head and typed on my Gizmo. **"Honey, I know what you're after, but I'm too tired for sex right now."**

"What are you talking about?" Svoboda responded. **"Oh, I see. You're being weird to find out if I'm being coerced. No, Jazz, I'm not setting you up."**

"Just being cautious. I have an obligation at the moment. Meet at your lab tomorrow morning?"

"Sounds good. Oh and if I am being coerced in the future, I'll work the word 'dolphin' into the conversation. Okay?"

"Copy," I responded. I put the Gizmo back in my pocket.

Dale pursed his lips. "Jazz . . . how bad is it?"

"Well, people want to kill me, so . . . pretty bad."

"Who are these people? Why do they want you dead?"

I wiped dew off my beer glass. "They're a Brazilian crime syndicate called O Palácio. They own Sanchez Aluminum and they know I did the Sanchez harvester sabotage."

"Shit," Dale said. "You need a place to hide out?"

"I'm good," I said. Then, after a few seconds, I added, "But if I need help I'll remember your offer."

He smiled. "Well, that's a start, anyway."

"Shut up and drink your beer." I emptied my glass. "You're two pints behind."

"Oh, I see how it is." He gestured to Billy. "Barkeep! Some little girl thinks she can outdrink me. We'll need six pints—three for the gay and three for the goy."

I awoke in my hidey-hole sore, groggy, and hungover. Probably hadn't been a good idea to get wasted in the middle of all this shit, but as I've established, I make poor life choices.

I spent a few minutes praying for death, then I drank as much water as I could stomach and emerged from the compartment like a slug.

I ate some dry Gunk for breakfast (you taste it less that way) and wandered off to the public bathhouse on Bean Up 16. I spent the rest of the morning there soaking in a tub.

Then it was off to a middle-class clothing store on Bean Up 18. I'd been wearing my jumpsuit for three straight days. It could almost stand up on its own at this point.

Finally I was sort of human again.

I walked along the narrow corridors of Armstrong until I reached the ESA lab's main entrance. A few scientists wandered the halls on the way to work.

Svoboda opened the door before I even had a chance to knock. "Jazz! Wait'll you see—whoa, you look like shit."

"Thanks."

He produced a package of mints and poured a few into my hand. "No time to mock your alcoholism. I gotta show you this ZAFO shit. Come on!"

He led me through the entryway and into his lab. The whole place looked different. He'd dedicated the main table to ZAFO analysis and shoved everything else to the walls to make room. Various pieces of equipment (most of it a mystery to me) covered the table.

He bounced from one foot to another. "This is so awesome!"

"Okay, okay," I said. "What's got you in such a tizzy?"

He sat on a stool and cracked his knuckles. "First thing I did was visual examination."

"You looked at it," I said. "You can just say 'I looked at it.'"

"By all accounts it's a normal, single-mode fiber-optic line. The jacket, buffer, and cladding are all routine. The core fiber is eight microns across—totally normal. But I figured there'd be something special about the core, so I cut up some samples and—"

"You cut it up?" I said. "I didn't say you could cut it up!"

"Yeah, I don't care." He tapped one of the devices on the lab table. "I used this baby to check the core's index of refraction. That's a pretty important stat for fiber optic."

I picked up a five-centimeter snippet of ZAFO from the table. "And you found something weird?"

"Nope," he said. "It's 1.458. A little higher than fiber optics usually are, but only by a tiny bit."

I sighed. "Svoboda, can you skip over the ways it's normal and just tell me what you found?"

"All right, all right." He reached over to a handheld device and picked it up. "This baby is how I cracked the mystery."

"I know you want me to ask what that is, but honestly I don't—"

"It's an optical loss test set! OLTS for short. It tells you how much attenuation a fiber-optic cable has. Attenuation is the amount of light that gets lost to heat during transmission."

"I know what attenuation is," I said. But it really didn't matter. Once Svoboda got going there was no stopping him. I've never known anyone who loved his work as much as that guy.

He set the OLTS back on the table. "Now, a typical attenuation for a high-end cable is around 0.4 decibels per kilometer. Guess what ZAFO's attenuation is."

"No."

"Go on. Guess."

"Just tell me."

"It's zero. Fucking. *Zero!*" He formed a circle with his arms. "Zeeeroooo!"

I sat on the stool next to him. "So . . . no light gets lost in transmission? At all?"

"Right! Well, at least, as far as I can tell. The precision of my OLTS is 0.001 decibels per kilometer."

I looked at the ZAFO snippet in my hands. "It has to have some attenuation, though, right? I mean, it can't actually be zero."

He shrugged. "Superconductors have zero resistance to electrical current. Why can't there be a material with zero resistance to light?"

"ZAFO . . ." I rolled the word around in my mouth. "Zero-attenuation fiber optic?"

"Oh!" He smacked his forehead. "Of course!"

"What's it made of?"

He spun to a wall-mounted machine. "That's where my spectrometer came in!" He stroked it gently. "I call her Nora."

"And what did Nora have to say?"

"The core's mostly glass. No big surprise there, most fiber-optic cores are. But there were also trace amounts of tantalum, lithium, and germanium."

"Why are they in there?"

"Hell if I know."

I rubbed my eyes. "Okay, so why is it so exciting? You can use less energy to transmit data?"

"Oh, it's way more awesome than that," he said. "Normal fiber-optic lines can only be fifteen kilometers long. After that, the signal's just too weak to continue. So you need repeaters. They read the signal and retransmit it. But repeaters cost money, they have to be powered, and they're complicated. Oh, and they slow down the transmission too."

"So with ZAFO you don't need repeaters."

"Right!" he said. "Earth has *huge* data cables. They run across entire continents, under the oceans, all over the world. Just think of how much simpler it would be without all those repeaters mucking shit up. Oh! And it would have very few transmission errors. That means more bandwidth. This shit is fantastic!"

"Great. But is it worth killing over?"

"Well . . ." he said. "I suppose every telecom company will want to upgrade. How much do you think the *entire planet Earth's* communication network is worth? Because that's roughly how much money ZAFO is going to make its owners. Yeah. That's probably murderin' money."

I pinched my chin. The more I thought about it the less I liked it. Then, the pieces all fell into place. "Oh! Goddammit!"

"Whoa," said Svoboda. "Who shit in your Rice Krispies?"

"This isn't about aluminum at all!" I stood from the stool. "Thanks, Svobo. I owe you one."

"What?" he said. "What do you mean it's not about aluminum? Then what's it about?"

But I already had a head of steam going. "Stay strange, Svobo. I'll be in touch."

. . .

The administrator's office used to be in Armstrong Bubble because that was the only bubble. But once Armstrong became all loud noises and machinery, she relocated. Nowadays she worked out of a small, one-room office on Conrad Up 19.

Yup, you heard me. The administrator of Artemis—the most important and powerful person on the moon, who could literally have any location rent-free—chose to work in the bluest of blue-collar areas. If I were Ngugi, I'd have a huge office overlooking the Aldrin Arcade. And it would have a wet bar and leather chairs and other cool powerful-people stuff.

And a personal assistant. A beefy yet gentle guy who called me "boss" all the time. Yeah.

Ngugi didn't have any of that. She didn't even have a secretary. Just a sign on her office door that read ADMINISTRATOR FIDELIS NGUGI.

To be fair, it's not like she was president of the United States. She was, effectively, the mayor of a small town.

I pressed the doorbell and heard a simple buzz emanate from the room beyond.

"Come in," came Ngugi's voice.

I opened the door. Her office was even less fancy than I'd expected. Spartan, even. A few shelves with family photos jutted out of raw aluminum walls. Her sheet-metal desk looked like something from the 1950s. She did at least have a proper office chair—her one concession to personal comfort. When I'm seventy years old I'll probably want a nice chair too.

She typed away on a laptop. The older generations still preferred them to Gizmos or speech-interface devices. She somehow carried grace and aplomb even while hunched over at her desk. She wore casual clothes and, as always, her traditional dhuku headscarf. She finished typing a sentence, then smiled at me.

"Jasmine! Wonderful to see you, dear. Please, have a seat."

"Yea-thank-yes. I'll . . . sit." I settled into one of the two empty chairs facing her desk.

She clasped her hands and leaned forward. "I've been so worried about you, dear. What can I do to help?"

"I have a question about economics."

She raised her eyebrows. "Economics? Well, I do have some knowledge in that area."

Understatement of the century. This woman had transformed Kenya into the center of the global space industry. She deserved a Nobel Prize. Two, really. One for Economics and another for Peace.

"What do you know about Earth's telecom industry?" I asked.

"That's a broad topic, dear. Can you be more specific?"

"What's it worth, you think? Like, what kind of revenues do they pull down?"

She laughed. "I could only hazard a guess. But the *entire* global industry? Somewhere in the five-to-six-trillion-dollar-per-year range."

"Holy shit! Er . . . pardon my language, ma'am."

"Not a problem, Jasmine. You've always been colorful."

"How do they make so much?"

"They have a huge customer base. Every phone line, every internet connection, every TV cable subscription . . . they all create revenue for the industry—either directly from the customer or indirectly through advertising."

I looked down at the floor. I had to take a moment.

"Jasmine?"

"Sorry. Kind of tired—well, to be honest, I'm hungover."

She smiled. "You're young. You'll recover soon, I'm sure."

"Let's say someone invented a better mousetrap," I said. "A really awesome fiber-optic cable. One that reduced costs, increased bandwidth, and improved reliability."

She leaned back in her chair. "If the price point were comparable to existing cables, it would be a huge boon. And the manufacturer of that product would be swimming in money, of course."

"Yeah," I said. "And let's say the prototype of this new fiber optic was created in a specially made satellite in low-Earth orbit. One with a centrifuge aboard. What would that tell you?"

She looked puzzled. "This is a very odd discussion, Jasmine. What's going on?"

I drummed my fingers on my leg. "See, to me that means it can't be created in Earth's gravity. It's the only reason to make a custom satellite."

She nodded. "That sounds reasonable. I take it something like this is in the works?"

I pressed on. "But the satellite has a centrifuge. So they do need *some* force. It's just that Earth's gravity is too high. But what if the moon's gravity were low enough for whatever process they're using?"

"This is an oddly specific hypothetical, dear."

"Humor me."

She put her hand on her chin. "Then obviously they could manufacture it here."

"So, in your expert opinion, where's a better place to manufacture this imaginary product: low-Earth orbit or Artemis?"

"Artemis," she said. "No question. We have skilled workers, an industrial base, a transport infrastructure, and shipping to and from Earth."

"Yeah." I nodded. "That's kind of what I thought."

"This sounds very promising, Jasmine. Have you been offered a chance to invest? Is that why you're here? If this invention is real, it's definitely worth putting money into."

I wiped my brow. Conrad Up 19 was always a comfortable 22 degrees Celsius, but I was sweating nonetheless.

I looked her in the eyes. "You know what's strange? You didn't mention radio or satellites."

She cocked her head. "I'm sorry, dear. What?"

"When you talked about the telecom industry. You mentioned internet, phone, and TV. But you didn't bring up radio or satellites."

"Those are certainly parts of it as well."

"Yeah," I said. "But you didn't mention them. In fact, you *only* talked about the parts of the industry that rely on fiber optics."

She shrugged. "Well, we're talking about fiber optics, so that's only natural."

"Except I hadn't brought up fiber optics yet."

"You must have."

I shook my head. "I've got a very good memory."

She narrowed her eyes slightly.

I pulled a knife from my boot holster and held it at the ready. "How did O Palácio find my Gizmo?"

She pulled a gun from under the desk. "Because I told them where it was."

11

"A gun?!" I said. "How did a gun get into the city?! I *never* smuggle weapons!"

"I've always appreciated that," she said. "You don't have to keep your hands up. You do, however, have to drop that knife."

I did as I was instructed. The knife floated down to the floor.

She kept the gun pointed at me. "May I ask, how did you come to suspect me?"

"Process of elimination," I said. "Rudy proved he wasn't selling me out. You're the only other person with access to my Gizmo location info."

"Reasonable," she said. "But I'm not as sinister as you think."

"Uh-huh." I gave her a dubious look. "But you know all about ZAFO, right?"

"Yes."

"And you're going to make a shitload of money off of it?"

She scowled. "Do you really think so little of me? I won't make a single slug."

"But . . . then . . . why . . . ?"

She settled back into her chair and relaxed her grip on the gun. "You were right about the gravity. ZAFO is a crystalline quartzlike structure that only forms at 0.216 g's. It's impossible to make on Earth, but they can make it here with a centrifuge. You're such an intelligent girl, Jasmine. If only you'd apply yourself."

"If this is turning into a 'You have so much potential' lecture, just shoot me instead, okay?"

She smiled. She could be grandmotherly even while holding a gun. Like she'd give me a butterscotch candy before putting a hole in my head. "Do you know how Artemis makes its money?"

"Tourism."

"No."

I blinked. "What?"

"We don't make enough from tourism. It's a large part of our economy, yes, but not enough."

"But the economy works," I said. "Tourists buy stuff from local companies, companies pay employees, employees buy food and pay rent, and so on. And we're still here, so it must be working, right? What am I missing?"

"Immigration," she said. "When people move to Artemis, they bring their life savings with them. Then they spend it here. As long as our population kept growing that was fine, but now we've plateaued."

She angled the gun away from me. She still had a good grip on it, but at least she wouldn't kill me by mistake if she sneezed. "The whole system has become an unintentional Ponzi scheme. And we're just cresting the top of the curve now."

For the first time, my attention was torn away from the gun. "Is . . . are we . . . is this whole city going bankrupt?"

"Yes, if we don't take action," she said. "But ZAFO is our savior. The telecom industry will want to upgrade, and ZAFO can only be cheaply made here. There'll be a huge production boom. Factories will open, people will move here for jobs, and everyone will prosper." She looked up wistfully. "We'll finally have an export economy."

"Glass," I said. "This has always been about glass, right?"

"Yes, dear," Ngugi said. "ZAFO is an amazing material, but like all fiber optics, it's mostly glass. And glass is just silicon and oxygen, both of which are created by aluminum smelting."

She ran her hand along the sheet aluminum desk. "Interesting how economics works, isn't it? Within a year, *aluminum* will be a by-product of the *silicon* industry. And that aluminum will be handy too. We'll have a lot of construction to handle the growth we're about to have."

"Wow," I said. "You really are all about economics."

"It's what I do, dear. And in the end, it's the only thing that matters. People's happiness, health, safety, and security all rely on it."

"Damn, you're good at this. You created an economy for Kenya and now you're doing it for us. You're a true hero. I should really be more grateful—oh that's right *you fucking sold me out!*"

"Oh, please. I knew you weren't stupid enough to turn on your Gizmo without taking precautions."

"But you did tell O Palácio where my Gizmo was?"

"Indirectly." She set the gun down on the table. Too far away for me to lunge at. She'd grown up in a war zone—I wasn't about to test her reflexes. "A few days ago, IT reported a hack attempt against the Gizmo network. Someone on Earth was trying to get your location info. I had IT deliberately disable security and let the hacker in. Actually, it was more complicated than that—they downgraded one of their network drivers to one with a known security flaw so the hacker had to work for it a little. I don't know the details—I'm not a tech person. Anyway, the end result is the hacker installed a program that would report your location if you turned on your Gizmo."

"Why the hell did you do that?!"

"To draw out the murderer." She pointed to me. "As soon as you turned on your Gizmo, I alerted Rudy to your presence. I assumed O Palácio would tell their man Alvarez as well. I hoped Rudy would catch him."

I frowned at her. "Rudy didn't seem to know anything about it."

She sighed. "Rudy and I have a . . . complex relationship. He doesn't approve of syndicates or indirect measures like I had taken. He'd like to be rid of me, and in all honesty, the feeling is mutual. If I'd warned him the killer was coming, he would've asked how I knew. Then he'd look into how the information got out, and that would cause trouble for me."

"You put Rudy on a collision course with a murderer and didn't warn him."

She cocked her head. "Don't look at me that way. It makes me sad. Rudy is an extremely skilled police officer who knew he was entering a potentially dangerous situation. And he almost caught Alvarez right then. My conscience is clear. If I had it to do over, I'd do the same thing. Big picture, Jasmine."

I folded my arms. "You were at Trond's a few nights ago. Have you been in on this from the beginning?"

"I'm not 'in' on anything," she said. "He told me about ZAFO and his plans to get into the silicon business. He wanted to talk about Sanchez's oxygen contract. He had reason to believe they were going to be in breach soon and wanted to make sure I knew he had oxygen if that happened."

"That didn't make you suspicious?"

"Of course it did. But the city's future was at stake. A criminal syndicate was about to control the most important resource on the moon. Trond offered me a solution: He'd take over the contract, but with six-month renewals. If he artificially inflated prices or tried to control too much of the ZAFO industry, he'd lose the contract. He'd rely on me to keep renewing and I'd rely on him to feed the ZAFO boom with silicon. There'd be a balance."

"So what went wrong?"

She pursed her lips. "Jin Chu. He came to town with a plan to make as much money as possible, and by God he succeeded. He'd told Trond about ZAFO months earlier, but Trond wanted a sample to have his people examine—proof that ZAFO really existed and wasn't just some fairy tale."

"So Jin Chu showed him the ZAFO and Trond paid him," I

said. "And then Jin Chu turned right around and sold the information to O Palácio."

"That's the thing about secrets. You can sell them over and over again."

"Slimy little bastard."

She sighed. "Just imagine what a revelation that was for O Palácio. All of a sudden, their insignificant money-laundering company was poised to corner an emerging billion-dollar industry. From that point on, they were all-in. But Artemis is very far away from Brazil and they only had one enforcer on-site, thank God."

"So what happens now?"

"Right now, I'm sure O Palácio is buying as many tickets to the moon as they can get. Within a month, Artemis will be swarming with their people. They'll own silicon production and that damned oxygen-for-power contract will ensure no one can compete. And they already started their next phase: taking over the glass-manufacturing industry." She gave me a knowing look.

"Oh fuck," I said. "The Queensland Glass Factory fire."

Ngugi nodded. "The fire was almost certainly set by Alvarez. Busy little fellow, wasn't he? Once O Palácio sets up their own glass factory, they'll have both production and supply line locked down. And of course, they'll kill anyone who tries to get in their way. That's the breed of 'capitalism' we can expect from now on."

"You're the administrator. Do something about it!"

She looked to the ceiling. "Between their financial base and physical enforcers, they'll own the city. Think Chicago in the 1920s, but a hundred times worse. I'll be powerless."

"It would be nice if you actually helped in some way."

"I *have* been helping," she said. "Rudy had you pegged as the saboteur right away. He showed me the video footage of that ridiculous disguise you wore to the Visitor Center."

I hung my head.

"He wanted to arrest you right then. I told him I wasn't convinced and needed more evidence. I knew that would buy you some time."

"Okay, so why did you become my guardian angel?"

"Because you're a lightning rod. I knew O Palácio would have at least one enforcer in town. You drew him into the open. Now he's caught. Thank you."

"I was bait?"

"Of course. And you're *still* bait. That's why I intervened yesterday and got Rudy to release you. I don't know what O Palácio will do next, but whatever it is, they'll do it to you."

"You . . ." I said. "You're a real bitch, you know that?"

She nodded. "When I have to be. Building a civilization is ugly, Jasmine. But the alternative is no civilization at all."

I glared at her with pure contempt. She wasn't impressed.

"So what the hell am I supposed to do now?"

"No idea." She gestured to the door. "But you better get started."

I crawled back into my hiding place and sealed the panel behind me. I curled up into a ball in the dark. I was so goddamn tired I should have fallen asleep right then, but I couldn't.

It all caught up with me. Constant danger, poverty, anger, and worst of all, sheer, unmitigated fatigue. I'd gone beyond sleepy into what my father used to call "overtired." He usually used that term while chucking my cranky, eight-year-old ass into my bunk for a forced nap.

I tossed and turned as much as I could in the cramped confines. No position was comfortable. I wanted to pass out and punch someone at the same time. I couldn't think straight. I had to get out of there.

I kicked open the panel. Who gives a fuck if someone sees me? I didn't.

"Where now?" I mumbled to myself.

I felt a wet droplet hit my arm. I looked to the ceiling. The frigid air of Bean Down 27 often made condensation points. Water's surface tension versus lunar gravity meant a bunch of it had to build up before it started dripping. But I didn't see anything above me.

Then I touched my face with my hand. "Oh, goddammit."

The source of the water was me. I was crying.

I needed a place to sleep. Really sleep. If I'd been thinking clearly I would have gotten a hotel. Ngugi wouldn't help O Palácio find me again.

Right that moment, I didn't trust anything electronic. I considered going to the imam's house, where Dad was. The imam would take me in, and at some feral level I wanted my daddy.

I shook my head and admonished myself. Under no circumstances would I tangle Dad up in all this shit.

Fifteen minutes later, I slogged down a corridor to my destination. I rang the door buzzer. It was past three in the morning, but I was past politeness.

After a minute, Svoboda opened the door. He wore full-body pajamas, because apparently he had just traveled to the moon from 1954. He looked at me through bleary eyes. "Jazz?"

"I need—" My throat closed. I almost fell prey to hysterical crying. *Get your shit together!* "I need to sleep. Svoboda, oh God I need to sleep."

He opened the door farther. "Come in, come in."

I trudged past him. "I'm. I need. I'm so tired, Svoboda. I'm just so tired."

"Yeah, yeah, it's okay." He rubbed his eyes. "Take the bed. I'll set up some blankets on the floor for myself."

"No, no." My eyes had already closed of their own accord. "Floor's fine for me."

My knees buckled and I collapsed. The moon is a nice place to pass out. You hit the ground very gently.

I felt Svoboda's arms pick me up. Then I felt the bed, still warm from his body. Blankets covered me and I nuzzled into the cocoon of safety. I fell asleep instantly.

I awoke to that few seconds of pleasant amnesia everyone gets in the morning. Unfortunately, it didn't last long.

I remembered the previous night's antics and winced. God. It's one thing to be a pathetic weakling, but it's another to do it in front of someone.

I stretched out in Svoboda's bed and yawned. It wasn't the first time I'd awakened in some guy's place worn out and full of regret. But I'll tell you what, it was the best night's sleep I'd had in a long time.

Svoboda was nowhere to be seen. A pillow and blanket on the floor showed he was quite the gentleman. It was *his* bed—I should have been the one on the floor. Or we could have shared.

My boots stood neatly together next to the nightstand. Apparently he'd taken them off while I slept. Other than that, I was fully clothed. Not the best way to sleep, but better than having someone undress my unconscious body in the night.

I pulled my Gizmo from my pocket to check the time.

"Holy shit!" It was well into the afternoon. I'd slept for fourteen hours.

The nightstand next to me had three Gunk bars in a neat stack with a note on top: *Jazz—Breakfast for you. There's juice in the fridge.—Svoboda.*

I noshed on a Gunk bar and opened his mini-fridge. I had no idea what the juice was, but I went ahead and drank it. Turns out it was reconstituted carrot-apple juice. It tasted like shit. Who the hell puts those things together? Ukrainians, apparently.

I pondered ways to pay him back. A really nice meal? A cool piece of lab equipment? Have sex with him? Just kidding on that last one, of course. I snickered at the thought. Then I stopped snickering but hung on to the thought.

Whoa. I needed to finish waking up.

I took a nice long shower and reminded myself what I was really working toward: a shower of my own. It's damned pleasant to walk three meters and be in a private shower. *Damned* pleasant.

I didn't want to wear my grungy, slept-in clothes so I raided Svoboda's closet. I found a suitable T-shirt and threw it on over my underwear (sadly, Svoboda had no women's undergarments in his closet. I would have had some questions for him if he had). The shirt hung on me like a short dress—Svoboda's considerably taller than I am.

Okay. I was rested, clean, and had a clear head. Time to settle down and do some serious thinking. How would I get out of this? I sat at the desk and plugged in my Gizmo. The desk's built-in monitor rose from its cubby and showed my desktop icons. I cracked my knuckles and extended the keyboard tray.

Over the next few hours, I sipped carrot-apple juice (it grows on you) and researched Sanchez Aluminum. Their operations, leadership, revenue estimates, you name it. Since they were a private company (owned by "Santiago Holdings, Inc." which I assumed was Brazilian for "O Palácio"), there wasn't much publicly available information.

I looked up Loretta Sanchez and found a paper she'd written about her refinements to high-temperature smelting. I had to take a break to learn some basic chemistry, but I found all that online pretty easily. Once I understood it, I had to admit: She really was a genius. She'd revolutionized the whole system and made it practical for use on the moon.

I'd still beat her ass if I met her. Don't get me wrong.

I must have been at it for a couple of hours because Svoboda finally came home from work.

"Oh, hey," he said. "How are you feeling—uh . . . uh . . ."

I tore my attention away from the monitor to see what had caused his mental reboot. He was just kind of staring at me. I looked down. I was still wearing just the shirt I'd liberated from his closet. I was pretty sexy, I have to admit.

"Hope you don't mind." I gestured to the shirt.

"N-no," he said. "No problem. It looks good. I mean, it hangs well. I mean, how your chest makes it, um . . ."

I watched him flounder for a second. "When all this is over, if I'm still alive, I'm going to give you woman lessons."

"Whu—huh?"

"You just . . . you really need to learn about women and how to interact with them, all right?"

"Oh," he said. "That could be really helpful, yeah."

He took off his lab coat and hung it on the wall. Why did he wear his lab coat home instead of leaving it at the lab? Because men like fashion accessories too. They just don't admit it.

"Looks like you slept well," he said. "What are you up to now?"

"Looking into Sanchez Aluminum," I said. "I have to figure out a way to shut them down. That's my only hope of survival at this point."

He sat on the bed behind me. "Are you sure you want to screw with them?"

"What are they going to do? Kill me harder? They're already after me."

He looked at the screen. "Ooh. Is that their smelting process?"

"Yeah. It's called the FFC Cambridge Process."

He perked up. "Oh, that sounds cool!"

Of course it did. Svoboda's just that kind of guy. He leaned in to get a better look at the screen. It showed the chemistry at each step of the smelting process. "I've heard of the process but I never learned the details."

"They're guarding the harvester now," I said. "So I'll have to go after the smelter itself."

"You got a plan?" he asked.

"Yeah. The start of one," I said. "But it means I have to do something I hate."

"Oh?"

"I have to get help."

He held out his arms. "Well, you got me. Whatever you need."

"Thanks, buddy, I'll take you up on that."

"Don't call me buddy," he grumbled.

I hesitated. "Okay, I . . . won't call you buddy. Why not?"

"Man lessons," he said. "Someday I'll give you man lessons."

I rang the doorbell for the fourth time. She was in there; she just didn't want to answer.

The main entrance to the Landvik Estate stood littered with flowers from well-wishers and mourners. Most of the flowers were synthetic, but a few wilting bouquets revealed how truly wealthy some of Trond's friends were.

I never thought I'd miss the sight of Irina's scowling face, but a sadness overwhelmed me when I realized she wouldn't be the one opening the door.

Then again, maybe no one would answer at all.

I rapped the door with my knuckles. "Lene! It's Jazz! I know this isn't a great time, but we need to talk."

I waited a bit longer. I was about to give up when the door clicked open. That was as much invitation as I was going to get.

I stepped over the consolation bouquets and through the door.

The once brightly lit foyer stood dark. Only the dim light from the sitting room filtered in to give any illumination at all.

Someone had drawn a dozen or more circles on one wall—where the blood spatter used to be. The actual blood was gone, presumably cleaned by a professional service after Rudy and Doc Roussel were done with the scene.

I followed the light into the sitting room. It too had changed for the worse. All the furniture was shoved against walls. The large Persian rug that once adorned the floor was nowhere to be seen. Some things just can't be cleaned.

Lene sat on a couch in the corner, mostly in the dark. As a wealthy teen girl she usually put hours into her appearance. Today she wore sweats and a T-shirt. She had no makeup on and dried tears streaked her face. Her hair was in a loose ponytail, the universal sign of not giving a fuck. Her crutches lay askew on the floor.

She held a wristwatch in her hands and stared at it with a blank expression.

"Hey . . ." I said in that lame tone people use when talking to the bereaved. "How you holding up?"

"It's a Patek Philippe," she said quietly. "Best watch manufacturers on Earth. Self-winding, chronograph, time zone, you name it. Nothing but the best for Dad."

I sat on the couch next to her.

"He had it modified by top watchmakers in Geneva," she continued. "They had to make a replacement self-winding weight out of tungsten so it would have enough force to work in lunar gravity."

She leaned over to me and showed me the watch's face. "And he had them change the moon-phase indicator to an Earth-phase indicator. It was tricky too, because Earth's phases go in the reverse order. They even modified the time zone dial to say 'Artemis' instead of 'Nairobi.'"

She clasped the band around her thin wrist. "It's way too big for me. I'll never be able to wear it."

She angled her arm downward. The watch slid off and fell to the couch. She sniffled.

I picked it up. I didn't know anything about watches, but it sure looked nice. Diamonds denoted each hour on the face except the 12. That had an emerald.

"Rudy has the guy who did it," I said.

"I heard."

"He'll rot in a Norwegian jail for life. Or be executed in Russia."

"Won't bring Dad or Irina back," she said.

I put my hand on her shoulder. "I'm sorry for your loss."

She nodded.

I sighed, just to fill the awkward silence. "Look, Lene, I don't know how much Trond told you about his business dealings . . ."

"He was a crook," she said. "I know. I don't care. He was my dad."

"The people who killed him own Sanchez Aluminum."

"O Palácio," she said. "Rudy told me. I never even heard of them before yesterday."

She put her face in her hands. I expected a crying jag—she was entitled to one. But it didn't come. Instead, she turned to me and wiped her eyes. "Did you trash Sanchez's harvesters? Did Dad put you up to it?"

"Yes."

"Why?" she asked.

"He wanted to take over the aluminum industry—well, the silicon industry, actually. Interrupting Sanchez's production would let him get a city contract he needed to make that happen."

Lene stared ahead blankly, then slowly nodded. "Sounds like him. Always working an angle."

"Look, I have an idea," I said. "But I need your help."

"You need a crippled orphan?"

"A crippled orphan *billionaire*, yeah." I pulled my legs up onto the couch so I could face her girl-to-girl. "I'm going to follow through with Trond's plan. I'm going to stop Sanchez's oxygen production. I need you to be ready to take over the contract. Once you do, O Palácio will be willing to sell you Sanchez Aluminum."

"Why would they sell to me?"

"Because if they don't, you'll make your own company, undercut their prices with your free power, and bankrupt them.

They're mobsters, but they're also businessmen. You'll be offering them a big payoff to walk away when their alternative is watching the company collapse. They'll take the deal. You own all of Trond's holdings, right?"

"Not yet," she said. "It's billions of euros, dollars, yen, and every other currency under the sun. Plus entire companies, stock portfolios . . . God knows what else. I'm on a trust until I'm eighteen. The probate's going to take months, maybe years."

"Not for his Artemisian slugs," I said. "Our lack of regulation works in your favor. His accounts became yours the instant Doc Roussel declared him dead. And I hear he converted a fuckton of money into slugs to prep for the Sanchez purchase. You have the money to make this happen."

She stared into the distance.

"Lene?"

"It's not the money," she said. "It's me. I can't do this. I'm not Dad. He was a master of this stuff. I don't know what the hell I'm doing."

I turned the watch over in my hands. The platinum back had Norwegian text engraved on it. I held it in front of her. "Huh . . . what's that say?"

She glanced over. "*Himmelen er ikke grensen.* It means 'The sky is not the limit.'"

"He was a confident man," I said.

"Got him killed."

I reached into my pocket and pulled out my Swiss Army knife. With the help of its tweezers, I detached the set pins from the metal watchband. I removed three links and put the pins back in.

I took Lene's hand and slid the watch onto her wrist. She gave me a confused look but offered no resistance. I snapped the clasp shut. "There. Now it fits."

She shook her arm and the watch remained in place. "It's heavy."

"You'll get used to it."

She looked at the watch face for a long time. She wiped a mote of dust from the glass. "I guess I'll have to."

"So . . . ?" I prompted.

"Okay, I'll do it." She stared straight ahead. "Take the fuckers down."

I'd never noticed before, but she had her father's eyes.

Dear Kelvin,

Thanks for helping me earlier. I was in deep shit. Now I'm in slightly shallower shit. Basically, I'm at war with a company called Sanchez Aluminum. I'll give you the full story later. For now, I need another favor.

Sanchez Aluminum's smelting facility is in a mini-bubble near the reactors. The reactor/smelter complex is a kilometer from town.

I did some research and found a twenty-year-old article about the "negotiations" between Sanchez and KSC. KSC got really hands-on in the smelter's design process and Sanchez didn't like it. They almost went to litigation in Kenyan court.

Sanchez's argument was "It's our smelter. We don't need approval from anyone. Fuck off."

KSC's counter was "It's 200 meters from our reactors. We need to know it won't blow up. Give us approval rights or we won't rent you the space, you little shits."

Ultimately KSC won because they own the mini-bubble. They never sell property—they're all about rent.

Anyway, the upshot is KSC must have detailed schematics of the Sanchez smelter somewhere. Like . . . super detailed with every potential failure case analyzed and covered. I need you to get ahold of those documents. I know you work in a totally different part of KSC, but you still have access most people don't. Feel free to spread some money around in the process. I'll pay you back.

Dear Jazz,

The plans are enclosed. They were surprisingly easy to get. No part of them was considered a company secret or industrial process. Sanchez kept the exact chemistry in the smelter to themselves, but everything else was right there in the architectural plans.

I have a drinking buddy in the metallurgy lab in Building 27. They'd been consulted as part of the safety overview. He pulled the plans up on his boss's computer (which has no password protection). All I had to do was buy him a beer.

So the cost was two beers (had to have one myself, of course). Call it 50 slugs.

Dear Kelvin

Thanks, buddy. Make it 75 slugs and have another beer on me.

12

CLOSED FOR PRIVATE EVENT read the sign.

"You didn't have to do that, Billy," I said.

"Nonsense, luv," he said. "You said you needed a meeting space, so this is it."

I closed the door to Hartnell's behind me and sat at my usual spot. "But you're losing revenue."

He laughed. "Believe me, luv, I've made far more from you than I'll lose by being closed for an hour in the morning."

"Well, thanks." I tapped the counter. "As long as I'm here . . ."

He poured me a pint and slid it over.

"Heya," said Dale from the doorway. "You wanted to see me?"

"Yeah," I said. I took a swig of my beer. "But I don't want to tell the same story over and over. So have a seat until everyone gets here."

"Seriously?" he groused. "I've got better shit to do than—"

"Beer's on me."

"A pint of your finest, Billy!" He hopped onto his seat.

"Reconstituted garbage it is," said Billy.

Lene Landvik hobbled in on her crutches. Yes, she was sixteen and Hartnell's was a bar, but there's no drinking age in Artemis. It's another one of those vague rules that's enforced with punching. If Billy sold teenagers the occasional beer it was no big deal. But if he strayed too far down the age bracket he'd get a visit from angry parents.

She sat at a nearby table and leaned her crutches against a chair.

"How are you doing, kiddo?" I asked.

"Better," she said. "Not cheerful or anything. But better."

"Step by step." I raised my glass to her. "Keep at it."

"Thanks," she said. "I don't know how to bring this up but—did Dad pay you? Or did he . . . not get a chance?"

Oh man, come on. I'd planned to approach Lene about it eventually, but not until she'd had time to mourn. "Well . . . no. He didn't. But don't worry about it."

"How much did he owe you?"

"Lene, let's talk about this later—"

"How much?"

Well, shit. I guess the conversation was going to happen right then. "A million slugs."

"Holy shit!" said Dale. "A million slugs?!"

I ignored him. "But I don't have any way to prove it, you've got no reason to take my word."

"Your word's good enough," she said. "Dad always said you were the most honest businessman he'd ever worked with. I'll transfer the money today."

"No," I said. "I didn't deliver. The job was to stop Sanchez's oxygen production. If you want, you can pay me after I do that. But you know this isn't about money now, right?"

"I know. But a deal's a deal."

"Billy!" said Dale. "All my drinks are on Jazz from now on! She's a millionaire!"

"Right now I'm a thousandaire at best," I said. "Buy your own drinks."

Dale and I had another couple of beers and Lene fiddled with her Gizmo. It would be a long time before her life had normalcy, but at least for the moment she got to be a teenage girl glued to her phone.

Bob Lewis showed up at exactly ten a.m.

"Bob," I said.

"Jazz," he said.

"Beer?"

"No."

He sat across from Lene at her table and said nothing further. Marines know how to wait.

Svoboda came in next, carrying a box of electronics. He waved and started setting up. The damn fool had brought a digital projector and roll-up screen. He connected his Gizmo and, as usual with technology, it didn't work. Unfazed, he twiddled settings. Happy as a pig in shit.

One person had yet to arrive. I stared at the door, getting more and more nervous as the minutes ticked by. "What time is it?" I asked the room in general.

Lene checked her wristwatch. "Ten thirteen a.m. . . . and there's currently a half-Earth, by the way. It's waxing."

"Good to know," I said.

Finally, the door opened and the last guest stepped in. He scanned the bar until his eyes landed on me.

I slid my beer glass away. I never drank in front of him.

"Hi, Mr. Bashara," said Lene.

Dad walked over to her and took her hand. "Miss Landvik. I was so sorry to hear about your father. I wept when I heard."

"Thanks," she said. "It's been hard. But I'm getting better."

Bob stood. "Ammar. Good to see you."

"And you. How's that rover hatch holding up?"

"Perfectly. Hasn't leaked at all."

"Glad to hear it."

Billy threw a towel over his shoulder. "Good morning, Ammar. Fancy some juice? I've got a few powder flavors back here. Grape is the most popular."

"Do you have cranberry?" Dad asked.

"I do indeed!" Billy pulled out a pint glass and reconstituted some cranberry juice.

Dale raised his glass. "Mr. Bashara."

Dad gave him a cold stare. "Dale."

"I forget," said Dale, "do you hate me because I'm gay or because I'm Jewish?"

"I hate you because you broke my daughter's heart."

"Fair." Dale polished off his beer.

Dad sat next to me.

"So a Muslim walks into a bar . . ." I said.

He didn't laugh. "I'm here because you said you needed me. If you're just having a drinking party I'd rather go back to the imam's."

"I'm not—"

"Mr. Bashara?" Svoboda popped his head between us. "Hi, we haven't met. I'm Martin Svoboda. I'm a friend of Jazz's."

Dad shook his hand. "One of those 'friends with benefits'?"

"Ugh." I rolled my eyes. "I don't do that, Dad. This may shock you, but I haven't had sex with anyone in this whole room."

"Well, it's a small room."

"Burn!" Svoboda said. "Anyway, I just wanted to say you did a great job raising Jazz."

"You think so?" Dad said.

"All right," I said. "Let's get started."

I walked toward the white screen. Svoboda got it to work, of course. He always got shit to work.

I took a breath. "A lot's been going on and some of you have questions. Like Bob, who wants to know who did an unlicensed EVA to blow shit up. And Dad, who wants to know why I've made him hide out at the imam's house for the last week. Settle in, I'm going to tell you everything I know. . . ."

So I told them the whole sordid tale. All about the Queensland Glass fire, how Trond hired me, how the job went wrong, and how it connected to the murders. That led to O Palácio, Lefty, and Jin Chu. I told them about Sanchez Aluminum's oxygen contract and Trond's plan to take it over. I turned the floor over to

Svoboda to explain ZAFO and how it worked. Then I finished up by telling the sea of shocked faces that dozens of mobsters were on their way to Artemis.

When I stopped talking, a general silence fell across the room.

Dale spoke first. "I think we can all agree this is pretty fucked up. But a couple dozen mobsters can't just take over Artemis. I mean, we've had bar fights bigger than that."

"This isn't a gangster movie," I said. "They're not going to waltz in and start bashing skulls. They'll just guard Sanchez Aluminum to make sure they keep the oxygen-for-power contract. We have a short window of opportunity before they get here."

"I assume whatever you've concocted will be illegal," Dad said.

"Very."

He stood from his stool. "Then I won't participate."

"Dad, this is my only chance to stay alive."

"Nonsense. We can go back to Earth. My brother in Tabuk could take us in—"

"No, Dad." I shook my head. "No running away. Saudi Arabia's your old neighborhood but it's not mine. There's nothing for me there but gravity sickness. Artemis is my *home*. I'm not leaving and I'm sure as hell not letting mobsters take over."

He sat back down. He gave me a mean look, but didn't leave. That was something, at least.

"Tell them about the plan!" Svoboda said. "I have all the visual aids ready!"

"All right, all right. Bring up the schematics."

He tapped his Gizmo a few times and the projector showed architectural plans. The text in the title box read SANCHEZ ALUMINUM SMELTER BUBBLE—METALLURGICAL ANALYSIS.

I pointed to the screen. "The smelter bubble is much smaller than a municipal bubble. It's only thirty meters across. But it still has the same double-hull construction as any other bubble. Wherever there are humans, KSC requires double hulls."

I walked in front of the screen and pointed to features as I spoke. "Over here is the control room. It's got a big window over-looking the facility, so I'll have to be sneaky."

"Is the control room its own air compartment?" Dad asked.

"No, it shares air with the rest of the facility. They have to access the main floor so often they didn't want an air-seal door in their way—that's my assumption, anyway. They have an air shelter in the control room if anything goes wrong. And if the train is docked they can just go in there too."

"Okay," Dad said.

I continued. "The grinders are outside and the grit comes in through this compression airlock. Then it moves downstairs to the lower level. The sorter centrifuge separates the anorthite out from the other minerals. Then it's sintered into anodes. From there it goes back upstairs into the smelter."

I tapped a large rectangle in the middle of the schematics. "This is where the magic happens. The smelter reduces anor-thite into its base elements by using an assload of electricity."

"FFC Cambridge Process," said Svoboda. "It's awesome! The anode is dipped in a calcium chloride salt bath, then electroly-sis literally *yanks* atoms out! Oh, and the carbon cathodes get eroded so they have to constantly re-sinter them from the carbon they recover off the CO_2 by-product. They use some of the result-ing powdered aluminum to make rocket fuel, but the rest—"

"Calm yourself," I said. "Anyway, I'm going to break in there and make the smelter smelt itself to death."

"You can't spell 'smelt' without 'melt'!" Svoboda added.

"How will you do it?" Dale asked.

"I'll crank up power to the heater," I said. "The bath is nor-mally nine hundred degrees Celsius, but if I can get it to four-teen hundred, the steel containment vessel will melt. Then the superheated salt bath will escape and destroy everything in the bubble."

Dad scowled. "What good will this petty vandalism do?"

"First off, Dad, it's not petty vandalism. It's *extreme* vandalism. Second off: With their smelter destroyed, Sanchez won't be able to make oxygen, and the contract with the city will be up for grabs. That's where Lene comes in."

Lene fidgeted as everyone turned toward her. "Uh, yeah. Dad had—er . . . I have enough oxygen to last Artemis a year. I'll offer to take over the contract as soon as Sanchez is in breach."

"And Ngugi will rubber-stamp it," I said. "She wants O Palácio out of Artemis as much as we do."

Bob snorted. "Why should I get involved in this?"

"Dammit, Bob," I said. "I don't want to spend time on the 'will you or won't you help me' part. If you don't understand why we have to do this, go stand in the corner until you do."

"You're such an asshole," said Bob.

"Hey!" Dad shot Bob a look that made the burly marine draw back.

"He's right, Dad. I am an asshole. But Artemis needs an asshole right now and I got drafted."

I walked to the middle of the room. "This moment—this moment right now—is where we decide what kind of city Artemis is going to be. We can either act now, or let our home degenerate into syndicate rule for generations. This isn't some theoretical scenario. They burned down a business. They murdered two people. There's a *huge* amount of money in play—they're not going to stop.

"This isn't a new thing. New York, Chicago, Tokyo, Moscow, Rome, Mexico City—they all went through *hell* to control their mob infestations. And those are the success stories. Big chunks of South America are *still* under cartel control. Let's not do that. Let's take care of the cancer before it can spread."

I looked each person in the eyes. "I'm not asking you to do this for me. I'm asking you to do it for Artemis. We can't let O Palácio take over. This is our one chance. They're bringing an *army* to town. Once those enforcers are here, we'll *never* be able to shut down Sanchez's oxygen flow. It'll be guarded better than Fort Knox."

I paused briefly just in case anyone wanted to argue that point. No one did. "Look, we've got a lot of planning to do so let's cut the bullshit. Bob: You're a marine. You spent half your life protecting the United States. Now Artemis is your home and it's in danger. Will you protect it?"

That hit him where it counted. I could see it in his face.

I walked over to my father. "Dad, do it because this is the only way to save your daughter's life."

He pursed his lips. "Sleazy tactic, Jasmine."

I turned to Dale. "Do I even need to explain why you have to do it?"

Dale dodged the question by gesturing to Billy for another beer. "You're not a *complete* asshole, Jazz. I assume you have a plan to keep the workers from getting hurt?"

Bob raised his hand. "And how will you get into the bubble? Even without mail-order goons on the way, Sanchez has tight security."

"And what about the safety systems?" Svoboda asked. "I looked over the schematics your Earth buddy sent. The smelter has three redundant temperature-control systems and a fail-safe copper melt plug."

"And why do you need me at all?" Dad asked.

"All right, all right." I put out my hands. "I can answer all of that. But first I need to know: Are we done with the convincing part? Are we all on board?"

The room fell silent. Even Billy stopped his morning prep to see how it played out.

"I'm not convinced you're right," Bob said. "But I can't risk Artemis having the future you described. And they killed two of our people. I'm in."

Dad nodded. "In."

"You know I'm in," said Svoboda. "I love a good caper!"

"Me too," said Lene. "I mean . . . the being in part. I'm unde-cided on capers."

"This buys me off," Dale said. "Done with the guilt about Tyler. No more of that shit."

I frowned. "I can't just stop being mad."

"No, but you can stop wallowing in it. And you can talk to me like a normal human being." He swigged his beer without break-ing eye contact. "That's my price."

"Fine," I said. I wasn't sure how I'd accomplish that, but for the sake of the city I had to swallow my pride.

Bob used his towering form and military bearing to clear a path through the Port of Entry. Dad and I followed behind, pushing a cartful of welding supplies.

I spotted Trigger in his parking space. I hadn't had opportu-nity to use him lately. I didn't have time for deliveries during all the chaos my life had become. I missed the little guy. Maybe I'd drive him around just for the hell of it when this was all over.

Bob led us to one corner of the huge chamber. He'd set up tem-porary walls. We went around them and into the ad-hoc work-room.

"I hope this'll do," said Bob. He gestured to the detached air shelter in the center of the room. "It's the biggest one I could find."

The cylindrical pressure vessel had a single manual hatch and four air tanks. On the back, there was a battery system to power internal fans and a chemical CO_2-absorption system. Over the main hatch a sign read MAX CAPACITY: 4 PERSONS. MAX DURATION: 72 HOURS.

"Where did you get it?" Dad asked warily.

"My house. It's my own family emergency shelter."

"Shit," I said. "You didn't have to do that, Bob."

"I knew Ammar wouldn't want me stealing one. Besides, you'll buy me a new one."

"Apparently I will." Dammit. That'd set me back a few thousand slugs for sure.

Dad inspected the shelter with his experienced eye. He walked a lap around it, looking every detail up and down. "This will do."

"All right. I'll leave you to it," said Bob. "Let me know if you need anything."

Bob walked around the temporary wall and out of the room. That left me and Dad staring at each other.

I picked up a welding mask from the cart. "Just like old times, huh? Been a while since we did a project together."

"Nine years." He threw a jumpsuit at me. "Wear the safety gear. All of it."

"Oh, come on. The suit's hot as hell and—"

He cut me off with a look. It's like I was sixteen again. I grudgingly climbed into the jumpsuit and started sweating immediately. Ugh.

"How are we doing this?" I asked.

He reached into the cart and hefted out a stack of aluminum sheets. "We'll cut the hole in the back. We'll have to move the tanks and batteries but that won't be a problem."

I put the welding mask on. "And then what? How do we make a connection point?"

He leaned the panels against the vessel. "We're going to weld these around the new hole to make a skirt."

I picked one of the panels up. I spotted the manufacturer's logo stamped in the corner. "Now, that is ironic. This is from Sanchez Aluminum."

"They make quality material," Dad said.

"Landvik Aluminum will make quality material too." I put the panel down. "Will a corner weld hold against a vacuum?"

He took out a Sharpie and uncapped it. "We won't have a

corner. We'll soften the panels with unfocused torches and bend them over the curvature of the pressure vessel. We'll assemble them into a cylinder." He looked up at me. "And how many panels will that take?"

Always a goddamned quiz.

"Well," I said, "we shouldn't bend five-millimeter stock more than a fifty-centimeter-radius turn. I'm guessing about six to make the full arc."

"Six would work," he said. "We'll use eight to be safe. Now, hand me the tape measure."

I did as he asked. He carefully measured and marked points on the shelter.

"So when's the lecture coming?" I asked.

"You're an adult. It's not my place to lecture you on anything."

"But you'll continue the passive-aggressive barbs, right? I wouldn't want to miss out on those."

He stood up. "I've never pretended to approve of your choices, Jasmine. I have no obligation to. But I don't try to control you either. Not since you moved out. Your life is your own."

"Yay me," I said.

"This is a terrible situation you've landed in," he said. "I'm choosing the lesser of two evils by helping you. I've never broken the law before in my life."

I winced and looked at my feet. "I really am sorry to drag you into this."

"What's done is done," he said. "Now, put your mask on and hand me a cutting head."

I put my mask on and gave him the desired tool from the cart. He fixed the head and checked it twice. Then he meticulously checked the gas-mixture valves. Then he rechecked the cutting head.

"What's up, Dad? You're slow as snot today."

"Just being thorough."

"Are you kidding? I've seen you fire up a torch with one hand and set mixture levels with the other at the same time. Why are you—"

Oh. I stopped talking.

This wasn't a normal job. Tomorrow, his daughter's life would rely on the quality of these welds. It slowly dawned on me that, to him, this was the most critical project he'd ever done. He would accept nothing short of his absolute best. And if that meant taking all day, so be it.

I stood back and let him work. After more fastidious double checks, he got started. I assisted and did what I was told. We may have our friction, but when it came to welding he was the master and I was the apprentice.

Very few people get a chance to quantify how much their father loves them. But I did. The job should have taken forty-five minutes, but Dad spent three and a half hours on it. My father loves me 366 percent more than he loves anything else.

Good to know.

I sat on the edge of Svoboda's bed and watched him set up.

He'd really gone all out. In addition to the normal monitor on his desk, he'd mounted four other monitors to the wall.

He typed on the keyboard and magically brought each monitor to life.

"A little overboard, don't you think?" I said.

He continued typing. "Two cameras on your EVA suit, two on Dale's, and I need a screen for diagnostics. That's five screens."

"Could have been windows on the same screen, though, right?"

"Pfft. Philistine."

I flopped back onto the bed and sighed. "On a scale from one to 'invade Russia in winter,' how stupid is this plan?"

"Risky as all hell, but I don't see what else you can do.

Besides"—he turned to me with a grin—"you have your own personal Svoboda. How can you lose?"

I snickered. "But have I covered every angle?"

He shrugged. "No such thing. But for what it's worth, you got everything I can think of."

"That means a lot," I said. "You're pretty thorough."

"Well, there is one thing," he said.

"Shit. What?"

"Well, it's half of a thing." He turned back to his computer and brought up the Sanchez bubble schematics. "The methane tanks bother me."

"How so?" I walked over and hovered behind him. My hair dangled on his face a little, but he didn't seem to mind.

"There's thousands of liters of liquid methane here."

"Why do they need methane?"

"The rocket fuel they manufacture is about one percent methane. It's needed as a combustion regulator. They import it from Earth in big-ass tanks."

"Okay, what's your concern?"

"It's flammable. Like . . . super-duper flammable." He pointed to a different part of the schematic. "And there's a huge staging tank of pure oxygen over here."

"And then I'm going to add a bunch of molten steel to the room," I said. "What could go wrong?"

"Right, that's my concern," he said. "But it shouldn't be a problem. By the time the smelter melts, there won't be anyone around."

"Yeah," I said. "And if the tanks do leak and explode that's great. Even more damage!"

"I guess," he said, clearly not convinced. "It just bugs me, you know? It's not part of the plan. I don't like things that don't match a plan."

"If that's the worst thing you can think of, I'm in good shape."

"Guess so," he said.

I stretched my back. "I wonder if I'll sleep tonight."

"You crashing here?"

"Eh . . ." I said. "Ngugi isn't going to sell me out again. Have I mentioned she's a bitch?"

"It's come up."

"Anyway, now no one can track me down by my Gizmo. So I can pay for a hotel. I'll probably be up late fretting, anyway. I wouldn't want to keep you awake."

"Okay," he said. Was there a hint of disappointment in his voice?

I put my hands on his shoulders. Not sure why, but I did. "Thanks for always being in my corner. It means a lot to me."

"Sure." He craned his neck around to look up at me. "I'll always be there for you, Jazz."

We looked at each other for a moment.

"Hey, did you try out the condom yet?" he asked.

"Goddammit, Svoboda!" I said.

"What? I'm waiting for feedback here."

I threw my hands up and walked away.

The huge door to the freight airlock lumbered open and revealed the desolate lunar landscape beyond.

Dale checked a reading on the rover's control panel. "Pressure is good, air mix A-okay, CO_2 absorption on automatic."

I looked over the screens in front of my seat. "Batteries at one hundred percent, wheel motor diagnostics are green, comms are five-by-five."

He grabbed the control stick. "Port of Entry Airlock, request permission to disembark."

"Granted," came Bob's voice over the intercom. "Take good care of my rover, Shapiro."

"Will do."

"Try not to screw it up, Bashara," Bob said.

"Bite me," I said.

Dale slapped the Mute button and shot me a look. "You know what, Jazz? We're breaking every guild rule in the book. If we get caught, Bob and I will both get kicked out. Forever. We're risking our livelihood here. Can you be a *little* more fucking considerate?!"

I unmuted the mike. "Uh . . . thanks, Bob. For . . . all this."

"Copy," came the clipped reply.

Dale piloted the rover out of the airlock and onto the regolith. I expected things to get bumpy but the suspension was very smooth. That, plus the area just outside had been flattened and smoothed over by years of frequent use.

Bob's rover was, simply put, the best rover on the moon. This was no dune buggy with awkward seats for EVA-suited passengers. It was fully pressurized and had a spacious interior with supplies and power enough to last for days. Both of our EVA suits were stored neatly in racks along the walls. The rover even had a partitioned airlock in the rear, meaning the cabin never had to lose pressure, even if someone went outside.

Dale looked straight ahead while he drove. He refused to even cast me a sideways glance.

"You know what?" I said. "It's the EVA Guild that's a threat to your livelihood, not me. Maybe protectionist bullshit isn't the best policy."

"You're probably right. We should let everyone play with the airlocks. I'm sure we can trust untrained people not to annihilate the city with the press of a button."

"Oh, please. The guild could have members operate the airlocks and let people manage their EVAs themselves. They're just greedy fucks running a labor cartel. Pimps went out of style a long time ago, you know."

He snickered despite himself. "I've missed our political arguments."

"Me too."

I checked the time. We had a fairly tight schedule to keep. So far, so good.

We turned southeast and headed toward the Berm a kilometer away. Not a long drive, but it would have been a very long walk, especially dragging the modified air shelter with us.

The shelter clanked against the roof as we entered the rougher terrain. We both looked up at the source of the noise, then at each other.

"It's strapped down tight, right?" he asked.

"You were there when we secured it," I said.

Clang.

I winced. "If it falls off, we pick it up, I guess. It would cost us time we don't have, but we could hustle."

"And hope it didn't break."

"No way it breaks," I said. "Dad did the welds. They'll last until the sun goes cold."

"Yeah, about that," he said, "will you be able to handle the next set of welds?"

"Yes."

"And what if you can't?"

"I'll die," I said. "So I'm fairly motivated to get it right."

He turned left slightly. "Hang on. We're crossing over the pipe."

The air pipeline that carried freshly minted oxygen from the smelter to Armstrong Bubble lay along the ground.

On Earth, no one would be insane enough to ship pressurized oxygen gas through a pipeline. But on the lunar surface, there's nothing to burn. Also, on Earth, they usually bury pipelines to protect the system from weather, animals, and idiot humans. We don't do that here. Why would we? We don't have weather or animals and all the idiot humans are mostly confined to the city.

Dale managed the controls as the front end of the rover bucked up and down, then the rear did the same.

"Is that really safe?" I asked. "Driving over a high-pressure line like that?"

He adjusted one of the wheel motor controls. "That pipe's walls are eight centimeters thick. We couldn't hurt it if we tried."

"I have welding equipment. I could hurt it."

"You're a pedantic little shit, you know that?"

"Yeah."

I looked through the roof porthole. Earth hung in the sky—a half-Earth, just like Lene's watch had said.

We'd strayed far enough from the city that the terrain became wholly natural. Dale navigated us around a boulder. "Tyler says hi."

"Give him my best."

"He really does care about—"

"Don't."

My Gizmo rang. I put it in a dashboard slot and it connected to the rover's audio system. Of course the rover had an audio system. Bob traveled in style. "Yo."

"Yo, Jazz," came Svoboda's voice. "Where you guys at now? I don't have a camera feed."

"Still en route. The suit cams are offline. Is Dad there?"

"Yup, right next to me. Say hi, Ammar!"

"Hello, Jasmine," said Dad. "Your friend is . . . interesting."

"You get used to him," I said. "Say hi to Dale."

"No."

Dale snorted.

"Call me when you're suited up," said Svoboda.

"Will do. Later." I hung up.

Dale shook his head. "Man, your dad really hates me. And it's not about Tyler either. He hated me before all that."

"Not for the reasons you think," I said. "I still remember when I told him you were gay. I thought he'd be pissed off, but he was relieved. He actually smiled."

"Huh?" Dale said.

"Once he found out you weren't nailing me, he warmed up to you a lot. But then, you know, then came the whole stealing-my-boyfriend thing."

"Right."

We crested a small rise and saw the flatlands ahead of us. The Berm stood a hundred meters away. Just beyond it would be the reactor complex and Sanchez's bubble.

"Fifteen minutes till we get there," Dale said, apparently reading my thoughts. "Nervous?"

"Shitting myself."

"Good," he said. "I know you think you're flawless on EVAs, but remember you flunked that test."

"Thanks for the pep talk."

"I'm just saying a little humility's good on an EVA."

I stared out the side window. "Believe me, this past week has been humiliating enough."

13

I looked at the silver dome of the Sanchez smelter bubble. Again.

My previous visit had been just six days earlier, but it seemed like forever ago. Of course, things were a little different this time. There'd only be one harvester out there doing its thing. That's okay, I wasn't after the harvester, anyway. That was old news.

Dale brought us up to the edge of the bubble, did a three-point turn, and pointed the rear of the rover at the wall.

"Distance?" he asked.

I checked my screen. "Two point four meters." Proximity read-outs are a frilly feature for cars on Earth, but critically important for lunar rovers. Crashing your pressure vessel into things is bad. It can lead to unscheduled dying.

Satisfied, Dale engaged the physical brake. "All right. Ready to suit up?"

"Yup."

We climbed out of our chairs and crawled to the rear of the vessel.

We both stripped down to our underwear. (What? I'm supposed to be demure around the gay guy?) Then we put on our coolant garments. The daylight outside could boil water—EVA suits need central cooling.

Next came the pressure suits themselves. I helped him into

his and he helped me into mine. Finally, we did pressure tests, tank tests, readout tests, and a bunch of other shit.

Once all the checks were done, we prepared to egress.

The rover airlock could fit two, though it was snug. We squeezed in and sealed the hatch.

"Ready for depress?" Dale asked via the radio.

"Pretty depressed, yeah," I said.

"Don't joke around. Not with airlock procedures."

"Sheesh, you really suck the air out of the room, you know that?"

"Jazz!"

"Copy, ready for decompression."

He turned a crank. Air hissed from the chamber to the vacuum outside. No need for a high-tech pump system. It's not like oxygen was in short supply; thanks to smelting, Artemis had so much we didn't know what to do with it all. . . .

For the moment, anyway (evil sardonic laugh).

He spun the handle, pushed the door open, and stepped out. I followed.

He climbed the ladder to the rover's roof and unhitched the rigging. I went to the other side and did the same. Then, together, we lowered the modified air shelter to the ground.

Weighing in at five hundred kilograms, it took both of us to make sure it came down gently.

"Try to keep dust off the skirt," I said.

"Copy."

Dad had done a number on the shelter. You could hardly recognize it. It had a large hole in the rear with a half-meter-wide aluminum skirt all around it. It looked like an engine bell. Some might say putting a huge hole in a pressure vessel is a bad idea. I have no rebuttal.

I clambered back up to the rover's roof and collected my welding gear. "Ready to receive?"

He positioned himself below me and held up his arms. "Ready."

I handed him the tanks, torches, tool belt, and other accessories I'd need for the job. He placed each on the ground. Finally,
I pulled a huge bag out of its dedicated container.

"Here comes the inflatable tunnel," I said. I shoved it off the
roof.

He caught it and laid it on the ground.

I hopped off the roof and landed next to him.

"You shouldn't jump down that far," he said.

"You shouldn't fuck other people's boyfriends."

"Oh, come on!"

"I could get used to this new relationship we have," I said.
"Help me get all this crap over to the bubble."

"Yeah, yeah."

Together we carried or dragged everything to the wall.

The arc of the dome, broken into two-meter triangles, was
vertical at ground level. I selected a reasonably clean triangle
and dusted it off with a wire brush. There's no weather on the
moon, but there is static electricity. Fine lunar dust gets everywhere and sticks to everything with the slightest charge.

"Okay, this one," I said. "Help me move the shelter into position."

"Copy."

Together, we hoisted the air shelter and shuffled it over to the
dome. We pressed the aluminum skirt against the shiny wall
then set the shelter down.

"Goddamn, Dad's good," I said.

"Jesus," Dale said.

He'd done an absolutely *perfect* job on the skirt. I mean, okay,
he just had to make the point of contact with the wall flat, but
holy hell. There was less than a millimeter of gap between the
skirt and the wall.

I brought up my arm readout, which was basically just a

fancy external screen for my Gizmo. The Gizmo itself was safely inside the suit with me (they're not made to handle the rigors of the outdoors). I tapped a few buttons and made the call.

"Yo, Jazz," said Svoboda. "How's tricks?"

"So far, so good. How's the camera feed?"

"Working perfectly. I've got your suit cams on the screens."

"Be careful out there," came Dad's voice.

"I will, Dad. Don't worry. Dale, you getting the phone audio?"

"Affirm," said Dale.

I walked back to the skirt and faced it so the helmet cam would point at it. "Good skirt alignment. Like . . . *really* good."

"Hmm," said Dad. "I see some gaps. But smaller than the bead you'll be making. Should be fine."

"Dad, this is some of the best precision I've ever—"

"Let's get to work," he interrupted.

I dragged the oxygen and acetylene tanks to the site and fixed the torch head.

"All right," Dad said. "Do you know how to start a flame in a vacuum?"

"Of course," I said. No way in hell I would admit I learned it the hard way just a few days ago. I set the oxygen mix very high, sparked the flame, and got it stabilized.

When I'd worked over the harvesters earlier I'd done very rudimentary joins. I just needed it to hold the pressure in long enough to blow up. These joins would be a lot more complicated. The job would've been trivial for Dad, but he didn't know anything about EVAs. Hence our teamwork.

"Looks like a good flame," Dad said. "Start at the crown and let the bead puddle downward. Surface tension will keep it aligned with the gap."

"What about the airflow pressure?" I said. "Won't it blow droplets into the skirt?"

"Some, but not much. There are no eddy forces around the flame in a vacuum. There's just the pressure of the flame itself."

I held a rod of aluminum stock to the top of the skirt and set the flame on it. It was awkward in my EVA suit, but not too bad. A bead of molten metal formed at the tip and dribbled down. Just as Dad predicted, it wicked along the gap and filled the crack.

By habit, I brought the flame down to the fill site to keep the bead molten.

"No need for that," Dad said. "The metal will stay liquid longer than you expect. There's no air to convey the heat away. Some gets lost through the metal, but the state-change soaks up most of the energy. It can't radiate too far."

"I'll take your word for it," I said. I returned the flame to the aluminum stock.

Dale stood a few meters away, ready to save my life.

And there I was again. Melting metal while in a vacuum. If a blob melted my EVA suit, my life would be in Dale's hands. If I sprung a leak, he'd have to haul me into the rover airlock. I wouldn't be able to do it myself because I'd be too busy dying of asphyxiation.

Bit by bit, I worked my way around the perimeter of the skirt. Dad told me when I went too fast or slow. Finally, I got back to the start of the seam.

"Whew," I said. "Time for a pressure test."

"No it isn't," Dad said. "Run another line. All the way around. Make sure you completely cover the first weld."

"Are you kidding me?!" I protested. "Dad, that weld is *solid*."

"Run another line, Jasmine," he said firmly. "You're not in any hurry. You're just impatient."

"Actually I *am* in a hurry. I have to get this done before the Sanchez shift change."

"Run. Another. Line."

I groaned like a teenage girl (Dad really brought that out in me). "Dale, hand me more rods."

"No," Dale said.

"What?"

"As long as you have that torch in your hand, I won't take my eyes off you, I won't be more than three meters away, and I won't have anything in my hands."

I groaned louder.

It took another twenty minutes, but I ran another seam around the skirt under Dad's watchful eye.

"Well done," said Dad.

"Thanks, Dad," I said. He was right. I'd done a good job. Now I had an air shelter perfectly welded to the smelter bubble's hull. All I had to do was cut a hole in the wall from inside the shelter and I'd have a ghetto airlock.

I set the torch down on a nearby rock and spread my hands at Dale. Now that I met his stringent requirements for safety, he ambled toward the inflatable.

The inflatable was the same kind I'd helped set up during the Queensland Glass fire—an accordion tube with a rigid airlock connector at each end. He and I each grabbed a hoop and backed away from each other. I headed toward the newly welded air shelter while Dale went to the rover.

I loaded all my welding equipment and tanks into the tunnel, then connected my end of it to the air shelter. Then I joined Dale and we both climbed into the rover airlock. Together we pulled the tunnel's other connector into place.

I stared down the tube toward the still-sealed air-shelter hatch.

"Time to test it, I guess," I said.

He reached for the valve. "Keep on your toes. Just 'cause we're in EVA suits doesn't make us safe. If we misconnected the tunnel, we could be in for an explosive decompression."

"Thanks for the tip," I said. "I'll be ready to jump out of the way if a pressure wave moving the speed of sound comes at me."

"You could be less of an ass."

"I could," I said. "But it's not likely."

He turned the valve and a foggy plume of air rushed in from the pressurized rover compartment. I checked my suit readouts and saw we were up to 2 kPa—about 10 percent of normal Artemis pressure.

An alarm blared from inside the rover.

"The fuck is that?" I said.

"Leak warning," Dale said. "The rover knows how much air it should take to fill the airlock, and we've gone way past that. We're filling this whole tunnel."

"Problem?"

"No," he said. "We've got plenty in the tanks. Way more than we need. Bob saw to that."

"Nice."

Slowly, the tunnel inflated. It held pressure perfectly, of course. This was exactly what it was designed to do—connecting one hatch to another.

"Looks good," Dale said. He turned the hatch crank and opened the rover's inner airlock door. He climbed into the main compartment and settled into the driver's seat. The rover was designed to accommodate a driver with or without an EVA suit.

He checked the control panel. "Twenty point four kPa, one hundred percent oxygen. Good to go."

"Here goes nothing," I said. I popped the vents of my EVA suit. I took a few breaths. "Air's good."

Dale joined me in the connector and helped me de-suit.

"J-J-Jesus." I shivered. When you release pressurized gas it gets cold. By filling the tunnel from the rover's high-pressure tanks, we'd made a goddamned meat locker.

"Here." Dale handed me my jumpsuit. I put it on faster than I'd ever put on clothes before. Well . . . second fastest (my high school boyfriend's parents came home earlier than expected one day).

Then he handed me his own jumpsuit. He was a big enough

guy that his clothes fit over mine easily. I didn't even argue. I leapt right in. After a minute, I warmed up to something bearable.

"You all right?" he asked. "Your lips are blue."

"I'm okay," I said through chattering teeth. "Once I fire up the torch, it'll be plenty warm in here."

I pulled my Gizmo out of its holster on the EVA suit, then popped an earbud into my ear. "You still there, guys?"

"We're here!" said Svoboda.

A thought struck me. "Did you watch me strip on Dale's video feed?"

"Yup! Thanks for the show!"

"Ahem," said Dad's voice.

"Oh, relax, Mr. B," said Svoboda. "She kept her underwear on."

"Still . . ." Dad protested.

"All right, all right," I said. "Svoboda, consider that payment for all the favors you're doing me. Now, Dad: Any prelim advice on this cut?"

"Let's get a look at the material."

I walked down the tunnel toward the air shelter and Dale followed close behind. I glanced back at him. "You going to be on my ass like that through the whole thing?"

"Pretty much," said Dale. "If there's a breach, I'll have to get your un-suited body down the tunnel and into the rover. I'll have three or four minutes before you get permanent brain damage. So yeah. I'm going to hang nearby."

"Well, don't get too close. I need elbow room to work and you don't want the flame anywhere near your suit."

"Agreed."

I turned the air-shelter valve and let air from the tunnel into the shelter. We listened to the hiss closely. If it stopped, that meant the skirt weld was airtight. If it just kept hissing that meant there was a leak and we'd have to go back out there and find it.

The hiss grew more and more quiet, eventually coming to

a stop. I cranked the valve open all the way and there was no change. "Seal's good," I said.

"Well done!" Dad exclaimed over the radio.

"Thanks."

"No, seriously," he said. "You made a three-meter-long airtight weld while wearing an EVA suit. You really could have been a master."

"Dad . . ." I said, a note of warning in my voice.

"All right, all right."

He couldn't see my smile, though. It really was a hell of a weld.

I cranked the hatch open and stepped in. The metal tube was freezing cold. Water condensed on the walls. I gestured Dale to the front. He turned on his helmet lights and got close to the weld site so Dad could see it through the camera.

"The inside edge of the weld looks good to me," I said.

"Agreed," said Dad. "Make sure Mr. Shapiro stays nearby, though."

"I'll be right behind her," Dale said. He stepped back into the connector.

I craned my head back to Dale. "Are we sure the pressure in here is *exactly* twenty point four kPa?"

Dale checked his arm readouts. "Yes. Twenty point four kPa."

We had pressurized to 20.4 kPa instead of Artemis's standard 21. Why? Because of how double-hull systems work.

Between the two hulls, there's a bunch of crushed rock (you knew that). But there's also air. And that air is at 20.4 kPa—about 90 percent of Artemis pressure. Also, the space between the hulls isn't a giant empty shell. It's partitioned into hundreds of equilateral triangles, two meters on a side. Each of those compartments has a pressure sensor inside.

So outside there's vacuum, between the hulls there's 90 percent Artemis pressure, and inside the bubble there's full Artemis pressure.

If there's a breach in the outer hull, the compartment's air will leak out to the vacuum outside. But if there's a breach in the inner hull, the compartment will be flooded with higher-pressure air from inside the bubble.

It's an elegant system. If the compartment pressure goes down, you know there's a leak in the outer hull. If it goes up, you know there's a leak in the inner hull.

But I didn't want a hull-breach alarm going off in the middle of my operation, so we made damn sure our air pressure matched the inside-hull pressure.

I made a quick inspection of my torch nozzle to make sure it hadn't warped in the temperature changes it had just been exposed to. I didn't see any problems.

"Dad, according to the specs, this will be the same as a city bubble hull—six centimeters of aluminum, a meter of crushed regolith, then another six centimeters of aluminum."

"All right," said Dad. "The initial breakthrough will be messy because of the thickness of the material. Just stay with it and try not to wobble. The steadier your hand the faster it'll breach."

I pulled the oxygen and acetylene tanks into the shelter and prepped the torch.

"Don't forget your breather mask," said Dad.

"I know, I know." I'd completely forgotten. Oxyacetylene fills the air with toxic smoke. Normally it's not enough to matter, but in a confined pressure vessel you need your own breathing apparatus. Hey, I would have remembered once I started coughing uncontrollably.

I reached into my duffel and pulled out a mask. The attached air tank had a little backpack rig to keep it out of the way. I put it on and took a few breaths just to make sure it worked. "I'm ready to fire up. Any other advice?"

"Yes," he said. "The regolith has a high iron content. Try not to linger in one place for too long or it might clump up around the cut site. Too much of that and you'll have a very hard time pulling the plug out."

"Got it," I said.

I put on my welding helmet and fired up the torch. Dale took a step back. However fearless EVA masters may be, there's still a deep, basic instinct in all humans to avoid fire.

I grinned. Finally I'd get some revenge. Time to cut a hole in Sanchez's gut.

14

I adjusted the gas mixture until I had a long flame. I picked a spot on the wall, dug in, and held the torch as still as I could. The massive heat plus the ready supply of oxygen dug away at the metal, boring a deeper and deeper hole.

Finally, it broke through. I can't tell you exactly how I knew. I just knew. Maybe it's the sound? The sputter of the flame? Not sure. In any event, the cut had begun.

"No airflow in or out," I said. "Looks like a pressure match. Good job, Dale."

"Thanks."

I moved the torch along at a deliberate pace and cut along a meter-wide circle. I beveled the edges so the plug could fall out a little easier when the cut was complete.

"Running a little behind now," said Dale.

"Copy," I said. But I didn't speed up. I was already going as fast as I could. Trying to go faster would just screw up the cut and end up costing me more time.

I finally completed the circle and the plug tilted forward. I turned off the torch and hopped back as an avalanche of gray regolith flooded into the chamber.

I threw off my welding helmet and pressed the breather mask hard against my face. I sure as hell didn't want to breathe that dust. I like my lungs without barbed death particles in them, thanks.

My eyes stung and teared up. I winced in pain.

"You all right?" Dale asked.

The mask muffled my voice. "Shoulda worn goggles," I said.

I reached up to wipe my eyes, but Dale caught my arm. "Don't!"

"Right," I said.

You know what's worse than having barbed rocks in your eyes? *Grinding* barbed rocks into your eyes. I resisted the urge, though just barely.

I waited for the dust to settle. Then, with stinging eyes and blurry vision, I stepped toward the hole. And that's when the electric shocks sparked off my body.

I yelped, more out of surprise than pain.

Dale checked his readouts. "Careful. The humidity is nearly zero."

"Why?"

"No idea."

I took another step and got another salvo of static discharges. "Goddammit!"

"Are you capable of learning?" Dale said.

"Aww shit," I said. I pointed to the slowly growing pile of regolith in front of the hole. "It's the fill material. Artemis air is humidified, but the air in hull compartments is bone dry."

"Why?"

"Water's corrosive and expensive. Why would you put that in your hull? That dirt acted as a desiccant and yanked all the moisture out of the air."

Dale detached the water-storage unit from his suit, opened the canister, and pulled out a quarter-filled plastic bag. He ripped the corner off the bag and pinched it with his fingers. It's amazing how much manual dexterity a true EVA master can achieve with those clunky gloves on.

He squirted me in the face with the water.

"What the fu—"

"Keep your eyes open. And look into the stream."

I did as instructed. It was hard at first, but the sheer relief at having the dust rinsed out kept me going. Then he sprayed my clothes, arms, and legs.

"Better?" he asked.

I shook my head to clear water off my face. "Yeah, better," I said.

Our ad-hoc wet T-shirt contest would protect me from any further discharges. At least for a while. Of course, dust collected on me and became a disgusting gray mud. I wouldn't be winning any beauty contests, but at least I was comfortable.

Next step: I had to dig the fill material out to expose the pressure sensor and, more important, to get at the inner hull.

I pressed my finger to my earbud. "Svoboda and Dad: I'm going to be digging for a while. I'll call back in a bit."

"We'll be here," said Svoboda.

I cut the connection. "Give me a hand digging this out," I said.

Dale held up a shovel. "There's two kinds of people in this world: those with EVA suits, and those who dig."

I snorted. "Okay, first off, if we're doing *The Good, the Bad, and the Ugly*, I get to be Clint Eastwood, not you. Second off, get your lazy ass to work and help me!"

"I have to be ready to drag your sorry ass back to the rover if things go wrong." He held the shovel out to me again. "Accept your inner Eli Wallach and get digging."

I groaned and took the shovel from him. This was going to take a while.

"We're running behind, you know," he said.

"I know."

Right around that time, Bob was being a pain in the ass, as usual. But this time he was doing it *for* me instead of *to* me. I wasn't present for any of this. I was busy digging dirt out of a wall. But I heard about it all later on.

Sanchez Aluminum owned dedicated train tracks from the Aldrin Port of Entry to their smelter. Three times a day, the train loaded up twenty-four employees and headed out to the facility. The short, one-kilometer trip only took a few minutes. They switched shifts, and the previous shift returned to Artemis on the same train.

I'd timed my little heist to coincide with their shift change. But I was running behind. I needed to be *inside* the facility before the train got there. And I still hadn't cut the inner hull.

The Sanchez workers conglomerated at the train station. The train had already docked and its hatch stood open. The conductor pulled out her Gizmo scanner in preparation to take fees for the ride. Yes, Sanchez Aluminum charged Sanchez Aluminum employees to ride a Sanchez Aluminum train to the Sanchez Aluminum smelter. Your basic 1800s-style "company store" bullshit.

Bob walked up to the conductor and put his hand on her scanner. "Hold up, Mirza."

"Problem, Bob?" she asked.

"We're doing a freight-airlock leak inspection. Safety protocols say no one can operate another airlock in the port while that's in progress."

"Are you kidding me?" Mirza said. "It has to be right now?"

"Sorry. We detected an anomaly and we have to run the test before tomorrow's lander."

"For chrissake, Bob." She gestured to the assembled crowd. "I've got twenty-four people here who need to get to work. And twenty-four more at the smelter waiting to come home."

"Yeah, sorry. The test ran long. We thought we'd be done by now."

"How much longer?"

"Not sure. Ten or fifteen minutes, maybe? I can't make any promises."

She turned to the crowd. "Sorry, folks. We've got a delay. Get comfortable—it'll be around fifteen minutes."

A collective groan arose from the crowd.

"I'm sure as hell not staying late to make up for it," one worker grumbled to another.

"Sorry about this," Bob said. "Let me make it up to you: I've got three tickets to the Artemis Acrobats show at the Playhouse. They're yours. Take your husbands out and have a good time."

Mirza's face lit up. "Wow! All right then. All is forgiven!"

A ridiculous overpayment, if you ask me. Those tickets cost 3,000 slugs each! Oh well. Bob's money, not mine.

After an eternity of digging and a great many profanities, I finally cleared out the dirt in the hull compartment. I flopped onto my back and wheezed.

"I think you invented new swearwords," said Dale. "Like . . . what's a 'funt'?"

"I think it's pretty clear from context," I said.

He loomed over me. "Get up. We're way behind and Bob can only delay the train for so long."

I flipped him off.

He kicked me. "Get up, you lazy fuck."

I groaned and got back to my feet.

I'd found the compartment's pressure sensor during the "dig a hole to China" phase of the operation. (Yes, that idiom still applies on the moon. I felt like I'd just dug a 384,000-kilometer hole.)

Our little "fool the pressure sensor" game had worked till now, but as soon as I breached the inner hull, the pressure on our side would go up to Artemis Standard. Then the sensor would say "Holy shit! Twenty-one kPa air! There's a hole in the inner hull!"

The alarm would go off, people would freak out, and the EVA

masters would come take a look, and we'd get caught. Dale and Bob would get drummed out of the guild, but I wouldn't live long enough to see it, because loyal Sanchez people would have stabbed me in the face.

Oh? You don't think a bunch of nebbish control-room nerds would do something like that? Think again. *Someone* at Sanchez tried to kill me with a harvester, remember?

The sensor itself was a metal cylinder with a couple of wires attached. The wires had a fair bit of play, which was handy. I pulled a steel can with a screw top out of the duffel. I'd modified it earlier for just this purpose by putting a little notch in the lid.

I put the sensor in the can and slid the cabling into the notch. Then I screwed on the lid. After that, I put six layers of duct tape over the point where the wires entered the lid. I didn't feel great about that part. Only an idiot relies on duct tape to maintain a pressure seal, but I didn't have a choice. At least the higher pressure would be on the outside so the tape would be pushed against the hole.

"Think that'll do it?" Dale asked.

"We'll know in a minute. Take us up to Artemis Standard."

Dale tapped his arm controls. Of course Bob's rover could be controlled remotely. If it was a luxury feature, Bob's rover had it.

Fresh air echoed down the inflatable tunnel, and my ears popped with the slight pressure change.

I watched the can intently. The tape over the hole bowed in slightly, but otherwise held. I pressed my ear to the inner hull wall.

"No alarms," I said. I called Svoboda back.

"Yo!" said Svoboda. "Criminal Support Team ready and waiting."

"I'm not sure I like that title," said Dad.

"I'm about to make the inner hull cut," I said. "Any last-minute advice, Dad?"

"Don't get caught."

I flipped my mask down. "Everybody's a comedian."

I got to cutting. The inner hull was the same as the outer hull: six centimeters of aluminum. And just like the outer hull, the cut only took a couple of minutes. This time I beveled the cut so the plug would fall outward instead of in. I didn't have a choice on the outer hull, but as a rule I prefer flesh-boilingly hot metal to fall *away* from me.

I waited for the plug to finish its slow fall to the ground, then peeked inside.

The factory floor was a large hemisphere full of industrial machinery. The smelter dominated the center of the room. It stood a good ten meters tall, surrounded by pipes, power lines, and monitoring systems.

I couldn't see the control room from my vantage point. The smelter was in the way. That wasn't a coincidence, by the way. I picked that part of the hull specifically because it was in a blind spot. No matter how absorbed the staff might be with work, it's unlikely that twenty-four people would all fail to notice a flaming hole in the wall.

I poked my head through the hole to get a look around. Without thinking, I put my hand on the edge for balance.

"Fuck!" I snapped my hand back and shook it.

"Welding torches make things hot," Dale said.

I grimaced and checked for damage. My palm was a little red but it would be fine.

"You all right?"

"Yeah," I said. "I just wish you hadn't seen me do that."

"We saw it too!" said Svoboda's voice.

"Super," I said. "And on that note, I'm hanging up. I'll let you know when the deed is done."

I cut the connection.

I stepped through the opening, being very sure not to touch the edges again. Dale handed my duffel through. But when I tried to take it, he held on.

"You know," he said. "This hole isn't big enough for me to get through with my EVA suit on. If something goes wrong, I won't be able to help you."

"I know," I said.

"Be careful."

I nodded and pulled the duffel away. He watched from the hole while I snuck over to the smelter.

The unit itself wasn't much to look at. Just a big block with heavy metal pipes leading in and out. A bucket conveyor rose through a hole in the floor and fed anorthite grit to a hopper atop the smelter. Inside, a maelstrom of heat, electricity, and chemistry turned rocks into metals. But the outside was calm, slightly warm to the touch, and had a gentle hum.

I sat on the ground and peeked around the corner.

The control room looked out over the facility. Through the large glass windows I could see the staff going about their workday. Some sat at computers while others walked about with tablets. The entire back wall was covered with monitors showing every detail of the facility and its process.

One woman was clearly in charge. People came to her, spoke briefly, and she gave quick answers. That's a boss. I estimated her age at around fifty, and she had a Latino complexion. She turned to speak to someone and I finally saw her face. It was Loretta Sanchez. I recognized her from the pictures I'd seen online while researching the company.

She was the one who designed the smelter. She'd started Sanchez Aluminum. And she was so thoroughly owned by O Palácio, she might as well have had a collar on. Interesting that someone like her would be in the trenches with her employees instead of in a comfy Aldrin office.

The other employees were just . . . people. No horns or black capes. No cackling with steepled fingers. Just a bunch of working schmoes.

I crawled to the other end of the smelter, but that was as far as I could go. The thermal control systems were visible from the control room. I called Bob on my Gizmo.

"Go," said Bob.

"I'm in position. Release the train."

"Affirm." He hung up.

I waited behind the smelter. After ten minutes of impatient fidgeting, I finally heard a clunk echo through the walls. The train had arrived. Right now, the outgoing shift was bringing the incoming shift up to date. I had a short window—maybe ten minutes—before the train loaded up and left.

I still had the breather mask and portable oxygen supply. But now I added a pair of goggles from the duffel. They'd be important for what came next. I duct taped both the mask and goggles to my face—I needed an airtight seal this time.

So now I was a mud-covered freak with random shit taped to my face. I probably looked like something out of a horror movie. Oh well. I was about to be horrible.

I pulled a cylinder of gas from the duffel. I gripped the valve, then stopped and did one more check on my duct-tape seals. Okay, everything was all right. Back to the valve. I gave it a quarter-turn.

The bottle released pure chlorine gas into the air.

Chlorine gas is lung-dissolvingly dangerous. They used it as a weapon in World War I, and it worked very well. Where did I get ahold of a tank of compressed death? I had my pal Svoboda to thank for that. He stole it from the ESA chemistry lab.

The FFC Cambridge Process involved a bunch of molten calcium chloride. In theory it was all safely contained inside the sealed, extraordinarily hot smelter. But just in case the smelter had a failure, the facility had chlorine gas detectors all over the place. Very sensitive ones too. They were designed to raise the alarm well before the toxic gas could harm people.

I left the valve open briefly then sealed it again. Within seconds, the chlorine gas alarm went off. And my, what a show!

Yellow lights flashed to life in twenty different places. An incredibly loud alarm blared throughout the facility. I felt a breeze. The emergency circulation vents had sprung to life. They would replace all the air in the facility with fresh oxygen from an emergency reserve.

In the control room, the employees scrambled to safety. Normally, their procedure would be to get into the air shelter in the back of the room. But why would you do that when there's a train right there? It's much better to be in a train that can go back to town than sitting in an air shelter awaiting rescue. It didn't take them long to make their decision—they piled into the train and sealed its hatch.

It was probably cramped in there. Both shifts were sharing the train—a total of forty-eight people.

I snuck a peek at the control room and fist-pumped when I saw it empty. They'd done exactly what I wanted.

Obviously, I had to get everyone out of there before making the smelter melt down. I could have let the pressure alarm go off when I was cutting the inner hull—that would have made people skedaddle. But a pressure leak would bring emergency crews to the hole in the wall. That'd raise a few eyebrows once they saw the rover, makeshift airlock, an awkwardly blushing Dale, et cetera. A toxic gas leak was much better. That was a purely internal issue.

I opened the valve to the chlorine tank again—just a trickle. That way the ventilation system couldn't clear it out. And as long as the chlorine alert blared, the workers would stay in their train.

I didn't have to hide anymore. I walked around to the front of the smelter. Then I shimmied underneath it and into the catch basin below.

As a last-ditch defense against meltdowns, the smelter had a copper plug at the bottom of its tank. Copper has a higher melting point than the operating temperature of the bath, but a lower melting point than steel. So if things got too hot (1085°C to be exact), the copper would melt. The superheated salt bath would drain into the cement basin below. There'd be a hell of a mess to clean up, but the smelter itself would be saved.

Can't have that!

I pulled the welding equipment and my duffel into the pit with me. Once again, I would be welding upward. Sigh. And this time I was joining steel to steel with steel rods as stock. So, in case it wasn't clear: steel. Yay. Well, at least this time I wasn't in an EVA suit. Any molten steel that hit me would just disfigure me for life instead of killing me. So I had that going for me.

I got to work. I stayed well to the side as I joined the plate to the underbody. I admit I lost the bead a few times, sending a blob of flaming death to the ground. But I kept at it. After fifteen minutes, I had a solid steel plate covering the copper plug.

I wasn't sure what grade of steel the smelter walls were made of, but most grades melt at or below 1450°C. So, just to be safe, my plate and stock rods were Grade 416 with a melting point of 1530°C. The smelter would melt before my patch would.

The patch was thin, so you'd think it would melt first, but physics doesn't work that way. Before the temperature could get up to the patch's melting point of 1530°C, everything that could melt at a lower temperature had to melt first. And the melting point of the smelter walls was 1450°C. So, even though the patch was thin and the smelter was thick, the bottom of the smelter would give out before the patch got anywhere near its melting point.

Don't believe me? Put ice water in a saucepan and cook it. The water temperature will stay at 0°C until the last ice cube melts.

I crawled out from the pit and checked the control room. Still empty. But not for long. The train had left.

With all that chlorine in the air, it made sense to send the workers back to town. But once they got there, a bunch of hazmat-suited engineers would board and come right back. I had ten minutes for the train to get to town, call it another five for the changeover, then another ten until the enemy cavalry arrived. Twenty-five minutes.

I hurried to the thermal control box. I unscrewed four bolts and took the access panel off. I yanked out the thermocouple management board and produced a replacement board from my duffel. Svoboda had spent the previous evening piecing it together. Pretty simple, actually. It acted just like the normal board, but it would lie to the computer about the bath temperature, always reporting it low. I inserted it into the slot.

For verification purposes, Svoboda's replacement board had LCD readouts showing the actual and reported temperature. The actual temperature was 900°C and the reported temperature was 825°C. The computer, believing the temperature was too low, activated the main heater.

There was an audible "click" even though there was no relay. The power conduit—thickest power line I'd ever seen, by the way—actually squirmed for a moment when the current began. So much electricity flowed through that cable, the resulting magnetic field made it bounce around while it ramped up power. It settled down once the current got to full amperage.

I watched Svoboda's board. Soon, the actual temperature clicked up to 901 degrees. Then, in far less time, it rose to 902. Then directly to 904. Then 909.

"Shiiit," I said. That was way the hell faster than I expected. Turns out a massive power line carrying the bulk of two nuclear reactors' output can heat things up pretty quickly.

I left the access panel on the floor and ran back to my private entrance.

Dale waited for me in the inflatable connector. "Well?" he asked.

I shut the air-shelter door behind me. "Mission accomplished. The smelter's heating up *fast*. Let's get out of here."

"All right!" Dale held up his gloved hand.

I gave him a high five (can't leave a fella hanging). He bobbled down the tunnel toward the rover.

I took one last look at the air-shelter hatch to make sure it was sealed properly. Then I turned back and started down the tunnel—wait a minute.

I spun back to the hatch. I could swear I'd seen movement behind me.

The hatch had a small, round window. I drew closer to it and looked through. There, inspecting equipment along the far wall of the smelter bubble, was Loretta Sanchez.

I put both hands on my head. "Dale. We have a problem."

15

Sanchez peered at the emergency air system. She wore goggles and a breather mask. Apparently a little chlorine gas didn't scare her.

Dale, halfway down the inflatable, gestured to the rover. "Come on, Jazz! Let's go!"

"Loretta Sanchez is in there!"

"What?!"

I pointed to the airlock window. "She's just wandering around like she owns the place."

"She does own the place," Dale said. "Let's get out of here!"

"We can't leave her there."

"She's a smart woman. When the meltdown starts she'll leave."

"Where will she go?" I demanded.

"The train."

"The train left."

"The air shelter, then."

"That won't protect her from molten steel!" I turned to the hatch. "I have to get her."

Dale stomped back toward me. "Are you out of your mind?! These people tried to *kill* you, Jazz!"

"Whatever." I checked the tape on my mask and goggles. "Get to the rover. Be ready for a quick exit."

"Jazz—"

"Go!" I snapped.

He hesitated for a second—probably to decide if he could physically force me back to the rover. He wisely chose not to and headed down the inflatable.

I spun the hatch valve and stumbled back into the facility. Sanchez didn't notice me at first—her attention was on the emergency air system. Probably trying to figure out why it wasn't cleaning the air.

How does one introduce herself in a situation like this? I don't think Emily Post covered "saving an enemy's life during industrial sabotage" in her etiquette books. I went with a tried and true method.

"Hey!" I yelled.

She whipped around and grabbed her chest. "Goodness!"

She panted a few times and regained her composure. She was a little older and more weathered than the pictures I'd seen of her. Still, she was spry and healthy-looking for a fifty-year-old. "Who on God's gray moon are you?"

"That's not important," I said. "It's not safe here. Come with me."

She didn't budge. "You're not one of my employees. How did you get in here?"

"I cut a hole in the wall."

"What?" She scanned the walls to no avail. The hole was on the other side of the smelter from her. "You put a hole? In my factory?"

"Why aren't you on the train!" I demanded. "You're supposed to be on the train!"

"I wanted to see if I could fix the problem. I sent the others to safety and—" She stopped and held up a finger. "Hold on a moment. I don't have to explain myself to you. *You* have to explain yourself to *me!*"

I took a step toward her. "Listen, dipshit. This whole facility is about to melt. You have to come with me *right fucking now!*"

"Language! Wait . . . I recognize you. You're Jasmine Bashara." She pointed an accusing finger. "You're the hooligan who ruined my harvesters!"

"Yeah," I said. "And I'm the hooligan who sabotaged your smelter. It's going critical as we speak."

"Nonsense. I designed it myself. It's infallibly safe."

"The heater's on full, the thermal system is hacked, and I welded a steel plate across the melt plug."

Her mouth dropped open.

"We have to leave!" I said. "Come on!"

She looked to the smelter, then back to me. "Or . . . I could fix it."

"Not gonna happen," I said.

"Do you plan to stop me?"

I steadied my stance. "You don't want to mess with me, Grandma. I'm half your age and I grew up in this gravity. I'll carry you out of here if I have to."

"Interesting," she said. "I grew up on the streets of Manaus. And I used to mug men twice your size."

Okay, I wasn't expecting that.

She lunged at me.

I wasn't expecting that either.

I ducked and watched her sail overhead. Earthers always underestimated how far a jump would take them. So it was easy to—

She reached down, grabbed my hair, and slammed my head into the ground with her landing. Then she straddled my chest and reared back to punch me in the face. I kicked up, bucked her off of me, and got to my feet.

Before I could get my bearings, she was on me again. This time she attacked from behind with a chokehold.

I have many flaws, but machismo isn't one of them. I know when I'm outclassed. Turns out Manaus is a much tougher town than Artemis. This woman could pummel me in a fair fight.

That's why I avoid fair fights.

I reached over my shoulder and pulled off her air mask. She released me immediately and backed away. She held her breath and fumbled with the dangling mask. That gave me an opening.

I spun around, ducked down, and grabbed her by the legs. Then I hoisted her into the air with all my might. She flew a good four meters straight up.

"Can you do that in Manaus?!" I yelled.

She flailed in the air and reached the top of her arc. I grabbed my acetylene tank from the ground as she began her trip down. She had no way to avoid what came next.

I swung as hard as I could. I made sure not to hit her head—I didn't want to kill her. I ended up tagging her left shin. She cried out in pain and landed in a heap on the ground. But, to her credit, she got right back up again. She started toward me.

"Stop!" I held out my hand. "This is ridiculous. Your smelter's getting hotter and hotter. You're a chemist. Do the math. Will you just come with me?!"

"You can't just—" She stopped. She turned slowly toward the smelter. The lower half of it glowed dark red. "Oh . . . my God . . ."

She spun back to me. "Where's that exit again?"

"Right this way," I gestured.

Together, we ran to the hole. Her a little slower than me because I'd just smacked the shit out of her shin.

She dove through and I followed her. We scrambled through the air shelter and into the connector tunnel. I closed the hatch behind us.

"Where does this lead?!" she demanded.

"Away from here," I said.

We ran down the connector.

Dale peeked his head through the rover airlock. He'd taken off his EVA suit.

Sanchez leapt into the rover and I followed immediately after. I slammed the rover hatch closed.

"We still have to detach the inflatable!" he said.

"No time," I said. "We'd have to suit up to do that. Drive away at max torque to rip the tunnel."

"Hang on," Dale said. He punched the throttle.

The rover lurched forward. Sanchez fell off her seat. I kept position at the rear window.

The rover had insane torque, but there's only so much traction to be had on lunar regolith. We only got a meter before the tunnel jerked us to a stop. Sanchez, just getting up, fell forward onto Dale. She grabbed him around the shoulders for support.

"We have to get away from here," she said. "There are methane and oxygen tanks in there—"

"I know!" I said. I shot a glance out the side window. A sharply sloped rock got my attention. I vaulted to the front of the rover and clambered into the shotgun seat. "I've got a plan. It'll take too long to explain. Give me control."

Dale flipped a switch in the center column to give my side priority. No argument, no questions, he just did it. EVA masters are very good at being rational in a crisis.

I threw the rover into reverse and backed up four meters.

"Wrong way," Sanchez said.

"Shut up!" I turned toward the angled rock and put the rover into drive. "Hang on to something."

She and Dale gripped each other. I threw the throttle to full.

We lunged at the rock. I steered the right front wheel over it and the whole rover bounced up at an angle. We hit the ground on the rover's left side and rolled. We gave that roll cage a workout. The cabin was like a tumble dryer—I tried not to puke.

Here's what I thought would happen: The inflatable would get all twisted up, which it wasn't designed to handle, so it would rip. Then I'd use reverse and forward motions to grow the rip all the way around. Then we'd be free.

Here's what actually happened: The inflatable took it like a champ. It was designed to have human occupants, so by God it would protect them no matter what. It didn't rip. But the connection point to the rover airlock wasn't as strong. The torsion from the twist sheared the bolts clean off.

The air inside the tunnel explosively burst forth, blowing the rover farther forward (note: lunar rovers aren't designed to be aerodynamic). We skidded on our side for another meter, then fell ponderously onto our wheels.

We were free.

"Holy shit!" Dale said. "That was genius!"

"Uh, yeah." I drove us away.

Whump!

The muted rumble lasted a fraction of a second. It was one of those sounds you feel more than hear.

"That was loud," Sanchez said.

"No, it wasn't." Dale pried her arms off his shoulders. "I could barely hear it."

"She's right." I kept my eyes on the terrain ahead as I drove. "That sound traveled through loose soil, up through the wheels, and into the cabin. The fact that we heard anything at all means it was loud as hell."

I checked the rear camera feed. The bubble was intact, of course. It would take something nuclear to crack that open. The surprising part was my air shelter. It was right where I'd left it.

I slammed on the brakes. "Holy crap! You see that! My weld held up against the explosion!"

Sanchez scowled. "Pardon me if I don't pat you on the back."

"Seriously?" said Dale. "You're going to brag right now?"

"I'm just sayin'. Hell of a weld."

"Goddammit, Jazz." He flipped the control switch back to his side.

He drove us back toward town. "You should call Svoboda and your dad to let him know you're okay."

"And you should call a lawyer," said Sanchez. "I'll see to it you get deported to Brazil to face charges."

"Think so?" I pulled out my Gizmo and called Svoboda. He didn't answer—it went to voicemail.

"Uh-oh," I said.

"Problem?" Dale asked.

"Svobo's not answering." I called again. Voicemail again.

"Maybe someone got to him?" Dale said.

I turned to Sanchez. "You got any more goons in Artemis?"

"I see no reason to cooperate with you."

"Don't fuck with me on this. If my dad or friend gets hurt I'll send you back to Brazil a piece at a time."

"I don't have 'goons' at all. Those types don't answer to me."

"Bullshit," I said. "Your nose is so far up O Palácio's ass you can see teeth."

She scowled. "They're the ownership. I'm not one of them."

"You're *partners*!"

"The bottom fell out of the aluminum market when Artemis stopped building new bubbles. I needed funds to continue. They offered rescue financing. I took it. They do their thing and stay out of my way while I run my smelter. A smelter I poured my life and soul into, which you just destroyed, you reckless puddle of exudate!"

"Don't think I won't look that up!"

I dialed Dad's number and held the Gizmo to my ear. Each successive unanswered ring raised my blood pressure.

"No answer from Dad." I drummed my fingers on the control console.

Dale drove with one hand and pulled out his Gizmo. "Try Lene, I'll try Bob."

I called Lene's number. It rang and rang. I hung up when it went to voicemail. "Nothing," I said.

"Bob's not answering either," Dale said.

We exchanged nervous glances.

"Maybe Rudy caught wind of it and arrested everyone. . . ." I pondered. I hovered my thumbs over the Gizmo and pursed my lips. Calling the police in the middle of a heist wasn't the best plan. Logically I should have waited until we were back in town—they'd be just as arrested then. But I couldn't wait.

I called his number. Four rings and out. I hung up.

"Jesus," I said.

"Seriously?!" Dale said. "Even Rudy's not answering? What the hell's going on?"

Sanchez pulled out her own Gizmo and tapped at the screen.

"Hey!" I grabbed at her Gizmo, but she pulled it away before I could get it. "Gimme that!"

"No," she said crisply. "I need to know if my people got back safely."

"Bullshit! You're calling for help!" I lunged at her. She dragged us both to the floor.

"Knock it off!" said Dale.

She tried to swing at me but only had one hand to work with— the other had a death grip on her Gizmo. I blocked and slapped her across the face. Oh God it felt good to get a hit in.

"Stop that shit!" Dale yelled. "If you idiots hit the wrong button we all die!"

"You told that harvester to kill me! Admit it!" I swung at her.

She dodged to the side and hammer-locked my arm. "Of course I did! How *dare* you try to destroy my life's work!"

"Goddammit!" Dale skidded the rover to a halt.

He waded into the fray and pried Sanchez and me apart. Despite what you see in action movies and comics, bigger really is better. A six-foot man just has too much of an edge over two slim women.

"Listen, assholes," he said. "I'm too gay to enjoy this catfight. Knock it off or I'll bash your heads together."

"Language." Sanchez resumed dialing her Gizmo.

"Would you stop her, please?" I said to Dale.

"If she can reach *anyone* I'll be happy." He let us both go, but kept a wary eye on me. Somehow he assumed I was the aggressor. Just because I wanted to claw that bitch's eyes out and shove them up her urethra.

Sanchez listened to the Gizmo for a response. Her expression grew fearful by the second. She hung up.

Dale looked to me. "Now what?"

"Since when am I the leader?"

"This whole heist is your deal. What do we do now?"

"Uh . . ." I flipped the radio frequency to Main. "This is Jazz Bashara calling any EVA master. Do you read?"

"Yes!" came the immediate reply. "This is Sarah Gottlieb. I'm here with Arun Gosal. We can't reach anyone else. What's going on?"

I knew both of them. Sarah was a master and Arun was a trainee. We'd put that Queensland Glass fire out together a few days earlier. "Unknown, Sarah. I'm in a rover outside and unable to get any response from town. What's your location?"

"Moltke Foothills harvesting ground," she said.

I muted my mike. "Oh right. They're guarding the harvester from me."

"Kind of irrelevant now," said Sanchez. "But it's nice to know the EVA Guild took the contract seriously."

I turned the mike back on. "Can you make it back to town?"

"We had planned to ride the harvester back to the smelter and walk from there. But we can't reach Sanchez Aluminum to ask them to send it home."

"Probably best to start walking," I said. I tried not to catch Sanchez's glare.

"Negative," said Sarah. "This could be a distraction to draw us away. We're staying right here."

"Copy that."

"Hey . . . you're still a trainee," she said. "You shouldn't be outside on your own. Is there a master with you? Who's with you?"

"Uh . . . you're breaking up . . ." I switched the radio back to our private frequency.

"That'll take some explanation later," said Dale.

"One fuckup at a time," I said. "Let's go to the Port of Entry and see what's going on there."

"Yes," said Sanchez. "That's where the train will be—where my people will be."

Dale took the driver's seat and got us rolling again. Sanchez and I sat in silence, avoiding eye contact for the rest of the trip.

Dale drove at breakneck speed back to town. As we approached the Port of Entry, we could see the train docked at its airlock.

Sanchez perked up. "How do we get in?"

"Normally you radio the EVA master on duty at the freight airlock," Dale said. "But since they're not answering I'd have to suit up and use the manual valves on the outside."

"Check out the train," I said. "We'll be able to see into the port through the train's windows."

Dale nodded and drove us across the well-trafficked terrain. We passed the freight airlock and stopped at the docked train. The windows were considerably higher than ours. All we could see from our vantage point was the ceiling inside.

"Hang on, I'll get us a better view." Dale tapped at the controls and the cabin began to rise. Turns out Bob's rover had a scissor-lift as well. Of course it did. Why wouldn't it? It had every other feature you could want.

We drew level with the train windows and Sanchez let out a gasp. I would have too, but I didn't want her to see me do it.

Bodies lay in disarray—some in their seats, others piled atop each other in the aisle. One had a pool of vomit around her mouth.

"Whu . . ." Dale managed to eke out.

"My people!" Sanchez frantically shifted around to look from different angles.

I pressed my nose against the glass for a better view. "They're still breathing."

"Are they?" she asked. "Are you certain?"

"Yeah," I said. "Look at the guy in the blue shirt. See his stomach?"

"Michael Mendez." She loosened up a bit. "Okay, yes. I see movement."

"They dropped right where they sat," I said. "They aren't crowded at the airlock or anything."

Dale pointed to the hatch connecting the train to the port. "The train airlock's open. See the Kenyan flag in the station?"

I furrowed my brow. "The air," I said.

Sanchez and Dale looked at me.

"It's in the air. Something's wrong with the air. Everyone in the train was fine until the conductor opened the hatch. Then they passed out."

Dale wrung his hands. "Right when we fucked up the smelter. That can't be a coincidence."

"Of course it's not a coincidence!" Sanchez said. "My smelter has an air pipeline directly to Life Support in Armstrong Bubble. Where do you think your air comes from?"

I grabbed her by the shoulders. "But your feeds have safeties, right? Valves and stuff?"

She slapped my hands away. "They're made to stop leaks, not stand up against a *massive explosion!*"

"Oh shit oh shit oh shit . . ." said Dale. "The explosion was contained in the smelter bubble. It didn't have anywhere to vent. You made your weld too good. The air pipeline was the only place for the pressure to go. Oh shit!"

"Wait, no," I said. "No, no, no. That can't be right. Life Support has safety sensors on incoming air. It's not like they pump it straight into town, right?"

"Yes, you're right," said Sanchez, calming a little. "They check for carbon dioxide and carbon monoxide. They also check for chlorine and methane, just in case there's a leak at my smelter."

"How do they check?" I asked.

She walked to another window to get a better look at her

fallen employees. "They have liquid compounds that change color in the presence of unwanted molecules. And computer monitoring to react instantly."

"So it's chemistry," I said. "That's your thing, right? You're a chemist, right? What if the explosion at the smelter made something else? Something Life Support couldn't detect?"

"Well . . ." She thought. "There would have been calcium, chlorine, aluminum, silicon . . ."

"Methane," I added.

"Okay, add that in and it could make chloromethane, dichloromethane, chlor—oh my God!"

"What? What?!"

She put her head in her hands. "Methane, chlorine, and heat will make several compounds, most of them harmless. But it also makes *chloroform*."

Dale sighed in relief. "Oh thank God."

Sanchez put her hands over her mouth and suppressed a sob. "They're going to die. They're all going to die!"

"What are you talking about?" I asked. "It's just chloroform. Knockout gas. Right?"

She shook her head. "You've watched too many movies. Chloroform isn't some harmless anesthetic. It's very, *very* deadly."

"But they're still breathing."

She wiped away tears with a trembling hand. "They passed out instantly. That means the concentration is at least fifteen thousand parts per million. At that concentration they'll all be dead in an hour. And that's the *best*-case scenario."

Her words hit me like hammers. I froze. I just plain froze solid. I shook in my chair and fought back the urge to puke. The world grew foggy. I tried to take a deep breath. It escaped as a sob.

My mind went into overdrive. "Okay . . . um . . . okay . . . hang on . . ."

Assets: me, Dale, and a bitch I didn't like. A rover. Two EVA suits. Lots of spare air, though not enough to feed a city. Welding equipment. There was also an additional EVA master and trainee (Sarah and Arun), but they were too far away to do any good. We had one hour to solve this problem, and they couldn't possibly get back in time.

Dale and Sanchez looked to me with desperation.

Additional asset: the entire city of Artemis, minus the people inside.

"O-okay . . ." I stammered. "Life Support's on Armstrong Ground. It's right down the hall from Space Agency Row. Dale, dock us at the ISRO airlock."

"Roger." He threw the throttle to full. We bounced over the terrain and skirted the arc of Aldrin Bubble.

I climbed to the airlock in the rear. "Once I'm in, I'll haul ass to Life Support. They've got *tons* of reserve air in the emergency tanks. I'll open all of them."

"You can't just dilute chloroform," Sanchez said. "The molarity in the air will be the same."

"I know," I said. "But bubbles have overpressure-relief valves. When I blow the reserve tanks, the city air pressure will go up and the relief valves will start venting. The good air will displace the bad."

She thought it through, then nodded. "Yes, that might work."

We skidded to a stop just outside the ISRO airlock. Dale threw the rover into reverse and performed the fastest, most skilled docking procedure I've ever seen. He barely slowed down to mate the two airlocks.

"Jesus you're good at this shit," I said.

"Go!" he implored.

I put my breather mask on. "You guys stay here. Dale, if I fuck up and the chloroform gets me, you have to take my place."

I turned the airlock crank. The hiss of equalizing air filled the cabin. "Sanchez, if Dale fucks up, you're next in line. Hopefully that won't . . ."

I cocked my head. "Does that hiss sound strange?"

Dale shot a look at the airlock door. "Shit! The rover airlock's damaged from ripping the inflatable tunnel off! Close the valve, we need—"

The hiss grew so loud I couldn't hear Dale anymore. The airlock was failing.

My mind raced: If I closed the valve what would we do next? Dale and I had EVA suits, so we could walk to the ISRO airlock and use it normally. But that would require us to leave the rover, which would mean using the rover's airlock, which would kill Sanchez. The only solution would be to drive the whole rover into town through the freight airlock at the Port of Entry. But no one was awake inside to let us in. We'd have to open the airlock manually, which would mean leaving the rover, which would kill Sanchez.

I made a snap decision and cranked the valve to full-open.

"What the hell are you—" Dale began.

The rover rattled from the force of escaping air. My ears popped. Bad sign—the air was escaping faster than the rover could replace it.

"Close the hatch behind me!" I yelled.

Four doors. I had to get through *four fucking doors* to get into Artemis. The rover's airlock had two and the ISRO's airlock had two more. Until I got through that last one, I'd be in danger. Dale and Sanchez would be fine as soon as he closed the first door behind me.

I opened Door Number One and hopped into the rover airlock. Door Number Two was the one trying to kill us. Ice condensed along the edges where a steady stream of air escaped. Just as Dale predicted, the aperture was warped where the inflatable tunnel had been attached.

I spun the crank and yanked on the hatch. Would the door even open in its fucked-up state? I prayed to Allah, Yahweh, and Christ that it would. One or more of them must have heard me because the hatch inched open. I used all my strength to widen the gap and finally opened it wide enough to slither through. Sometimes being small is awesome. I'd made it into the collet— the one-meter tunnel between the two airlocks.

Both the rover outer door and the collet had been badly warped. Both leaked air like a sieve. But at least there weren't any big holes. The rover's air tanks were keeping it pressurized for the moment, though they were losing the battle. And if you're wondering about my breather mask: No, it wouldn't help in a vacuum. It would just blow oxygen onto my dead face.

I cranked the ISRO outer hatch handle and threw it open. I stumbled into the ISRO airlock and glanced back to check up on the others.

I'd assumed Dale would already be closing the rover's inner hatch. I'd assumed wrong. If he'd closed the hatch, my air supply would've been gone until I got into Artemis. Was that on his mind? Was that idiot being noble?

"Close the fucking hatch!" I screamed over the wind.

Then I saw them. They both looked pale and woozy. Dale fell to the floor. Shit. The ISRO airlock had chloroform in its air. In the heat of the moment and all my deep planning I'd forgotten that little detail.

All right. One thing at a time. First, get the last door open. The rover had limited air, but Artemis had plenty. I spun the final hatch's crank and tried to push it open. It didn't budge.

Of course it didn't. The rover was at lower pressure than the city because of the constant leak.

"Fuuuuck!" I said. I cranked the hatch's central valve to equalize the airlock with the air on the other side. The ISRO equalization valve battled the leak. Which one had a higher air-flow rate? I didn't wait to find out.

I braced my back against the airlock outer wall and used both legs to kick the hatch. The first two attempts jarred it, but didn't break the seal. The third did the trick.

The hatch clanked open. A whoosh of air rushed into the airlock and rover beyond. I wedged a foot in the opening to keep the hatch from closing against the airflow.

Dale and Sanchez were saved . . . sort of. If you consider breathing poison gas in a leaky pressure vessel to be "saved."

My back hurt like hell. I'd be paying for all this tomorrow. If there was a tomorrow.

I pulled off my shoe and left it in place to keep the hatch open. I returned to the rover. Dale and Sanchez were completely unconscious at this point. Goddamn. Note to self: Don't take the mask off.

Both of them were breathing steadily. I closed the rover's inner airlock hatch to seal them in, then returned to the ISRO inner door. I shoved it open again (much easier because my shoe kept the door from re-sealing) and fell into the lab.

I retrieved my shoe and the hatch shut automatically against the rushing air.

I was in.

I sat on the floor and put my shoe back on. Then I checked the seal on my air mask. It seemed good. And I wasn't puking or passing out, which I figured was a good sign.

The ISRO lab was littered with unconscious scientists. It was an eerie sight. Four of them had passed out at their desks, while one lay on the floor. I stepped over the one on the floor and made my way to the hall.

I checked my Gizmo. It had been twenty minutes since the chloroform leak started. So, if Sanchez's estimate was correct, I had forty minutes left to fix the city's air or everyone would die.

And it would be my fault.

16

I needed Rudy. Or, more accurately, I needed Rudy's Gizmo.

Remember, Life Support is a secure area. You have to work there to get in—the doors won't open unless they recognize your Gizmo. But Rudy's Gizmo opens any door in town. Secure areas, homes, bathrooms, doesn't matter. There's *nowhere* Rudy can't go.

His office on Armstrong Up 4 was just a few minutes' run from the ISRO lab. And holy shit was that a surreal trip. Bodies littered the halls and doorways. It was like a scene from the apocalypse.

They're not dead. They're not dead. They're not dead. . . . I repeated the mantra to keep from losing my shit.

I took the ramps to get from level to level. The elevators would probably have bodies blocking the doors.

Armstrong Up 4 has an open space just near the ramps called Boulder Park. Why is it called that? No clue. While passing through, I tripped over a guy lying on his side and face-planted onto a tourist holding her unconscious toddler. She'd curled her body around the boy—a mother's last line of defense. I got back up and kept running.

I slid to a stop at Rudy's office door and barged in. Rudy was slumped over his desk. Somehow he looked poised even while knocked out. I searched his pockets. The Gizmo had to be in there somewhere.

Something caught my eye and bothered my brain. I couldn't

figure out what. It's one of those warnings you get that's more a sense of "wrongness" than anything else. But hell, everything was "wrong" at the moment. I didn't have time for subconscious bullshit. I had a city to save.

I found Rudy's Gizmo and slipped it into my pocket. My inner Jazz made another appeal to me, this time with more urgency. *Something's wrong, goddammit!* it screamed.

I spared a second to look around the room. Nothing awry. The small, Spartan office was just as it had always been. I knew the place well—I'd been in there dozens of times when I was an asshole teenager, and I have a very good memory. Nothing was out of place. Not a single thing.

But then, as I left the office, it struck me: a blunt object to the back of my head.

My scalp went numb and my vision blurred, but I stayed conscious. It had been a grazing blow. A few centimeters to the left and I would have been leaking brains. I stumbled forward and turned to face my attacker.

Alvarez held a long steel pipe in one hand and an oxygen tank in the other. A hose ran from the tank directly to his mouth.

"You fucking kidding me?!" I said. "One other person awake and it's *you*?!"

He took another swing. I dodged away.

Of course it was Alvarez. That's what my subconscious had tried to tell me. Rudy's office was the same as I always remembered. But it was *supposed* to have Alvarez locked up in the air shelter.

The whole sequence of events played out in my mind: The shelter had protected Alvarez from the chloroform. Once Rudy conked out, the now-unsupervised murderer had wrenched a meter-long pipe loose and used it to force the hatch handle. The lock and chain on the other side stood no chance against that kind of torque.

Alvarez might not be a chemical engineer, but it wouldn't

have taken a genius to work out something was wrong with the air. Either that or he'd spent a second almost passing out before realizing. Either way, the shelter had air tanks and hoses. So he'd rigged up a life-support system.

And hey, as an added bonus, the pipe had a jagged, sharp end where he'd broken it off. Wonderful. He didn't just have a club. He had a spear.

"There's a gas leak," I said. "Everyone in town will die if I don't fix it."

He lunged without hesitation. He was an assassin with a job. Got to admire his professionalism.

"Oh, fuck you!" I said.

He was bigger, stronger, a far superior fighter, and armed with a pointy metal stick.

I turned as if to run, then kicked backward. I figured it would throw off his attack and I was right. He ended up swinging the pipe around me instead of bashing my head in. Now I had his hand in front of me and my back to his chest. I'd never get a better shot at disarming him than this.

I grabbed his hand with both of mine and twisted it outward. Classic disarming move, and it should have fucking worked, but it didn't. He just reached around me with his other hand and pulled the pipe up to my throat.

He was strong. *Very* strong. Even with the injury to his arm he easily overpowered me. I got both my hands between the pipe and my neck, but it still dug in. I couldn't breathe. There's a special kind of panic that overwhelms you when that happens. I flailed uselessly for a few seconds, then used every ounce of will-power I had to get myself under control.

He'd either break my neck or choke me out and then break my neck. The breather mask was useless—it couldn't force air through a closed throat. But the air tank on my hip might help. Solid metal blunt object. Better than nothing. I reached down for it.

Pain!

Taking my hand off the pipe was a terrible idea. It got rid of half my resistance. Alvarez dug it deeper into my throat. My legs gave out and I sank to my knees. He followed me down and kept the pipe perfectly in place.

Darkness closed in around me. If only I had another hand.

Another hand . . .

The thought echoed in my increasingly foggy mind.

Another hand.

Another hand.

Too many hands.

Alvarez had too many hands.

What?

My eyes shot back open. Alvarez had too many hands!

A second ago he'd had the pipe in one hand and an air tank in the other. But now both hands were on the pipe. That meant he'd set the tank *on the floor*!

I summoned the tiny amount of strength I had left, coiled my legs, and lurched forward. The pipe dug into my throat even deeper but that was okay—the pain helped keep me awake. I pressed again, harder this time, and finally brought him off balance. The two of us toppled forward, me on the bottom, him lying atop me.

Then I heard the sweetest sound I'd ever heard.

He coughed.

His grip relaxed slightly and he coughed again. I got my chin under the pipe and finally my throat was free! I wheezed and took great gasping breaths from my mask. The black fog around me receded.

I held on to the pipe with both hands and pushed forward, dragging Alvarez with me. He held on, but his grip grew weaker with every passing moment.

I wriggled out from underneath and finally turned to face him. He lay crumpled on the ground and coughing violently.

Just as I'd hoped, he'd put the tank down to strangle me. When I'd dragged him forward, the air line had popped out of his mouth. He could either hold on to the pipe or grab the air line. He'd chosen the pipe. He'd probably hoped he could choke me out then get the air back before falling unconscious himself.

He reached back with one hand for the air line, but I grabbed his collar and dragged him along the floor. He gasped again and the color drained from his face. I reached down and pulled the pipe out of his hands once and for all.

His face fell to the floor—he was finally down for the count. I panted for a few seconds, then stood up.

The rage boiled inside. I stepped forward with the sharp end of the pipe ahead of me. Alvarez lay helpless on the ground—a known murderer who had just tried to kill me. One thrust between the fourth and fifth ribs . . . right into his heart . . . I considered it. I *really* considered it. It's not something I'm proud of.

I stomped his right upper arm with my heel. The bone crunched underneath.

That was more my style.

I didn't have time to waste, but I couldn't let that asshole escape again. I dragged his unconscious body into Rudy's office. I shoved Rudy aside and rummaged through his desk until I found handcuffs. I handcuffed Alvarez's good arm to the air-shelter handle and threw the key out into the hall. You're welcome, Rudy.

I checked my Gizmo to see how much time I had left: thirty-five minutes.

And it wasn't like I had until 0:00. That was just an estimate. Hopefully a little on the safe side. Nevertheless, with over two thousand people in town, some were sure to die ahead of schedule.

I "sheathed" the pipe by slipping it between my belt and jumpsuit. Alvarez was knocked out, breathing chloroform, had a broken arm, and was handcuffed. But I still wasn't taking any chances. No more fucking ambushes.

I ran toward Life Support. I wheezed harder and harder and

my throat swelled up—still pissed off about the recent strangu-
lation. I probably had a hell of a bruise there but it hadn't swollen
shut. That was all that mattered.

I tasted the bile on my breath, but didn't have time to rest.
I powered through the obstacle course of bodies. I cranked up
the flow rate on my air tank to get more oxygen into my aching
lungs. It didn't help much (that trick doesn't work when the entire atmosphere is already oxygen). But at least the slight over-
pressure kept me from sucking in chloroform-riddled air around
the edges. That was something.

I reached Life Support and waved Rudy's Gizmo at the door.
It clicked open.

Unconscious Vietnamese guys lay everywhere. I glanced at
the main status screens along the wall. As far as the automated
systems were concerned, everything was hunky-dory! Good
pressure, plenty of oxygen, CO_2 separation working perfectly . . .
what more could a computer ask for?

Mr. Đoàn's seat at the main panel was empty. I hopped into it
and looked over the air-management controls. The writing was
in Vietnamese, but I got the general idea. Mainly because one
wall showed a map of every pipe and air line in the system. As
you can imagine, it was a pretty big schematic.

I gave it a long, hard look. Right away, I picked out the emergency air system. All its lines were marked in red.

"Okay . . . where's the actuation valve?" I said. I traced my
finger along various red lines until I found one that entered Life
Support itself. Then I found something that looked like a valve
icon. "Northwest corner . . ."

The room was a maze of pipes, tanks, and valves. But I knew
which one I needed now. The third from the left in the northwest
corner. On my way there, I passed Mr. Đoàn lying on the floor.
From the looks of things, he'd tried to get to the valve himself,
but hadn't made it.

I grabbed the valve with both hands and turned. The throaty roar of pressure release echoed throughout the room.

My Gizmo rang in my pocket. It was so unexpected I drew my pipe, ready for a fight. I shook my head at the silly move and re-sheathed my weapon. I answered the call.

"Jazz?!" came Dale's voice. "You all right? We passed out there for a minute."

"Dale!" I said. "Yeah, I'm fine. I'm in Life Support and I just opened the flush valve. You okay?"

"We're awake. Feel like shit, though. No idea why we woke up."

Sanchez spoke in the background. "Our lungs absorbed the chloroform out of the rover's air. Once the ppm's dropped below twenty-five hundred, it stopped working as an anesthetic."

"You're on speaker, by the way," said Dale.

"Sanchez," I said flatly. "So glad you're well."

She ignored my bitchiness. "Is the flush working?"

I ran back to the status screens. Each bubble now had multiple blinking yellow lights that hadn't been there before.

"I think so," I said. "There are caution and warning lights all over the place. If I'm reading this right, they're probably the relief valves. It's venting."

I prodded a technician in the chair next to me. He didn't stir. Of course, even with perfect air, it would take these guys a while to wake up. They'd been breathing nineteenth-century anes-thetic for half an hour.

"Hang on," I said. "I'm going to take a sniff."

I pulled the mask away from my face for a second and took a very shallow breath. I *immediately* fell to the floor. I was too weak to stand. I wanted to puke but resisted the urge. I held the mask against my face again.

". . . no good . . ." I murmured. ". . . air still bad . . ."

"Jazz?" Dale said. "Jazz! Don't pass out!"

"'m'okay," I said, getting up to my knees. Each breath of canned air made me feel better. "I'm . . . okay . . . I think we just have to wait. It takes a while to replace all this air. We're good. We're doing good."

I guess-the gods heard that and laughed their asses off. No sooner had I said it than the sound of air through the pipes quieted down and fell silent.

"Uh . . . guys . . . the air stopped."

"Why?" asked Dale.

"Working on it!" I shot a look at the status screens. Nothing obvious there. Then I went back to the line schematics on the wall. The main valve was right there in Life Support and it led to a staging tank in that room. It read empty.

"Ugh!" I said. "We ran out of air! There's not enough!"

"What?!" Dale said. "How can that be? Life Support has air to last months."

"Not quite," I said. "They have enough air to refill one or two bubbles and they have enough battery power to turn CO_2 back into oxygen for months. But they don't have enough oxygen to flush the entire city. It's just not something anyone thought of."

"Oh God . . ." said Dale.

"We've got one chance," I said. "Trond Landvik stockpiled huge amounts of oxygen. It's in tanks right outside."

"That bastard," said Sanchez. "I *knew* he was after my oxygen-for-power contract."

I looked over the control board again. Thank god Vietnamese uses a superset of the English alphabet. One section of the schematic was labeled LANDVIK.

"Trond's tanks are on the schematic!" I said.

"Of course they are," said Sanchez. "Trond would have had to collude with them to make sure his air system could interface with theirs."

I ran my finger along the map. "According to this, Trond's

tanks are already connected to the system. There's a whole com-plicated set of valves in the way, but there's a path."

"So, do it!" Dale said.

"The valves are manual cranks and they're outside," I said.

"What?! Why the hell are there manual valves out on the sur-face?!"

"Safety," I said. "Trond explained it to me earlier. Doesn't matter. I just memorized the pipe layout. It's complicated as hell and I don't know what state the sub-valves will be in. I'll work out what to do when I'm there."

I bolted out of Life Support into the corridors of Armstrong.

"Wait, you're going out?" Dale said. "Wearing what? Your EVA suit's in here."

"I'm on my way to Conrad Airlock and I've got a big pipe. I'll pry open Bob's locker and wear his gear."

"Those lockers are centimeter-thick aluminum," said Dale. "You'll never get through in time."

"Okay, good point. Uh . . ." I hurtled through the Armstrong–Conrad Connector tunnel and checked my Gizmo. We had twenty-five minutes left. "I'll use a tourist hamster ball."

"How will you turn the cranks?"

Goddammit, right again. Hamster balls had no arms, gloves, or articulation points at all. I'd have no way to grip anything outside.

"I guess you'll have to be my hands. The tanks are in the triangle between Armstrong, Shepard, and Bean. Meet me at the Bean–Shepard Connector. I'll need your help to get into the triangle."

"Roger. Driving to the connector now. I'll get as close as I can and walk the rest of the way."

"How will you get out of the rover without killing Sanchez?"

"I'd like to know that too," Sanchez added.

"I'll put her in your suit before opening the airlock," he said.

"*My* suit?!"

"Jazz!"

"Fine, yeah. Sorry."

I plowed through Conrad Ground as fast as I could. My home bubble had some of the most Byzantine passageways in town. When you put a bunch of artisans in one place with no zoning rules, their workshops expand to fill every nook and cranny. But I knew the layout by heart.

Naturally, the tourist airlock was the *farthest point* from the Armstrong Connector tunnel. I mean, where else would it be?

I finally got there. Two EVA masters lay on the floor in front of sixteen tourists who'd passed out in their chairs. The leak had caught them in the middle of orientation.

"Dale, I'm at the airlock."

"Copy," came his voice. He was far from his Gizmo's microphone. "It's taking a while to cram Sanchez into your gear. She's kind of tall—"

"I beg your pardon," she said. "I'm 164 centimeters—exactly average for a woman. I'm not tall, your saboteur friend is short."

"Don't stretch out my suit," I said.

"I'll defecate in your suit!"

"Hey—!"

"Sanchez, shut up!" Dale said. "Jazz, save the city!"

I charged into the large airlock and pulled a deflated hamster ball from its cubby. "I'll let you know when I'm outside."

I spread the flaccid plastic on the ground with the zip hatch facing up, pulled a scurry pack off the wall, and put it on. Time for some Rudy Gizmo Magic. I closed the inner airlock door, waved the Gizmo across the airlock control panel, and it granted me access.

Next problem: Airlocks are meant to be operated by EVA masters wearing suits with gloves. This was going to take some finesse.

I deactivated the computer controls and switched to manual.

First thing I did was spin the outer door's crank. The door (like all airlock hatches) was a plug door—the air pressure behind it pushed it into its seal. So, while I made it possible to open the door, you'd have to be Superman to actually pull it open against the pressure. But I'd moved the physical latches out of the way, at least.

I very slowly turned the venting valve. As soon as I heard the hiss of escaping air, I stopped turning it. At full-open, the valve would let all the airlock's air vent into space in under a minute. But at this rate it would take a bit longer—long enough for me to not die, hopefully.

I hurried to the hamster ball and crawled inside. It was an awkward affair, like getting into a collapsed tent, but that's just how these things worked.

I closed the zip seals (there are three layers of them for safety), then cranked the airflow valve on the scurry pack for a few seconds. The ball grew just enough for me to move around.

Normally you do this shit when the airlock's *not* venting. You take your time, inflate, and wait for the EVA master to check your seals. I wouldn't have that luxury.

The pressure in the airlock decreased, so my ball grew like a balloon in a vacuum chamber. That's not an analogy. It was literally a balloon in a vacuum chamber.

I crawled forward (it's hard to move in a partially inflated ball) and reached out for the hatch handle. Since my ball wasn't fully rigid, I could bend the skin just enough to grip the hatch. I held on with both hands as the pressure tried to pry me loose.

The ball grew more rigid as the airlock vented, making it harder and harder to hang on to the handle. That rubber *really* wanted to be a sphere now. It didn't approve of me wrapping it around a handle.

I came close to losing my grip a couple of times but managed to keep hold. Finally, the airlock pressure got low enough that I could pull the door open.

The remaining air whooshed out and my ball sprang into full rigidity. It slapped my hands away from the edge so hard I actually fell on my ass. But it didn't matter. I was safely in my hamster ball and the airlock was open.

I got back up and something scraped against my leg. It was the pipe I'd appropriated from Lefty. In all the excitement I'd forgotten I even still had it. Generally not a good idea to bring a pointy stick into your inflatable life support system, but it was too late to do anything about that now. I tightened my belt to make sure the pipe was secure. Wouldn't want it slipping out.

I checked the scurry pack. All was well. Remember, they're designed to be worn by tourists. They take care of everything on their own.

I ventured out onto the surface.

For all its limitations, a hamster ball is great for running in. No clunky boots, no thick suit legs to push around, no lugging around a hundred kilograms of gear. None of that. Just me in normal clothes with a moderately heavy backpack.

I got up to speed and rolled across the terrain. Whenever I hit a bump, I bounced into the air (well, not "air," but you know what I mean). There was a reason tourists paid thousands of slugs for this. In other circumstances it would have been fun as hell.

I ran along the arc of Conrad Bubble until Bean came into view. I beelined for Bean, then followed its perimeter.

I tapped my earpiece to make sure it was on. "How's it coming, Dale?"

"Sanchez is suited up and I've driven us to the Shepard–Bean Connector. About to exit the rover. You?"

"Almost there."

I rounded the edge of Bean and saw Shepard come into view. I kept following Bean's wall to the connector tunnel. Dale, at the wall of the connector, spotted me and waved. Bob's rover stood parked nearby. Through the windows, I could see Sanchez sitting awkwardly in my suit. I scampered to the connector and checked my Gizmo. Fifteen minutes left.

Dale crouched down and put both arms under my bubble. "On three," he said.

I coiled, ready to leap.

"One . . . two . . . *three!*"

We timed it perfectly. I jumped a fraction of a second before he flung the bubble upward with all his strength. So I kicked against the ground, flew up, and Dale threw the ball to match me. My ball and I vaulted over the connector with ease. Of course, I bounced around like an idiot when I landed on the other side.

Dale climbed over the connector with practiced ease by using its many handrails. He landed next to me just as I got back up.

With Bean and Shepard behind us, we faced the smaller dome of Armstrong ahead. The external tanks stood to one side, partially hidden by their complicated network of pipes and valves.

"My face itches," said Sanchez over the radio.

"Sucks to be you," I said. Dale and I headed for the tanks.

"This suit is quite uncomfortable," Sanchez continued. "Can't I just close the rover hatch, pressurize, and wait for you in comfort?"

"No," said Dale. "Always have the rover ready for quick entry. That's how we do things."

She grumbled to herself but didn't press the issue.

I rolled to the first line of pipes. Three huge, looming pressure tanks dominated the structure. Each one had LANDVIK stenciled along the side.

I pointed to the middle of four valves on the nearest pipe. "Turn this valve all the way off."

"Off?!" Dale asked.

"Yeah, off. Just trust me. These pipes have blowout zones, cleaning access, and a bunch of other shit that makes it a mess to deal with."

"Gotcha." He grabbed the crank with his thick gloves and muscled it closed.

I pointed to another valve, this one on a pipe three meters above the ground. "Now open that one to full."

He jumped up and grabbed the pipe with both hands. He monkey-barred to the valve, braced his feet on a pair of lower pipes, and turned the valve. He grunted with effort. "These valves are *tight.*"

"They've literally never changed state," I said. "We're using them for the first time."

The valve handle finally gave and Dale gasped with relief. "There!"

"Okay, down here." I gestured at a mess of pipes with four valves on it. "Close all those except the third one. That one should be full-open."

I checked my Gizmo while Dale worked. Ten minutes.

"Sanchez, how accurate is that one-hour estimate on chloroform toxicity?"

"Quite accurate," she said. "Some people will already be in critical condition."

Dale redoubled his pace. "Done. Next."

"Just one more," I said. I led him away from the pipe maze to a half-meter-wide outflow pipe and pointed to a valve that controlled it. "Turn this to full-open and we're done."

He grabbed the handle and tried to crank it. It didn't budge.

"Dale, you have to *turn* the handle," I said.

"The hell you think I'm trying to do?"

"Try harder!"

He turned around, gripped with both hands, and pushed against the ground with his legs. The crank still refused to move.

"Dammit!" Dale said.

My heart nearly beat out of my chest. I looked at my useless hands. With the hamster ball surrounding me I had no way to grip the valve. All I could do was watch.

Dale strained as hard as he could. "God . . . damn . . . it . . ."

"Does the rover have a toolbox?" I asked. "A wrench or something?"

"No," he said through gritted teeth. "I took it out to make room for the inflatable."

That meant the nearest wrench was in town. It would take way too long to retrieve one.

"What about me?" Sanchez said over the radio. "Can I help?"

"No good," said Dale. "It takes hours to learn how to climb in an EVA suit. I'd have to go get you and carry you here. That would take a long time and even then you're not very strong. You wouldn't help much."

This was it. This was as far as we'd get. One valve away from victory, but no further. Two thousand people would die. Maybe we could get back into town and save a few by dragging them into air shelters? Probably not. By the time we got in, everyone would be dead.

I looked around for anything that could help. But the surface around Artemis is the definition of "nothing." Lots of regolith and dust. Not even a friendly rock to hit the valve with. Nothing.

Dale fell to his knees. I couldn't see his face through the visor but I heard his sobs over the radio.

My stomach tied into knots. I was about to throw up. I welled up—about to cry. That just made my throat hurt even more. That pipe had really done a number on me and . . .

And . . .

And then I knew what I had to do.

The realization should have panicked me. I don't know why it didn't. But instead I just felt a great calm. The problem was solved.

"Dale," I said softly.

"Oh God . . ." Dale rasped.

"Dale, I need you to do something for me."

"W-What?"

I pulled the pipe from my belt. "I need you to tell everyone I'm sorry. I'm so sorry for everything I did."

"What are you talking about?"

"And I need you to tell Dad I love him. Okay, that's the most important thing. Tell Dad I love him."

"Jazz." He stood up. "What are you doing with that pipe?"

"We need leverage." I gripped the pipe with both hands and pointed the sharp end forward. "And I've got it. If this won't turn it, nothing will."

I rolled my ball over to the handle.

"But the pipe's inside your hamster ba—oh. No!"

"I probably won't last long enough to turn the handle. You'll have to grab the pipe and finish for me."

"Jazz!" He reached toward me.

It was now or never. Dale had lost focus. I can't blame him. It's hard to watch your best friend die, even if it is for the greater good.

"I forgive you, buddy. For everything. Goodbye."

I thrust the sharp end of the pipe through the edge of my ball. Air hissed out through the pipe—I'd just given the vacuum a straw to suck on. The pipe grew cold in my hands. I pushed harder and wedged the pipe into the valve handle's spokes.

My hamster ball stretched and ripped near the puncture site. I had a fraction of a second left, at best.

With all my strength, I shoved the pipe to the side and felt the handle give.

Then physics showed up with a vengeance.

The ball ripped itself to shreds. One second I was pushing on the pipe, the next I was flying through the void.

All noise stopped immediately. Blinding sunlight assaulted my eyes—I squinted in pain. The air fled from my lungs. I gasped for more—I could expand my chest but nothing came in. Weird feeling.

I landed faceup on the ground. My hands and neck burned

while the rest of my body, protected by clothing, roasted more slowly. My face ached from the onslaught of burning light. My mouth and eyes bubbled—the fluids boiling off in the vacuum.

The world went black and consciousness slipped away. The pain stopped.

Dear Jazz,

According to the news, something's very wrong with Artemis. They say the whole city went offline. There's been no contact at all. I don't know why my email would be the exception but I have to try.

Are you there? Are you okay? What happened?

17

I awoke to darkness.

Wait a minute. I awoke?

"How am I not dead?" I tried to say.

"Huu m uh nn' d'd?" I actually said.

"Daughter?!" It was Dad's voice. "Can you hear me?"

"Mmf."

He took my hand. It didn't feel right, though. The sensation was dulled.

"*C . . . can not . . . see . . .*"

"You have bandages over your eyes."

I tried to hold his hand, but it hurt.

"No. Don't use your hands," he said. "They're also injured."

"She shouldn't be awake," said a woman's voice. It was Doc Roussel. "Jazz? Can you hear me?"

"*How bad is it?*" I asked her.

"You're speaking Arabic," she said. "I can't understand you."

"She asked how bad it is," Dad said.

"It's going to be a painful recovery, but you'll survive."

"N . . . not me . . . the city. How bad is it?"

I felt a pinprick on my arm.

"What are you doing?" Dad asked.

"She shouldn't be awake," Roussel said.

And then I wasn't.

. . .

I drifted in and out of consciousness for a full day. I remember
snippets here and there. Reflex tests, someone changing my bandages, injections, and so on. But I was only semi-alert until they
stopped groping me, then I'd return to the void.

"Jazz?"

"Huh?"

"Jazz, are you awake?" It was Doc Roussel.

". . . yes?"

"I'm going to take the bandages off your eyes."

"Okay."

I felt her hands on my head. The padding on my face unwrapped and I could finally see. I winced at the light. As my eyes
adjusted, I saw more of the room.

I was in a small hospital-like room. I say "hospital-like" because Artemis doesn't have a hospital. Just Doc Roussel's sick
bay. This was a room in the back somewhere.

My hands were still bandaged. They felt awful. They hurt,
but not too bad.

The doc, a sixtysomething woman with gray hair, shined a
flashlight in each of my eyes. Then she held up three fingers.
"How many fingers?"

"Is the city okay?"

She wiggled her hand. "One thing at a time. How many fingers."

"Three?"

"Okay. What do you remember?"

I looked down at my body. Everything seemed to be there.
I wore a hospital smock and I'd been tucked into the bed. My
hands were still bandaged. "I remember popping a hamster ball.
I expected to die."

"By all rights, you should have," she said. "But Dale Shapiro
and Loretta Sanchez saved you. From what I hear, he threw your

body over the Armstrong–Shepard Connector. Sanchez was on the other side. She dragged you into a rover and pressurized it. You were in vacuum for a total of three minutes."

I looked at my gauze mittens. "And that didn't kill me?"

"The human body can survive a few minutes of vacuum. Artemis's air pressure is low enough that you didn't get decompression sickness. The main threat is oxygen starvation—same as drowning. They saved you just in time. Another minute and you'd be dead."

She put her fingers on my throat and watched a clock on the wall. "You have second-degree burns on your hands and the back of your neck. I'm assuming they directly contacted the lunar surface. And you have a pretty bad sunburn on your face. We'll have to check you for skin cancer once a month for a while, but you'll be all right."

"What about the city?" I asked.

"You should talk to Rudy about that. He's right outside—I'll get him."

I grabbed her sleeve. "But—"

"Jazz, I'm your doctor, so I'll take good care of you. But we're not friends. Let go of me."

I released her. She opened the door and stepped out.

I caught a glimpse of Svoboda in the room beyond. He craned his neck to look in. Then Rudy's impressive build blocked the view.

"Hello, Jazz," Rudy said. "How do you feel?"

"Did anyone die?"

He closed the door behind him. "No. No one died."

I gasped in relief and my head fell to the pillow. Only then did I realize how clenched up I'd been. "Thank fucking God."

"You're still in enormous trouble."

"I figured."

"If this had happened anywhere else, there would have been deaths." He clasped his arms behind him. "As it is, everything worked in our favor. We don't have cars, so no one was operating vehicles at the time. Thanks to our low gravity, no one got hurt falling to the ground. A few scrapes and bruises is all."

"No harm, no foul."

He shot me a glare. "Three people went into cardiac arrest from chloroform poisoning. All three were elderly with preexisting lung conditions."

"But they're okay now, right?"

"Yes, but only through luck. Once people woke up they checked on their neighbors. If it weren't for our tight-knit community, that wouldn't have happened. Plus, it's easy to carry an unconscious person in our gravity. And no part of town is far away from Dr. Roussel." He cocked his head toward the doorway. "She's not thrilled with you, by the way."

"I noticed."

"She takes public health seriously."

"Yeah."

He stood quietly for a moment. "Care to tell me who was in on this with you?"

"Nope."

"I know Dale Shapiro was involved."

"Don't know what you're talking about," I said. "Dale just happened to be out on a drive at the time."

"In Bob Lewis's rover?"

"They're buddies. They lend each other stuff."

"With Loretta Sanchez?"

"Maybe they're dating," I said.

"Shapiro's gay."

"Maybe he's not very good at it."

"I see," Rudy said. "Can you explain why Lene Landvik transferred a million slugs to your account this morning?"

Good to know! But I kept a poker face. "Small business loan. She's investing in my EVA tour company."

"You failed the EVA exam."

"Long-term investment."

"That's definitely a lie."

"Whatever. I'm tired."

"I'll let you rest." He walked back to the door. "The administrator wants to see you as soon as you're up and about. You might want to pack some light clothes—it's summer in Saudi Arabia right now."

Svoboda slipped in through the door as Rudy left.

"Hey, Jazz!" Svoboda pulled up a chair and sat beside the bed. "Doc says you're doing great!"

"Hey, Svobo. Sorry about the chloroform."

"Eh, no big." He shrugged.

"I'm guessing the rest of town isn't as forgiving?"

"People don't seem that mad. Well, some are. But most aren't."

"Seriously?" I said. "I knocked the whole town out."

He wiggled his hand. "That wasn't just you. There were a lot of engineering failures. Like: Why aren't there detectors in the air pipeline for complex toxins? Why did Sanchez store methane, oxygen, and chlorine in a room with an oven? Why doesn't Life Support have its own separate air partition to make sure they'll stay awake if the rest of the city has a problem? Why is Life Support centralized instead of having a separate zone for each bubble? These are the questions people are asking."

He put his hand on my arm. "I'm just glad you're okay."

I put my hand on his. The effect was kind of lost with all the bandaging.

"Anyway," he said. "The whole thing gave me a chance to bond with your dad."

"Really?"

"Yeah!" he said. "After we woke up we formed a two-man team to check on my neighbors. It was cool. He bought me a beer afterward."

I widened my eyes. "Dad . . . bought a beer?"

"For me, yeah. He drank juice. We spent an hour talking about metallurgy! Awesome guy."

I tried to imagine Dad and Svoboda hanging out. I failed.

"Awesome guy," Svoboda repeated, a little quieter this time. His smile faded.

"Svobo?" I said.

He looked down. "Are you . . . leaving, Jazz? Are they going to deport you? I'd hate that."

I put my mittened hand on his shoulder. "It'll be all right. I'm not going anywhere."

"You sure?"

"Yeah, I have a plan."

"A plan?" He looked concerned. "Your plans are . . . uh . . . should I hide somewhere?"

I laughed. "Not this time."

"Okay . . ." He was clearly not convinced. "But how are you going to get out of this one? Like . . . you knocked out the *whole town.*"

I smiled at him. "Don't worry. I got this."

"Okay, good." He leaned down and kissed my cheek, almost as an afterthought. I had no idea what possessed him to do that—honestly I didn't think he had it in him. His bravery didn't last long, though. Once he realized what he'd done, his face became a mask of terror. "Oh shit! I'm sorry! I wasn't thinking—"

I laughed. The look in the poor guy's eyes . . . I couldn't help it. "Relax, Svobo. It's just a peck on the cheek. It's nothing to get worked up about."

"R-Right. Yeah."

I put my hand on the nape of his neck, pulled his head to mine, and kissed him full on the lips. A good, long kiss with no ambiguity. When we disengaged, he looked hopelessly confused.

"Now, *that*," I said. "*That* you can get worked up about."

. . .

I waited in a blank, gray hallway next to a door labeled CD2-5186. Conrad Down 2 was a little classier than the usual Conrad Down fare, but not much. Strictly blue-collar, but without that smell of desperation the lower levels had.

I opened and closed my hands a few times. The bandages were off, but both hands were littered with red blisters. I looked like a leper. Or a hooker who gave handjobs exclusively to lepers.

Dad rounded the corner, following his Gizmo's directions. He finally noticed me. "Ah. There you are."

"Thanks for meeting me, Dad," I said.

He took my right hand and inspected it. He winced at the damage. "How are you feeling? Does it hurt? If it hurts, you should go to Dr. Roussel."

"It's okay. Looks worse than it feels." There I was, lying to Dad again.

"So I'm here." He pointed to the door. "CD2-5186. What is it?"

I waved my Gizmo across the panel and opened the door. "Come in."

The large, mostly bare workshop had stark metal walls. Our footsteps echoed as we walked. A worktable stood in the center covered with industrial equipment. Farther back, gas cylinders mounted along the wall fed pipes leading throughout the room. A standard air shelter stood in the corner.

"One hundred forty-one square meters," I said. "Used to be a bakery. Fully fireproof and certified by the city for high-temperature use. Self-contained air-filtration system, and the air shelter seats four people."

I walked over to the tanks. "I just had these installed. Central acetylene, oxygen, and neon lines accessible from anywhere in the shop. Full tanks, of course."

I pointed to the worktable. "Five torch heads, twenty meters

of feeder line, and four sparkers. Also, three full sets of protec-
tive gear, five masks, and three filter-shade kits."

"Jasmine," Dad said. "I—"

"Under the table: twenty-three aluminum stock rods, five
steel rods, and one copper rod. I don't know why you had that
copper rod back then, but you had one, so there it is. Rent's pre-
paid for a year, and the door panel's already keyed to accept your
Gizmo."

I shrugged and let my arms fall to my sides. "So, yeah. Everything I destroyed back on that day."

"It was your idiot boyfriend who destroyed it."

"I'm responsible," I said.

"Yes, you are." He ran his hand along the worktable. "This
must have been very expensive."

"It was 416,922 slugs."

He frowned. "Jasmine . . . you bought this with money that—"

"Dad . . . please, just . . ." I slumped down and sat on the floor.
"I know you don't like where the money came from. But . . ."

Dad clasped his hands behind his back. "My father—your
grandfather—had severe depression. He committed suicide when
I was eight."

I nodded. A dark corner of our family history. Dad rarely dis-
cussed it.

"Even when he was alive, he wasn't really 'alive.' I didn't grow
up with a father. I don't even know what it is. So I've tried my
best—"

"Dad, you're not a bad father. I'm just a shitty daughter—"

"Let me finish." He got to his knees then sat on his heels.
He'd prayed in that position five times a day for sixty years—he
knew how to make it comfortable. "I've been winging it, you
know. As a father. I had nothing to work from. No blueprint.
And I chose a hard life for us. An immigrant's life in a frontier
town."

"No complaints here," I said. "I'd rather be a hardworking pauper in Artemis than a rich woman on Earth. This is my home—"

He held up his hand to silence me. "I tried to prepare you for the world. I never went easy on you, because the world certainly wouldn't go easy on you, and I wanted you to be prepared. We've fought at times, of course—find me a parent and child who haven't. And there are certainly aspects of your life I wish were different. But in the grand scheme of things, you became a strong, self-reliant woman and I'm proud of you. And, through extension, proud of myself for raising you."

My lip quivered a bit.

"I've lived my life by the teachings of Muhammad," he said. "I try to be honest and true in all my decisions. But, like any man, I am flawed. I sin. If your peace of mind comes at the price of a small tarnish on my soul, then so be it. I can only hope I've built up enough good grace with Allah that he will forgive me."

He took both my hands. "Jasmine. I accept your recompense, even though I know the source is dishonest. And I forgive you."

I gave him a firm handshake and we called it a day.

Not really. I collapsed into his arms and cried like a child. I don't want to talk about it.

Time to face the music. I waited outside Ngugi's door. The next few minutes would determine whether I got to stay or had to leave.

Lene Landvik hobbled out on her crutches. "Oh! Hi, Jazz. I transferred the money to your account a few days ago."

"I saw that. Thanks."

"O Palácio sold me Sanchez Aluminum this morning. It'll take weeks to work out the paperwork, but we agreed on a price and we're good to go. Loretta's already designing the next smelter.

She has some improvements in mind. The new one will prioritize silicon extraction and—"

"You're keeping Loretta Sanchez?!"

"Ah," she said. "Yeah."

"Are you fucking crazy?!"

"I just paid half a billion slugs for a smelting company that can't smelt. I need somebody to rebuild it. Who better than Sanchez?"

"But she's the enemy!"

"Anyone who makes you money is a friend," Lene said. "I learned that from Dad. Besides, she helped save your life like *four days* ago. Maybe you guys are even now?"

I folded my arms. "This is going to bite you in the ass, Lene. She can't be trusted."

"Oh, I don't trust her. I just need her. Big difference." She cocked her head at the doorway. "Ngugi says KSC's eager to get oxygen production back online. The city won't be too strict with safety regulations. Weird, huh? You'd think they'd get *more* picky, not less."

"Sanchez in charge . . ." I sighed. "This isn't what I had in mind when I came up with the plan."

"Well, neither was knocking out the whole city. Plans change." She checked her watch. "I have to get to a conference call. Good luck in there. Let me know if I can help."

She hobbled away. I watched her go for a moment. She seemed taller than before. Probably a trick of the light.

I took a deep breath and walked into Ngugi's office.

Ngugi sat behind her desk. She glared at me over her glasses. "Have a seat."

I closed the door and sat in the chair opposite her.

"I think you know what I have to do, Jasmine. And it isn't easy for me." She slid a piece of paper across the desk. I recognized the form—I'd seen it a few days earlier in Rudy's office. It was a formal deportation order.

"Yeah, I know what you have to do," I said. "You have to thank me."

"You must be joking."

"Thanks, Jazz," I said. "Thanks for keeping O Palácio from taking over. Thanks for eliminating an outdated contract that would have stood in the way of a massive economic boom. Thanks for sacrificing yourself to save Artemis. Here's a trophy."

"Jasmine, you're going back to Saudi Arabia." She tapped the deportation order. "We won't press charges, and we'll cover your living expenses until you adjust to Earth gravity. But that's the best I can do."

"After everything I just did for you? You'll just chuck me out with yesterday's trash?"

"It's not something I *want* to do, Jasmine. I *have* to do it. We need to present ourselves as a community that lives under the rule of law. It's more important now than ever before, because the ZAFO industry is coming. If people think their investments can be blown up without the perpetrator facing justice they won't invest here at all."

"They don't have a choice," I said. "We're the only city on the moon."

"We're not irreplaceable. We're just convenient," she said. "If ZAFO companies don't think they can trust us, they'll make their own lunar city. One that protects its businesses. I'm grateful for what you've done, but I have to sacrifice you for the good of the city."

I pulled out a paper of my own and slid it to her.

"What's this?" she asked.

"My confession," I said. "Notice I left out any mention of you, the Landviks, or anyone else. It's just me. I signed it at the bottom."

She gave me a puzzled look. "You're helping me deport you?"

"No. I'm giving you a 'Deport Jazz for Free' card. You're going to put that in a drawer somewhere and keep it for emergencies."

"But I'm deporting you right now."

"No, you're not." I leaned back in the chair and crossed my legs.

"Why not?"

"Everyone seems to forget this, but I'm a smuggler. Not a saboteur, not an action hero, not a city planner. A *smuggler*. I worked hard to set up my operation and it runs smoothly. In the beginning I had competition. But not anymore. I drove them out of business by having lower prices, better service, and a reputation for keeping my word."

She narrowed her eyes. "You must be going somewhere with this, but I don't see where."

"Have you ever seen guns in Artemis? Other than the one you have in your desk, I mean?"

She shook her head. "No."

"How about hard drugs? Heroin? Opium? That sort of thing?"

"Not at any scale," she said. "Sometimes Rudy catches a tourist with a personal stash but it's rare."

"Ever wonder why that shit doesn't get into town?" I pointed to my chest. "Because I don't let it. No drugs, no guns. And I have a bunch of other rules too. I keep flammables to a minimum. And no live plants. Last thing we need is some weird mold infestation."

"Yes, you're very ethical, but—"

"What happens when I'm gone?" I asked. "Do you think smuggling will just stop? No. There'll be a short power vacuum then someone else will take over. No idea who. But will they be as civic-minded as me? Probably not."

She raised an eyebrow.

I pressed on. "This city's about to have a ZAFO boom. There's going to be jobs galore, construction, and an influx of workers. There'll be new customers for every business in town. New companies will open to keep up with the demand. The population will spike. You've already got estimates, right?"

She peered at me for a moment. "I think we'll have ten thousand people within the year."

"There ya go," I said. "More people means more demand for contraband. Thousands of people who might want drugs. Shitloads of money flying around, which means more crime. Those criminals will want guns. They'll try to sneak them in through whatever smuggling system and black market is in place. What kind of city do you want Artemis to be?"

She pinched her chin. "That's . . . a very good point."

"All right. So, you have my confession. That'll keep me from getting out of line. Checks and balances and all that."

She thought about this for an uncomfortably long time. Without breaking eye contact, she pulled the deportation order off her desk and put it in a drawer. I sighed in relief.

"We still have the problem of punishment, though . . ." She leaned forward to her antiquated keyboard computer and began typing. She ran her finger along the screen. "According to this, your account balance is 585,966 slugs."

"Yeah . . . why?"

"I thought Lene paid you a million."

"How did you kno—never mind. I paid off a debt recently. Why is this relevant?"

"I think some restitution is in order. A fine, if you will."

"What?!" I sat bolt-upright. "Artemis doesn't have fines!"

"Call it a 'voluntary contribution to the city's funds.'"

"There's nothing 'voluntary' about it!"

"Sure there is." She settled back into her chair. "You can keep all your money and get deported instead."

Ugh. Well, this was a win for me. I could always make more money, but I couldn't get un-deported. And she had a point. If she didn't punish me, any asshole could do what I did and expect to get away with it. I'd have to take a slap on the wrist. "Okay. How much?"

"Five hundred fifty thousand slugs should cover it."

I gasped. "Are you fucking kidding me?!"

She smirked. "It's like you said. I need you to control smuggling. If you have a bunch of money, you might retire. And then where would I be? It's best to keep you hungry."

Logically I came out way ahead. I'd cleared my conscience. But still, the prospect of my account balance going from six digits to five physically hurt.

"Oh!" She smiled with a realization. "And thanks for volunteering yourself as Artemis's unpaid, unofficial, import regulatory body. Of course, I'll hold you responsible for any dangerous contraband in town, regardless of how it got here. So, if some other smuggler crops up and lets guns or drugs in, you can expect a chat with me."

I stared blankly. She stared back.

"I'll expect that slug transfer by the end of the day," she said.

My bluster was completely gone. I stood from the chair and walked over to the door. When I reached for the door handle, I paused.

"What's the endgame here?" I asked. "Once the ZAFO companies start up, what happens then?"

"The next big step is taxes."

"Taxes?" I snorted. "People come here because they don't want to pay taxes."

"They already pay taxes—as rent to KSC. We need to change over to a property-ownership and tax model so the city's wealth is directly tied to the economy. But that's not for a while."

She took off her glasses. "It's all part of the life-cycle of an economy. First it's lawless capitalism until that starts to impede growth. Next comes regulation, law enforcement, and taxes. After that: public benefits and entitlements. Then, finally, overexpenditure and collapse."

"Wait. Collapse?"

"Yes, collapse. An economy is a living thing. It's born full of vitality and dies once it's rigid and worn out. Then, through necessity, people break into smaller economic groups and the cycle begins anew, but with more economies. Baby economies, like Artemis is right now."

"Huh," I said. "And if you want to make babies, somebody's got to get fucked."

She laughed. "You and I will get along just fine, Jasmine."

I left without further comment. I didn't want to spend any more time inside the mind of an economist. It was dark and disturbing.

I needed a beer.

I wasn't the most popular gal around town. I got some dirty looks in the hallways. But I also spotted a few thumbs-ups from my supporters. I hoped the excitement would fade in time. I don't want fame. I want people not to notice me at all.

I walked into Hartnell's, not sure what to expect. The regular crowd were in their usual seats—even Dale.

"Hey, it's Jazz!" Billy called out.

Suddenly, everyone "passed out." Each patron tried to outdo the others with ridiculous displays of being unconscious. Some lolled their tongues, others snored with a comedic whistle on the exhale, and a few lay spread-eagle on the floor.

"Har-har," I said, "very funny."

With my acknowledgment, the prank was over. They resumed their normal quiet drinking with a few subdued giggles.

"Heya," said Dale. "Since you forgave me, I figure I can just show up anytime and hang out with you."

"I only forgave you because I thought I was going to die," I said. "But yeah. No take-backs."

Billy put a fresh, frosty beer in front of me. "The customers took a vote and decided this round's on you. You know, to make up for almost killing everyone."

"Oh, is that so?" I scanned the bar. "Can't be helped, I guess. Put 'em all on my tab."

Billy poured himself a half pint and raised it in the air. "To Jazz, for saving the city!"

"To Jazz!" the patrons called out, and raised their glasses. They were happy to toast me if I bought the beer. I guess that was a start.

"How are the hands?" Dale asked.

"They're burned, blistered, and hurt like hell." I took a sip. "Thanks for saving my life, by the way."

"No problem. You might want to thank Sanchez too."

"Nah."

He shrugged and took another sip. "Tyler was really worried about you."

"Mm."

"He'd like to see you sometime. The three of us could grab lunch, maybe? On me, of course."

I bit back the obnoxious comment that swelled up. It was going to be a doozy too. Instead, I heard myself say, "Yeah, okay."

He clearly didn't expect that answer. "Really? Because—wait, really?"

"Yeah." I looked at him and nodded. "Yeah. We can do that."

"Wow," he said. "G-Great! Hey, you want to bring that Svoboda guy?"

"Svobo? Why would I bring him?"

"You two are an item, right? He's clearly crazy about you, and you seemed a little—"

"No! I mean . . . it's not like that."

"Oh. You're just friends, then?"

"Uh . . ."

Dale smirked. "I see."

We drank quietly for a moment. Then he said, "You're totally going to bang that guy."

"Oh, shut up!"

"A thousand slugs says you two get freaky within a month."

I glared at him. He glared back.

"Well?" he said.

I finished off my pint. "No bet."

"Ha!"

Dear Kelvin,

Sorry for the slow response. I'm sure you've read all about the chloroform leak in the news. People around here call it "The Nap." There were no deaths or serious injuries, but I'm shooting you an email just to confirm I'm okay.

I did spend three minutes sizzling on the lunar surface without a spacesuit. That kind of sucked (no vacuum pun intended). Also, everyone knows I was responsible for the Nap.

Which leads me to my next problem: I'm broke. Again. Long story short, the city took most of my money to bitch-slap me for my indiscretions. Unfortunately, I hadn't transferred your share of our profits this month, so I'm going to have to owe you. I'll pay you off the moment I can, you have my word.

I have some legwork for you: There's a guy named "Jin Chu" (might be an alias) headed back to Earth right now. He claimed to be from Hong Kong and that's probably true. He works for a Chinese materials research company. I don't know which one.

He got sent home from Artemis for being naughty. They shipped him out a few days ago, so he must be aboard the *Gordon*. That means you've got four days before he arrives at KSC. Hire a detective or whatever to find out where he works. We need that company's name.

Because Kelvin, old buddy, this is the opportunity of a lifetime. That company is about to make billions. I'm going to invest as much as I can in it and I suggest you do the same. Long story—I'll send you a more detailed email later.

Aside from that, we're back to business as usual. Keep the goods coming. Also, we'll be ramping up our smuggling volume soon. Artemis is going to have a population boom. More customers coming our way!

We're going to be rich, buddy. Filthy rich.

And hey, once that happens, you should come visit. I've learned a lot about the value of friends lately and you're one of the best friends I've ever had. I'd like to meet you in person. And besides, who doesn't want to come to Artemis?

It's the greatest little city in the worlds.

ACKNOWLEDGMENTS

People I want to thank:

David Fugate, my agent, without whom I would still be blogging my stories on nights and weekends.

Julian Pavia, my editor, for being a pain in my ass at exactly the right times.

The entire team at Crown and the Random House sales force for their hard work and support. You're an army too numerous to name individually here, but please know I'm incredibly grateful to have had so many smart people believe in my work and get it out into the world.

A special shoutout is due to my longtime publicist Sarah Breivogel, whose efforts have been instrumental in keeping me sane over the last few years.

For their smart feedback in various arenas, but most especially for helping me tackle the challenge of writing a female narrator, Molly Stern (publisher), Angeline Rodriguez (Julian's assistant), Gillian Green (my UK editor), Ashley (my girlfriend), Mahvash Siddiqui (friend, who also helped make sure the portrayal of Islam was accurate), and Janet Tuer (my mom).

ABOUT THE AUTHOR

ANDY WEIR built a career as a software engineer until the success of his debut novel, *The Martian,* allowed him to pursue writing full-time. He is a lifelong space nerd and a devoted hobbyist of subjects such as relativistic physics, orbital mechanics, and the history of manned spaceflight. He lives in California.